GW00645437

PARIS IS THE PITS

by

Brigitte Downey

**Grosvenor House
Publishing Limited**

All rights reserved
Copyright © Brigitte Downey, 2009

Brigitte Downey is hereby identified as author of this
work in accordance with Section 77 of the Copyright, Designs
and Patents Act 1988

The book cover picture is copyright to Anna Issa Sotolova

This book is published by
Grosvenor House Publishing Ltd
28-30 High Street, Guildford, Surrey, GU1 3HY.
www.grosvenorhousepublishing.co.uk

This book is sold subject to the conditions that it shall not, by way of
trade or otherwise, be lent, resold, hired out or otherwise circulated
without the author's or publisher's prior consent in any form of binding or
cover other than that in which it is published and
without a similar condition including this condition being imposed
on the subsequent purchaser.

A CIP record for this book
is available from the British Library

ISBN 978-1-907211-75-1

With love for
Eileen and Andrew Downey
Abbeyfeale, Co. Limerick

ONE

Dublin 1985

I worked as a cashier for six months in Tipps Topvalues of Ireland Ltd. It's RIPPS they should have called that dump with its worldwide reputation as Ireland's Emporium of the Rejects - First for Everything in Seconds. Like nighties with necks so snug they'll garrot you in your sleep if you so much as twitch. Or men's trousers with the crotch two inches from the pockets which must be a blessed relief for men with their privates perched on their upper pelvis.

Not even in my most florid nightmares did I think I'd end up in a kip like Tipps when I left the grassy outpost of home in Dun-mo-Croi (population aiming for the 2,000 mark) and off to Dublin to blind them on stage and screen with my acting genius. The minute I arrived I alerted all the theatres and RTE TV that Nellie Flanagan was gracing the metropolis with her presence and was available for suitable leading parts. They said feel free to send in my glossy, my cuttings and an SASE which I thought was something fancy but only turned out to be a Self Addressed Stamped Envelope.

Cuttings? That was a good one. At 17 they expect me to have a suitcase of cuttings like some teen star. My solitary cutting was from The Kerry Monocle. It went: 'The Dun-mo-Croi Players did a solid job of ploughing through a ho-hum production of '*You, Me and the Others*'. Nicolas Feeney showed definite merit in providing unexpected comedy in a dreary play. (*This was when Fr. Feeney dropped the iron on his toes and howled the house down.*) And Nellie Flanagan who tended to overwhelm her small part, nonetheless gave us her rendition of Atlas as she propped up the back wall of the set during the final act, thus obviating the total collapse of both play and stage.'

OK! So I saved all on stage from being brained by a collapsing set. That wasn't the point. I had a supporting role in that play and that donkey reviewer Donnelly has the audacity to classify me as some kind of prop holder. It's not the kind of review that is going to startle the makers and shakers in theatre land to come screeching over with sirens blaring to haul me away from the cash register in Tipps. I hate critics and when I become a household name I am going to blow the whistle on that lot.

When I hopped on the train to Dublin gasping for my first taste of freedom, I knew it wouldn't be plain sailing before I became Ireland's answer to Meryl Streep. I was prepared to suffer like all the greats had done before they hit the big time. I was ready to sleep on floors so I could share flats with exciting people my age who lived for the theatre, film and TV. Who did I end up with? Mad Auntie Betty who squeezes more praying into a single day than the Pope and the College of Cardinals combined. It wasn't easy living with Auntie Betty no matter how much my Mam went on about how 'very kind' it was of her to put me up for free when any other girl from the country would have to pay through the nose to live in digs in Dublin. But I paid and how!

Instead of falling into bed at dawn after all night parties, Auntie Betty is dragging me out of bed and off to first Mass. Even in Holy Dublin this is neither the time nor the place you'll meet exciting theatre people who'll give you a part. This is where you'll find the lunatic twins who spend hours taking turns kissing the feet off all the statues in the Church. One of these days those saints will just topple over and kill them since those statues have hardly anything left to stand on from all the kissing. But daily Mass at dawn is only a tiny taster to Auntie Betty. Before breakfast we have to thank the Lord effusively and at length for the bounty we are about to receive. By the time the prayers are over, the eggs are stone cold and the tea is stronger than Guinness. During breakfast Auntie Betty tells me all about the suffering children in Africa, India and Latin America and reminds me how lucky I am to be eating Irish eggs instead of infected grass.

Then it's into work with Valerie Vaughan who waits for me at the bus stop every single morning. Valerie thinks that knitting is on a par with walking on water for excitement, and believes that Superman is going to fly into Tipps and whisk her away from her cash register to Happy Bunny Land. I don't blame her. Anything would be better than working in Tipps. The only way I can get through the day with my sanity intact is to rehearse my favourite Shakespeare speeches out loud and beam myself away from dreadful reality to a more sublime zone. No matter how busy I am at that cash register I can declaim 'To Be or not To Be' without losing a beat and put more feeling into it than any actor living or dead. Because I have suffered so many slings and arrows just by living in this Emerald nightmare isle of 24-hour prayers and kips like Tipps. Plus I've got an extra edge being a woman. From what I've witnessed, it's the women who get slung at more often.

Most times I never get to finish my soliloquies. Some cretin of a woman with more children hanging off her than jewellery off an Indian Princess wants to know where she can find a size 7 for Gary who's chewing his way through his buggy. I feel like telling her to go home, get in a large supply of Mr. Hefty, the heavy duty garbage bags, and wrap Gary the Gobbler in them until such time as he can distinguish between food and his buggy. That way she'd save money and I wouldn't have to interrupt a divine Juliet speech and show her where the number 7's are - right in front of her eyeballs of course.

Some days I feel like hanging a sign around my neck - 'Don't ask me. I don't know.' This would be appreciated in the US where things are more advanced I'm told, and where they'd realize it would be far, far better for me to hone my art and get prepared for Broadway instead of acting like some signpost illuminating the way to the booties, the bonnets, and the bras.

During the afternoon we get a fifteen-minute break. I race to the phone to call every place in Dublin where they might give me an acting job. Even the phone is against me. It's either broken, engaged, temporarily out of sorts, or it swallows my precious money. On those rare days when I get through to somebody in drama, they ask me how old and how tall I am. When I say I'm almost 18, five feet eleven inches, green eyes and luscious brown hair, there's a long pause before they say 'Thank you, dear,' like I'm some kind of seconds myself, as if it's my fault I'm as tall as I am. After six months they had me convinced. Pigs would be dancing minuets around the moon before they'd give Nellie Flanagan a break.

By the time I'm through phoning I'm so depressed I know I'll be flat out dead before I ever get to play Juliet. But then it gets to five and Tipps is swarming with the lucky girls who come dashing in for their cheap tights so they can get all fussed up for an evening out on the town. In the rush I forget about dying from depression and shooting and maiming all those low lives who keep rejecting me by saying that horrible phrase – 'we'll keep you in mind' - when what they really mean is 'Take a hike, freak!'

Then I'm really busy clicking away on the cash register. That clickety click CLACK (that's me stapling the bill to the plastic bag) becomes second nature and takes my mind off everything. It whisks me away to another zone and I'm a great actress being pelted with bouquets on Broadway and the West End. I'm so mesmerized by the clickety click CLACK it's a joy to be spouting my Shakespeare speeches out loud.

Finally it's quitting time and the end of a nightmare day at Tipps. The lights of Dublin are all shining red and the Guinness signs are glowing in front of cosy pubs. Even the rain has a thrill to it that you'd never get in our village of Dun-Mo-Croi. And I have a choice. I can either hide out in the toilet to escape getting on the bus with Valerie Vaughan the knitting maniac or risk getting locked in for the night.

Most evenings I walk around Dublin in the rain trying to think of excuses why I shouldn't go home to Auntie Betty for supper and endless prayers. 'I promised your Mother I'd look after you and I want you home immediately after work.' But I want to be like the students who are always living it up in the pubs near the Green. When the despair overwhelms me, I go in there just to feel the young excitement. I buy a small gin & tonic and it's an awful price to pay especially when all my money is going into the bank so I can go to Drama School one day. But in the student pubs, the boys and girls my age all stick to their own little groups, and never talk to outsiders like me.

One evening, however, I did meet two drama students from Trinity College which is where I'd be going if there were any money in our family. The students were friendly as could be until I mentioned that I came from a village in Kerry where my Dad had a grocery shop and that I was working as a cashier in Tipps. They edged away from me with false smiles before I could tell them I was a genius actress waiting to be discovered. Another evening I met a nice medical student who was from the country like me. He chatted about autopsies and having to cut into a dead person's eyes. He was in the middle of a great grisly story about a head that went missing in the hospital when his girl friend waltzed in. There were javelins shooting out her eyeballs when she saw the two of us laughing. That was that. They left me gazing down at my expensive gin & tonic and wondering what happened to the missing head.

Instead of going to parties, discos, films and plays I linger like an old lady over a G & T radiating non-threatening smiles all around. I'm a brilliant actress so I can hide the heart crying inside me with loneliness and manage to look as if I've just won the lottery. But with the exception of the barman nobody says anything to me. I cut my losses, buy strong mints to cover the smell of gin and drag myself home for supper. Auntie Betty says Grace Before, Grace in Between and Grace After. I have to listen to Tales of Starvation and Horror worldwide while we do the dishes. This merriment is followed by a few rosaries on our knees. After that I no longer care if I live to see 18. l hunch in front of the TV and watch all those people acting. Zillions of actresses - younger than me, older than me, prettier than me, uglier, more exotic, less gifted than me, but none taller than me. So when they're casting around for 'The Return of the Giants' I may get my break.

Before we go to bed I have to traipse all over the house with Auntie Betty while she goes from room to room drenching everything with Holy Water to ward off burglars and rapists. She always warns me not to forget to say my Act of Contrition … in case I make medical history and die of a heart attack at 17. Before I fall asleep I always beg the Good Lord to please get me into acting soon before I die of depression in Dublin where all my dreams were supposed to come true.

My prayers were heard. I didn't die from depression. They fired me from Tipps.

TWO

'Just explain to me again how they could possibly give you the sack?' my Dad has asked me about fifty times now. If my Dad were in his dotage I wouldn't mind. But I've already explained to the last detail how I got fired.

I was honing my craft, rehearsing Shylock behind the cash register when that fat fart of a Manager's wife came in to ferret around for her seconds in bras like some hog that hadn't had his mash in months. Tipps is the only place you'll find bras to suit the O'Toole tits, which I'd say are like two slippery pythons she has to coil up into a bun before she can clamp them into anything.

Mrs. O'Toole was so surprised to hear my superb rendition of Shylock's '*Do we not bleed?*' that she stopped snorkelling for bras. I was in perfect pitch that afternoon and Mrs. O'Toole was most fortunate to catch the entire speech. Shylock is of course an old man's role. But 'Be Prepared' is Nellie Flanagan's motto. One day I might be an extra in *The Merchant of Venice.* Shylock and his understudy could take a dive into the gin bottle and they'll be desperate for somebody to step into the breech. With a bit of makeup and a wig (hey, if Dustin Hoffmann can play *Tootsie,* then Nellie Flanagan can do Shylock) I'll bring the house down. My Mam says I spend too much time day dreaming and that this could become a problem later on in life. But she doesn't understand. I want to play all of Shakespeare and not just Juliet (kills herself for love), Ophelia (goes off her rocker from love) or Desdemona (murdered for love).

What was the mangy Manager's wife's opinion of my stunning interpretation of Shylock? She pulled her snout out of the bras and cantered off to complain to her Manager husband that one of 'his girls' was indulging in 'disgraceful rowdiness'. This was the monster who got me fired from Tipps and the miscreant who defiled the English language by using the word 'raving' to describe my Shylock tour de force. The manager said he had to fire me because it lowered the store's standard to have one of 'his girls hollering out Shakespeare all day long'. First of all, I'm not one of 'his girls'; second that dive doesn't have a standard to lower and third neither the Manager nor his mutt of a wife could spell Shakespeare let alone appreciate his work.

They asked me to leave before closing time which solved the problem of hiding in the loo to avoid taking the bus home with Valerie Vaughan updating me on her latest knitting triumphs. I used my free time to double check all acting opportunities. But as if being fired wasn't enough, the people at RTE TV 'implored me to stop pestering them' (their very words!). I walked out of Tipps and strolled along the streets of Dublin smoldering about the injustice of the world and wondering what to do next. I didn't want to go home to Auntie Betty who'd have me on my knees praying for forgiveness for breaking my parents' hearts by deliberately losing a great job at a time when the economy had collapsed yet again and jobs were like gold dust.

Or else she'd come out with one of her philosophical saying like: *'The Lord is testing you for greater things'*. Auntie Betty is full of gems like that. Her top favourite is: *'The Good Lord never closes one door but He opens another'*. That's what she told Clare Foley after she set the house on fire making flaming tinned peaches as a treat for her boyfriend. He's a picky eater because he works in a sausage factory and is on intimate terms with the blood and guts that go into Ireland's favourite food. Clare was a bit too generous with the brandy. One flick of the boyfriend's lighter and the peaches, the tablecloth and half the kitchen went SWOOSH! SWOOSH! The curtains disappeared. (Never buy nylon curtains from Tipps!) The flames devoured all their wallpaper. By the time they remembered the number of the fire brigade the place was half gone. And what was Auntie Betty's reaction to the tragedy where both the back and the front doors had been burnt off the hinges? '*The Lord never closes one door, but He opens another.*' If their neighbour Mr. Donovan, who is very active in the St. Vincent de Paul Society hadn't given them two doors for free, the Foleys would still be sitting in their shell of a home with the breezes swirling around them waiting for the Lord to deliver a few doors (and windows) down from the Above.

I walked by those student pubs where luckier and richer kids my age were laughing and drinking before heading off for all their all night parties. They would never know the pain of taking the bus back to Kerry with their tails between their ankles and their dreams smashed to smithereens. Of course My Dad would be thrilled to see me. He'd tell me to take it easy after the excitement of Dublin and help him in the shop if I felt like it. My Mam wouldn't be angry at me for losing that job, just very disappointed I wasn't promoted to head cashier which was her dream for me. She'd try and cheer me up by reminding me that most of Ireland was unemployed and that things were so bad in England, the Irish workers were returning home in droves.

How would I survive in the Kerry wilderness without even a sniff of an acting job let alone the role of Juliet? The ache in my heart was suddenly so bad I had to stop walking. I found myself standing in front of a travel agency with posters plastered over the windows for exciting flights to all parts of the world. There were at least five for Paris – showing the glittering nightlife, the culture and the gorgeous theatres. That was the moment I had the brainwave of the century. Why not try my luck in culture packed Paris? It wasn't like I had meticulously planned to emigrate or anything.

THREE

'Mam, I'm going to Paris. I'm going to get a job there and become an actress.'

We were out in the garden drinking tea and enjoying the seven and a half minutes of Irish Summer sunshine when I unveiled my exciting plans to my Mam. Her mind was on its usual slug and caterpillar patrol so my news didn't sink in first time around. My Mam is grounded in her own reality and Paris isn't part of it. What's real for my Mam are caterpillars wiping out all her cabbages or a supermarket opening up in Dun-mo-Croi and bankrupting us. Stuff like me going to Paris to be an actress is in the realm of the Pope having his belly button pierced and tangoing out the Mass.

'I'm going to Paris,' I said again.

'Those cursed things,' snarled my Mam, and swooped down on her precious flower bed. She had spotted a fat caterpillar sunning itself on the back of a half-gnawed dahlia leaf. She shook it off and squished the living daylights out of it with the heel of her sandal.

'If you see any more of those pests, will you please stop them, Nellie?' she said, and settled back into her deckchair again.

'I'm going to Paris,' I repeated. 'When I'm all fixed up you and Dad can come and visit me.'

'That would be lovely,' said my Mam in a dreamy voice. You could see she didn't believe me. She had the look she gets when she and Dottie O'Connor are discussing what they'll do when they win the Sweepstakes.

'I really am going to Paris.'

Just what is the problem with my parents? Every night of my life I see people on TV telling their parents they've been impregnated by aliens, they've robbed a bank and accidentally killed a few guards, they put the house on a sure thing and the horse had to be put down during the race. All those TV parents understand first time around. Why can't my parents?

'I'll need a bit of money to get me started,' I said, and waited with my hand out in case my Mam dropped her tea cup. If she did, I'd have to listen to incantations to broken china and how it was a wedding present from Helen Dempsey who went to Australia and disappeared without a trace. In other countries people 'emigrate'. In Ireland they 'disappear without a trace'. Until they 'come back from the dead' in the form of a Christmas card fifteen years later.

'Nobody goes to Paris to be an actress, Nellie,' said my Mam and began to sip her tea again. Now that was a very bad sign. It meant she was slipping into her own reality zone and it was going to be a real tug-of-war to haul her back into mine.

'Oh, when I think of that lovely position you had in Dublin. How could that shop have let you go? I just don't believe it.'

Here she goes again. My Mam is worse than a starving bulldog gnawing a bone when it comes to my six months of Hell in Dublin.

'I'm going to Paris,' I muttered between my teeth.

'Paris is a very cold city,' said my Mam. Her face brightened. 'You wouldn't know anyone. You'd be awfully lonely. It wouldn't be a bit like Dublin.'

Welcome news!

'Now didn't your Dad and I say we'd pay for a secretarial course in Dublin? You'd stay with Auntie Betty. She loves having you. And after you pass your tests, you'll be in such demand.'

My Mam's eyes glinted like a woman having a vision.

'You'll get a nice job in a nice office. You'll meet nice people and have a really nice life. You can still think of acting on the side.'

I don't know why my family thinks acting is weird. They'd almost prefer to see me on the dole because that's 'normal' when there isn't a spare job to be had for love or money in all of Ireland or the UK.

'Mam, does Dad still have that old FCA rifle?'

She gave me a quizzical look. When my brother Brian and I were very young we used to fight for the privilege of polishing the long wooden handle.

'Of course your Dad still has his rifle. It's in his workroom where it always is. Why?'

She smiled and tilted her face up to the sun, pleased to know that things were looking normal again.

'I'd just like you to know,' I said, raising my face up to the sun too, 'that I'd prefer to use that rifle to blow my brains out than do a shorthand and typing course in Dublin and get a nice job with a nice firm and live for another half hour with Auntie Betty and her incessant ding-dong psalming. So please, can I have a loan of a few pounds?'

My Mam sighed, sipped her tea and gazed out at the sea which was winking up at us from about a mile below.

'I'll discuss it with your Dad this evening.'

'Oh thank you, Mam.'

I threw my arms around her and kissed her. She really was the person I loved and treasured most in the world - and not just because she was the only one who could persuade my Dad to part with a bit of money for my Paris enterprise.

In a way I felt sorry for my Mam sitting there looking down at the sea with her eyes skinned in that death-watch for caterpillars. I wanted to swear to her that one day I'd show her Paris, so she'd get a bit of real living, and real excitement and real thrills.

But it wouldn't be any use. If there is anything my Mam dreads in life, it's real excitement and real thrills. All my Mam wants is peace and quiet. The way I see it, she should be comatose from all the peace and quiet she gets from running this shop with my Dad in the back of beyond in the wilds of Kerry.

FOUR

That evening I decided to be gone while the 'discussion' was underway, so I cycled over to Granddad and Belinda's cottage. Granddad used to live with us until he married Belinda and moved into a cottage three years ago. I am crazy about my Granddad and the less I see of him the crazier I am about him. It seems to be the same with him, because every time I see him, he insists on contributing to my 'drama fund'. If my parents ever found out, they'd make me give it back accusing me of 'depriving' Granddad of his miniscule pension. Whereas Granddad always emphasizes that I'd be 'depriving' him of the pleasure of giving if I didn't take it. Naturally, I don't want to deprive either of us of the pleasure of giving and the pleasure of receiving. Granddad and I understand each other. There is none of this complicated, round-and-round-the-mulberry-bush fifty times before the penny drops.

The two of them were outside sitting in the tepid twilight with rugs wrapped around their legs. Even though it was after six they still wore straw hats to avoid any risk of sun-stroke. On the table between them there was a small box of Black Magic chocolates, probably a gift because they only buy soft marshmallows. They have a horror of hard centres in case their dentures lock onto the chewy substance and they run the risk of choking to death.

This happened to Granddad once when they were having dinner in a glamorous restaurant. At the end of the meal when the bill arrived with a selection of mints, Granddad chose the green one thinking it would be soft. But it turned out to be the gooey kind that welded his dentures together. He nearly died of suffocation right there at the table in that fancy eatery. So as not to kill off the rest of the diners by extracting his dentures there at the table with the green goo stuck between them Granddad, being the gentleman he is, shuffled his way across the dining room, taking gigantic snuffles through his nostrils like an asthmatic stallion. With his lips curled back to get the maximum of air through his cemented green dentures, he looked nuttier than a wild boar.

When he sauntered back a little later breathing as normal as could be through his separated dentures, the other diners looked at him as if he were some kind of lunatic who broke out in short lived attacks. He is now very careful about what he eats in public places. The two of them have never-ending discussions about the pros and cons of different denture glues. Belinda is forever trying to persuade Granddad to go over to her brand, which keeps her dentures stuck to her gums no matter what she bites into. She sleeps with them in. Granddad says she is flirting with death by having dentures welded to her gums. He warns her that one fine night (never one rainy night or one snowy night) Belinda's dentures could become unstuck, drop into her gullet and choke her; when he wakes up she'll be gone. Thanks to Granddad and Belinda old age will hold no mysteries for me. I know exactly what to expect.

I made sure I didn't come up on them too suddenly. That's another thing you don't do to old folk. Startle them and you are liable to murder them on the spot. In all the murder mysteries I've read, I've yet to come across two old fogies being surprised to death. Did Sherlock Holmes ever pronounce the solemn words, 'They were startled to death'?

'It's me-e-e-e-e—e!' I called out as I came into view - in case they thought I was some kind of extra-terrestrial vision against the setting sun.

'Get yourself a chair, get yourself a cushion,' they chanted.

'I'm grand on the grass,' I said.

'That's how you get arthritis,' Granddad warned. 'Damp grass.'

'You get arthritis because the synovial fluid between the joints is no longer being produced. The dry bones grate against one another because they aren't being lubricated properly and it's that friction that causes the pain.'

'You get it that way too,' said Granddad, handing me the box of Black Magic.

As he leaned out of his chair Granddad let off a giant fart and then pretended to have a coughing fit to try and cover it up. I felt like telling him that I knew he couldn't help farting every time he moved. 'It's very natural in old people,' is how my Mam put it when Granddad came down with his wind affliction about two years ago. Since then she has said, 'Flatulence is natural' about three thousand times and 'It's nothing to be embarrassed about' twice as often. I know Granddad isn't embarrassed when only Belinda is around. Once when I was visiting, treading softly as usual so as not to startle them into an early grave, I heard Granddad literally go Quack! Quack! Quack! as he walked across the kitchen. Then he turned to Belinda and said: 'Oh, the indignities of old age, my dear.'

'I'm going to Paris to be an actress,' I told Granddad,

instead of saying that I knew flatulence was natural at his age.

'When exactly?'

He stopped coughing.

That's why Granddad and I are on the same wavelength. He has the kind of mind that sifts the information through immediately.

'As soon as my Dad gives me the fare. Of course, I do have my drama fund in case he doesn't.'

'I've always dreamt of going to Paris,' said Belinda. Her eyes lit up as much as any old person's can. Something happens to their eyes at a certain age: the colour just fades away like clothes that are left out in the sun for too long.

'We'll go and visit her, of course,' said Granddad, as if I were already installed in Paris with a guest suite at the ready.

'Imagine painting by the Seine,' said Belinda. 'What a dream!'

Belinda paints. That's how she came to Ireland. She used to be a hairdresser in England. When her husband fell off a construction site and died, she came into a bit of insurance money. She decided to use the money to make her life's dream come true and capture Ireland in oils and canvas. That's how she met and married Granddad. She's been painting full-time now for three years. Even though she still does the odd mess there is something in her paintings that pulls you into the colours. Something 'magical', as Granddad puts it. But the magic was missing in the portrait she did of me. I thought I looked like a bent telephone pole but Granddad pronounced it a 'work of art' and hung it over the fireplace in their living-room.

'Every painter has to go to Paris - at least once in her life,' said Granddad. He squished a chocolate between his fingers until the liquid came through and there wasn't a trace of a doubt that this was a softie.

'See Paris and live life to the hilt,' he said and slurped back the red ooze.

That sure would make a change, I thought and gazed up at the blazing pink clouds near the setting sun. They looked like giant strawberries that had been tossed out of God's giant fruit basket (I'm quoting Belinda here).

'You'll surely get to Paris,' said Granddad and winked.

I knew from that little wink that even if my Dad didn't hand over the money at least Granddad was good for a few pounds. And if that was the case he could most certainly come and visit me in Paris when I was properly installed and working as an actress at a very prestigious theatre.

'Picasso, Cezanne, Van Gogh, Renoir, Matisse,' Belinda chanted and wafted along in a zone all her own. 'What splendid lives they must have had.'

'They were all artists who lived and worked in Paris,' said Granddad for my benefit, in case I got the impression they were talking about the latest Irish rock bands.

'Oh really!' I said.

Never say 'I know that' to an oldie. It only reinforces their self doubt that they're useless and can't tell you anything new.

'Berthe Morisot, Van Dongen ….' Belinda was still chanting away like Father Denis who almost goes into a trance when he's saying Mass.

'Shall I make us all a drink?' I asked.

'It's just lovely to be served,' said Belinda, coming down to earth.

'What'll it be?'

'A nice G & T for me,' said Belinda. 'And you know what your Granddad's favourite is.'

'An inch and a half of Paddy,' I said as I got up from the grass, feeling a bit on the stiff side. Maybe there was something to Granddad's arthritis theory after all.

'A Paddy a day keeps the Doctor at bay,' said Granddad, and I really had to hand it to Belinda. She can still smile as if she's hearing it for the first time. Every time he has his evening drink he says the same old thing. And every night she gives him the same wide smile.

While I was fixing the drinks in the kitchen I began thinking of an article I had read about an island in the South Pacific. Every year all the old folk over a certain age were forced to scamper up coconut trees. When they reached the top (if they reached the top at all) their sons and daughters at the bottom shook the living daylights out of the tree. If the old geysers came tumbling down it was too bad, because they were dead as dodos from the fall. But if they managed to stay put in the tree they were allowed to live for another year. It was part of their island tradition.

Whenever Granddad and Belinda get on my nerves - which is practically every time I set eyes on them - I force myself to think of that tribe and their cruelty. Because if I don't watch out I'll be worse myself. However, by the time I had fixed the drinks and filled a little bowl with chips just like they do in Horgans' pub, I was feeling positively saintly. Here was the future famous actress being kind to oldies and ignoring their farts. Surely the Lord Above would note it down in the Golden Book and see to it that my Dad forked over the necessary dough. Once on French soil I'd be discovered by a talent scout and never look back again.

The three of us sipped our drinks and watched the sun slide slowly into the Atlantic. The seagulls loped across the blood red sky and the strawberry clouds went a deeper red and clustered into one another so that they looked like an ad for haemorrhoid cream. Every time he sipped his drink, Granddad said, 'A Paddy a day keeps the doctor at bay'. Belinda said, 'Ah Paree! Paree! Paree!' eleven times.

I concentrated on the sound of the waves lapping the shore below. It was in tune with all the applause I was hearing in my mind. That evening, Paris was over the sea, a dream yet unlived, the pot of gold at the end of the rainbow which could never turn out to be the setting sun shining on shattered glass.

FIVE

My Dad coughed up the necessary. Granddad slipped me another hundred pounds and warned me not to breathe a word to anyone. He didn't have to worry. Nobody would ever get a whiff of that bonus.

'Oh Nellie, you're going so far away from me,' Granddad said, like I had been picked as the first Irish astronaut to go to Mars, never to return in his lifetime. 'I wish I were young enough to go with you.'

Then wouldn't you know it? I was bawling and so was Granddad and our tears were going plop, plop, plop. Granddad ended up consoling me, telling me he didn't mind about being old and beyond it. I wasn't to worry on his account. We both felt better after our little cry.

I can't say the same for my Mam. She took to singing 'She is gone from the Land' even though she didn't know the tune. The rest of the time she was like a leaking tap and went around clutching gigantic packets of Kleenex.

'Nellie is leaving us,' my Dad informed every customer who came into the shop, irrespective of whether they knew who he was talking about. Naturally, with the exception of passing tourists, most people did.

'Isn't it a tragedy?' they all said.

Oh yes, indeed, my Dad agreed. It was a tragedy when Ireland couldn't find jobs to keep its youngsters at home because of a pack of greedy politicians who were only interested in lining their own pockets and to hell with the rest of the country. It is nice to know one is loved, but only an Irish family could turn my departure for Paris into a 'tragedy'.

My little brother Billy asked for my radio and my records since I wouldn't be taking them with me. I warned him I'd be back so he'd better take good care of them. But you could see in his eyes he was hoping he'd never lay eyes on me again and that way he'd get to keep all my stuff. It was a relief to see there was somebody normal in the family besides myself. Even though I knew in my heart I'd miss them all a little I was itching to leave. The ferry was booked. There was only one week to survive the 'tragedy' and the 'Oh to be young again!' litany. But I was saved from more tears and melodrama when my older brother Brian announced that he was bringing a girl home for the week-end.

'A girl?' said my Mam. There was a look of complete astonishment on her face, as if my brother had telephoned to say he had adopted a kangaroo and could my Mam make up a spare bed for it.

'How did we get so old so suddenly?' my Dad wondered.

'Nellie is going to Paris. Brian is going to get married,' chanted my Mam.

For the rest of the week the tragedy of my leaving Ireland took second place. They were too busy marrying Brian off to this unknown girl. It came as a major blow when he arrived on Saturday without the girl. Well, he sort of forgot to inform them of the change in plan. My Mam said never, never to do that to her again. She'd had her hair done a different colour for the future bride. We were going to have roast duck and trimmings to celebrate and then Brian dares to appear without any bride.

We all went to Horgan's for my going away celebrations. The old folk got drunk as coots. Brian and I sat at the bar and he told me about being a student in Galway. He owed his landlady seven weeks rent and ate nothing but eggs and bread. He even had to cut out the food if he was meeting the girl so he could afford to pay for a drink. But he couldn't tell my Dad he was stone broke and in debt. I assumed he was angling for a donation from my Drama Fund.

'I don't want any kind of a loan from you,' said Brian.

He looked more offended than an Irish setter who's been expecting a juicy bone and gets kicked in the jaw instead.

'I just wanted to tell you if you're ever short in Paris let me know and I'll see what I can do to help.'

I nearly expired there on the spot. Of course in retrospect I understood. Brian had gone away to University to become an engineer. In the process he had grown a heart, something I'd been convinced he'd been born without.

'What happened to the girl?' I asked.

'She preferred the guy with the MGB,' he said sadly and slouched over the bar as if life was weighing him down. 'The usual. You'll find out soon enough.'

I pulled out a tenner and gave it to him.

'When you're in Galway have a pint on me,' I said, trying to be hard because I was pretty sick of the ocean of sentimentality that was surging around me.

He took the money and clasped me clumsily to him. I was on the verge of sobs. But then Belinda appeared behind us, tottering on her high heels.

'Give the children whatever they want,' she told the barman, and plonked down another tenner. 'It's so nice to have you all together, isn't it?'

Belinda floated back to the oldies. I had a Babycham,

which is as close as you can get to Champagne. Brian had a pint. He told me all about Daphne and how nothing but eggs made his breath go off and maybe that's why she preferred the guy with the MGB. It made me feel so sad. All of a sudden I felt mature. It was weird. I hadn't even left the Green Isle and I knew I'd finally reached that awful stage they'd been threatening me with for years - grown up, age of reason, understanding broken hearts. It was all there.

SIX

I had more food than clothes in my luggage when I left home for Paris. My Mam and Dad packed in about 10 pounds of Barry's tea because 'the French don't have real tea like us.' I had pounds of Irish bacon, Irish black puddings, a small side of Irish smoked salmon, an Irish fruitcake and a selection of Irish chocolates. Granddad ordered ten pounds of Irish sausages from the O'Learys, informing them that his granddaughter was going abroad and would need their special sausages to keep her strength up. I had to remind him that I was going to France, Land of Food, and anyway I'd be staying in a hotel until I found long-term lodgings. Granddad had the answer. Ask the hotel manager to put the goods in their freezer. It was the least they could do for a traveller. Especially since the French had learnt how to make sausages from the Irish.

I said my goodbyes to Granddad and Belinda in Dunmo-Croi.

'See you in Paris then,' Granddad said merrily. Then he kissed me and rushed away saying he'd been caught short. I knew he was crying.

My Mam and Dad drove me to the ferry and I tried not to look too happy when I finally got on the boat. They looked heartbroken: their eyes were red as radishes. I kept telling them that Paris was only an hour away - if they took the plane.

'We'll fly, we'll fly one day,' my Dad said mopping his tears. Since he is not given to gushiness like the rest of them, that made things worse and waves of tears came crashing down all our cheeks.

'Keep moving now, would you, please,' hollered the guard who was in charge of getting folk onto the ferry with the least amount of fuss. I was crying so hard I couldn't move.

'D'you mind if I go ahead of you?' said an American voice in my ear.

Through my tears I could see this blur of teeth, the American kind that half-blind you the first time they unsheathe them. He also had orange lips. That sort of stopped my tears for a moment. It isn't every day you find a guy walking around with orange lips. Later I found out it wasn't a permanent affliction but due to the orange ice lollies he'd been sucking on.

'I've got a very heavy knapsack,' he whined.

'You're not the only one with heavy luggage,' I told him, and started moving as fast as I could with my ton of pig parts. I didn't stop until I had reached a zone where the guard was no longer hollering at us to keep on moving. I looked back and couldn't see my parents. In fact it would be ever so long until I saw them again.

'This is your first time leaving home then?' asked the American, as he tried to plonk his gear down on the space I had my eye on.

'What's it to you?' I said nastily. He had spoilt my going-away picture of myself. Because of him I had missed standing there waving at my parents for another poignant minute.

'Where are you going?' he asked.

I looked at this guy. I mean, really, really looked. Here we were on a ferry to France with a connecting train to Paris and he was wondering about my destination.

'I'm going where the boat's going. You're going somewhere different?'

'No. I'm going back to Paris,' he answered, friendly as could be. 'But I was just like you the day I left home. You feel so guilty about leaving them. It's like if you want crispy fried chicken, somewhere down the line somebody's got to murder that chicken. It's the same leaving home. You murder your parents. It's like a mini-death. They die inside as they see their little fledging fly away.'

'I didn't fly away,' I reminded this runaway mouth. 'This is a ferry, right?'

'That's just a detail. Right as we speak your parents are crying on one another's shoulders. Their little girl has left home.'

'Just how would you know?'

What is it about Americans that the minute they say 'Hello' they immediately assume they know you and how you are going to react. When you don't even know yourself. Because the last thing I expected to do that moment was burst out crying again. In fact when my tears started to flow I thought it was rain.

'What did I say?' said the American guy, and patted my shoulder. 'It's terrible. It's the price we all have to pay for our freedom.'

'Oh, just shut up,' I told him and continued sobbing.

There was a screeching noise as the anchor was lifted. We began to move. No, we began to - lurch, lurch, lurch - out to sea. I had to stop crying because all my insides were on their way up.

'Why didn't you take your Dramamine?' he called after me as I galloped to the toilets.

When I came out the Green Isle had disappeared from view. I limped back to my seat looking and feeling worse than an animal who has been skinned and is watching her own pelt being stretched onto a frame. He was still there, standing tall with flashing gnashers.

'Feeling better now I guess! My name's Paul,' he said and proffered a packet of pills. 'Have a Dramamine.'

'No thank you.'

I might look bright green but I knew all about the risks of taking strange pills from strangers.

'These do not contain aspirin.' he said meaningfully, as if that nugget of information was going to impress me.

'I don't actually need them. I'm a real sailor. I never get sea-sick.'

The words were scarcely out of his mouth when the boat gave a nasty lurch and he went green in the face which didn't even clash with his orange lips. He just had time to jettison himself into the men's loo. It made me feel miles better. I hate guys who strut around saying they never catch colds, they never get the 'flu, they never get sea-sick - like they've got heavy, heavy influence with the Powers Above.

The ferry ride was as enjoyable as you could expect when the two of you are yo-yoing to and fro to the toilets and vomiting. In between trips to the loo Paul told me he was from Philadelphia, a graduate in Eng. Lit. and a writer (he hadn't been published yet, because like Hemingway, he was going through the rejection process first). He had invested the last of his cash to go to Ireland and trace his ancestors and write an article about that riveting experience and break into magazine writing. Unfortunately, not even the Records Library in Dublin could detect a whiff of his relatives. So he was writing an article about *not* finding his relatives in the Green Isle.

When we changed from the boat to the train we both looked about ten years older. I was so weak I felt like tossing those heavy pig products overboard. But I didn't have the energy. Paul had to almost heave me and my bags onto the train for Paris. We shared a compartment with a pack of wild drunks who hadn't been remotely affected by the choppy boat ride. This bunch of drunks were not Irish which is something the BBC and all the other TV companies should take note of. In most films you get the impression that the Irish hold the world monopoly on drinking skills. These were French rugby supporters on their way back to their native land, having victoriously belted the shit out of the Irish team. Yes, I thought, looking at that pack of French drunks, I appreciate my good fortune that God made me a woman, and not a half-baked man with an obsession for kicking balls of all shapes and sizes.

'Goutez! Goutez!' One of the drunks waved the bottle of champagne right under my nose. ('Goutez' is French for 'taste' or in this case 'Have a swig'.)

'Non merci!' I said adamantly.

The drunk almost shoved the bottle into Paul's mouth.

'Vive La France! Vive l'USA!' said Paul, in between swigs from the common trough.

'Goutez! Goutez!' Another drunk waved a wine bottle into my face.

'NON!'

This time I left out the 'merci' part. The drunk burped and toddled away to molest a few more passengers.

That was my first conversational exchange in the land of Molière, Baudelaire, Rimbaud, Voltaire, Balzac and Victor Hugo. I had been preparing myself for profound philosophical discussions in the Land of Class. Instead I was feeling sicker than a gutted duck, besieged by yelping, burping French drunks and an

American who smelt of recent vomit and had absolutely no compunction about drinking from a stranger's bottle of booze.

'Look! Look! That's the Sacré Coeur!' Paul yelled and jumped up from his seat. 'We're home.'

In the distance I could just make out a white building of sorts sticking up from a mass of concrete. The drunk made a reappearance. Paul whipped the bottle out of his hand, guzzled half of it and roared:

'Ah Paree! Paree! Enfin chez moi!' (That's French for 'Oh Paris, Paris, I'm finally home.') It struck me as an odd thing for an American from Philadelphia to chant. When the train pulled into the Gare du Nord he blew kisses to all the other trains outside the window. Gare du Nord is French for 'Station of the North' meaning that the trains leaving from this station are either coming or going from a Northern direction. The French make things easy. You don't have to take a history course to find out which station to take, as Granddad says about London, with its Trafalgar, Waterloo and Piccadilly stations.

Paul grabbed my bags and said: 'Follow me, mademoiselle.'

You can bet I followed him in case he ran off with all my Irish groceries.

'I know just the hotel for you,' he said.

'I can get my own room, thank you,' I told him, and tried to stop him dialling the number. But the journey had slowed my reflexes

'You've got a room here,' he said.

He pointed to one of the hotels listed in my guide book - the hotel St. André. Then with giant strides and still holding my bags he marched out to the taxi rank and bundled me into the first one. In impressive French he ordered the cabbie to help me with my bags at the other end, because I had a bad back. He whispered sotto voce in English that French cabbies wouldn't help their own grandmothers with their luggage but were a nation of hypochondriacs and would be most understanding about a bad back.

'Take care. See ya!'

SEVEN

That cab shot from its spot faster than a rocket taking off from NASA. We went from the North of Paris to the South in a blur of speed. The driver was a lunatic who chain smoked and swore non-stop. His favourite word was 'con' (that's French for shithead, or dickhead or bastard - take your pick). In my first ride across glamorous Paris I heard that word 'con' approximately 75 times.

I had visualized my first trip across Paris with a handsome driver who would point out a golden statue, tell me the history of a famous bridge and pause at spots where people had been guillotined during the Revolution. Just the regular stuff you see on film and TV. Instead I'm locked in with a maniac who takes direct aim at anyone on the pedestrian crossing and is only capable of saying 'con'.

We screeched to a halt in front of the Hotel St. André. It happened so fast I was slammed right up against the back of the front seat. Another few inches and my breasts would have poked through my back and I'd be wearing my bras back-to-front for the rest of my life and buying them at Tipps, the only place that caters to such irregularities. The driver didn't help me with my bags: he was too busy hollering out a torrent of 'cons' at a driver who was trying to ease by him. A couple staggered backwards out of the bar across the way yelling out a stream of 'cons, connards' and 'enfoirés,' - a more advanced version of 'dickhead'. I must have arrived on a bad day. Here I was in the most romantic city in the world surrounded by irate Parisians all shouting 'shithead' at one another.

The foyer of the hotel was an oasis of tranquillity after that cab ride. It had old beams, crooked windows, antique carpets and a beautiful Frenchman at the reception desk who said 'Bonjour Mademoiselle' as he bowed politely. He kindly corrected a grammatical mistake I made as I filled in the registration form and gave me a very useful tip about gender. Most of the professions in French, he explained, took the male form 'le' with the exception of nurse and teacher, which could take either 'le' or 'la'. That titbit shook me. I had erroneously thought that it was the French who had introduced 'egalité' a few centuries back.

He complimented me on my quick grasp of French. We were getting along so well I asked him if he could put some food in their deep freeze. His eyebrows quivered as if he couldn't quite understand what I was talking about.

'Just some Irish bacon and sausages and smoked salmon,' I explained. 'I don't want them to go off.'

'Irish food? You brought Irish food to Paris?'

He bowed and took my groceries. He smiled widely, implying that he would do everything in his power to serve a hotel guest. But the silent query was: when did this include preserving half a ton of Irish pig parts?

My room was so sweet. It had a tiny shower fitted into the space behind the bed. The fat tourists who had passed me on the stairs wouldn't have fitted into those showers. They must have had rooms for the slim and the fat in this hotel - the way they have smoking and non-smoking bedrooms. I was hoping I'd see a famous landmark from my window like the Eiffel Tower so that I could stand decorously at the window sighing 'Ah, Paree, Paree'.

But the view I had from my window was a giant ad for beer that was about five stories high. It showed a woman naked from the waist up chasing her blouse. Underneath I read … (the excitement!! My first Parisian words) … 'my shirt for a beer'. I stood at the window and thought how exotic it all was. Then I noticed a gross error in the ad. Being a genius actress, I have a keen awareness of the little details that can let a production down. For instance, if Julius Caesar is wearing a Rolex or if Cleopatra starts yelling for her 'lady shave' while she's swimming in her goat's milk. It's inaccurate. So was this ad for beer.

The woman's hair was standing straight behind her implying that she was going at one mighty clip. She was racing after that beer. Is she were going at 90 miles an hour like the ad implied then her boobs couldn't be projecting from her like two spikes. They'd be under her arms or at least have been flattened a bit from the wind resistance. I stood at the window pondering this glaring mistake on the part of the graphic artists when three men strolled by. The area under the ad was badly light. But I could still see the outline of the three guys as they piddled against the wall. In the half light you could see the dark liquid snaking it's way across the pavement. I closed my shutters and went to bed reminding myself that I really and truly was in Paris. And when I woke up the next day I'd get to see the REAL Paris – the one I'd always seen on TV and in the movies.

I had my first French breakfast in the tiny dining room. Two American girls sat at the next table talking about the water level in the shower. One of them said according to a market survey the French only used one bar of soap as opposed to the five bars used by the rest of Europe during the same test period. I wondered how on earth people could take such a personal survey.

'That's why the French are great for making perfumes,' said the blonde one. 'They need something to cover the smells.'

'You're so gross!' said the other girl. 'We're eating this fantastic bread, this fantastic jam, this fantastic coffee and all you can think of is odours! Just why did you come to France?'

'Unfortunately it's one of those things you just gotta do.'

'You are Vile!'

After that total silence prevailed and I finished my six helpings of bread, all the jam and five cups of coffee. It was included in the price of the room.

Fortified by my breakfast, I sallied forth to find a job and long term lodgings. It was a grey and drizzly day. The first thing I did was buy an umbrella - a fiercely red one because my mood had brightened when I left the hotel and saw I was in the quaintest looking section of streets you could imagine. Overnight the streets had changed into a market and it was brimming over with exotic fruit and vegetables and more colours than even the Impressionists had used.

I also discovered in a tiny back street this ancient café with the most beautiful etched glass windows. The décor was like something out of an old painting. A few men in overalls from the market were drinking tiny glasses of calva with their espressos. I sat down at one of the tiny old brown tables and ordered an espresso without the Calvados. I felt so Parisian sitting there with my red umbrella particularly since not an American or an Irish accent could be heard in the entire place. I almost had to control myself from blowing kisses to all and sundry the way Paul had done when he had caught sight of the Sacré Coeur.

A man came in with drenched hair. He shook himself, laughed and said: 'Oh la la la la!'. This was the real Paree! I was in love with the whole scene ... the sheer exoticism of it all ... the smoke even ... the vibrancy of these market guys who had been up half the night and were now treating themselves to a café and a calva. The noisy group in the corner looked like young artists who had worked through the night and were now thinking of going to bed. And the man with the wet hair who had 'oh la la'd' and was only having an espresso like myself could have been a drama critic. He'd handed in his review, finished his work and was now going to drop exhausted into bed.

Soon I too would be just like these people, doing exotic things, experiencing wonders and laughing through life shaking the rain from my hair. It was a great feeling. Like I was living the most truly exotic moment of my life. From that day forward I would hear symphonies in my heart the way Beethoven had heard them in his head. I would have invisible wings on my ankles and glide through the rest of my life.

Who was the playwright who wrote: 'It is only our illusions that keep us tramping on from day to day?'

EIGHT

A week later I had a job and a roof over my head. In exchange for my own 'apartment' and meals I would give two hours of English every day to 10 year old twins, Maude and Claude. It sounded great when their mother Madame Duchamps interviewed me in her stunning salon. The room was as big as an art gallery and dripping with silk yellow drapes, tassles two feet long, and a chandelier bigger than a sofa. The delicate carpet was a wisp of pink silk, and Madame skirted it instead of walking across it. My Mam would have had a fainting fit just looking at that carpet. There were little lamps dotted all over the room with glass lampshades that drooped like exotic blooms over golden holders. It made our living room at home look like something that had been flung up during a hurricane.

The walls were covered with silk wallpaper and real oil paintings of ancestors. The males bore a strong resemblance to pugs/beagles and the female side looked like scrawny Afghans. They must have been from Monsieur's side of the family because Madame was gorgeously French – chic, groomed, elegant, not a wisp of a blonde hair out of place. Madame sat on the pink sofa - again of the most delicate shade and texture - and it was a toss up as to which was more stylish – the sofa or Madame. She pointed me in the direction of a more robust petit point armchair. This, I might add, was the most refined piece of furniture I had ever sat on - with the exception of the chair in Cork Castle. I'd plonked myself on it before I'd noticed the *FORBIDDEN TO SIT* sign.

This was the Paris of my imagination. Elegance oozing all over the place. The chandelier was a bit on the fancy side but I could get used to it. I settled into the armchair wondering if Madame would lend me a camera so that I could take a photo to show my Mam and my Dad where I would be spending my leisure hours - when I wasn't performing on classy stages. That's when Madame informed me that 'my quarters' were not within the apartment. They were on a higher level. I thought I'd misunderstood what she was saying to me in French. But there was no mistake. Madame asked me if I wanted to view my 'accommodation' before I committed myself. I said I was game.

We left the pink salon with the chandelier twinkling like a chunk of starry heaven that had dropped through the window on a particularly spectacular night. Madame ushered me down a long hallway (more ghastly ancestor portraits) through a restaurant sized kitchen and into a mini laundry. She undid the four bolts on the back of the door and we walked out onto a back staircase that was like something out of Dickens. The stairs hadn't been swept in years. There were cobwebs the size of the chandelier in the salon. Madame did not look at her ease, leading me up those dingy back stairs to my 'apartment'.

The first time I saw that place under the roof I nearly dropped dead. It was beyond unreal especially after overdosing on silk sofas and old portraits in the salon. I'd seen loads of views of the famous roofs of Paris. But this was my first view of life as lived under those arty roofs. There were about ten little rooms on either side. Most of the doors were open, so you could see who lived there. It was heaving with different nationalities. African and Arab kids ran up and down in the middle of the corridor and in and out of rooms. There was a Chinese guy chanting a mantra. In one of the rooms there was an ancient, wrinkled old man who looked twice as old as Granddad. I had to blink a few times. I just couldn't believe I was seeing a Turkish cobbler with a red fez tip tapping away at an old shoe. His room was stacked high with shoes of all kinds waiting to be repaired.

Madame clearly disapproved of anyone who was housed up here in all the chambres de bonne (that's French for 'maid's rooms'). These rooms went back to the heyday of the bourgeoisie, when the servants were tucked up under the eaves at a safe distance from their masters. People don't have that many servants anymore and these rooms were rented out to the poor (as know-it-all Paul told me later). Two laughing little boys flew past us on a squeaking skateboard.

'Go away!' said Madame. Her voice had an edge to it, as if the kids were aliens who had melons growing where the rest of us have teeth.

'Do hurry!'

There was panting urgency in Madame's voice. We were passing a tiny room where about ten faces stared out at us.

'There are more people living up here than in the rest of the building combined,' said Madame. Her nostrils quivered with distaste as she turned the key in a closed door. Marie Antoinette and Madame would have had a lot in common.

'This is it.'

Madame pushed the door open with her foot.

'It' .. the room .. was the biggest shock of all. I was looking at a dog box. An Irish setter would have come down with claustrophobia immediately.

'There are no cooking facilities here,' said Madame grandly.

You'd have to remove the bed to get anything else into that pen.

'But you will have your meals in our apartment. You may eat on your own, or with the children or with Francesca.'

Francesca was new. It could have been the dog, the cat or a mad relative they wheeled out at meal times.

'Francesca is our maid. You haven't met her yet,' said Madame, clearing up that little mystery.

The bed had a very odd look to it. It seemed unnaturally high. I know I'm taller than most. But that doesn't mean I like beds higher than my waist.

'Aha! Now you see you have two mattresses.' said Madame, pulling away the duvet to show me. 'We will be taking the extra mattress with us to the country house in the Spring.'

'In the Spring?' - Spring being a long way off.

Plus I'm not keen on heights. That bed looked so high it almost gave me vertigo. If I ever fell out of it, the floor was such a long way down I'd definitely break an indispensable part of my anatomy. Even Madame could see I was not about to break into a frenetic flamenco of enthusiasm.

'I suppose it is on the small side,' she said. She walked the six spaces to the window where two pigeons were simultaneously billing, cooing and crapping. Those were my first Paris Pigeon Lovebirds. I thought they looked so romantic on that windowsill. Later I would drastically revise my attitude. I wouldn't go so far as to say that I'd love to blast every last one of them from the face of the planet. But it would become open war between me and those pigeons.

'It sure is small. You can say that again,' I said, so there would be no misunderstanding.

'You don't have many clothes,' Madame announced. It was difficult to know whether this was a question or a statement.

'Just enough to see me through.'

'Good! The last American girl was a problem. She had to put some of her clothes in my closet.' Madame paused, and pointed to the thinnest excuse of a wardrobe I had ever seen. 'If you don't have enough room, you can use the broom closet in the apartment.'

The broom closet? Wow! Come to Paris for a bit of class!

'I'll have Francesca clean it out. We don't use it for anything.'

I could see that in these 'accommodations' I'd be real fit in no time. Running up and down those stairs for my three meals. Running up and down every time I had to wash - because as Madame had pointed out, there were no washing facilities. And if I wanted a change of clothes just take a dive into the former broom closet.

'Eh bien?' she asked me.

The Chinese wailing mantra chant suddenly stopped and we both jumped. In the silence you could hear a very strange tapping noise that could easily shred your nerves to tatters. It was the old Turk mending all those shoes.

'You are interested?' asked Madame. She eased over to the door as if it were beyond her endurance to spend any more time up here in Pauvreville.

'I'll take it.'

It was free and it wasn't like I'd be spending much time up here in Pigeon City once I'd found work at a classy theatre.

'Good. That's settled. The children come home at 3. They will eat a little snack and your lesson will commence at 3.30. You will finish at 5.30. Monsieur usually comes home at 6.30 so you should have your last meal before then. Monsieur has a very, very demanding job.'

Hey, I wasn't exactly bursting to spend quality time with Monsieur.

'OK by me,' I replied and that's how I ended up living in a dog-box in one of the fanciest parts of Paris with untold nationalities, all of us living squashed up together like an armada of rabbits in hutches.

I asked Madame if I could deposit my Irish goods in her ample freezer. When she had given me the tour of their giant apartment I had been introduced to the vast freezer that was bigger than the butcher's in Dun-mo-Croi and certainly roomier than my 'accommodations.'

'Are they safe?' Madame wanted to know.

'I didn't know the pig personally. But we always get our bacon from O'Leary's and there has yet to be a complaint.'

I watched as she cleared out a large space in the freezer for the foreign goods so they wouldn't come into contact with the native stuff. Europe might be on its way to becoming One, but not with Madame's approval.

'I'll give you a taste,' I offered.

'Oh, that won't be necessary,' said Madame with a slight shudder.

I remembered how carefully, mournfully and

lovingly my Mam, my Dad and Granddad had selected and wrapped those parting gifts for me. I had to resist giving the frozen packets a little pat – like a sort of a long distance caress to them all. It was my first brush with homesickness.

NINE

I was hauling my bags out of the Hotel into a cab when who should loom up in front of me but Paul - teeth shining and gleaming in the sunshine. Since I wasn't throwing up my guts and being sea-sick, this 6'3' American with bouncy brown hair and velvety eyes suddenly struck me as rather dishy.

'Hey, what's happening?' he shouted, picking up one of the bags with the frozen pig parts and tossing it into the boot of the cab.

'I could ask the same of you.'

'I'm available,' Paul announced. He leaned against the cab much to the blatant displeasure of the cab driver who took offence at the sight of anyone daring to lean on his carrosserie. 'I've finished my article so I'm a relatively free man now.'

'Well, I'm not. I'm moving to my new place.'

'Hey, no problem! Meet me later in this café. It's our local,' he said and whipped a notebook out of his tattered old rucksack, scribbled the address of the café on it and gave it to me.

It wasn't in my grand design to become matey with English speakers in Paris. If I had wanted to meet Americans I'd have saved up and gone to New York. But after a week of pounding the Parisian pavements looking for a job and a room, I was more than ready to celebrate my success. Sitting in a café with the only person I knew in Paris was also preferable to lying in my hutch watching a platoon of pigeons having a go at one another in between pooping all over my windowsill.

'OK. See you later.'

The café's full name was Café de Marie Hélène de Beaulieu. 'Beaulieu' is French for 'beautiful place'. There are millions of 'beaulieus' in France. People find it too cerebrally taxing to be a bit more specific or descriptive. They slap on the 'Beaulieu' the way painters put 'untitled' under canvases they can't be bothered finding a name for.

Whoever had originally christened the café a beautiful place would have gone into terminal shock to see it now. Over the decades millions of Gauloises had kippered everything in sight to a dull brown. The walls, the ceiling, the floor, the curtains were all brown. The teeth of most of the habitués were smoked to a deep mahogany. The TV screen had a sepia glow to it. Amber light fell through the bronzed windows. I felt as if I had just walked into that morose painting, 'The Absinthe Drinkers'. Of all the cafés in Paris, I thought, he has to choose this one. Just too typical!

Most of the tables lined against the wall (brown on brown) were occupied by people reading. One elderly woman was writing music and she tapped out an occasional beat against her cup (also in the sun-tanned zone). Paul sat at a corner table with books piled high on either side of him. A small espresso (the cheapest thing you can order in a Parisian café) was perched on top of a pile of books. He was busy scribbling in a notebook. I sat down opposite him and made my presence known.

'Just lemme get this idea down on paper. Otherwise it will evaporate.'

He held up his left hand, like a policeman halting traffic. I ordered myself a citron pressé from the not very pressé garcon. (That's a nifty play on words even if I say so myself). The verb 'presser' in French can mean both 'squeezed' and also 'in a hurry'. 'Citron Pressé' is the sophisticated Parisian version of freshly squeezed lemon, water and sugar. It is always served in a tall glass in a silver holder sitting on a saucer with the spoon over the top. My citron pressé was the only elegant looking thing in that brown dive of a café.

'My new book,' said Paul as he slapped his notebook shut.

Not even as much as a 'Hello and how are you' or 'What d'you think of Paris?' from the guy.

'I'm going to call it – '*What They Ate*'.'

'What did who eat?'

'The Greats! Hemingway, Fitzgerald, Picasso. If I can get enough material I'll just do Hemingway. He was the Great of Greats after all. And Fitzgerald never felt the lash of hunger and poverty the way Hemingway did.'

There was abject reverence in his voice every time he said 'Hemingway'.

'They're all dead. Who's going to be interested in what those guys ate?'

'The entire world as we know it,' said Paul with that overpowering confidence you will only find in a true American. 'After they read what I've written. When he lived here in the 20's, Hemingway had to go to the Tuileries and shoot pigeons so his wife and son could have something to eat. I'm trying to find what recipes they used for the pigeons. Can you believe the greatest nearly starved in Paris?'

'Why didn't he get a job?'

Paul's eyes gave a little hop in their sockets.

'A job? Hemingway was a writer.'

Paul was so astonished he could hardly squeak out the words.

'Well, I'm an actress and you wouldn't find me shooting dirty pigeons in any Park let alone eating them.'

'Hey, we're talking Great writers here, not stupid AKtors!'

Paul poured out a giant glass of free water and gulped half of it down as if the very thought of anyone lumping his sacred Hemingway in with actors was too much to bear.

'We're talking … Hem . ing . way,' he repeated, reverence oozing from every syllable. 'I'm going to spend the next few months researching how Hemingway and all the other greats managed to survive on nothing – and I mean *NOTHING* – during the 20's right here in Paris. Then I'm going to compile all their favourite recipes. It will make a dynamite history, art cum cookbook.'

'That's about the nuttiest thing I've heard in years,' I said so there would be no misunderstanding.

Paul smiled patiently at me like I was some half brained cocker spaniel he was trying to toilet train.

'My book will have everything,' Paul continued smugly. 'The romance of Paris in the '20's. The literary and artistic greatness of the Lost Generation, the flower of American writers scratching by on pigeon pie.'

'Scratch the other one!'

'Plus it will have my brilliant style brimming with verve and brio,' Paul blithely waffled on. 'And don't overlook the food and recipe factor. Americans adore cookbooks. They're right up there next to diet books. My book will take the US by storm.'

Paul flung his arms wide and threw himself back in his chair, full of overbearing self-satisfaction. The chair wobbled and he lost his balance. He fell back against the wall. The resounding wall and brain contact knocked the wind out of him. While he was getting his breath back I talked about my passions.

'I'm going to start out in the fringe theatre, and in a no time at all I'll be ready for the Académie. Paris also has an American theatre and ..'

A giant plonked himself down at our table. This guy was a human shag carpet and could have played King Kong without the costume. His tattered jacket was held together by a tapestry of safety pins that glittered in the café's amber light.

'Hi Hansi,' said Paul, flashing a wide smile of relief. 'Meet my friend Nellie Flanagan.'

Hansi grunted into his beard.

'Hansi is one of the few authentic painters left in Paris,' Paul said, rather grandly.

Aha! So that was *his* problem. And not his only one either.

Hansi from Berlin lived with two giant dogs (a mixture of Dalmatian and Afghan and burdened with the names Carnation and Schopenhauer), and six cats (also tending to the large of bone and hard to pin down lineage and colouring) in a caravan parked in a field in Paris South West, West. The cats all worked as art elves because Hansi let them prance and 'paint' across his wet watercolours or fish paste collages.

'Hansi is constantly pushing back the boundaries of art,' said Paul proudly.

'That's cruelty to cats,' I told him, imagining those poor animals with their painted paws and technicoloured tongues trying to lick the paint off one another.

'Tell her they get double shrimp rations for working,' said Hansi and slouched over to the bar. He sat there looking like a sad gargoyle.

'Now look what you've done,' said Paul angrily.

'Hansi adores animals. He wouldn't hurt a flea. And he's very sensitive especially since Jelly Bean's accident.'

Jelly Bean is Hansi's favourite cat – his soul mate. But one day while Hansi was in the local café having a coffee, a leak and a crap (there are NO modern facilities in Hansi's caravan) an oil painting fell off its perch in the caravan and Jelly Bean had a long artistic roll in the wet canvas. The only way to remove her dried fur was to shave it all off. The fur grew back but it was now white instead of black! Hansi kept the shaved off fur and interspersed it with another masterpiece which he signed - Hansi and Jelly Bean.

'He'll never forgive himself for poor Jelly Bean,' said Paul winding up his tale. 'So quit referring to animal cruelty. OK?'

Eventually the hairy painter lumbered back to us. When he crossed the café the amber light caught his safety pins and he twinkled like a walking Christmas tree.

'What are you doing in Paris?' Hansi grunted when he had settled himself at our table again.

I had only made two references to Shakespeare when another unwashed looking weirdo came in and Hansi immediately got up and bummed a few cigarettes off him.

'That's Michel the sculptor,' said Paul and got out his notebook and started scribbling again.

I sipped my citron pressé and looked around the café. It was just the kind of place I'd read about where the creatives hang out before all their dreams come true. In future years maybe one of Hansi's paintings would be up on the wall near the loo. They'd be a plaque to Paul the writer listing all his works. And they'd have a portrait of

Nellie Flanagan - world renowned actress replacing the mirror behind the bar.

How was I to know that in Paris this café was a famous landmark hangout for losers and rejects? And I was about to become a fulltime member.

TEN

My early letters home were filled with beautiful descriptions of Paree: the flamboyant bridges, the ornate green and gilded roof of the Opéra de Paree, the hundreds of varieties of cheeses, the pastry shops which drove me nuts with desire every time I walked past, and the blood red geraniums that dangled from black wrought iron balconies on practically every street in the city. I wasn't too graphic when it came to my own living conditions, sans geraniums, sans balcony. I concluded each of my letters with: 'Things are looking extremely promising on the acting front.' This was perhaps verging into the non-truth as opposed to my 'new and improved' CV which was a complete pack of lies invented by Paul.

I asked him to cast a writer's eye over my CV before I sent it out to every agent, theatre, film and TV producer in Paris (251 in all) to alert them to the news that Nellie Flanagan was available for auditions. By the time Paul had finished re-writing my CV I had 'starred' in a vast array of Irish and BBC productions and had made cameo appearances in the Abbey and in Stratford-on-Avon. Paul convinced me that only dumb assholes didn't 'enhance' their CVs. Nobody, he said, ever actually went to the bother of checking references – especially the French, and particularly in my case since they could audition me on the spot. We made 251 photocopies of Paul's masterpiece and I spent

Granddad's bonus on glossies. Only the really important people got my expensive large sized 8x 10 glossy. The others had to do with a passport sized photo until I came into another wad of cash.

I also decided to pay a personal visit to several agents and dazzle them. This turned out to be a very bad idea. They carelessly tossed my letter and expensive glossy onto a pile so high it quivered in the breeze. One good draught and the whole lot would topple conveniently into the wastepaper basket. The cruellest agent of all was called Jean-Thomas Moineau (which most aptly translates into John Thomas Sparrow). This was the specimen who had the gall to say to me, 'You're all wrong!!' Why didn't he just keep a baseball bat on his desk and whop it across all the prospective hopefuls who made the mistake of going into his office? But I kept on. The Irish lot hadn't defeated me. But man, how those French tried to squish out every scintilla of hope, ambition and dream that my Irish bosom might dare to harbour. Some complimented me on my French and told me to come back again in 5 years. Others said I didn't have a chance unless I went to Drama or Film School. Tell me news, not history! None of them had any advice on how to pay for either. One man said to me: 'You want to be an actress? My dear, it would be easier to jog barefoot to the South Pole and back. But that's your decision, isn't it?'

I went to CAT – the renowned Association which caters for people in the arts and theatre and helps them get jobs. Madame Flore, a very kind employee who was about as old as Belinda told me I reminded her of herself when she was young and hopeful. She did everything she could to help and gave me a long list of theatres, agents and film producers – all of whom had already been honoured to receive a Nellie Flanagan CV and glossy. Madame Flore also advised me to check the bulletin board where they regularly posted 'small' acting jobs. 'Small jobs' sometimes lead to leading roles in the acting world. She tried but failed to sound convincing.

I waited with my tongue hanging out for the offers to come pouring in. But only a few of my own letters came back with 'address unknown' stamped on them. It was bitterly disappointing – not to mention the waste of my precious money. Here I had arrived in Paris, expecting to be discovered and welcomed with open arms into the finest acting community in the world. The French are noted for their finesse and nose for talent. They are supposed to have the gift just as hogs can sniff out elusive truffles buried deep in the earth. Let me tell you the truth about those French! Their snouts were well and truly clogged when it came to detecting my talent. Paris was a closed shop. Paul said, 'Welcome to the real world, kid.' Then he spent a week wondering whether he could place an article on 'How *not* to get work as an actress in Paris.'

However, my 'job' turned out to be far more satisfying than I anticipated. Maude and Claude were easy kids to teach. It isn't often you come across a pair of 10 year olds who want to lace into *Macbeth* with more gusto and brio than the *Royal Shakespeare Company*. I even enjoyed those two hours because I could pretend I was rehearsing and not drumming English into two French kids. As a teacher I was a regular dynamo although Paul disagreed thoroughly with my teaching methods. He said he couldn't see how two 10 year olds could usefully apply a sentence like: '*Not all the perfumes of Arabia shall sweeten this little hand.*' He said I should be dinning things into them like: '*How do I get to the nearest métro station from here?*' But my kids already knew the banal and useful stuff.

However, I did concede there would be few opportunities in life for either Maude or Claude to say '*Now o'er the one half-world Nature seems dead and wicked dreams abuse the curtained sleep.*' But the kids loved *Macbeth* – especially the witches. For those who need to brush up their Shakespeare, *Macbeth* opens with three ugly witches cackling over a cauldron: '*when shall we three meet again, in thunder, lightning or in rain?*' The three of us hunkered down on the floor of the study, around the biggest saucepan in the house with Monsieur's dark jackets draped over our heads. Naturally we didn't ask his permission because even if Monsieur looked calm as a goldfish in a murky bowl he might object to his expensive dinner jackets being used as witches' capes. And we certainly didn't want Madame to get a whiff of our rehearsals.

One day we had a very close call. Maude was applying abundant ketchup to her hands to show the blood oozing from Lady Macbeth's hands when suddenly the bottom fell out of the plastic bottle of ketchup and all the contents *PLUPPED* onto the Persian carpet. The two went whiter than all the ghosts in *Macbeth*.

'Mamman will murder you,' said Claude.

'Papa will kill me,' whimpered Maude.

That was the precise instant we heard the front door open followed by the tinny sound as Madame tossed her keys into the silver Louis XIV bowl on the hall table. Maude gave a sob as if she were going to be sick. Claude was trembling. I could never remember being that terrified of my Mam and Dad and suddenly felt a surge of protective affection for these kids. That was most unusual because I honestly can't stand most children.

'Sit down and start the dagger speech.'

They immediately went into a squat like defeated ducks on an oil slick. The parquet let out squeals of pain as Madame's high heels pranced across it. In half a second I had whipped off my jacket and placed it nonchalantly over the other props (Madame's lacy negligee, her chunky ruby necklace and gold chains that Maude had made into Lady Macbeth's crown). I put my Complete Shakespeare on the floor between the three of us and spread my skirt over the pool of ketchup.

When Madame passed by the door we looked so innocent, sitting cross-legged like lazy students lounging on a lawn. Madame had a quizzical furrow on her brow when she caught a glimpse of my Complete Shakespeare.

'Maude and Claude are extremely gifted,' I said. 'Little philosophers really. Shakespeare is perfect for them.'

'My little philosophers!' said Madame.

It was the only time I heard Madame coo. She beamed like a slim swan proudly paddling across a pond with her gifted brood in tow.

'Don't let me interrupt you! I had to come back for my dry cleaning ticket. *Incredible*! The girl wanted proof. They know those silk blouses are mine. I've paid more to have them cleaned in that establishment than I paid for them originally. I am going to sever all connections with those cleaners.'

Three pairs of eyes gazed up at her. It was to be the longest monologue Madame would ever spout in my presence. Not knowing or caring anything about dry cleaning silk blouses I kept my best stage smile glued to my face.

'Continuez!' Madame ordered. But her brisk tone

was milder than usual. The way a fresh Spring breeze isn't as sharp as a Winter wind.

We heard her open a drawer in the kitchen to retrieve the dry cleaner's ticket. The hall parquet moaned again under her heels and then the front door howled as she gave it her usual confident bang. The curtains in the study quivered with the vibrations.

'We can all resume breathing again,' I told the kids, and began to investigate the ketchup damage to my skirt.

I was about to stand up when the two of them threw themselves on top of me - literally. I was quite overwhelmed. Up to that day I'd never been smothered with kisses by two 10 year olds. Maude put her lips to my ear.

'Je t'aime, Nellie. Je t'aime beaucoup!'

I was most taken aback. But I rose to the occasion beautifully.

'I love you too, sweetie,' I told her. 'And you too, Claude,' so that he wouldn't feel left out.

After that we switched to *Romeo and Juliet*. In the balcony scene Claude showed remarkable mountaineering skills scaling to the top of the book shelves where he pretended Juliet's balcony was located. I applauded his inventiveness but I agreed with Maude who refused to perch herself up there. She didn't want to risk toppling off right in the middle of her *'good night, good night parting is such sweet sorry'* speech. One tumble off those shelves and it would have been good night Maude and Claude! Instead we set up a balcony on Monsieur's desk. Again I had to applaud their prop making inventiveness even if Monsieur was quite peeved when he noticed the scratches and asked Francesca to please stop polishing his delicate antique desk with such vigour. Nobody ever caught us off guard again because we always locked the study door. When

Mercutio was killed there was a brief debate about re-introducing the ketchup. But I ruled that one out. You could still discern the stain on the Persian carpet.

My life settled into a regular trot. Down the stairs first thing in the morning for my shower in the apartment two floors below. Then up the stairs to dry my hair. Down the stairs for my breakfast. Up again to rehearse '*The Glass Menagerie*', or *Cyrano*' in front of the tiny mirror, accompanied by the rooftop bedlam of Mr. Uno howling out his mantras, the Farkas boys trying to kill themselves with skateboard obstacle races in the corridor and Mr. Turk's incessant shoe hammering (his real name could have choked you so everyone called him Monsieur Turk). Down for lunch with Francesca, who was a hypochondriac and did her best to put me off my meal. Out to CAT to check the offers on the board. Back up the stairs for the kids' lesson. A quick dinner before Monsieur arrived from his super demanding job. Up to get my coat and down to the café to meet Paul, Hansi and the other motley crew of regulars.

Some nights the cigarette smoke wasn't at smog level and you could see the last of the losers propping up the bar (in France it costs a little more if you sit down at a table for your five minute or five hour espresso). Paul's girl friend never came to this café. 'Colette' was upper drawer French - Paul's words - and her chic sensibilities would have been offended by the rawness of the place. Paul also said that it was a mistake to mix friends and lovers until they were both which is the kind of garbage only a writer could come up with. Every evening Hansi offered to buy me a carafe of wine which was a contradiction in terms because he had never bought anything in his entire life. He didn't believe in money. If he wanted something he just asked for it – cigarettes, food, wine, newspapers, paint. His tab with Henri the owner was legendary. He got away with murder because 'he's Hansi' and because nobody wanted to get on the wrong side of the Son of Kong who carried photos of his zoo in his tattered wallet.

Once a week, usually on a Friday night, Hansi grunted if I wanted to see his caravan. So in my letters home I could honestly tell my Mam and Dad that a very gifted painter was eager to date me and he wasn't the only one either. Michel the sculptor asked me to model for him (Paul explained that this was his artistic way of asking a girl out on a date). Even though everyone in the café said he was France's answer to Michelangelo, he couldn't afford materials so I'd have to pay *him* for the honour of modelling for him. Some nights I almost had to hypnotise myself into still believing that I and my weirdo pals were on the threshold of Fame & Fortune and not the Loony Bin.

Going up those stairs last thing at night I wondered if I'd ever get to be an actress in Paris. The days were flitting by. I'd wake up one morning and I'd be too old to even play Juliet's mother who doesn't exactly have the most jaw dropping lines Shakespeare ever penned.

ELEVEN

After the first month I knew in my bones that I was wasting time and effort going to CAT. The offices were in Pigalle - that dreadful part of Paris where busloads of sub-humans come to goggle at breasts and simulated sex. It's amazing how that place pulls them in. They could go to any sea-side resort in France and do a PHD in mammaries if they were so interested. The only reason I continued going to CAT was because I had promised Madame Flore not to give up even if all the offers on the board were always for other people. Needed: Actor, male, acrobatic, forties. Or: White, female, late teens, not over 5' (Planet of the Dwarfs?); Mediterranean, male, 20-22; female, 19, ballet dancer. I'd have qualified for that one if I'd only had the foresight to take up ballet at the age of 5.

One afternoon I was in CAT waiting for the rain to stop and thinking how the Paris rain had a cruel, sulking quality to it as if it objected to leaking over such stunningly gorgeous buildings. It wasn't like the sparkling, silver rain we have in Ireland which gave us the Emerald Isle, arthritis, damp, mould and a legitimate excuse for the Irish to dip their beaks into troughs of Guinness at the drop of a hat. That's when this blonde whirled in. She was about my age. She shook the rain off her hair and coat with the vigour of an irritated Afghan. Under her breath I heard her mutter; 'I hate this fucking

city.' Then she pulled out a bundle of cards from her bag
and stuck them onto the nearest notice board.

LEARN TO DAZZLE WITH THE DAGGER
LEARN TO DUEL TO THE DEATH
FROM LEONORE THE LEOPARD.

At the bottom there was a name of a café and a
telephone number. The blonde saw me looking at her
notice and gave me her card with a flourish and a smile.

'I already know how to dazzle with the dagger,' I
told her.

'This is for stage duels,' she insisted.

'I know how to duel, thank you.'

'I bet you a hundred francs I could beat you,' she said.

'I should hope so. You're supposed to be a teacher
aren't you?'

'The things we say to make a buck!' she said and
shook my hand.

Her real name was Diana and the duelling business
wasn't exactly wallpapering her place in sables.

'No phone either?' I asked, pointing to the number
for a café on her card.

'I'm lucky I got hot water in my chambre de bonne. I
only have a sink but at least I get hot water regularly. But
I got a dead fridge at the end of my bed.'

I put her card in my pocket and thought how exciting
and different it might be to have a pal in Paris with a few
normal mod cons. It's a mystery why only the talented
artistic strivers are expected to live without extra rooms,
phones and showers.

'I'll have to kill myself if anyone from New Jersey
ever sees how I'm living in Glam Paree,' Diana said. 'I
mean, everyone back home has at least two bathrooms.'

'Have you been in Paris long?' I asked Diana to veer her away from the Poverty in Paris theme.

'Only two years,' said Diana. 'But that's nothing. You gotta give Paris at least five years before you begin to know useful people. It's all about contacts! D'you think you'd have any problem breaking into the theatre if your name was Deneuve?'

For a second I thought I was listening to Valerie Vaughan reminding me in between knitting tips that I'd never get anywhere because my name was Flanagan, not Fonda. So the Paris version was - give it five years.

The rain finally stopped and since neither of us had gold embossed invites to premieres, vernissages or first night to the Opéra de Paree we decided to treat ourselves to a 'pot'. (That's pronounced 'po' and is real French for 'a drinkie'.) I suggested we go to my local, Café de Marie Hélène de Beaulieu. Diana looked most impressed. On the way over I had to burst her bubble. My Montmartre local was an ancient dump of a café owned by weirdo Henri who put up a small, plastic Christmas tree on the bar on New Year's Eve and took it down again on the 14th of July, the French National Holiday.

Paul and Hansi took to Diana like ducks to slugs. Diana is bold, blonde and pert so men immediately slobber over her the way kids zero in on the cute looking puppy as opposed to the poor animal with the great personality, three paws, half an ear and only one eye. Diana probably took up fencing to ward off hordes of fawning men.

With grandiloquent flair Paul introduced Hansi with his usual garbage.

'This is Hansi. One of the few good painters now working in Paris.'

'I'm good and I don't have to wait for some half blind critic to tell me what I already know,' Hansi grunted.

Diana was still reeling at the lack of elegance in my Montmartre local so I was kind and didn't acerbically set the record straight on Hansi's status in the art world. I didn't repeat that:

A. No art critic with a sanity certificate would want to track down Hansi's caravan in that godforsaken field in Paris South West, West.

B. Any art critic would have to be suicidal to confront Hansi's two horse sized dogs and six ill-tempered cats.

C. Any art critic with half an eye would detect something hairy about Hansi's work. But none of them would be smart enough to figure out that a poor cat had donated all its fur to one particular painting or that the 'Jelly Bean' signature was not attributable to a person but a cat.

Paul ordered a carafe of red wine he couldn't afford while Diana waxed lyrical about the deficiencies in Parisian bathrooms. Paul listened. It's amazing how a bosomy blond can change a man. This was the same guy who complained to me ad nauseum how he hated Americans moaning about Parisian plumbing. Why couldn't they say 'Have you seen the Seine by twilight?', or 'Have you walked across the Alexander Bridge and seen the moon glinting off the gold statues?' Why was it always a case of 'What's the shower in your room like?' or 'What's the pressure like?' or 'Does your water run cold too?' And here he was listening entranced to Diana's ode to non plumbing.

But I have to give the guy credit. Paul quickly lost interest and resumed his scribbling. Diana tried to involve Hansi in the topic of the French Bath not realizing that Hansi's contact with soap, water and baths is zero and if Henriette, the owner of the local bistro, didn't allow Hansi to avail of her washing facilities he would be walking around smelling higher than the caves where they breed Roquefort.

'Before I came to Paris, I thought a French Bath was something elegant,' said Diana, tossing back her abundant blond locks à la Monroe. 'You stand in front of the sink with your legs in a plastic tub we'd wash the dog in back home. How did that get to be a French bath? There's a real knack to having a shower with just a sink and your feet in a plastic tub. At first I just couldn't get the hang of it. Now I'm a real pro.'

'And that's going to change the world,' Hansi snarled with a double grunt to indicate that the topic of conversation wasn't to his liking. Even if he doesn't like to converse, Hansi is very picky about the topics he chooses to listen to.

'Living conditions are important to some people,' said Paul, leaping to Diana's defences.

'Bien sûr!' said Hansi and gave us that threatening look to say he would launch into his tirade against materialism unless there was a change of topic real quick. Hansi's speech on the evils of materialism is a real bore if you hear it once. If you've heard it about 20 times like I have, it's enough to make your eyeballs melt. I was about to change the direction of the conversation. But Diana wasn't a duelling expert for nothing.

'I am speaking!' she informed Hansi with eyes as penetrating as the points of a rapier. She went on speaking for the next ten minutes sharing with us her impressions of Paris. They should have called it - The Trials and Tribulations of Duelling Diana in Paris.

By the end of those ten minutes, Hansi was pounding one of Paul's pen into the table trying to suppress the urge to crack something larger like Diana's skull. Paul's eyes had glazed over because there was nothing in

Diana's woeful tale that Paul could use in any future work. The only time Paul's eyes sparkle is when somebody tells him something he can use in some literary work or other. He 'uses' everything. Once he even asked me if he could write a story about my two mattresses.

'Plus I got this enormous old fridge at the end of the bed that gave up the ghost about 30 years ago. The métro lines run directly under my building and I gotta wake up every morning with vibrating walls and the fridge wobbling in the breeze at the end of my bed. I keep telling that slum landlord to take it away. I only use it to store stuff in. I don't need that fridge. It's dangerous because of the way that métro sends it into a frenzy. Any morning that gigantic thing could easily topple over on top of me in my bed.'

Hansi's eyes lit up. Diana flattened by a frenetic fridge. What a delectable thought! That should put an end to her obsession with showers and French Baths! Paul's eyes sparkled. Diana flattened to a pancake by a vibrating fridge at the end of the bed. Here was something he could possibly use in a literary oeuvre! Diana, of course mistook this lighting up of 4 eyes as entrancement and flung herself into more minute detail about her miserable abode.

I look around the café and try to propel myself into my dazzling future. But it's hard to concentrate when Henri the owner is yelling at a regular to stop spitting out the bits of tobacco from his unfiltered Gauloises. Normal people who smoke those non filtered Gauloises also pick at their tongues to delicately remove the odd bit of tobacco. But they don't cough up half their lungs while they're doing it like our moth-eaten regulars.

I look at Paul, Hansi, Michel and Duelling Diana and think: these are my Paris friends. I try to defy reality and tell myself: 'These are my exotic Paris friends.' I think of my Man who uses the word 'exotic' as a euphemism for anything beyond her realm of understanding. I suddenly miss my Mam terribly and wish I could propel myself back in time and be back home at the age of 10 being tucked up in my bed with warm cocoa and lots of kisses.

Hansi puts his hairy paw over my hand and says: 'Little One, you mustn't cry.' I take a dive into his jacket to hide my tears. I have a long sniffle thinking how sweet it is to be called 'Little One', which is the only nice thing that Paul and Hansi ever say to me. Then I begin counting all the safety pins that hold Hansi's signature ragged jacket together. I stop at 23 and start laughing hysterically. Diana finally shuts up about her dead fridge, her French Bath and her medieval living conditions.

I dry my tears. Hansi grunts and Paul orders another carafe of red wine he can't pay for.

TWELVE

Then one morning everything changed. Most mornings I was ushered into the new day by Mr. Uno wailing his 'release me and never send me back to Paris' Nirvana mantra in the room next to me. Mr. Uno walked half way around the globe thinking that Paris was the answer. Now he spends all his time chanting to avoid the risk of being reincarnated and sent back to Paris for second helpings of pain and loneliness. The first thing I always saw when I opened my eyes was that exclusive panorama of pigeons' bottoms on my windowsill. But this particular morning I was awake before Mr. Uno and there wasn't as much as a pigeon feather to be seen. All was serene and lovely under my Paris rooftop with its vista of thousands of terra cotta chimneys. I lay on my high bed and watched the swallows slicing through the pink dawn sky and diving for midges. I could hear the dawn concert of swallows squeaking happily as they swooped and looped over Paris. They sounded exactly like the swallows who thronged the fields that go sloping down to the sea behind our home in Dun-mo-Croi. Suddenly I was choking to death on homesickness in that dog box. I raced down the back stairs to try and get some fresh air and get over it.

On the streets of Paris the pink of the dawn sky was slowly fading but the clamour of the swallows up in the sky could still be heard. The red geraniums festooning the black wrought iron balconies seemed to be crooning with contentment. Bursts of laughter echoed from the café down the street where all the food market people went for their dawn breakfasts. A huge ornate double door - probably the same one they had during the Middle Ages - swung open in the millionaires' apartment building across the street. A bent old concierge tottered out and struggled to wheel inside the gigantic, green garbage bins that had been emptied by the Sanitation people during the night. She looked twice as old as Granddad. Seeing that crooked, old woman shoving and panting over those bins it didn't seem right that some people had it so very easy in life and others so darn rotten. I wanted to telephone my brother Brian and ask him if the world had become more cruel and sadder after he had left home permanently. Instead, I bought the Herald Tribune just to read words in English and went into the café to treat myself to a coffee.

And there it was on page 5 – the ad that would change my life!

BUSY ACTOR NEEDS ENGLISH LESSONS. TEACHER MUST COME TO THEATRE. IRREGULAR HOURS.

There was a telephone number.

I waited until 8 o'clock in that café where the market people were having their usual Calvados and espresso. Then I called the number. I had to let it ring about 17 times before a half dead husky voice answered.

'You're looking for an English teacher? I'm an English teacher. When would you like to start?'

Silence at the other end of the phone. I had visions of this guy falling asleep with the phone in his hand and my precious franc gone up the spout.

'English lessons. You want English lessons?

'Vous parlez francais?' he finally asked.

'You bet I do.'

And he was off! Rattling away at a fierce clip like all the French even though he was only half awake. It was hell trying to understand him. The French all talk so fast you'd think the whole nation was battling permanent diarrhoea.

'It's like this,' he said. 'I'm playing the lead in a play called '*No Fun at the Wake*'. It's at the *Théâtre du Zivot*. We're in rehearsals at the moment. But I'd like to have lessons at the theatre every day. I'm learning English because I want to go to Hollywood and be a star.'

The pips on the phone were coming fast and furious. I got the address from him just before my franc ran out. We arranged to meet in the theatre at 13.00. My hand was trembling when I put the phone down. Visions darted in front of my eyes. I'd be at the theatre giving the usual English lesson. The lead and her understudy would both come down with flash liver attacks (they get these weekly, I'm told, from the amount of wine they swill). Nellie, who'd know every line by heart would spring to the rescue and save the play. The Irish Times would do a huge spread on the young, unknown Kerry actress who had shot to the top in Paris. The lads from the Irish Television would send a crew over to beg me for an exclusive interview. I'd tell them to stuff their cameras back into their vans because they'd made my life a misery when I was an unknown in Dublin. The offers would pour in from Broadway and the West end. Top agents in London, Paris and New York would bribe me to let them represent me. My life would be a whirlwind of first nights, film making and attendance at super glamorous events in Cannes and Hollywood. I could hear the sound of enthusiastic clapping. Amazing how the dream of applause could be so real, so vibrant, so near. Then I realized that two market workers were banging on the telephone booth.

I hadn't heard of the *Théâtre du Zivot* so it wouldn't have the cachet or reputation of the *Comédie Française*. Maybe it was one of those gorgeous baroque or rococo theatres that are tucked away in the most charming parts of Paris. But it wasn't listed among the hundred odd theatres I'd sent my CV and glossy to and was located in a remote part of Paris North. My heart gave a little sauté! This was part of Mitterrand's plan to revitalize all the districts of Paris and not just the touristy, chic parts? He was almost bankrupting Paris building a vast beyond modern Opera house in the run down Bastille district. Maybe this was going to be a new revolutionary theatre in an equally decrepit district of Paris North?

I agreed with Mitterrand. The district could definitely do with a bit of a make over. There wasn't a geranium to be seen for miles. All the little balconies were cluttered with household goods and lines of washing. When I got off at my stop even the language had changed. So had the people. They didn't have that Parisian sniffy snarl that the likes of Madame have patented. I passed a café with beautiful intricate writings over the door. Next door was a butcher's with more hieroglyphics. Odd animal parts were on display. I'm not saying there were hyenas or skinned bats dangling from hooks but the meat was cut differently. The greengrocer allowed his customers to poke and prod the vegetables. This verged on the extraordinary. Normally in a Paris greengrocers if you dare so much as let a finger caress the fruit or veg the shopkeeper will have a 'crise'. 'Crise' (pronounced Kreeeeze) is the French word for 'attack' and covers every ailment which may or may not be tagged in the Medical Dictionary. You can also have 'petite crise' (small attack) or 'grande crise' (big attack). The French have more kinds of kreeezes than they have cheeses.

When I finally found the theatre I nearly had a flat out major kreeze myself. This was not a blindingly modern edifice to glorify Mitterrand for posterity. *Théâtre du Zivot* was a run-down cinema with tattered posters of a Kung-Fu film - pictures of guys leaping all over the place with their legs at unnatural angles, and naked women smirking at this cretinous activity. But maybe they were preserving the derelict exterior so it would add more edge to the post modern jewel inside. A lot of Mitterrand's 'grands projets' were controversial. But as I pushed the wooden entrance doors all illusion died and I knew I'd have to postpone faxing the boyos in Irish TV telling them to go screw themselves.

There were pinpricks all over the door. The place was riddled with woodworm. I'm an expert on woodworm, which is something not every 18 year old actress can claim. Granddad used to take in bits of old furniture badly in need of being reborn. But not before my Mam went on her woodworm, termite, and beetle hunt and shared her findings with all members of the family. My Mam would have shrieked to see the condition of that door. I had to stifle a shrieking fit myself when I walked into the 'theatre' proper. It was worse than any dump I'd seen in the grassy outposts of rural Ireland. The place smelt like mothballs marinated in onions and brandy and flambéed. There were seats missing in every row. Obviously, if one of the wooden seats gave up the ghost, they just removed it.

On stage a rehearsal was in progress. There were three people on stage. One was stretched out motionless on the bed in the centre of the stage. I surmised this was the '*Wake*' in question. Except the two people cavorting around the bed were acting in a most unwakelike manner.

The man was chasing the woman around the bed trying to kiss her. At one point the woman had a laugh attack and fell against the bed. The corpse levitated a bit from the mattress. Now that was really bad acting. Because a good actor playing a corpse does not leap or levitate. Body control is an essential element of the actor's bag of instruments. The man flung himself onto his knees in front of the laughing woman. The floorboards went into a quake. If they'd been in as bad nick as the door he'd have gone right through them. Again the corpse did a lift-off from the bed. I walked closer to the stage to have a better view of this weird *'Wake'*.

The man grabbed the laughing woman (again the corpse did a little sauté off the bed) and hurled her onto the floorboards. He stuffed his face into her ample bosom with great élan. By accident two ringlets from his wig (it looked like Regency) dropped into the woman's open mouth. When she tried to scream another ringlet just plopped in. The man had his face in her ample bosom and couldn't see that the woman was turning blue in the face. She couldn't move her hands and take the ringlets out of her mouth because he had both her arms pinned down. If this went on for much longer the actor on the bed playing the corpse would be out of a job.

Suddenly the corpse sat up in bed and announced:

'Midi! On mange! Lunchtime! I'm starving.'

She hopped out of bed, walked over to the two, pulled out a cigarette and started smoking. This upset the guy who was snorkelling in the woman's bosom. He stood up and finally the ringlets stopped choking the woman. She coughed up a few bits of ringlets and then started shrieking about what she was going to do to all the soft parts of his anatomy.

The Director strolled out of the wings and started pointing to marks on the floor where the actors should have been. Nobody paid any notice to him. He was rather handsome with that wan and wistful air of dead poets. He'd have made a super corpse. In fact he was cut out to play that part instead of the beer barrel of a woman they'd hired who looked like a giant bumble bee without wings and very obviously only had food on her mind and not her craft.

'I am speaking to you all, now,' said the Director. Well, he might look faint and wan but when it came to the crunch this guy had a clear, strong voice that commanded instant attention. In fact it seemed as if another soul inhabited that emaciated body.

The man and the woman stopped arguing. The Director spoke.

'Antoine, please try not to impale yourself on top of Valerie. You reminded me of a starving huntsman throwing himself on a side of venison. Yes, your character is crazed with love. But you do not wish to dispatch the subject of all your desires into the next world by crushing the last living breath out of her. Do you understand?'

Valerie obviously understood. Valerie being the one who'd almost been done in by the ringlets. She gave Antoine a belt that sent him spinning half way across the stage.

'Espèce de cochon,' she hurled after him.

Antoine wearily sat down on the edge of the rickety old bed and the mattress gave a little leap.

'Where are we going to eat?' he asked in a defeated voice which I recognized as the one I'd spoken to on the phone.

'Maybe you'd like to fly us all to Lyons for a change?' asked Valerie with the arrogance and the disdain that the French have patented.

'I'm getting a bit tired of Mahmoud's couscous,' said

the young Director. It was a pity he wasn't looking for English lessons. He was in his twenties whereas Antoine was as old as my Dad.

'Try the sheep's heart,' said Antoine. 'I had it yesterday and it was excellent.'

'How can anyone eat heart?' simpered Valerie who had the build of a woman who could down combine harvesters and not suffer indigestion.

'Have a taste of mine and you'll see how exquisite it is,' said Antoine, in a very friendly way for a guy who's just been flung across the stage and called 'a type of pig'

'Oh, and aren't you the little love?' said Valerie and blew him a kiss.

They were poised to exit stage left. I rushed to the front and announced myself:

'I'm the English teacher.'

THIRTEEN

In Mahmoud's I ordered tripe in an onion and white wine sauce instead of sheep's heart, brains or couscous. They all applauded my choice, telling me I had done the right thing, since Mahmoud's tripe was famous in Paris. They also mentioned how adventurous I was for an Irish person. I didn't want to burst their admiration bubble and admit that it was the only halfway recognizable thing on the menu and that we used to have it at home once a month when Granddad lived with us. Tripe was Granddad's favourite and my Mam, being the kind and fair cook that she is, allowed us all to have our favourites once a month. But she was most certainly not going to cook separate meals. When Granddad had tripe we all had it. Oddly enough, after a few years of gagging over the tripe I got very fond of it. As Granddad pointed out, with most gourmet food you have to choke over it a lot in the beginning before you can appreciate the subtlety.

The tripe was indeed delicious. So were the chips. The French, of course, eat far more potatoes that the Irish. Yet, it's the Irish who get called 'spuds' and the French get praised for their cuisine.

'You're not drinking the wine, Nellie.'

It's the French who also drink more than the Irish and half of Europe combined. Yet it's over the Irish that they hoist the flag of inebriation. While the troupe knocked back untold bottles, I sipped half a glass of white, crushed my frites into the tripe sauce and basked in the eyes of the Director, who was gazing intensely at me across the table over his sheep's heart.

At the next table a group of four were having roast chicken which was something that hadn't been even mentioned to me. But this particular chicken arrived on a platter with its head still on and its eyes still intact - well, as much as they could be after two hours in the oven. Its claws were decorously poised on a mound of roast potatoes. All that was missing from that chicken were its feathers! Only the soft eyes of the Director took my mind off that poor chicken and the fact that tripe is actually the lining of a cow's stomach. 'Tripes' is French for 'guts'. So as long as I could focus on the Director's melting eyes I could stop wondering how cow's guts ever became a gourmet delicacy.

They spent the first half hour analyzing the worthiness of this meal as opposed to the others they had consumed at Mahmoud's in the past. They then eased into a discussion of the herbs that should and should not go into a proper couscous. They compared the wine with that of Spain, Morocco, America and Australia. When they had critiqued every facet of the food and wine we had consumed, the Director told me his name was Jean-Claude. I thought it was the most romantic sound I had ever heard. It fell off his tongue like a lush, sweet kiss.

'So you are Antoine's English teacher?' His silver voice made me think this was how a star would sound if and when stars should ever speak.

'You don't mind the hours?' asked Antoine, referring to the classes now that he was no longer chewing on his sheep's heart.

'No problem,' I lied, wondering how I could persuade

Madame to agree to 'flexible' hours, since she and concrete came with the same degree of flexibility.

'You can be Chantal's understudy,' said Valerie, thinking she was being witty. She was still sucking and gnawing the marrow out of a hunk of bone. Lassie would have left more on the bone than she did. But then Lassie had class.

'I hate being that fucking corpse. Why did I ever let myself be talked into that role?' moaned Chantal.

'But it's so *YOU*!' Valerie shrieked.

'How much are you going to pay for the classes?' I asked Antoine.

Silence fell on the table as suddenly as night in the Tropics. There was no more chewing, crunching or sucking on bones.

'We'll have to come to an arrangement, of course,' said Antoine evasively.

'The schools charge at least 100 francs an hour. I'll teach you for 50. But it will have to be cash.'

'Nellie can talk money too,' said the silver voice, oozing admiration. He raised his glass to me. 'Slainte!'

'What a show-off!' snarled Valerie. 'He goes to Ireland a few times and thinks he is impressing us with his 'Slaintes'. I've been to Russia and do I go around saying 'Dos Vidania' all the time?'

'I go to Ireland to compose,' said Jean-Claude, ignoring Valerie. He was a brave man. Valerie could have played Rambo with only a bottle of suntan oil for make-up.

'He's into that new wave, new sound shit,' said Valerie.

'I'll play it for you sometime,' said Jean-Claude, in a low voice with delicate promise in his satiny brown eyes.

After lunch we went back to the theatre and I met the rest of the cast and the author - Maurice de la Tour

Tournant. Maurice had intense black eyes. He also had a face littered with giant blackheads, teeth yellow as catarrh and blood streaked stubs of what had once been fingernails. Even the semi-gutted theatre looked better than mouldy Maurice with his ever-wrinkle clothes. They ran through the play which took place on a ship on its way to the New World of America in the middle of the 17th century (hence all the wigs). There were three different couples. The corpse had been servant to all six. Was it any wonder she kicked the bucket? Maurice pompously told me that the dead maid was a metaphor for the lack of freedom in 17th century Europe at a time when so many people fled to the US.

Well, all I can say is that I must admire his breath of imagination and self delusion. You only had to watch that bilge about those couples flinging themselves at each other after they had tried to have it off with the poor maid and it was crystal clear that Maurice had major, major problems. Having spent 17 years in the company of real writers like Shakespeare, O'Casey, Synge and Tennessee Williams I can immediately recognize piffle when I hear it on stage. Somebody must have bribed them to put on this moronic claptrap. Maurice interrupted the rehearsal about fifty five times clamouring for more passion, more blood, more involvement. He did it once too often for Chantal's liking.

'I'm not playing this fucking corpse any more,' she shouted and flounced off the bed.

This shocked all the cast because for an hour and a half Chantal had been dead out in a post prandial siesta.

'It's after 5 and I want to go home and get the dinner going.'

This was too much for Maurice's fragile sensibilities.

He stopped gnawing his bleeding fingers for half a second. Then he stormed out.

'Tell that guy to stop coming to rehearsals,' said Valerie, using her most Ramboesque voice. 'I'm going to kick him into the balcony the next time he tries to show me how to act.'

Jean-Claude sighed, turned to me and said softly:

'Where are you dining?'

'Who? Me?'

'If you haven't a previous engagement, I'd like to invite you back to my place for supper.'

I thought I had died, grown gossamer wings and flown to a suite in Paradise. A French composer/director had invited me to dine at his apartment!

FOURTEEN

Outside the theatre the troupe broke up with more kissing than I'd seen in my entire life. In Paris they're different - naturellement! They kiss four times. Left cheek, right cheek, left cheek, right cheek. Valerie gave Antoine double the dose asking for his forgiveness: she was suffering from a 'little kreeze' that day. They all lavished kisses on me like I was a long lost cousin suddenly returned to the fold. By the time I got into Jean-Claude's car I was practically worn out from all the kissing and embracing.

Jean-Claude lived in a massive apartment in the ritzy section of Montmartre which was galaxies away from our brown café. He had the largest windows I'd ever laid eyes on. They slanted like one enormous side of a tent and you could see down into the tiny, twisting streets and the zillions of steps that lead up and down all over the hill of Montmartre. From the windows on the other side you could see the whole of Paris in all its concrete splendour.

'Montmartre has the only city vineyard left in Europe,' said Jean-Claude, and pointed to a dark part of the hill outside. He stood behind me and his breath on my neck gave me all sorts of shivers. 'In the old days a lot of wine was produced around here. Now it's just one carpet of concrete.'

'Yes, but beautifully done, don't you think?' I was talking rubbish because of that breath on my neck.

'Paris is beauty,' he said. 'You have so little manmade beauty in Ireland.'

His very words!

'But you have beauty that is so elusive, so transient. You experience it and then you wonder if you've only dreamt it.'

I was way out of my depth there. Beauty, aesthetics and the like were not the everyday topics at our dinner table - not with my little brother Billie clamouring to know why cats only cried at night and why dogs got stuck together.

'I love the elusiveness of the beauty you find in Ireland.' said Jean-Claude, concluding his little ode to Ireland.

I was thinking that if he was so hung up on Ireland and could nail down elusive beauty, then he'd have no problem spotting the very tangible acting talent in one of its native daughters.

'You like champagne?' he said before I could ask him to get me a job as an actress.

'Sure!'

At least I think I do. Except I've never tasted enough to know for sure. At home we always had a bottle of champagne for Christmas. I was 16 before I was allowed to taste it. That means I've had two glasses so far in my life and I couldn't fully enjoy those. Not with my Mam giving us a detailed account of what it did to her gastric juices, followed by her endorsement of champagne as a diuretic since it really 'flushed out' her system. Brother Brian thought he was suave repeating – 'Beats Guinness any day' like some half brained chimpanzee. 'We shouldn't get too fond of this stuff,' Granddad repeated at least fifteen times as we sipped our meagre prelude to Christmas dinner. I could hardly explain to Jean-Claude how limited my relationship had been with champagne.

The lights of Paris flickered up at us as Jean-Claude proffered me a glass of champagne and led me to the white couch. The entire living room was in black and white and looked really, really classy. The walls were covered with giant black and white photographs. The piano was black and so were a vast array of speakers and synthesizers. Jean-Claude served the champagne in cloudy white glasses that went like a dream with the black tray. For the first time I noticed that Jean-Claude was also dressed in black from top to toe. In my best Marks and Spencers Summer Flower Collection number (you could recognize half a dozen of the bright flowers) I felt as out of place as a skunk at a bunnies' party.

'Now, do tell me all about you and what brought you to Paris.'

Somehow, because of the champagne I had expected him to do something weird. Like ask me to take off my fussy dress because the wild colours were giving him a migraine. I was wearing my black slip and 'silk' underwear. Sipping champagne on the sophisticated white sofa I felt like suggesting to Jean-Claude that I'd blend in much better with the décor if I took off my dress and sat there in my £9.0 black slip from Marks. While all these nutty things were going through my head I told him about my life in Dublin, trying to be an actress and we finished the champagne.

Then he took me into the kitchen and made us Spaghetti Primavera (that's not French but Italian for 'Spring' Spagetti). His kitchen was white but the trimmings were all in a lush blue, like Matisse's favourite tone. His cutlery and picture frames were the same exotic blue. I felt more in tune with the kitchen and forgot about my black underwear for a while. He put on some light and breezy music that was piped into the kitchen. I wondered how he could afford such refined surroundings. Being a Director at the worm-infested *Zivot* would barely cover the spaghetti. Instead of asking him to clarify his cash flow situation I said I liked the music and he beamed.

'It's one of my better pieces,' he said proudly. 'I can't decide whether to call it 'Melancholy Mountain' or 'Ocean of Torment'. I'm lousy with titles.'

'Sounds like swallows at dawn,' I told him, because I could almost see the swallows diving and shrieking across the morning sky. Just like there are pieces of music that remind you of the sea or the wind or summer, this sounded just like Autumn dawn over Paris.

'You are remarkable', said Jean-Claude and he put his face very, very close to mine. He was a quarter of an inch shorter than me. 'I composed that at dawn sitting by an Irish lake.'

'So why don't you call it 'Sitting by an Irish Lake'? That sounds a hell of a lot better than 'Ocean of Torment'.'

He did a strange thing then. He put one arm around my shoulders, kept tossing the salad with the other and gave me a soft kiss on my right ear. I nearly fainted into the boiling pot of spaghetti with the emotion that surged through me.

'We'll have a hearty red. Take one from the wine rack - top row. The top is for spaghetti, the second is for fish, the third for fowl and the fourth for birthdays. When is your birthday?'

One peck on the ear and for the life of me I couldn't remember when my birthday was.

'Not for some time yet.'

The spaghetti was the best I ever ate and I'm not wild about pasta. I had three glasses of the hearty red and I could almost hear Granddad pontificating: 'Don't get too fond of it, darling girl.' Jean-Claude finally clarified his financial situation. He had inherited a small fortune from his grandparents. Two years earlier they had been killed in a messy railway accident. Up to then he had been working as a lawyer for a French company that installed nuclear energy plants in Africa. He hated it and said 'Adieu' the minute he got the cash from the railway company. He was spending the money wisely, composing in Ireland and getting hands-on experience as a Director. He still hadn't made up his mind if he wanted to devote his life to being a major composer or a major director.

'All I want to be is a major actress,' I told him.

'You're with the right crowd then,' he said.

This didn't exactly fill me to the brim with confidence. Smelly carpet of blackheads Maurice, bumblebee Chantal and Rambo Valerie – the right crowd? Only Antoine had the makings of an actor.

The sky was as black as it ever gets in Paris as we moved back into the living room. A moon had come up and was pouring yellowish light into the room which conflicted somewhat with the stark black and white decor. But when Jean-Claude lit a barrage of thick candles the room was tone in tone with the moon. I was giddier than the proverbial goat when he sat down at the piano and played his 'Sitting by an Irish Lake' for me.

I cannot quite describe what it was like to be draped over the white couch in the moonlight listening to this wan French composer/director playing the piano with his gorgeous fingers and making music as silvery as sunlit water. He stopped playing and instead put on a recording of more silvery music. He came over and sat on the floor next to the couch. He put his hand on my right knee (my heart had a belt of the gallops) and left it there as we listened to the end of the piece. Then he kissed my knee. I nearly passed out with the excitement. What was next on the romantic menu?

'I'll call you a cab,' he said.

FIFTEEN

My first week at the *Théâtre du Zivot* was very painful
on several fronts. My passionate knee kisser did not
invite me to dine with him again. He explained he was
beyond busy, supervising re-writes with Maurice who
clung onto every word in the play and had to be almost
bludgeoned into changing as much as a comma. I told
him I understood perfectly how maniacally attached
writers could get to their 'babies'.

'You are remarkable, you know,' Jean-Claude cooed
and nonchalantly kissed my left ear. 'I will play for you
soon.'

'That would be nice,' I told him instead of hollering
out 'Soon isn't soon enough.'

If things were painful on the romance front, they
were beyond agonizing on the Antoine front. It would
have been easier to teach English to Godzilla, Lassie
or a demented goat. In fact, I'm convinced that if
Lassie, a wild racoon, the same demented goat and
Antoine were all thrown together and taught English
under strictly controlled laboratory conditions where
every breath is monitored I would bet my last pound (I
never, ever bet!) that Lassie would be first, the racoon
second and maybe, with extensive private round-the-
clock coaching, Antoine would tie with the demented
goat.

One of Antoine's major problems was that he

couldn't manoeuvre his lips around a simple 'w'. Up to then I never realized what an important role 'w' plays in the English language. But two of the simplest phrases have that fatal 'w' in them. I am referring to 'How are you?' and the lesser used 'Who are you?'. Coming out of Antoine's mouth 'How are you?' sounded exactly like *AU-WOO-AHAHAH -RRRRRR- - UUUU*? Of course the 'r' always poses a major challenge for the French. They like to gargle with it. Antoine's 'How are you?' sounded worse than a forest full of croaking toads.

Having identified Antoine's block with regard to the 'w' and the English tongue in general I decided to take the bull by the horns and concentrate on: 'Who', 'What', 'When', 'Where' and 'Why' - the essential quintet in 'w'. The objective was to get him to reach the point where he could pronounce something remotely akin to a 'w'. This approach was not a good idea. Nor shall I ever again endorse the saying 'Practice makes perfect'. Because in Antoine's case it made it much, much worse.

Antoine practiced 'How are you?' until his lips practically fell off and it still sounded like ... *WUUU-AHAHA-WO000*. Being a perfectionist he had no intention of letting go until he got it right. He was capable of repeating *'wuu-ahaha-wuu'* until he sounded worse than Godzilla giving painful birth in the wild. We moved on to 'where'.

His interpretation of 'Where are you?' was a howl from the bowel of some tortured elephant hollering to his mate over the jungle tree tops. He'd start out sort of OK. He'd go *'wa wa wa wa'* trying desperately to get the knack of fitting in the 'h' after the 'w'. When he finally got the two together, i.e. 'WH', he sounded as if his tonsils had grown together and were choking him. By the time he got the entire combination of that one word 'Where' off his chest he was reminding me of a camel chewing off its hump. The camel would have made less contortions than Antoine.

He was also a virtuoso in introducing hitherto unheard of nuances into the simple 'when'. He'd go through the usual contortions and let loose alarming shrieks and squeals until he'd finally choke out something that sounded like 'a – hen'. He'd be so pleased with himself he'd go on repeating *'a hen, a hen, a hen'* until I felt like hollering out at the top of my lungs – *'My Kingdom for a hen.'*

I went out and spent precious money on the most highly recommended Manual on How to Teach English. Chapter One: introduce the student to the many facets of the little word 'What' as in 'What is this?' and 'What is that? There was no advice on what to do with a student who was congenitally unable to say 'What'. It was a case of conquering those 'w's' or break the news to Antoine that he'd be starring in American movies when Madonna was made honorary Member of the College of Cardinals in Rome.

The Manual said it would be easy to widen the student's vocabulary by pointing to pictures of a cat, a table or a dog. I pointed to a picture of a dog and asked Antoine 'what is this?'. The answer *'it's a dog'* coming out of Antoine's mouth was worse than Godzilla having unwanted dentistry. And that wasn't the worst. His mutilation of *'where is the dog?'* nearly finished me off entirely. If, on some rare occasion in his life, Antoine will need to question the whereabouts of the dog i.e. *'where is the dog?'* it will still sound like this. *WWWWWWW-EEEEE-RRRRRRRR* (that's just the *'where'* bit) repeated at least four times just to be sure it was perfect. Then he'd continue *HISSSSSS ZEEEE*

ZEEE ZEE ZZZOGG (translated that's '*is the dog*').
By the end of those two hours I felt like shaving off
my ears and screaming – 'Will somebody just tell him
where the fucking dog is'.

But that would have distressed Antoine no end. He
already had a mild notion that he would never be
among those people who smile out from those lying
ads, claiming they have learnt English, Dutch or Greek
in only 36 hours. At the end of our two hours Antoine
sat and clutched his head like Hamlet in his speech of
deepest despair whether or not to top himself. Even
though I felt more drained than if I'd spent the two
hours teaching ten leopards to tango, I had to rustle up
the last of my strength to boost his tattered confidence.

'It's early days, Antoine. You've only just started.'

What about his six years of school English?

'Did you have a teacher like Nellie Flanagan? Non!'

More agonizing minutes reassuring Antoine that he
was doing fine, making progress and that he'd be
fluent in no time. After that, I barely had enough
energy left to lift my glass of red in the café. But were
any of my so-called friends worried about my terminal
exhaustion? Were any of them interested in debating
why my kids could rattle off: '*Round about the
cauldron go, in the poisoned entrails throw*' (first
witch in Macbeth) but Antoine couldn't ask where the
bloody dog was? Paul was wallowing in the throes of
rejection and was blind to everything except his own
self-pity. He had sent off his outline and a first chapter
of '*What They Ate*', now re-christened '*The Losers*'
(meaning that even the Greats had been Losers when
they were poor and struggling). He got back a
rejection letter which loosened the last of his hinges.
The letter said: '*This is a no-frills rejection. I don't see
any dollar signs. The idea is pathetic. I hate the title.*

Nobody in their right mind would rush out to buy a book called 'The Losers'. Most people are losers. We've had too many books on Hemingway and I personally loathe and detest the guy.'

I can't mention the name of the publishing house or the editor because Paul swore he'd demolish the entire company, even if he had to spend his life doing so. He was going to go to the editor's office the next time he was in New York and shoving that no-frills rejection letter down her gullet. Actually he was going to shove it someplace else, but that is the kind of 'jolly' vulgarity only Americans can pull off.

'No frills rejection! Jerks! They rejected Hemingway 29 times so what else could I expect? No frills rejection!'

He was in a bad way, nattering away like a machine-gun gone berserk. I made no attempt to stem this froth of rage. Paul had yet to reach that very important stage in the life of an artist which is - forget, never forgive the bastards, and go on. I could have written a thesis on those rejections which had made me feel lower than a worm that's been flattened to nothing by a bus. But now was not the moment to rhapsodize on how I had found the fortitude to go on to the next kick in the jaw.

'Oh what's the use of talking?'

I agreed. What was the use of asking anyone why Jean-Claude who had kissed my ear twice, my knee once and called me 'remarkable' on two occasions couldn't find the time to join me for a cup of coffee?

'You didn't expect them to snap up your outline just like that, did you?'

The words were out of my mouth before I could stop them.

'You don't think it's any good either, do you?' he

said and shrugged the way people do when they are trying to pretend that things don't matter when it is actually the most important thing in life to them. They shrug to make more room around their hearts so the pain won't crowd in too much and make them explode with sadness.

'That's not what I meant,' I said, backtracking as fast as I could. 'That's the first and only one you sent out, isn't it?'

Paul nodded as miserably as a man who's just passed several gallstones through his John Thomas without anaesthetic.

'So what's the Big Deal? It's like you always say. First you have to survive Rejection City.'

He didn't look convinced so I had to give him a Nellie Flanagan tour de force in the 'don't let the bastards get you down' department.

'It's a wonderful idea! It will make a fantastic book! Just because one half wit editor can't see its potential doesn't mean it's the end of the world. You gotta keep sending it out. You'll find the right publisher in no time.'

Mercifully, I was rescued by Diana who stormed in and announced the latest in her Parisian Purgatory.

'That slum landlord cut off my hot water.'

Hansi had the answer. Join him in the caravan and they'd both have a shower in Henriette's bistro. I didn't even smile when Diana retorted that she'd prefer to snorkel in the sewers than go within a mile of his caravan. After Diana arrived on the scene, The Prince of Primates had stopped inviting me over to his caravan on a Friday night. What were the chances a washed, suave French composer/director would ask me out on a real date?

SIXTEEN

Every loser in the café offered Diana the use of their shower or that of a relative if they themselves didn't have one.

'Jerks!' was Diana's unanimous response.

'That's a bit harsh,' I said.

'There's no such thing as a free wash,' said Diana and laughed at herself. 'I'm not that easy.'

This was a new side to Diana. It was alarming to see her laughing at herself in her direst hour of need.

'So what are you going to do?' I asked.

'Well now, let's see. I could borrow Hansi's dogs and have them chew on my landlord's balls except he doesn't have any.'

'Wouldn't it be easier to just move somewhere else?'

'You got the address of a place I can afford on my income?'

'Sorry.'

'I'll buy an electric kettle. That'll keep me going unless he decides to cut off the electricity as well,' sighed Diana with tired resignation in her voice which wasn't a bit like her. 'Paree, Paree, my ass!'

Diana defeated? There wasn't room for another one in that particular boat.

'Why don't you pop by when I'm giving the kids their lessons and have a shower?' I said recklessly, knowing quite well if Madame ever got a sniff of free showers for friends I'd be out on the Paris streets before nightfall.

"I couldn't let you risk it,' said Diana.

Duelling Diana not willing to risk an illicit shower? You think you've heard it all.

'Madame is never there in the afternoon,' I said.

'Where is she?'

'How do I know? She picks the kids up from school and disappears again until Monsieur comes home.'

'She's having an affair'

'Madame? At her age?'

'Of course she's having an affair. You're so naïve, Nellie.'

'Fine! Go out and buy your kettle then.'

That's how Diana spent the next week washing in the Duchamps guest bathroom and dazzling my kids with duelling advice. Naïve Nellie had come up with a blindingly brilliant plan. If Madame ever did change her schedule and make an unexpected reappearance during the afternoon we would simply explain that Diana was giving her little philosophers an extra edge in life by teaching them self-defence plus the duelling skills needed in *Romeo and Juliet*. Everything went like clockwork for that one week. Maude and Claude adored Diana. She told them hair raising stories of guys she'd almost gutted and promised to find some fake blood for them to use in their duels.

With Diana around I had a legitimate excuse to skip the romantic Romeo and Juliet scenes which the two loved because of the danger involved. They had built their Verona balcony on Monsieur's drinks cabinet. If that had toppled over with its collection of priceless crystal it would have been adieu Nellie. But I was beginning not to really care. All I could think about was Jean-Claude and the pain of seeing him for a few fleeting moments every day after my two hours of torment with Antoine. He always gave me an apologetic, lopsided smile as if he longed to spend time with me but was trapped by theatre obligations. When I tried to discuss the matter with Diana, all she said was: 'Men are dipshits. Screw him. He's not worth it.' But I felt he was. Apart from the fact that he was a theatre director I only had to touch my knee and my insides melted at the memory of that magical evening I had spent in his Montmartre penthouse. It was a draw which pain was worse – seeing him or teaching Antoine. I wanted to quit. But having admitted the situation to Diana I knew she'd keep reminding me that I'd given up a 'lucrative teaching position' because of some ass of a man.

But then three things happened. Monsieur came home early with the flu and saw Diana exiting the bathroom. She was washed and dressed and looking even more blindingly beautiful. He stopped dead in his tracks and the last complication Diana needed in her life was yet 'another married bozo stalking her' (her words). She invested in a kettle which in the end wasn't necessary because that same day the landlord explained the gas fault had been repaired. The gas was included in the rent but not the electricity. Diana went back to the store to get her money back. But items on sale were not returnable. For weeks afterwards she couldn't shut up about that kettle. The second major event of that week was that Antoine managed to say 'the book is on the table' without sounding like parts of the Paris sewers exploding.

And Jean-Claude asked me if I was free for dinner on Friday.

I spent three days getting ready with Diana's help. We were the same size and she had a wardrobe (or in Diana's case a fridge) full of exquisite outfits. I'd never seen her in any of them but as she said herself 'they were wasted on the café losers and she had enough stalkers'. I wore her marine blue ensemble and my black underwear. That way I'd be tone in tone with the kitchen on the outside and underneath I'd blend in with the living room. When he picked me up Jean-Claude blinked and called me 'stunning' instead of 'remarkable'. He took me to his local, Chez Gustin, a most superior fish restaurant. He had to explain almost everything on the menu to me. He laughed when I told him I could quote most of *'Cyrano'* but didn't know the names of any French fish except for salmon. He taught me. By the end of the meal I could reel off sixteen different fish in French. Jean-Claude said I had a 'remarkable' facility for the French language. I felt like gently breaking the news to him that the French tongue had more adjectives than 'remarkable' and maybe he should brush up his *Cyrano*.

Afterwards we strolled around old Montmartre. Jean-Claude gave me a tour of the area and I nearly expired from the romance of strolling around the tiny moonlit, cobbled streets holding hands with my heart's desire.

'You do know that Montmartre means - Mont des Martyrs (That's French for Martyrs' Mountain)?' he asked me and gave my ear kiss number five.

Martyrs' Mountains? No. I always thought Montmartre was the original homing grounds for boozed-out artists.

When Jean-Claude walked me to the little park I thought the next stage of the evening was about to begin – i.e. kissing and smooching amongst the flowers and vegetation. Instead he showed me this most gruesome statue of a beheaded guy holding his own cut-off head in his hands. A more macabre statue you could not imagine and it was right in the middle of a children's playground. Jean-Claude pointed to the Bishop's mitre on the lopped off head. This was how Montmartre got its name he explained. St. Denis who wanted to introduce Christianity to Paris in the 3rd century was beheaded on this very spot. But he became famous because he picked up his own head, washed it and walked four miles holding it in his hands. His headless stroll ended in a village in the North of Paris. He dropped dead and that's where today they have the famous Basilica of St. Denis. Even Auntie Betty hadn't mentioned this gruesome walking miracle when she indulged on her marathon speeches on the lives of saints. I thanked Jean-Claude for this amazing tidbit but didn't add that I would file it under 'erase and forget'.

And finally under the Montmartre moon next to the statue of the headless bishop, Jean-Claude really kissed me for the first time. It stopped me thinking why the French topped the list when it came to chopping heads off. He ran his hands over my cheekbones with the intensity of Chopin composing a love symphony and gazed dreamily into my eyes as if I was more wondrous than all the stars over Paris. I lapped it all up like a hungry old hound who hasn't had a whiff of a bone in months. This was better than all the love films about Paris. He kissed my hair a few times. I wasn't too sure if he expected me to do the same to him. But then he said 'on rentre?' which is the very beautiful French way of saying: 'fancy coming back to my place?'

Jean-Claude took my hand and we giddily romped down the hill and up to his penthouse. Every single part of my body was tautly tingling like a trapeze artist about to cha cha cha her way across a high wire without a safety net. Therefore, I was a bit disappointed when he opened a bottle of red wine, poured out two glasses and perched himself at the piano. I took up my admiring position on the sofa and sipped my wine. He played a new piece - 'Crickets Under the Sun' - twice because he was changing the ending and wanted my opinion. I was his muse he told me and blew me a kiss from the piano. This was slightly bewildering since blowing kisses also means goodbye. Was he hinting it was call the cab time? He stood up, put on another recording of his better pieces and finally came over to the sofa and sat on the floor next to me. He ran his manicured hand up my left leg, kissed my right knee and I waited. What would a Frenchwoman have done under the circumstances? Leaned over and kissed his hair? Stood up and said 'good night' before he did?

'Sit down here with me,' he whispered in a voice drenched in moonlight and tapped the carpet next to him. I slid off the sofa and joined him on the floor. He kissed me long and passionately. I reciprocated with increased passion. He unbuttoned my dress and I willingly whipped it off. Finally I was lying in my black slip on the white carpet feeling splendid as Cleopatra and tone in tone with the décor. The moonlight streamed in. Jean-Claude ran his hand up and down my bare arms and let his fingertips glide over the part of my bosom that was sticking up from my under wired black bra. He was elegance personified in all his movements. He didn't rip my straps, or go into that frenzy of licking and chewing that some guys go in for. Personally I don't know. But my best friend Deirdre had this guy in Cork who wanted her to lick his entire chest like she was some kind of sponge. But Jean-Claude, being a French composer/director, had delicacy in every aspect. He removed his shirt. He didn't have too much hair so it wasn't like kissing the carpet.

All the while I just copied what Jean-Claude was doing to me - taking a mouthful of his neck into my mouth, swirling it around gently as if his skin were expensive ice cream I was savouring. This obviously went down quite well. Because he was moaning. I was moaning at the sheer wonder of it all, being on the floor with this French composer/director, in Montmartre, Paris, France. His hands scampered up and down my body. The black bra and the black undies went sailing through the air. Likewise his jockey shorts. They were black with a white waistband.

When I felt his bare body on mine I wanted to melt into him forever. Nobody had ever warned me that the hot contact between a man and a woman could be like walking through flames and cold water all at the same time. Up to then all the other contacts had included some kind of fabric or wool from the guy's sweater. When I let out the yelp of pain it sort of destroyed the magical atmosphere.

'Oh God,' said Jean-Claude. 'I should have known.'

The pain brought me back to the floor for a bit.

'It's too late. I'm sorry,' said Jean-Claude. That's as much as I understood from all the moaning he did in my ear.

When he stopped moving the pain wasn't too bad. He kept kissing my neck and face, saying I should have told him. I restrained myself from saying I was glad. Because it had to happen one day anyhow, and what better mise-en-scene than lying on a romantic Montmartre floor under the magical light of a Paris moon and a sensitive Frenchman who didn't leap up hollering about getting blood all over his white carpet. Even if he felt like rushing out to the kitchen for a vat of salt, or mineral water, or whatever else is supposed to take out blood stains, Jean-Claude had the delicacy not to do so. He kept on kissing and caressing me. Of course he could have felt put out about not recognizing a virgin when he met one. But then again, maybe he just didn't feel like rummaging around in the kitchen when things were so terribly romantic on the white if flawed carpet.

I wanted to burst into song and not stop until I had finished the entire repertoire of songs about falling in love with love and magical Paris, the most glorious city on the globe where dreams always came true.

SEVENTEEN

For weeks afterwards, every time I caught a glimpse of myself in a passing bus or shop window I didn't quite recognize myself. I'm not saying that Love had changed me into a beauty goddess overnight but there was a new and improved glow to my hair and skin. I was dying to tell somebody about my thrilling love life so I wrote a long letter to Deirdre. All through school she had been my best friend but we faded apart when she went to Galway University while I served the braying masses in Tipps. I didn't send the letter to Deirdre because she's also the kind of person who would carelessly leave a letter in a library book and then I wouldn't have to worry about the whole country not knowing that I was no longer a virgin.

I couldn't tell Diana because she and I are at different stages in our sexual lives. She is very keen for me to read a book called 'Men are Just Desserts' but Jean-Claude is my first starter. Plus, Diana was back to obsessing about money wasted on a stupid kettle, the injustice of living in a hole with no phone, no shower, a fridge cum wardrobe and the constant fear of having to commit hari-kari if somebody from New Jersey turned up in Paris and discovered her appalling living conditions. I certainly couldn't tell Paul because to him anything he heard was only 'material' he would distort in a future oeuvre. Besides, I rarely went to the café since I was spending most evenings with my exquisite French lover who had finally introduced me to his king sized bed in his black and white bedroom. At first I had major doubts about those particular choices for any bedroom. To my mind black sheets were ominous but black walls would have been even worse. Very slowly I began to accept that this kind of décor was real Paree sophistikay and not rural Kerry! But it sure took some getting used to. When I opened my eyes in the morning the first thing I saw out the window was the Eiffel Tower in the distance. That definitely beat pigeons' bottoms any day.

My kids came down with whooping cough so I had even more free time. Madame spent an hour quizzing me as to how they could have contracted that disease, which she seemed to think was an affliction of poor children. She suggested that I use the apartment as little as possible until the infection passed - for my own good, she emphasized. This was Madame's way of saying that if I did get sick, she wouldn't be rushing up and down the stairs to me with bowls of fortifying chicken soup. I told her not to worry.

I had bigger problems like not going off my rocker trying to introduce Antoine to the possessive case. When he tried to wrestle with those simple words: 'my', 'your', 'his' and 'hers', Antoine still sounded like a train going over a herd of hyenas. My ears were in a permanent state of numb pain. Antoine only had to attempt to usher the little sentence 'This is my coat' out of his mouth and wild hound dogs choking on bones in mean alleys immediately sprang to mind. One day I made the unfortunate mistake of wearing earrings and Antoine wanted to know the English word for them. Then of course he had to actually say 'ear-ring' - a pretty innocuous word. But it has the double 'R' in there. And to hear Antoine erupting with those two 'R's' was like listening to the sound track of a John Wayne movie at the point when the buffalo start to stampede and the cowboys start yelling their guts out and shooting after them.

By now I knew all the members of the troupe and enjoyed helping out in the theatre, making cups of peppermint tea, moving the scenery, prompting. Valerie and Chantal both thought I had the makings of a great slave - somebody who would drop everything to run out and buy their cigarettes. The only ones who appreciated my voluntary work and always said: 'Merci, Nellie. You're so good, Nellie,' were Pierrette and her real life husband Armand. They were super mild and looked like two docile mice flitting across the stage. When Valerie became temperamental or had her brawls with Chantal, Pierrette and Armand would discuss what they would make for the kids' dinner. Should they risk having corn again and establish if this gave little Sophie the hives? Where would they go for Sunday dinner, and what would they do with heir respective Mammans during the Christmas holidays? Every week they had a different home project, like new cushions or curtains. Pierrette hand sewed the pre-cut material while Armand removed the pins and talked her through it, so to speak. They were the typical bourgeois couple you'd see in TV ads for loo paper. Yet they loved the theatre the way they loved their children. They didn't have any raving histrionics like Chantal and Valerie. One day Valerie said that Pierrette and Armand were a disgrace to the acting profession by being so normal, when it was as obvious as the day was long that no actor could ever be half way normal.

One afternoon during rehearsal Chantal waddled over to me and began to stroke my hair with her fat fingers. Chantal, like I've said, looked just like a human bee - all rounded. Except she had flat fingers - just like the fish fingers you eat. Chantal went into her stroking mode whenever she wanted something.

'Nellie, chérie, Nellie,' she cooed me. 'You'd love to be my understudy, wouldn't you, chérie?'

After her one little speech at the beginning of the play before she kicks the bucket, Chantal didn't have anything to do except try and play dead on the bed.

'Why do I have to lie there for hours during all those rehearsals,' she whined to Jean-Claude. 'Put a dummy there. Can't you just pretend there's a corpse in the bed?'

'Correction! Correction!'

This was Valerie at her simpering best. Watch out when Valerie simpers. She's just like a rattlesnake that gives a gentle rattle, then *WHAM, BANG* and you're *DEAD.*

'I don't think any of us true actors have difficulty in pretending you're dead. It's you, sweetie, who has difficulty in acting dead. Correct me if I'm wrong, Antoine.'

She eyeballed Antoine who was feeling somewhat spent after hours of English looking for the dog and torturous grappling with 'his coat', and 'my hat'. If he contradicted Valerie she'd maul what was left of him to bits during the play. He whimpered like a puppy owned by over affectionate youngsters. But Jean-Claude came to his rescue.

'This is the theatre, Chantal,' Jean-Claude said with frost in his silver voice. 'You can't play Madame de Stael every night.'

'A corpse is not a very challenging role. You understand, don't you Jean-Claude?' Chantal asked, fluttering her eyelashes at him. She pouted and blew her lips out a few times. It's a trick only French women can pull off. I've been assiduously practicing that lip pouting routine in front of the mirror but I still look like a baboon dissatisfied with the quality of her banana. However, when French women pout and blow their lips in and out a few times, they always get what they want.

'Chantal if you're not satisfied say so now. We'll hire somebody else.'

Those trips to Ireland had done Jean-Claude the world of good. It had helped him cut through the layers of French posturing and pouting. But Chantal wasn't giving up that easily. She oozed closer to me.

'Nellie, chérie. You love the theatre and you'd love to be my understudy, wouldn't you, chérie?'

She pouted pleadingly. Obviously if Chantal wanted something she would pout for men, women and even the spider in the bath if she had to. She cocked her head to one side.

'Eh? You'd love to be on stage, wouldn't you?'

'*UFF,*' I replied.

UFF is not a French word you will find in the dictionary. But it is extensively used and very useful. To get it right, just pretend you're a dog with a lisp trying to woof. Push both lips out – *UUFFF.* It's amazing in how many ways this one simple sound can be interpreted by the French.

My own '*UUFFF*' was multi-layered with meaning. I was able to express my disdain for the bitch Chantal who was blatantly not a committed actress and not antagonise the others who wanted to keep that corpse up there on stage during rehearsals. My '*UUFFF'* was also a non-committal grunt. It was up to the director to decide. But inside my heart was going – uff, uff, uff, uff. Because if Chantal dropped out entirely I'd get to say that poignant speech at the beginning before she goes into convulsions and dies.

'You want Nellie to do your dirty work, is that it?'

Antoine asked and put a protective arm around my shoulders.

'What I want is not to die of fucking boredom pretending to lie there dead for hours on end,' snapped Chantal. 'I got one little, bitty speech and then I croak. It's not what you'd call a part.'

'Chantal do remember, there are no small parts. Just small actors.' This was Valerie pontificating.

Chantal looked as if she could have shoved spears right up Valerie's wide nostrils when she said that. Jean-Claude was just about to raise his Director's pencil and the whole episode would be forgotten. Opportunity doesn't knock often. Even if it is only understudying a corpse - get in there - fast.

'I'd love to be your understudy, Chantal,' I said sweetly.

'Oh, aren't you the sweetie? Oh, mais qu'elle est gentille!'

'In that case maybe we should all have understudies,' sniffed Valerie as she flung back her thick auburn hair like Rambo doing drag.

You do have an understudy, Valerie, I said mentally, as I strolled over to the bed. I already knew Valerie's part from playing prompter. When Valerie came down with the inevitable French Kreeze I'd hop to the rescue and be an overnight sensation. I could already see the headlines:

NELLIE CONQUERS PARIS.
IRISH STAR IS BORN IN ARABIAN PARIS

EIGHTEEN

All the members of the cast were given free tickets mainly because it was going to be murder to fill up that decrepit theatre during the play's run. I went to deliver the free tickets to Madame and Monsieur but mainly to my kids, who were not yet fighting fit. I had to ring at the back door bell several times because it was after 6 and Madame had put on all the locks.

'Who is it?' Monsieur called out. His voice sounded suspicious.

'It's Nellie.'

There was silence from behind the door. To jog his memory I shouted (Those backdoors are very thick. Probably a hangover from the Revolution when the servants turned out to be real brutes and chopped people's heads off):

'I'M YOUR ENGLISH TEACHER!'

Monsieur undid the locks and stood there with a wide and totally artificial smile on his face. I showed him the tickets.

'They're for my play. I'd like to invite Maude and Claude,' I said.

Monsieur didn't say anything. He looked perplexed as if I was some kind of fungus that had drifted down from the roof after the rain.

'They're free tickets,' I repeated, in case he thought there might be money involved.

'What's the matter, Henri?' Madame's whining voice drifted around the corner. She sounded like a cat upset about having its delicate parts caught in a door. Madame was in the kitchen drilling Francesca into the evening routine of serving. Nothing interested Francesca, the hypochondriac, apart from her various ailments and pains and she had the tendency during a dinner party to have minor and major Kreezes.

'Nothing, dear,' said Monsieur. 'I'm just speaking to Nellie.'

Obviously that met with Madame's approval. Even if I didn't totally applaud the 'nothing' bit.

'Do come in, Nellie,' said Monsieur, suddenly becoming very jolly and opening the door wide. 'Join us in an apéro.' ('Apéro' is real French for 'apéritif'.)

You could have felled me with a feather. But with the tickets in his hand, I suppose Monsieur felt duty bound to reciprocate in some way.

'This way, please,' he said very politely and lead me into the pink salon with the chandelier the size of my dog box.

'What can I offer you, Nellie? Kir, vermouth, gin tonic, champagne?'

'Champagne.'

While he strolled to the distant recess of the massive sized salon I had a good look around. It was truly amazing that a paltry two floors separated this opulence from the Fourth World under the eaves.

'Are you participating in this play?' said Monsieur, as he handed me my glass. There were three glasses on the silver tray, which was a relief. I wasn't relishing a tête-à-tête with Monsieur.

'I understudy to all the three leading actresses - in case of illness.'

I only lie when absolutely necessary. This was one of those times. In these opulent surroundings I felt I had to live up to the satin walls and the velvet curtains with the gold tassels. Pounding 'What', 'Why' and 'When' into Antoine wasn't smart enough for those walls to hear.

'Marie-Ange tells me you teach the children Shakespeare,' he said. For a moment I had difficulty identifying Marie-Ange. Well, of course he'd call his wife by her first name.

'Yes. We like Shakespeare.'

'I work in a bank.'

'Yes, Madame told me.'

'I've worked in the same bank for 19 years.'

'I'm not even that old.'

All the pretty champagne bubbles were having an enchanting effect on me. My bones felt floppy, so I languidly lounged over the chaise longue (of which there were four!!!!). Let's face it. I can do a fabulous lounge. A short person just cannot pull off a proper lounge. It's like comparing a lounging Afghan and a lounging hamster. When Monsieur refilled my glass I gave him my French throaty laugh – the one I was perfecting – and fluttered my eyelashes at him. I had just splashed out on a new mascara that was going to 'revolutionize' my life.

'Life goes by so quickly,' sighed Monsieur. He slumped over his champagne like it was the end of the world.

'My dear, life is always going by one.'

For a second I wasn't sure where this voice was coming from. Then I realized it was coming from the lounging lizard - moi. I'd been looking at the portrait of the lady over the fireplace and thinking of a suitable voice for her.

'One must simply go with the flow. If life is dull, then just rev up the engine, old boy.'

I was in total character with the portrait lady, fluttering my eyelashes with the new mascara I'd bought so that when I got to play the corpse at a real performance I'd have long, luscious lashes which would show up beautifully against the white make-up.

Monsieur was frozen to his seat. I had called him 'old boy' (that's 'mon vieux' in French. It is most familiar and old geysers approaching 40 don't go for it in a big way). I wanted to explain about the lady in the portrait. Then he smiled - the sad smile of poets who know they will never be famous until they are long dead which is pretty useless.

'That's very good advice, Nellie. Rev up the engine. It is something we forget all too often. My wife thinks entertaining and having parties every second night is living. Do you?' Monsieur had that same hangdog look Paul gets after a rejection letter.

'Don't know. I've never been to any parties. I was hoping to get to a few in Dublin but Auntie Betty wasn't exactly a party demon.'

'But at your age life is still one long party.'

'My life is definitely not one long party.'

'We are having three couples over for dinner tonight. One is Marie-Ange's oldest friend. But they don't move in our circles any more so we have to get them out of the way occasionally. We'll waste all evening talking about their kids. I don't want to know about their kids. I hardly know my own. And you think it's easy to rev up the old engine?'

'Henri?'

Madame's voice was like a bowl of crushed ice flung across the room.

'What on earth are you doing?'

If Henri had been perched naked on the windowsill juggling four dead pigeons she couldn't have been more surprised.

'I'm about to rev up the old engine of life,' said Henri, and topped up our glasses with more champagne.

'How are you, Nellie?' Madame said to me. As always in French homes - politesse oblige. In the honest-and-true normal version it would have been - 'Why in hell are you swilling our most expensive champagne with the help?'

'I gave Monsieur the tickets for our play.'

'But of course,' said Madame briskly. Then she looked at her watch with that very obvious flourish of people who don't need to know the time but are very eager for you to hit the street.

'I must be going,' I said, and finished my champagne.

'Oh, and who is the play by?' said Madame, much more relaxed now that I was standing and they wouldn't have to rent a removal convenience to get rid of me before their guests arrived.

'Maurice de la Tour Tournant,' I said.

'I've never heard of him,' said Madame politely.

'Well, Marie-Ange, if you haven't heard of him he can't really exist, can he? It's just as well you've heard of Voltaire and Mordillat or they wouldn't exist either,' said Monsieur.

He sloshed more champagne into his glass and tried to aim for mine. Several drops splashed onto the carpet and Madame let out a yelp worse than a dog who has managed to get himself locked into a slaughter house. Then she went into her total control mode.

'Thank you for the tickets, Nellie. The children are not totally recovered yet. I will check my agenda and inform you if we can come on that evening.'

'We can change the evening if you like,' I told her.

'We'll have to see,' she snorted through clenched teeth as she propelled me out the door like I was some undesirable substance. The nerve!

I was so annoyed with Madame that I forgot to do my usual duck down and hide routine as I floated past Madame Favela's quarters. Madame Favela is the last of a dying breed in Paris - the ever vigilant concierge who gets a low-rent pokey flat in exchange for policing the building, acting as warden and delivering the mail. You are dead meat if she doesn't like you. Paul didn't get along with one of his concierges. She said he couldn't hang out his wet underwear on a string from his window because it lowered the tone of the building. He told her it was his right to do so. He kept hanging out the washing; she kept telling him he had no mail. He stopped hanging out his washing. Three dozen rejection letters arrived in the next post. Personally, I've never had any problems with my concierge. Quite the contrary. Madame Favela dotes on me. She is always trying to drag me into her flat for tea and cakes so she can weep about her children in Peru. I certainly wouldn't mind doing that sort of stuff occasionally. But not every time I pass the entrance.

Madame Favela waved a letter to me as I rushed past her lookout. I had to stop then. The letter could be from a French producer, Irish TV or the Abbey. They had realized my loss to the nation and wanted to lure me back. Madame Favela kept a claw like grip on my arm as I looked at the writing on the letter.

'From Mama?' she asked with huge tears in her eyes. She had them on tap.

'No. It's from my Granddad.'

'Oh so lucky. Lucky!' said Madame Favela. 'Mio Granddaddy - he is …' and she made a huge sign of the cross and kissed her fingertips. Since Madame Favela is way over 70 it was a safe guess that the gesture meant that her Granddad was no longer tangoing the Saturday nights away in downtown Lima.

'Lucky! Lucky!'

Madame Favela's vocabulary is limited but 'lucky' is top favourite. It seems that every other living person is luckier than she is. I can't judge. She has never clarified to me how she could afford the fare from Peru to Paris.

'Grandpa!' said Madame Favela and the tears were rolling down her cheeks. She shoved me into that room for tea and more tales of woe. Life ain't easy as Paul says repeatedly. I concurred that evening. Being pushed out of one room and shoved into another.

'I'm late. Late,' I said, and hit my watch so as to facilitate Madame Favela's understanding. The French for late is 'tard'. It's not like trying to remember a word like 'calembour'. You would think that after 25 years in France she could understand that one little word especially since she has no problem following every single syllable of 'Miami Vice' in French.

Thirty excruciating minutes later I was on my way to my lover in Montmartre. Granddad's letter was very short and not a bit like his usual longwinded chronicle of the week's happenings and events in Dunmo-Croi.

'Darling girl, (that's how he always started his letters).

Guess what? Belinda and I are coming to Paris for two weeks. Don't worry. We're not looking for a bed from you. We'll be staying in a nice hotel Mr. Horgan found for us. If you have time - and only if it doesn't interfere with your dazzling theatre career - could you give the hotel the once over to see if it's alright for Belinda's sake? I don't mind much myself. Just being in

Paris and seeing you will be enough. I hope I'll recognize you when I see you.

Loads of love from Belinda and your Granddad.'

Somehow you know when things are going to shift. I had a premonition that night when I got Granddad's letter. Things were shifting. They'd shift and shift and never, ever be the same again.

NINETEEN

Some nights when Jean-Claude needed to compose or meet and schmooze critics and investors or rest his brain, I slept in my own hutch. It was on one such night that I got the emergency call from Paul. Naturally I had given Madame's number to the very select few, with the stipulation that it was to be used only in the direst of emergencies. Madame - apart from not wanting to rush up to the ethnic warren under the eaves every time the phone rang for me - believed that too many people abused the phone. It was a convenience, she used to say, and abused far too often for tittle-tattle. Paul was also a firm believer in not using the phone. It cost a franc. For two francs he could buy a whole baguette and for three francs he could sit and scribble all day in a café over an espresso.

Spending a franc is something most normal people don't think twice about. But in Paul's case he only had 150 dollars a month (his trust fund from his Grand-father) and being a writer he couldn't run the risk of impairing his writing ability by taking a job. I had mentioned to Paul that he should write about the deprivations of being a writer in the 80's instead of harping on about Hemingway hunting pigeons in the Tuileries. But Paul said that the poverty and writers combination was not fashionable in the 80's, it was the writer-wealth combination people wanted to read about.

By the time I got downstairs Paul's franc was almost gone and there was that pip-pip-pip sound to remind you to pop in another franc.

'I've been evicted. I'm homeless. Can I have the loan of your second mattress for the night? Meet me outside your place in fifteen minutes.'

The line went dead.

Madame hovered in the background waiting for me to evaporate back upstairs.

'A friend of mine is in trouble,' I told her.

'I'm sorry,' she said and looked at her watch. 'Goodnight, Nellie.'

While I waited outside for Paul to arrive I pondered his words. 'Loan' he had said. The usual meaning of that is 'taking away and bringing back'. We'd have to haul the mattress down 127 stairs and past Madame Favela's lookout. Even though she says I am more like a daughter to her, she'd still want to know where the mattress was going. She is paid to keep track of what comes in and out of the building. Plus, Madame would not take too kindly to the mattress taking a stroll before Spring.

When Paul arrived he was wetter than a drowned rat. His jacket was a different colour because it had absorbed so much rain. His face looked greyer than the rooftops of Paris.

'Sorry about this,' he panted and we trudged up the 127 steps.

He had to pause after the 52nd to get his breath back. Naturally with all the jumping up and down I did on those stairs I didn't have to pause. Paul, I could see, was real impressed.

He couldn't speak for five minutes after he reached the top. Then he was struck speechless a second time when I took him on a tour of the premises. Mr. Turk was in residence, with the door open, tip-tapping away, so we went in and said 'hello' to him. Half of Africa was in the communal kitchen cooking up some godawful smelly stuff. As always they were most cordial and invited us to taste some. I said 'No way' and they said I didn't know what I was missing. Then we went into my dog box and Paul said:

'There must be least 50 people living up here.'

'Sometimes more.'

'Well, at least they have a roof over their heads,' he said bitterly.

'What happened?' I asked.

'I should sue that son of a bitch,' said Paul vehemently. 'There was nothing in our arrangement that I couldn't use my typewriter during the night. I know my rights.'

It was a toss-up between 'rights' and 'Hemingway' as to Paul's favourite topic.

'People like to sleep at night.'

'That Jean-Pierre is a philistine,' said Paul, and ground his teeth. Paul had an arrangement with Jean-Pierre. In exchange for free rent in Paris, he could stay with Paul's parents in Philadelphia when he spent his year in the USA. Paul's parents have yet to be advised of this exchange.

'So where are you going to stay?' I asked, before I gently broke the news to him that he'd have to wait for the arrival of a solar eclipse before he could smuggle the mattress out of the building without Madame Favela knowing.

'I haven't solved that one yet,' said Paul, and paced the three steps over to the window. There were five pigeons swaying in the breeze looking like they needed the Last Rites. They looked pathetic as hell, their heads all scrunched up into their necks as if this would keep the rain from plopping down on them. For a moment I was distracted from Paul's dilemma and wondered why some birds' necks weren't flexile enough to tuck their heads under their wings for comfort when it rained. Ducks and swans could snuggle their heads under their wings. Why couldn't pigeons, sparrows and robins? Maybe Paul could have clarified that bird query. But it wasn't the moment to pick his brains.

'I was hoping I could stay with you,' said Paul, still with his back to me looking out into the wet night.

Hey! The guy was secretly in love with me and had to resort to this eviction and homeless charade because he was … shy? Although Paul 'shared' most things with me, he was annoyingly discreet when it came to his love life. He had an on-and-off relationship with Colette whom I met once and hated on sight. She came into the café wearing black stockings, an old weather-beaten sixties dress and a few rows of straggly pearls. She looked fabulous. Even the special way she crossed her legs yelled out: 'I'm French! So French!' Dressed in that same getup I - or anyone else - would have looked worse than Liz Taylor in the final act of 'Who's Afraid of Virginia Woolf' when she was a woman ready for the garbage truck.

'Paul, I do like you, you know that.' I was getting ready to break his heart and demurely reject the only tall guy who had ever come my way.

'I'm not aiming to jump on your bones, if that's what you're thinking. No way,' he said, and banged on the window to see if that would stop the pigeons in mid-crap.

'That's not what I was thinking,' I said, and acted all insulted. The nerve of the guy! 'I just meant there isn't room for two of us in this room.'

'Paris! We're living in Paris! I've got 26 dollars left for the month. We're living like rats.'

'Thank you,' I said sarcastically.

However it did strike me that at that particular moment Paris was not living up to its glamorous image. A wet, homeless American was dripping all over my dog box. The drenched pigeons looked so pathetic I almost wanted to open the window and let them in to dry off. Suddenly almighty shrieks either in Turkish or in African erupted out in the corridor. Paul's eyes doubled in size. He spoke in hushed tones.

'Are we safe?' he asked, looking at the door as if he expected spears with scalps dangling from them to come cutting through the wood. The usual bedlam continued outside.

'Are they allowed to make all that racket? Do they have the right ….'

'Just zip it with your bloody rights,' I said in an annoyed voice. Here he was asking for shelter and at the same time insinuating that the premises weren't up to standard. 'You're homeless. Remember?'

If I had poked out both his eyes he couldn't have looked more wounded. Standing there with his wet hair he reminded me of a poor old horse who used to live in a field near us. When it rained there was no tree he could shelter under. The poor old wet horse used to whinney mournfully at the top of his lungs, calling out to the country at large to please take it out of the rain and bring it into a warm, dry barn.

'We'll figure something out,' I told Paul. 'Now sit down and get dry.'

I pulled the towel from a hook near the window. When I removed it there was a movement of sorts from the pigeons. I looked out. There were only four left. The really sick looking one was gone. I could only hope it had flown away and not just plopped off the sill and onto the pavement below.

'Right then, let's figure out your options,' I said, slipping into Paul's jargon and adopting my most upbeat voice. That's the glory of being an actress. You can fool people. You can even fool yourself into feeling optimistic and not thinking about poor birds floundering around in the gutter, letting out their last gasps before they died.

'I can't stay at Martin's because he's back with that hybrid Hélène.'

'I understand.'

Hélène (whom Paul always referred to as either Hybrid Hélène, Helen of Hades, or Handgrenade Hélène) once told Paul to 'get real, there was *NO NEED* for writers any more. There were enough books in the world already and most people preferred the film version'.

'Well, there's Hansi of course.'

He didn't have to explain about Hansi's inability to house even as much as an extra flea. The caravan was so cramped the cats had to sleep on top of one another. Paul couldn't even sleep on top of the caravan because that was where Hansi kept the interior décor that had once been inside his caravan.

'Ok, so we can eliminate Hansi and the Paris Zoo,' I said and offered my hairdryer to Paul. But he declined it and just combed back the wet hair. He looked rather astonishingly handsome with his wet hair. Or maybe because he was looking so sad. Men look better when they have a touch of melancholy to them. Not all the time of course.

'What about Colette?'

'Colette?' Paul wrinkled his brow as if I had asked him to give me the square root of 7985. 'Oh that's been over for ages now.'

'Really! And what's the name of the new one?'

'Monique. But she's living with her parents. And I'd prefer to stay out of their way. They're very protective of her.'

'Fine. No room at Monique's.'

'It's a pity about Colette. Her sofa was really comfortable,' said Paul.

I wondered if one day I would ever say something like that about Jean-Claude, like how I missed his white sofa more than him. In fact sometimes I could remember more details about his apartment than I could about Jean-Claude. I could conjure up a very exact image of his piano, right down to the scratches on the left leg. I couldn't have done the same with, say, Jean-Claude's toes. But I did spend more time looking at the piano. Maybe that was the answer.

'Anyone else? What about Jacques?'

'Connard! I showed him my last story and he said it was like chewing through a slab of granite. Espèce de con! The nerve! He thinks writing is all about inventing a new kind of structure and never using adjectives. I'd get a terminal disease just by sitting on that guy's sofa. He writes shit.'

'So we can safely eliminate Jacques in that case,' I said, but the sarcasm flew way over Paul's head.

'Why does it have to be like this? Merde, troisfois merde.'

He threw the towel on the bed and paced the two paces to the window. He banged on the window and startled the four wet pigeons from their unhappy slumbers. He stood there with his shiny hair in bright contrast to the grey dreariness outside. But it was the sagging of his shoulders that tightened my heart. They sagged as if his heart was too heavy for him to stand up any straighter. He looked exactly the way I used to feel when those voices at Irish TV and the Paris agencies told me in those false, cheerful tones that broke my heart: 'Sorry, we can't use you. But best of luck, dear.' That's why I said it.

'There's an empty room down the hall. It's locked but we could open it during the night and take the mattress over there. Then you could just bring it back in the morning.'

'You mean there's an extra room here?' he asked and turned away from the window. His eyes were all lit up. As if I had given him the kiss of Life and put the colour back into his baby blues.

'Well, it's got a bit of a history. An old African woman tried to do herself in with the bread knife. She was depressed about her condition. The police saved her even if they had to arrest her for attempting suicide. She's in a home now. The owner doesn't want to rent it out and risk people ruining his property and reducing the value of it.'

'Jesus!' said Paul, and ran his fingers through his hair to get it back to its usual ruffled state. 'You'd have to evacuate the whole colony up here before you could even think of property value. Most of those bourgeois would be afraid to come here anyhow.'

It was not the moment to tell him that I could see similarities between his eyes and those of Madame when she walked up here. I, myself, could have thought of more 'normal' accommodations. But to me this room was my place of freedom, my first independent home, and now I could also offer shelter to a fellow suffering artist. Even if he wasn't an actor and only a writer.

'Will it work though?' asked Paul.

That's the worst thing I've noticed about writers. No optimism. They always concentrate on the snags. Not like actresses, the superior breed. To me there was nothing simpler than walking down that corridor in the middle of the night and undoing that lock. With the entire colony snoring their guts out, a platoon of *UFO's* could be landing in the corridor and nobody would notice. Maybe one or two of them would try and turn over in the bed. And I mean 'try'. Because when there are five of you in a single bed, it's quite a feat to turn unless all five of you do so simultaneously like so many sausages on a spit.

'Nothing will go wrong,' I reassured him.

We went to the café to while away the hours. I took my Complete Shakespeare with me. Paul took three notebooks. He splurged on a hot chocolate for me. I almost refused but then I decided there was no reason why he shouldn't express his thanks in this way. We stayed in the café for 5 hours. It was packed with the usual suspects. Occasionally Paul would reach over and tap me on the hand and tell me that I was distracting him by rehearsing out loud. Of course the boyos breaking the slot machines and the drunks brawling at the bar didn't even enter his sphere of consciousness. But my soft mutterings of a superior writer adversely affected his Muse. I bore it all with exemplary fortitude. Then I said I'd have another hot chocolate, thank you.

At 2.30 that morning Paul broke the lock on the door of the little room. It had a combination lock which I thought would be a bit of a challenge but Paul had it cracked in twenty-five seconds flat. It was nothing, he said. At school he and his pals used to practice breaking their bicycle locks to jazz up the day. You think you know people and then it turns out you don't know them at all.

He hauled the top mattress off the bed and heaved it down to his room.

'Bring it back in the morning,' I reminded him. In case he had any ideas of doing a bunk with the mattress.

'Of course I will,' he said and moved away. Then he turned back and blew me a happy kiss. 'Thanks, little one.'

Well, that was that, I thought. How wrong could any one person be?

TWENTY

A letter arrived from my Mam with a list of all the things Granddad was forbidden to do while in Paris. He was not to eat any of the rich French food (which would eliminate everything except the expensive dry toast they call 'biscottes'). He was not to drink endless cups of that vile coffee which would make his arthritis flare up again. And he was not to overdo it. In my Mam's vocabulary the verb 'overdo' applies to every single activity known to humankind. I wrote back, told her to forget her worries and to tell Granddad that I had checked out their Paris hotel to make sure it was as good as Horgan's.

Their hotel was located on the semi touristy side of the hill of Montmartre. The lobby was most tastefully furnished in grey and burgundy. But a few shades either side and the place would have looked like a shipwrecked brothel. When I strolled in the receptionist was bowed over a stack of bills. She snapped upright like a toy doll when she heard me approach. She smiled the way people do who are in the profession of serving the public. The smile that said – 'just what are you going to bother me with, this time?'

'Je suis Irlandaise,' I announced. (i.e. I am Irish)

That little phrase can prove most helpful in France. Her smile veered towards the genuine. Mentioning the fact that you are Irish to a French person immediately consolidates a kind of rapport. The French really like the Irish, the way a kind, sophisticated city cousin has a fondness for a poor, charming country cousin.

'My grandfather is coming to the hotel on Friday. He wanted me to check out his room.'

The smile vanished. The one thing the French cannot abide is another nation questioning their ability. She had the look of a woman who suddenly didn't give a flying fuck if I was Irish or Dracula's granddaughter.

'Why? What's wrong with him?' she snapped.

Oh, why can't the French be more like the Irish? Go with the flow! When the Americans who stay in Horgan's Hotel moan about the lack of ice makers in their rooms Mr. Horgan doesn't have a fit. He's all charm and says something like it would spoil the old world, authentic feel of the room or some such garbage. Then he'll tell them they can have as much ice as they want. Just say the word. No song and dance. No daggers shooting out of the eyeballs like this French woman who is longing to see my blood on the burgundy carpet.

'Oh, I suppose it's because he has his own hotel. He has standards.'

That took the wind out of her sails!

'They have room 317,' she said, almost contritely.

I felt bad about lying but couldn't help but admire my inventive wits. I almost advised: 'Madame, unless you want to croak at 35, take it easy, OK?' But I certainly didn't want to antagonize her any further. Knowing how expensive nice rooms can be in Paris. Knowing the shortage of decent rooms reminded me that Paul had been in residence for a week and was 'settling in despite the odds' to quote himself.

Madame gave me the keys to Room 317. It was Parisian perfection. The geraniums frolicked on the balcony and the whole view of Montmartre with the

Sacré Coeur perched on top was framed in the French windows. There was a small balcony with a table and chairs. It was almost a shame to waste this most romantic room on Granddad and Belinda. There was a writing desk in the corner and this was probably the kind of room that inspired people to stay in Paris and paint and pen their hearts out. I strolled out onto the balcony. The scent of croissants and true coffee wafted up to me accompanied by the sound of French chat and laughter. I had a premonition of sorts. Room 317 was the kind you wouldn't willingly leave. It was too romantic. Even the bed was heavenly. I lay down for a while and looked out at the Sacré Coeur framed in the fluttering white curtains and wished I could swap this view for my panorama of pigeons' bottoms. But the main asset was the elevator. The two wouldn't have to expire walking up the stairs with which Paris has an ever enduring love affair.

'The room is very beautiful,' I told the woman on the desk.

'Of course it is,' she hissed with a full artificial smile.

'I like the geraniums. Lovely colour. And the view is divine and so is the bed,' I rhapsodised.

But you could see the damage was irreparable. By coming here to check the place out I had blatantly insinuated that the place might not be up to standard. Now this is more than a French person can tolerate. They give themselves ulcers and liver attacks to make life beautiful, to make the food glorious, the drink heavenly, the ambience romantic, the environment harmonious. That should be enough. It is unfathomable and unbearable for them to have their efforts questioned.

'The room is just gorgeous!'

She gave a disdainful shrug with her shoulders – a Gallic version of Paul's 'tell me something I don't already know.' It's very stressful living with the French. I racked my brains for every admiring adjective I knew in French. By the time I left, the woman had almost reached normality again. But I needed a double espresso to scrape together enough energy to get me onto the métro and over to theatre to go a few rounds with Antoine.

I had reached that state of mind which I had honestly thought could only possibly occur in a Shakespearean tragedy, i.e. where the heroine wishes to throw herself on a sword to end it all. Believe me, two hours daily with Antoine was enough to make impalement at the end of a rapier an acceptable alternative. But such a decorative death would have killed my Mam, my Dad and my Granddad straight off, so I just had to find the fortitude to soldier on in the battle to thump some English into Antoine. Just what was his problem? Why couldn't he say 'this', 'that', 'these' and 'those' without sounding like a backed up drain? Paul had even insinuated that the fault could lie with my Irish accent. That really got me steamed up. Nellie Flanagan with the perfect pitch, impeccable delivery, enviable resonance was being accused of not being crystal clear! We had progressed (I use the term very euphemistically) to the problem of asking a question in English – i.e using those little words 'do' and 'does' as in 'Do you like Paris? Does he like Paris?' Antoine preferred his own version minus any 'do' or 'does'.

I'll give you an example. One day he came in with a box of marrons glacées (that's French for their gorgeous 'sugared sweet chestnuts'). He held out the box and announced: 'Jew lucky?' I smiled back at him wondering if maybe 'Jew Lucky' was a horse he'd put a bet on. Or maybe he was referring to himself and wanted to say 'Lucky Jew', that's if he was Jewish. I didn't know since we had never discussed religion. He kept repeating 'Jew Lucky' while I tried to figure out the connection to the marrons glacées. A haunted look of despair rushed across Antoine's face. He changed his tune. 'You lickey?' he asked and took the lid off the box of chestnuts. And the penny finally dropped. The 'Lucky Jew' and the 'You Lickey?' were one and the same thing. And they both meant: 'Like you' and 'You like?' And just forget about the addition of anything sophisticated such as 'Do'. Fifty hours of pounding him with the simple expression – 'do you like … marrons glacées?' and 'you lickey … marrons glacées' was the disheartening result.

But I had to hang in there. Antoine might be a bit slow. I kept reminding myself about the Australian woman who had taught that chimpanzee 250 words which was more than Antoine had absorbed so far.

Hope which is supposed to spring eternal would have to keep flowing a little longer.

TWENTY-ONE

It was almost curtain up time on Opening Night. Being different of course, the *Théâtre du Zivot* didn't have a curtain. The moths had chewed it off the rail decades earlier. In this theatre it was a return to the blackout. All the lights would go off on stage and in the auditorium to signal that the play was about to start. However they still hadn't perfected the dazzling Opening Sequence. This involved Antoine staggering across the stage carrying a gigantic carved naked lady tied to a pole. This, believe it or not, was supposed to symbolize a ship leaving a harbour in the Old World and sailing away to the brave New World of America. No matter how he tried Philippe, the lighting director, who didn't know the difference between voltage and wattage, couldn't get the spots to focus on the statue of the woman. You could still see most of Antoine puffing and huffing under the weight of the carving. By the time Antoine reached the other end of the stage the naked lady was wobbling dangerously. Jean-Claude didn't object to the wobble. He said it evoked images of a storm tossed ship at sea. This was true 'l'art à la française'. I really had to admire the depth of their self delusion.

The cast were all indulging in mini breakdowns. Armand decided he had amnesia and would never remember his lines. Pierrette had a fit of pique and ran her knitting needles into the pillow missing Chantal by three inches. Antoine protested that his back wasn't up to hauling the heavy lady across the entire stage. He flounced onto the bed. And with one almighty twang it collapsed under him. It took them about an hour to repair the bed. Everyone blamed Antoine and told him to shut up about his back.

Because it was Opening Night I wasn't even playing the corpse any more. I lingered enviously on stage and Jean-Claude came over and stood next to me. We gazed out at the empty theatre. Behind us on stage Pierrette and Armand were still trying to mend the bed and swearing their guts out. In the wings Antoine was whimpering about his back. Philippe was trying to get the lights to go and off when he flicked the switch and not just when the electricity wires felt like it.

'It's this fabulous?' said Jean-Claude. His eyes glowed like two giant rubies in an Indian goddess. 'It's not the Académie but it's a beginning.'

Then without missing a beat he reminded me that it was time to open the Box Office. I had the exalted position of Box Office Director keeping track of the stream of Francs that would come cascading into our coffers. It was drizzling dourly onto the grey pavement. The headlights from the passing cars gave the impression that they were large eyes crying in the mist. I sat in the booth and fantasized that this was all part of a French film and any second now the Director would shout 'cut'. The minutes passed. I watched the raindrops dancing off the pavement and scooting down into the gutter. Finally a car stopped and a couple got out. But I couldn't sell them tickets. They already had free ones.

After that things picked up. At one point the lobby was packed with people and there was a hum in the air of excitement and anticipation. Cars drew up and people ran into the theatre to escape the rain. The two critics arrived. One was a woman in her late seventies the size of a battleship. Jean-Claude groaned when he saw her. She wrote for a local newspaper which was published by a group of bitter old folk who found fault with everything. The other critic was a tall thin man. Jean-Claude said it didn't matter what the guy wrote since everyone knew he only had the job because his uncle owned the paper. But I was to be on a watch out for anyone else who might be scribbling in the theatre so I could describe them to him. A lot of Parisian critics, he said, sometimes took side trips to the fringe to ferret out the fine from the fiascos.

The play went off as planned. There was raucous applause at the end of every scene because the audience was 100% family and friends fulfilling their duty by clapping frenetically. They didn't waste their time wondering what in hell was happening up there on stage. The fat lady critic looked slightly stunned by it all, as if a tree had toppled over on top of her. She was so huge it would have to be an oak of true substance to rattle that woman. But Maurice's play had obviously left its mark. Half way through the first act she was a woman defeated, and packed away her notes. The skinny tall guy sucked his pen the entire time as if he hadn't had a bite in months.

Nothing happened that wasn't supposed to happen. When they all went out for their bows, Jean-Claude and Maurice joined them. Even the corpse got a loud round of applause. I was in the wings standing next to Philippe who was still trying to tame the lights. For a second I nearly pushed him aside and plunged the place into darkness. Such was my sudden envy to see all those people out there on stage, bowing and basking in the applause that somehow always eluded me.

Afterwards we all went to Mahmoud's with a few of the relatives. For another two hours they regurgitated everything that had happened on stage. In a moment of total exuberance Jean-Claude said I should have taken a bow for the 'remarkable' work I'd done. They all agreed. Chantal went one better. She gave me one of her special French pouts, stroked my hair and said she wished she had green eyes like mine. She wanted something.

'Nellie, chérie,' she said still stroking my hair. 'I must leave early on Saturday week. You can have my part in the second act.'

I am a sublime actress and can control my temper and my words. I did not turn to Chantal and hiss: 'Part? What part? You're dead by then and covered with a sheet. Take a dive into the Seine, sister.'

'Thank you, Chantal,' I said. She immediately stopped stroking my hair. I raised my glass and like a true heroine said:

'Here's to all of you. Well Done!'

I nearly croaked on those words, because the envy of not being a working actress is a terrible affliction. It can do more damage to your tonsils and tongue than the 'Where, when, whys and whose' can do to Antoine. They all raised their glasses and drank heartily and then ignored me for the rest of the evening while they analysed, rehashed and repeated their lines. I had three glasses of wine before I came to my senses and realized that it was no good trying to drown my sorrows. Booze was not the magic key to the kingdom of success. If it were Antoine and failed actors the world over would be paddling in booze from dawn to dusk. Pierrette and Armand didn't use booze. Their trick was to fuss incessantly about the children and their Mammans to stop them realizing that the *Théâtre du Zivot* in the dreariest part of Paris was forever going to be their only moment of glory in the theatre. And Jean-Claude probably sat at his piano with one hand on the bottle sipping in that elegant way of his to stop himself from knowing that he was not Rachmaninoff and that he was not Jourdheuil and that he would always be Jean-Claude - a nice, average composer director while being neither really.

Jean-Claude drove me home. He informed me that I wouldn't be staying overnight with him. He needed his rest. He jabbered all the way without once asking me what I was thinking. I was too depressed at not being a working actress to be too put out about it. Which proved that even though I had the hots for Jean-Claude he was not the burning passion of my life. That too was a very depressing thought.

I trudged up the 127 steps. I even had to pause at number 74. Which goes to show the detrimental effect three glasses of wine can have on a healthy constitution. Under the roof everyone was sleeping and the symphony of snores sounded like the rhythm of a rough sea breaking against cliffs. A light was shining in Mr. Turk's room. I stopped to make sure he was ok. Sometimes he fell asleep face down in the middle of his shoes and pots of glue. Mr. Turk always left his door ajar. For some reason he couldn't tolerate to have the door shut entirely. I looked into his room. Mr. Turk was fast asleep on his narrow bed with a huge smile on his face. He looked so very happy. Naturally that depressed me even more. Here was a demented old geyser who spent his last days on earth making shoes for poor people who couldn't afford normal shop shoes, who took occasional dives into the glue and polish when he was exhausted, who was too weak to go downstairs into the sunshine, who suffered from the fear of being alone behind a closed door... and he looked sublimely happy. How could he smile in his sleep?

When the hand came on my shoulder I let out a shriek and went all clammy with terror.

'It's only me,' said Paul. 'I waited up for you. How did it go?'

'It was fantastic,' I told him. 'Simply out of this world amazing.'

Paul produced half a bottle of wine and two wine glasses Henri had lent him from the café so we could properly celebrate my brilliant debut on a French stage.

TWENTY-TWO

I didn't recognize Granddad when he walked into the Arrivals Hall of Charles de Gaulle Airport. I had been expecting my Granddad - not this man with a brand new moustache and a red beret pushing a cart in front of him with more luggage than the Vienna Boys Choir on a World Tour. Belinda was the same 65 year old with a fresh tint and perm.

'Darling Girl! Darling Girl!'

When Granddad put his arms around me I could feel his heart jumping all over the place with excitement like a soccer ball being dribbled by a super professional.

'You've decided to emigrate?' I said and pointed to the luggage.

'Your Granddad wouldn't let me come without my paints and my easel,' said Belinda apologetically.

'A painter couldn't come to Paris without her utensils, could she?' said Granddad.

'We're in Paris, Jimmie Joe', said Belinda with wonderment. 'We're really here.'

'We brought you lots of sausages to keep your strength up,' said Granddad, patting an enormous bulging bag. Madame would yet again have to clear a space in the freezer, just when she thought she'd seen the last of those Irish goods.

'But of course you've been spoilt by all that French food.'

'No complaints,' I said because despite her hypochondria, Francesca was a superb cook and Jean-Claude always took me to bistros frequented only by French gourmets.

'I like the beret, Granddad. It makes a new man out of you,' I said, which was exactly the right thing to say. You don't live with your parents and your Granddad for years without knowing that the thing they want most in the world is to be somebody else, or somebody totally new, or somebody different.

We took the *RER* (which is the super fast train in Paris) to the Gare du Nord (figure that one out for yourself). I had to cart all those suitcases up and down the escalators since I didn't want either of them having heart attacks from the strain. It took four trips.

'I must say Paris is certainly agreeing with you,' said Granddad. 'You're as fit as a fiddle. All that Parisian partying and high life!'

There was a different woman at the hotel reception desk which meant I didn't have to exhaust myself with another adjective fit. The two were enchanted with the grey and burgundy decor. It took three trips up and down in the slim elevator to deliver their luggage and bags of duty free booze. Granddad requested the lady at the desk for a bowl of ice cubes and a bottle of tonic. By now Granddad had eased into his version of French and had so far said 'jolie' (nice') about 55 times to the woman at the desk. The woman was smiling genuinely. She even divulged her name to Granddad: Madame Roussard, owner. Granddad invited her to join them for drinkies. It was probably the first time in decades that anyone had asked Madame Roussard for a drink. She was more than ecstatic to have such generous guests in her small hotel as opposed to the usual crop who emptied the shelves of every last drop of shampoo and took the toilet paper with them.

The two practically expired when they saw the view. Granddad let out a stream of 'jolies' even though there wasn't a French person present. Belinda said: 'so this is Paris' fifteen times. I lay on the bed and wondered if you could damage your heart before you were 19 by hauling half of Ireland up and down stairs and elevators.

'This calls for a little celebration,' said Granddad when he felt up to tearing himself away from the view.

They had brought enough booze to knock out half of Paris - four large bottles of Irish gin, four large bottles of Irish whiskey and 6 bottles of French champagne. Neither of them had ever heard of 'Duty Free quotas.'

'Of course you'll take a few bottles back to your place for your friends,' said Granddad while I was pouring out the usual weak G & T and a small Paddy.

'I'll leave them till later,' I said. 'Right now I've got to hotfoot it over to the theatre.'

They were most impressed. They didn't give me time to add that I was going there to thump the present tense into Antoine and then to sit in a freezing box-office to try and harass passers-by into buying a few tickets.

'To the theatre! How thrilling!' said Granddad.

'Well, that's Paris, isn't it?' said Belinda. 'A different world altogether.'

'That's the main reason we came to Paris. To see you tread those boards,' said Granddad.

'Grandad, I told you I only have a miniscule part. Hardly a part at all.'

'But darling girl, that's not a bit like you!' said Granddad, looking quite elevated from the combination of the Paris view and the two inches of Paddy. 'They would never waste your talent on a nothing role.'

'It's small, Granddad. You'll see,' I told him firmly. 'It's very small.'

'I said it to your Mam before we left. Leave it to the French to make a star of our Nellie.'

'I can hardly believe we'll be watching you up there on stage - in Paris!' said Belinda, wafting over with the gliding motion of an aging ballerina towards the gin bottle. 'What a pity your Mam can't be here to see you performing in Paris!'

'Off you go now,' said Granddad, shooing me out the door. 'We can't have our star running late for the theatre.'

As it turned out Antoine and I didn't have an English lesson that particular evening. This time he asked me if I would go over one of the scenes with him. We rehearsed the part in the beginning of the play where he is badgering the poor maid to inform on the other couple. She's on the verge of convulsions, approaching her dying moment. This was Chantal's one big speech. Antoine at this point in the play is a snivelling shit. Later he changes into a man of conscience.

It gave me an ache to be rehearsing with Antoine in the recesses of that broken down old dressing room. If there were any justice in the world I should have been in a proper theatre flaunting my talent for the world to enjoy. It also crossed my mind that it was at moments like this that people poisoned other human beings. A few sleeping tablets in her coffee and Chantal would snore through the first act. And Nellie would leap onto the breech.

'Magnifique! Magnifique!' Antoine exulted when we had finished rehearsing. Sure he was impressed but not to the point of demanding that I replace Chantal. That's another thing that's rampant in the acting profession. Actors are exclusively preoccupied with their own performances and roles. Oh sure, they can recognize an extraordinary performance and comment on it. But their thoughts are always on their own roles, their own voice, their own place on the stage. It has to be like this. So it was only natural for Antoine to say 'Merci, chérie' and scoot off instead of helping me murder Chantal for that miserable part. Such was the theatre.

The theatre wasn't quite so full that night. This was a blow and a disappointment to all concerned. Pierrette said it was because it was Tuesday. Nobody could be expected to come out on a wet Tuesday. Nobody in their right mind who wasn't a complete masochist, I felt like adding. It was the truth but it's the code never to inflict unnecessary hurt on others in the acting fraternity. The applause was less than lukewarm. Very few relatives were present among the audience. I didn't see anyone scribbling away furiously from my vantage position in the back. So it didn't look as if there would be major reviews in Le Monde or Le Figaro the next day.

There was a near miss with the bed at one point when Valerie threw herself energetically on top of it. Before each performance Jean-Claude appealed to the players to take the bed into consideration as if the bed had now been raised to the status of cast member. But in their enthusiasm the actors forgot about Jean-Claude's admonishments and Chantal did her usual series of lift-offs, quivers and jumps from the bed. Once the thought did cross my mind that if the bed were to disintegrate under Chantal she might be slightly brained for a while (not really hurt) and I'd be able to take over her part for the rest of the run.

It was like a wake at Mahmoud's after that particular performance. None of them were very hungry which induced a fit of pique in Mahmoud. Instead they drank gallons of wine. Mahmoud plied them with salty olives. They drank some more. I had 2 glasses to their 12. Antoine finally decided to order a couscous and Mahmoud told him the kitchen was closed. Antoine had a 'crise de nerves' - that's actually a fit of shouting, but they call it an attack of nerves. Mahmoud delivered the couscous with more invective and swear words than in all of the Complete Shakespeare.

Jean-Claude drove me home and drummed his fingers against the steering wheel the entire time. He gave me a kiss that seemed to drain the last of his energy from him. He sighed and said: 'It's disappointing, isn't it?' I didn't know if he was referring to the production, me, or the weather.

The bulb had gone in my room. The rain had stopped and a large wet moon seemed to be weeping over Paris. Five plump pigeons were nestled peacefully on the windowsill. I stood in the dark at the window. Under the watery moon the rooftops had an eerie glow to them and the chimney pots were exactly like a scene out of untold movies about magnificent Paris.

Paris, I thought. Mystical City. City of Light. Penninsula of Pain as Paul had mentioned to Hansi one night recently in the café. I hoped the two in Room 317 were seeing a different Paris.

TWENTY-THREE

The rest of that week was hectic. Every day I
accompanied Granddad and Belinda to see the usual
stuff like the Eiffel, the Arch, the Louvre, the M'0, the
Picassos. We saw it all. Granddad always wore his red
beret and French people came up to him in the street
asking for directions. Belinda wittered on about Monet,
Manet. Renoir, poor Utrillo and poor Toulouse. My kids
recovered from their whooping cough and we resumed
our lessons. To suit my gloomy mood I decided we'd
chuck in *Romeo and Juliet* and do *Hamlet* who wanted
his too, too solid flesh to melt – a feeling I could more
than relate to every night in that dump of a theatre.
Maude and Claude were gutted they wouldn't be seeing
me on stage (Madame decreed it was too late for them
and too far north for her) so to cheer us all up I went a
bit overboard about my own involvement in '*NO FUN
AT THE WAKE*'. I spent the week enchanting my kids
with tales of the fabulous leading role I had in an
extraordinary play in a most glamorous theatre. I am
fully aware I should not have done so. It was barefaced
lying to innocent children. But I convinced myself it was
justified compensation for the fact that I wasn't already
a world famous actor. And we mustn't forget that theatre
is all fantasy and these particular fantasies delighted
both my kids and myself. If I had been able to get
away with it, I would have spun the same set of lies for

Granddad and Belinda to save them witnessing with their own eyes that the supremely talented grand-daughter could only cut it as a corpse.

Saturday night arrived as it had to inevitably. I parked myself in the box office to let in those few Parisians who were daft enough to come to this forlorn part of the city on a rainy night to see a play by a freak who ate and slept in a coffin while writing the play. Maurice believed this helped him infuse the true feeling of death into his corpse character. Did it? If the tub sized critic's reaction was anything to go by she'd have willingly sat on that coffin with Maurice inside to give him his answer and pay him back for the agony he had inflicted on her.

It was about ten minutes to curtain time - or light and launching time in our case. To help the audience understand that this was a ship leaving Le Havre, Philippe had added lights that went haywire and a sound machine that emitted yelps of waves and wind so that people wondered where the burning kennels were. Seven minutes to Opening and I was thinking that maybe Granddad and Belinda had forgotten the name of the theatre and I wouldn't have to endure the mortification of having them witness their star relative lying 'dead' on a bed for an hour. Just as I was cheering up, this taxi pulled up and Monsieur, Madame and the two kids hopped out. Madame hugged her fur tightly, as if she was afraid somebody would shave it off her back and said plaintively:

'They insisted on surprising you.'

Monsieur shoved a 500 franc note through the little hole in the glass, saying he was sorry they couldn't come on the night I'd given them tickets for and did I have the four reserved for 'Duchamps'? There are fifty million Duchamps in France. How was I to be inspired it could have been them? If I'd only known I'd have alerted my kids that Nellie the Super Star was giving the others a chance that evening and would not be playing the lead. I wanted to be stretched out on that bed well and truly dead watching my kids jumping all over the lobby like pepped-up puppies. I was just closing up the box office when another taxi pulled up and out tottered Granddad and Belinda. They had time to tell me that they had taken a long nap that afternoon so they'd be fresh for my performance and could report back home in minutest detail how Nellie Flanagan had trodden the Parisian boards and wowed the natives. I gave them the two seats in the front row next to the Duchamps family.

I locked up. For a second I thought of pocketing the 500 francs. It would help after I'd be fired from my job for misleading and disappointing young children. Paul and I would be homeless. But theft was theft and 500 francs wouldn't help much so I turned the key on the cash box. Just as I was sliding inside to take up my position near the door so that I could be helpful to latecomers, three shadows pulled in behind me.

'We waited until there was nobody around,' whispered Paul. From the smell of paint I knew one was Hansi and the perfume was Diana's. 'Can you get us in for free?'

'We couldn't miss your first performance in Paris,' enthused Duelling Diana.

Dear God, have the entire place cave in, now. Do that, Lord, and I'll never bother you again, I swear.

The lights went into their opening frenzy of flashing and dimming which was supposed to symbolize a busy port on a stormy night. As usual the audience kept looking around, wondering what the hell was wrong with the electricity. The naked figure of a lady loomed up on her pole carried by a very visible Antoine. The illusion of a ship taking off from Le Havre was not recognizable at that moment. The soundtrack of a busy port sounded like fifty angry bears savaging their cages. The audience looked perplexed. Nothing new there!

However, halfway across the stage Antoine stumbled, which was a new twist. That's the beauty of the theatre. You never know what the night is going to cough up. The naked lady on the pole waved frantically to and fro while Antoine tried to regain his balance. There was a shout of laughter and applause from Maude and Claude for this astonishing juggling feat. Antoine continued wrestling with the heavy naked lady statue. The house exploded with laughter. The lady won the round and came crashing down onto the stage, rolling towards the edge of the stage. Philippe and Jean-Claude dashed out from the wings and between them they tamed the lady and prevented her from smashing into the front row and maiming Granddad, Belinda, and the Duchamps. I reversed my prayers. Forget about wrecking the theatre, God!

The play began. Pierrette and Armand did their to-and-froing, speechifying and exiting without any major mishaps. The audience was puzzled. They were probably wondering what had happened to the rabid bears. Next came Antoine's Grand Entrance! But it was evident he still hadn't recovered from the opening fiasco. He rushed on stage, whirled by the bed and left his crowning glory of ringlets dangling from one of the bed posts. There were roars of appreciative laughter from the audience. If he'd practised a thousand times he couldn't have done that again. The ringlets added a touch of 'je ne sais quoi' to the rickety bed. Antoine didn't notice that he had lost his crowning glory. He pranced around the stage with his own hair tied back in the black net. The net had a few holes in it and tufts of grey hair peeked through. He forgot his lines. Valerie had no intention of helping him. She let the wig dangle there, thinking he'd done it on purpose to upstage her.

When Antoine finally saw the wig, he yelped and plonked it back on his head sideways. The whole place shook with laughter. Antoine looked so forlorn with his crooked wig he was visibly on the verge of tears. Not so Valerie. She wasn't going to be upstaged by a smelly wig and a hair net full of holes. She was going to get her own back. They had reached the point in the play where Chantal does her dying speech. Valerie, instead of replying to this speech in a dignified manner decided instead to flounce onto the bed. This was not in the script. Neither was the total collapse of the bed. It gave one massive quiver and quake and broke into its component parts. With the shock Chantal and Valerie howled like scorched tomcats which was also not in the script.

Philippe and Jean-Claude rushed on stage from the wings. The audience couldn't make head or tail of the whole thing. The two in modern dress and all the others in 17th century garb. But who cared what the point was? The audience hadn't seen such magnificent farce in a long time. Jean-Claude was frantically yelling to Chantal to lie down anywhere – just start dying. Chantal was still yelping at the top of her lungs and didn't look a bit like a character who was supposed to die in the next 5 seconds. Philippe did what he could with the bed. In the end they moved the old mattress centre stage and shoved Chantal down onto it so they could get on with the play. Then Jean-Claude and Philippe did a quick dive back into the wings.

The show went on. Chantal died. She had to if the rest of the play were to have any thread of coherence to it. The audience were not thrilled with this. How could somebody croak so early in a comedy? About five minutes before the intermission Paul's head lolled forward in a quick snooze.

'Sorry about that,' he whispered to me when he woke up again. 'I suppose things will liven up when you're up there.'

Oh absolutely, Paul.

By intermission you could almost chew on the audience's disappointment. The comedy had fizzled out and the audience was bored and ill-tempered. I knew I had a choice. Creep out into the night and disappear, or lie up there on stage and endure … the slings and arrows … and the long stemmed roses that my kids had tried to hide behind their father's back as they skipped into the theatre. I wasn't even going to be spared that one. In my fantasizing with the children I had mentioned the mountains of flowers the cast – but mainly Nellie Flanagan - got after the show. How high exactly were the bouquets, wide-eyed Maude wanted to know? I had positioned my hand just above her head. Take me now, God!

TWENTY-FOUR

Backstage Antoine was yowling like a madman. He'd put his fucking back out because of a fucking wooden woman on a fucking pole that the fucking Director had made him cart across the fucking stage every fucking night when you'd have to be a fucking idiot to associate a fucking woman on a fucking pole to a fucking ship being launched in fucking Le Havre.

'Mais, chéri, chéri, chéri!' Valerie was rubbing his back, secretly delighted about the state of Antoine's back and matching one effusive 'Chéri' for every 'fuck' that Antoine unleashed.

Philippe was sulking over the electricity switches and letting loose so many 'Merdes' we should have been throat deep in shit. Pierrette and Armand were arguing at the top of their voices. It was like watching Joseph and Mary brawling in the Nativity Play about what to name the baby.

'You have massacred my masterpiece. Shoot me now,' wailed Maurice. There would have a rush on the gun if one had been handy.

In this wailing ocean of merdes and curses, Chantal calmly applied abundant lipstick, smacked her lips together and informed Jean-Claude and Maurice that if her gentle anatomy had sustained any injuries from the collapse of the bed she would sue them for every last royalty they were likely or more unlikely to see in her lifetime. Then she walked out leaving me to take over her enviable role of corpse. Jean-Claude, embroiled in sticking the bed back together told her to fuck off and go to dark places which are too rude to mention here. I changed into my dull coloured corpse costume, applied my new, revolutionary mascara and several layers of scarlet lipstick. Maurice was struck mute when he saw the flamboyant moi in corpse's garb. Up to that moment he was yelling to himself about maiming actors and cutting out their guts because of the damage they did to his immortal words When he recovered the gift of speech he unleashed his poison darts in my direction.

'This is the final insult,' he shouted at me. 'You are not satisfied with making a mockery of my soul, you are now changing around my people. Oh Mon Dieu! Mon Dieu!'

He fell on his knees near the bed and looked like somebody mourning the end of the world as we knew it. Jean-Claude was embroiled in mending the bed and winked over at me to indicate I was not to take the insults to heart. Maurice saw this wink.

'And now my so called Director is in cahoots with this person!'

He pointed to me as if I were some kind of skunk.

'You have ruined my masterpiece. Now you are replacing people. Do you think that the people out there who came to see my work won't notice this travesty?'

Antoine gallantly rode to my rescue.

'That fucking audience out there hasn't a fucking clue about what's going on in your so-called fucking play. So why the fuck are you so fucking concerned about one fucking corpse taking over from another fucking corpse?'

Antoine's back was still giving him grief. He lifted

his arms up wide to see if that would help with the pain. It didn't.

'Nellie, forget that fucking asshole, go out there and have a nice nap. Because I'm sure that's what the audience would prefer to be doing instead of trying to figure out his fucking twisted soul.'

Antoine pointed derisively at Maurice who was beyond whimpering by this stage. Still with his arms outstretched, Antoine backed away letting loose a resounding string of 'fucking' insults ... and unwittingly walked on stage.

The lights were still on. The audience hadn't been expecting such a flood of 'fuckings' to come from the stage. They had come back refreshed from the intermission spent outside smoking on the dreary sidewalk. They were fortified and ready to enjoy la comédie. They gave a round of applause to Antoine and his stream of expletives. Antoine looked aghast into the wings, realized that he had walked on before the Props (i.e. me and the bed) and sheepishly slouched off the stage. The audience tittered.

There was hope in that titter.

TWENTY-FIVE

Philippe finally managed to switch off all the lights and plunged the place into total darkness. Antoine and Valerie walked onto the dark stage and settled in at the end of the bed. I groped my way onto the bed. Under cover of darkness I was supposed to nestle down under the covers and nobody would notice the corpse switchover. Unfortunately it is impossible to nestle anywhere if all the sheets are sealed up. I tried my best but when the lights snapped on the audience had a full view of me sitting up still wrestling with the sheets, one leg in and the other one out of the bed. Antoine and Valerie both gasped when they saw me.

Nellie Flanagan rose to the occasion. My superb acting instinct told me to act dead. Let the audience come to the conclusion that during the intermission the corpse had been moved into this sitting up and half in and out of the bed position. I waited for Antoine's opening lines. Unfortunately these were: 'She is dead, dead, dead.' I could commiserate with Antoine. It was a trying situation to be in. After all Chantal had been lying down dead for most of the first act. And with the exception of Lazarus not too many people have sat up in the bed again. If only Antoine's acting reflexes had been up to their usual standard he could have said something like: 'What was she trying to flee? Oh spirit, rest, rest.' That would have given him the opportunity to get up, shove me back onto the bed and pull the sheet over me - that's if he could untangle those sheets.

But no! Silence hung heavy over that stage. An even heavier silence hung over the audience. Everyone waited for something to happen. Not as much as a sigh from Antoine. It was up to Nellie Flanagan to save the day and ingeniously, even if I say so myself! Still with my eyes closed and in my unusual semi sitting, one leg in and leg out rigor mortis position I began to slowly and dramatically incline myself sideways. Why? Because if I were lying down even with one stiff dead leg out of the bed, then maybe Antoine could get on with the first lines of the second act - i.e. 'She is dead, dead, dead!'.

I began to incline sideways very slowly, relishing every second. This was going to be my only moment of actual acting up on that stage and my imitation of a dead person keeling over for the second time was going to be dazzling. I was feeling mighty pleased with myself. I was saving Antoine who couldn't digress from the script if his life depended on it. My kids would see my face for a few fleeting seconds. I continued my keeling over act. Oh the pleasure of acting is too incredible to explain. At that moment I was fully alive for the first time in months. Even though I was keeling over dead, inside I was feeling immortal, allowing the Flanagan talent to pour out and dazzle the audience. Then I misjudged the edge, fell off the bed and nearly killed myself for real right there in the *Théâtre du Zivot*, Paris, France.

The howls! The shrieks! The laughter! I could hear my kids gurgling the way kids get when they are delirious with delight. I could hear Granddad yahooing out loud and almost expected to hear the plink plonk of his dentures being projected up onto the stage. Once when he was watching a particularly enjoyable TV cartoon his false teeth shot out of his jaws and landed on

top of the set. I could hear Paul's most distinctive
guffaw. He was laughing the way he used to, way back
when I had just met him on the boat over from Ireland,
when his literary hopes were higher than Everest, when
he had visions of becoming Hemingway's rightful
Parisian successor.

Meanwhile on stage, I wondered if my left elbow was
broken. My jaw was definitely damaged. It had taken
the brunt of the fall. My body hadn't felt this bad since
the day five years ago when the brakes on my bike gave
up the ghost and I'd landed in the ditch. And still they
went on laughing. Oh yes indeed! It is so true that it
takes tragedy and injury (i.e. of others) to make most
human beings laugh. It did cross my mind that I could
play the rest of the act lying there scrunched up on the
floor next to the bed. I was supposed to be dead. What
was the point of getting up again? I waited for the
audience to calm down and for Antoine to get on with it.
But, obviously, Antoine wasn't quite ready yet. Being
half dead wasn't good enough for him. He needed more.
I did my best to deliver the goods.

I struggled up a bit, stretched out both my legs, put
both my arms out straight, and then at the top of my
lungs I screamed: 'I'm dying, dying. I'm dead.' Even
that got a laugh from the audience which wasn't the
effect I was aiming for. I tried to look my most deathly
gruesome with my mouth wide open just like that
woman in 'The Scream' painting. God, but I was a
fantastic actress. To come up with another idea like that
was only a tiny indication of the wells of talent just
waiting to explode through Nellie Flanagan's body. Not
even Meryl Streep could have surpassed me in my
portrayal of a dying person, arms out wide, bidding one
last farewell to the world.

I had saved Antoine. He could now proceed with the

opening line - 'She is dead, dead, dead.' Very gently I lowered my head to the floorboards (I wasn't going to inflict any more injuries on myself). I let out a kind of a rattle to make things more plausible. And that was the exact second the huge pillow came toppling off the bed. It flopped right down on my face and scared the living shit out of me. I reacted the way any actor would have done under the circumstances. I let loose a blood curling shriek, leapt up and before I knew it I was standing in the middle of the stage, clutching my heart so that it wouldn't jump clean out of my rib cage. Then I heard it. That sweet swell of applause and the satisfied gurglings of my kids in the front row. I could even distinguish Granddad's gargle. He had removed his false teeth. He was settling in for a continuation of great acting from his darling girl! Granddad had always believed in my talent. And in this woodworm riddled dump of a dive in Paris I suddenly thought there was no reason why I shouldn't demonstrate a little more of the Flanagan talent.

'I'm dead. I'm really and truly dead,' I said as I walked over to where Antoine and Valerie were still glued to the floor.

'This is my *GHOST!*'

Never let the side down. The bed could conspire against me, the sheets attack me, the pillow try and smother me ... Nellie the actress would conquer all. I was saving this piece of shit of a play so I decided I'd add a touch of class to it. I spoke in both French and English. That way the French audience would be impressed no end and Granddad and Belinda would understand what I was saying. Maybe I did get carried away.

'Go on!' I urged Antoine in both languages. 'I am only the Spirit, wafting here, wafting there. Wafting everywhere. But what I'm going to do now is lie down, get comfy and take it easy. And you can continue.'

Now if that wasn't as clear as the shining mid day sun in the desert, what was? But Antoine was still wafting in his own wordless zone probably caused by excruciating back pain. In the wings I saw Jean-Claude and Maurice gesticulating that I should shut up and exit stage left. But if the second act had to have any sense at all the corpse had to be there on the bed. So I ignored the two windmills in the wings and proceeded with my bi-lingual tour de force.

'I am a dead person,' I said again. This got a great giggle from my kids. It is amazing how just the mention of the word 'Dead' can make kids laugh. I smiled down at them. They let out another peal of pleasured laughter.

'A very dead person.'

Out of the corner of my eye I could see Jean-Claude frantically pointing to my shoes. What was wrong with my shoes?

When I tripped over the trailing end of my shroud, landed snout down in the middle of the bed I understood. My lithe body toppling onto the bed sent the stage into a minor quiver. The bed quaked, shivered but endured.

This finally jolted Antoine out of his coma.

'If she's a fucking spirit, then I'm a fucking pig's ear,' he bellowed at the top of his lungs and pointed into the wings. 'And I hope that poor girl sues you for endangering our fucking lives. And if you think you can fucking write, you are out of your fucking mind.'

This was too much for Maurice. He had already seen his play mutilated by bad lighting, an uncontrollable naked lady statue, a collapsing bed, a corpse who refused to die. He was not going to endure any more insults. He gave one giant leap in the direction of Antoine's throat and arrived centre stage totally unmindful of the fact that the public had paid to see his work performed and not Maurice murdering Antoine right there in front of their eyes. Lord only knows what would have happened if Jean-Claude hadn't done a lateral arabesque in from the wings to haul Maurice away from Antoine's ready fists.

The audience clapped with appreciation at this turn of events. Antoine puffed and huffed and tried to get his breath back.

'Being a spirit could practically kill you,' I said. Keep the flag flying no matter how tattered, is the Flanagan motto. 'But even a dead person likes a well made bed.'

I proceeded to make the bed. That got gurgles of appreciation from the audience. I was glad. Some people think that making a bed while you're on stage is no big deal. Let me tell you it requires the ultimate in acting craft to duplicate those little gestures we do every day without thinking twice. I also added that touch of genius. While I made the bed I sang one of Granddad's old favourites - 'Up in the morning, out on the job.' At the end of the song I got into the bed and flopped gently to my well deserved rest.

'I am now officially dead.'

If Antoine couldn't take it from there he might as well hang up his acting threads and retire.

'She's dead,' said Antoine.

Finally, 13 minutes into the Second Act, Antoine set the ball rolling. But not for long. Valerie decided that since everyone else was indulging in a mental breakdown she might as well have one too. Instead of kissing Antoine as she was supposed to do, she told him if he put his face next to hers he wouldn't live to see the end of the play. Amazingly that too, got a ripple of laughter. That drove Valerie into further flights of fancy. When Antoine tottered against the bed, she screamed:

'Go on, wake up the dead again.'

I obliged, hopped out of bed and took a little stroll around the stage, interjecting Hamlet's comments about dear Yorrick's skull in both languages. My kids chimed in because this was the bit of Hamlet they knew off by heart. Always trust kids to remember the gory bits.

Pierrette and Armand arrived, bang on cue. They continued their fight. It had something to do with little Sophie's hives and Armand's Mamman's casserole being to blame for this latest outbreak. This inspired Valerie to grab Antoine's wig and fling it into the wings. Jean-Claude tossed it back. Valerie caught it and again sent it sailing back. For a long silent minute Antoine gazed at the wings waiting for the re-entry flight of his ringlets. None appeared.

'Well, fuck this,' said Antoine and ripped off his hairnet. 'I'm going to Mahmoud's. I need a sheep's heart after this shit.'

Valerie followed him, fearing that she had finally driven him over the verge. I was alone on stage. When I turned my head I could see that Maurice and Jean-Claude were trying to force Antoine back on stage. But he had already torn off half his costume. I hopped out of bed and launched into my unique rendition of that wonderful song from 'Fiddler on the Roof' called 'To Life! To Life!'. Even if I do say so myself, Nellie Flanagan doing a jig in a shroud singing 'To Life! To Life!' was a stroke of genius.

The Finale was also quite spectacular in its own way. The scripted Finale was the re-appearance of the naked lady on the pole, drifting across the stage to the sound track of horns hooting and breezes blowing. This was to symbolize the ship's safe arrival in the port of New York, land of Freedom and Liberty. The lady was supposed to be borne in by Armand. But he was too busy kissing Pierrette and begging her forgiveness.

Jean-Claude tried to inveigle Antoine to give it another go. But Antoine said something with a dozen 'fucks' in it, like he wasn't going to have his fucking back put out another time. This was the crucial moment when Philippe finally got the lights to do what they should have been doing for weeks. They flickered merrily on and off. It didn't take much imagination to know that this was some kind of German air attack during WW2. Maurice went loony at that point. He grabbed the naked lady and tried to hit the actors with it. They all fled onto the stage. There was no other place of refuge.

The Finale was Maurice and the naked lady being pounded into submission by the rest of the cast while the lights gave an imitation of the World at War. Gentle Armand, totally out of character, gave Maurice a good kick to express in the flesh his opinion of Maurice's play. Maurice and the statue fell onto the bed which collapsed one last time. Pierrette stood at the end of the bed and said:

'I've had enough. Let's go home, chéri.'

She turned to the audience and bowed. They clapped. Exit Pierrette and Armand.

'Let's go eat,' said Antoine and linked arms with Jean-Claude and Phillipe. 'I want two sheep's heart.'

The trio gave a most elegant bow to thunderous applause. But Antoine had one last parting word of loathing for Maurice who was still prostrate on the broken bed with his arms around the naked lady.

'Eat shit and die, bozo!'

Maurice snapped to life and did the five yard dash after Antoine. The sound of a crash came from the wings. Then silence. And I was alone on stage. The lights went all funny. Then the spotlight focused fully on me. I stood up.

'*Now o'er the one half-world ……*
Maude and Claude yelled out the rest with me:
'*….. Nature seems dead and wicked dreams abuse the curtained sleep.*'

Paul later apologized for saying my kids would never get an opportunity to say those immortal lines. I never admitted to him that I was a bit confused at that point. I had intended quoting Hamlet and not Macbeth. The spotlight moved and I hopped behind it and tried to disappear elegantly into the wings. But Philippe chased me with that spot and I was still in full glow, so to speak. I just couldn't resist it. I hopped in and out of the spotlight and did my Woody Woodpecker imitation.

'That's all folks.'

That would have made the perfect finale for one dog's dinner of a so called play. But Philippe still hadn't found the off switch. The spot left the stage and settled on Claude who was flapping his arms in a bird imitation. He leapt up from his seat.

'I wish you were my bird,' he yelled out. (a little saying that will come in quite handy when he visits Ireland where 'girlfriend' is synonymous with 'bird')

At ten Claude had the makings of an actor. The actual lines in Romeo and Juliet's balcony scene are: '*I would I were thy bird*' quoted by Romeo when he doesn't want to leave his Juliet. But I had made the lines more accessible for them. Ok, so Claude sometimes got the '*I wish I were your bird,*' the wrong way round.

The spot suddenly swooshed between myself and Maude. It was the ideal opportunity for both of us to follow up on Claude's line.

'*Good night, good night. Parting is such sweet sorry,*
That I shall say goodnight till it be morrow.'

Philippe finally found the right button. The house was plunged into darkness and then the lights came on.

I was alone on centre stage and the audience was giving me a standing ovation. Then they whistled for Antoine who returned on stage in his underwear. Valerie aka Rambo got more applause than on any other night. My lovely kids dashed forward and plonked their giant bouquet at my feet. The audience let out the biggest hurrah of the evening, egged on by Paul, Hansi and Diana who were whistling like hooligans. Despite more potential injuries to his back Antoine bent down and lifted the two up on stage. Audiences only have to look at cute kids and they dissolve. More thunderous clapping. I could see Granddad wiping his nose and going all sentimental. I took a rose from the bouquet and tossed it down to him in a most dramatic fashion. Then one to Belinda, since I couldn't very well exclude her from all the emotion. My kids then tossed a rose each to their parents. Madame and Monsieur smiled and almost looked human. And all the while the audience clapped and clapped and finally began to move out towards the lobby, most reluctantly.

As I stood up there on stage I felt as if I had lived. If nothing else happened to me in my entire life, I would always have this to remember. I had wowed them on stage in Paris, France and experienced the meaning of life.

TWENTY-SIX

I've mentioned before that 'crise' (pronounced kreeze) is the French for attack. That evening in Mahmoud's at the closing party, every possible shade of attack was trotted out. Mahmoud himself had a gigantic one when he saw 25 in the party instead of the reserved 15. Did they expect miracles? Antoine pulled Mahmoud's cheek and said: 'Ever heard of the loaves and fishes?' Mahmoud scowled and said: 'Fish is off,' and sallied away to kitchen to hack up a few more sheep hearts.

Everyone thought they were merry. But in fact there was a thick veil of mourning in the air, a knowledge that we were taking a fond farewell to a segment of our lives. 'Tristesse' is the French word for sadness. Although very few French words can outdo the wonder of the English tongue, nonetheless in a contest between tristesse and sadness, French win hands down. Sadness has a clunkiness to it, like a heavy copper saucepan falling on a stone floor. Whereas tristesse has a whispering melancholic elegance, like thin snow falling on Irish fields. You can savour tristesse the way you can taste the end of summer in those first fall mornings tinged with the snap of ripe apples. Sadness is corrosive. It leaves tracks in the heart like the ones left behind when our favourite dog Butch died. Whereas tristesse is a sadness you can even enjoy.

Tristesse was what we were all feeling that evening in Mahmoud's in between the various kreezes. Valerie was having a kreeze de passion. The Love subject was Antoine. Now that she would never see him again, Valerie was in love with Antoine and gave him all the passionate kisses and embraces she should have been bestowing up there on stage. Jean-Claude was having a 'remarkable' kreeze. He hadn't used his favourite word all evening.

'So, what's our next play going to be?' I asked, expecting nothing less than the leading role.

'There's been a change of plan, mon amour,' he said in his amazing silver voice. 'I'm going to Ireland for a while to compose.'

That's when I had my kreeze de coeur ('coeur' is French for 'heart').

'Can I house sit for you?' I asked breezily. It was the second thing that popped into my mind. The first was: Gee, thanks for the warning, bozo.

'I've sub-let it to some Americans.'

'Right! right!' I answered the way people always do when things are wrong! wrong!

Expelled from the Island of Love in Montmartre! Blow out the silver candles. Farewell white sofa. Thanks for the memory, piano. Adieu scallops in Pernod Chez Jean. You could have warned me, you tight-lipped bastard.

'Of course I will be back - for you, mon amour.'

He looked so beautiful when he said that. I wanted to have a quick weep - to complete the scene.

'I'll miss you every minute,' he said.

That cheered me up no end. The tristesse swooshed right through my ribcage and rattled at my heart. It almost made me feel good inside. That's the real test of tristesse.

Antoine and Granddad hit if off big time. Granddad immediately understood the mangled mush that poor Antoine thought was English. To give you an example. Antoine lisped, hissed and spat his way through:

'*Yuri - YURI - FIFE .. yes, fife, vat hiss zee zooing?*'

While I'm still trying to figure out who Yuri is and if Antoine has mentioned him to me before, Granddad has already answered Antoine's question.

'Belinda is a painter.'

My Shakespeare saturated brain cells would never immediately equate '*Yuri fife vat hiss zee zooing?*' with the English equivalent of 'Your wife what is she doing?'

Other snatches of their conversation ('verbal battering of the English tongue' would be more accurate) drifted over to me.

'How long you learn English?' This was my Granddad speaking.

Back snaps Antoine's immediate response. None of this having to repeat the question 25 times before he accepts that 'how long?' has absolutely nothing in common with 'how are you?'

'Two and a half months.'

OK! So it sounded like he was referring to 'Two in an eel's house.' But Granddad didn't hesitate.

'That's fantastic! And you never spoke any English before.'

Up to the word 'spoke' so far so good. Antoine glowed. He finally had proof that he was no longer linguistically on the same wavelength as the radiator. But the glow faded as he tried to tackle the word 'spoke'.

'Spooky?' he queried.

'No. Before you never speak English? Before the 2 and a half months?'

Antoine's face lit up like the Champs-Élysées on the

14th of July. He radiated so brightly a few more degrees and he'd have been carted off as radio active.

'NAFF her. NAFF her. But Nellie of course (which Antoine as always massacred into 'off curse') is teaching me.'

Recognition at last! I went into a mild wilt and raised my glass to Antoine who had finally accepted the existence of the present continuous tense. But trust Antoine to ruin everything. *BANG! THUMP!* The clenched fist trying to wallop a hole through his forehead.

'Mais non! Is wrong! Nellie, she teaches me.'

'She teaches you beautifully,' Granddad finished the sentence for him and they went onto the next topic.

'Je vous aime. Oh, mes amis! Mes meilleurs amis, que je vous aime.'

Valerie had downed a substantial amount of red. Her eyes were doing a tipsy dance in her sockets like two seasick ducks on a stormy pond. Granddad turned to Antoine and asked him to please translate. Antoine nearly expired with the pleasure of interpreting for the Irish visitor.

'She say she love you. You is friend.'

'Ah! Isn't that lovely? The French are so emotional.'

'Yes, we are.... (he still pronounced it *AAAAAARRRRGGHHHH).*'

'I like a bit of emotion myself,' said Granddad.

'A bit?' asked Antoine and the deep furrows crossed his brow.

'A bit?'

The English pronunciation of the word 'bit' is a dead runner for the French word 'bite' which is French for 'penis'. Antoine's eyebrows quivered as he tried to figure out how those dangly bits had sneaked into the conversation. The other fascinating thing about the

French word 'bite' is that it is feminine - as in 'la bite'. Most of the professions with some rare exceptions like teacher and nurse are masculine. But a man's member is feminine.

Antoine went on nodding. 'Emotion' was the same in both languages. So maybe that was the case with 'bit'. He was a man struggling.

'Life is grand, isn't it?' said Granddad and raised his glass to Antoine. Granddad sighed with a hint of tristesse. Old people always sigh when they are sublimely happy.

'Life is grand, isn't it?' repeated Antoine in a thick Irish accent.

Belinda blithely chatted away to Hansi, a fellow artist who wasn't listening to a word she said. He was too busy feeding slivers of sheep's heart to Mahmoud's flea ridden cat Bogart.

'What a dream you are living, Hansi,' said Belinda. 'Five years in Paris. Your own atelier in Paris! Just like Sisley. Just like Monet. And poor Utrillo and poor Toulouse.'

Belinda's eyes weren't as bad as Valerie's. But they were still drifting like two fat fish in a murky bowl.

'How romantic it must be to have you own studio in Paris.'

'Hansi's set-up isn't exactly romantic,' said Paul diplomatically, instead of giving his usual description of Hansi's caravan - i.e. that two giant hounds, and six obese cats dumped more shit in a day than he did in a month.

'Oh, the romance, the romance!' rhapsodized Belinda, pouring out more vin rouge.

'Hansi hasn't begun selling his work as yet.'

'Just like poor Utrillo and poor Toulouse. Even Monet had to beg for money all his life. Have you seen his lovely lilies at the Marmatton Museum?'

Hansi let out a growl that shocked both Belinda and Bogart.

'Hansi isn't too keen on Monet's lilies,' Paul explained diplomatically instead of repeating Hansi's opinion of the lilies. They were 'wallpaper for fat Texans, or for a Sear's catalogue for obese Germans and the same fat Texans.'

Diana ended the lilies debate by proffering her card.

'Thank you, dear,' said Belinda, as if she might one day urgently need Diana's duelling specialty. Diana's face was flushed brighter than the carafe. To date this had been her most successful evening - professionally speaking. Everyone had taken her card and said they'd love to have lessons - one day. Antoine said he needed duelling lessons but couldn't afford them until he was fluent in English - which will be in the 25th century. But the minute things eased up … The heavy scent of promise hung in the air. Even Mahmoud took her card and said duelling skills could come in handy in his business. Diana was on such a high she didn't once mention the expensive kettle or moan about living in a hole with no phone, no shower and a giant fridge at the end of the bed. It was a milestone for Diana.

The eagerly awaited moment finally arrived. Jean-Claude called for champagne and dessert and said the magic words: 'Tonight it's all on the theatre.' Pop, pop, fizz, fizz and Belinda hugged Granddad and said:

'Let's stay in Paris, shall we, Jimmie Joe?'

'My very thoughts, my dear,' said Granddad and kissed her cheek.

'I shall paint in Paris,' said Belinda, not sounding in the least like the old Belinda. But that's Paris for you. Arrive as one person and become another.

'I shall paint in Paris - just like Renoir and Valadon. And poor Utrillo. And poor Toulouse.'

'But you …' said Antoine to Granddad, with a worried look on his face. 'Vat you do?'

'I shall LIVE!' said Granddad, rather on the grand side, a bit like Napoleon on his return to France from his foreign forays.

'Vive la Vie!' said Granddad, and got to his feet like an old general leading the toast at a Regimental Dinner.

The whole group noisily quaffed to Life, to Love, to Mahmoud. I broke my sacred vow and poured myself a fourth glass of red plonk.

TWENTY-SEVEN

I got another emergency call from my Mam. It came just after our re-enactment of Ophelia's mad scene which Maude and Claude adored. It was their idea to use the flowers that were scattered in giant bouquets all over the apartment to get the full effect of mad Ophelia covered in blooms. They stuck gladioli, freesias, lilies and super expensive passion flowers up their sleeves, into their belts, down their blouses and tied them around their legs. If Madame had ever witnessed the two walking gardens she'd have freaked. We tried our best to re-arrange the flowers the way the florist had. But you could see the querying look on Madame's face when she returned from her afternoon appointments. When she left the house not a petal had been out of place. When she returned a few hours later, the bouquets looked as if they'd been trampled on by rabid rhinos. She called the florist and gave him hell.

The day I got the call from my Mam, Madame had just returned and was standing in front of the bouquet in the hallway, gazing in a most disturbed way at the droopy arrangement. I was hoping she wouldn't ask me if anyone had been tampering with the flowers because the kids and I had agreed to dump Ophelia and her flower-tossing phobia. We had scheduled Polonius's murder for the following day. A new scene that included a bit of murder and violence might help me concentrate on something other than missing Jean-Claude. The phone rang and Maude and Claude ran out of the salon screaming that it was my Mamman, calling from Ireland. At least it distracted Madame from wondering about the semi dead bouquet.

'I want you to tell the truth,' were my Mam's first words. I really felt insulted. As if I was in the habit of spouting nothing but lies, when I do try and walk the straight and narrow when life permits me.

'Who gave your Granddad and Belinda the daft idea to stay on in Paris?' Her voice was full of silent accusations. 'Your Dad and I are sick with worry.'

So what else was new? Now, apart from worrying about me and that 'acting', Brian never bringing home a suitable bride, Billy not passing his exams, my Mam had this additional worry about Granddad. All he had to do, she told me, was topple over on his weak ankles and fall into the middle of the Paris traffic. Even though he was covered with a medical card and free travel in Ireland this wouldn't extend to France. There would be substantial expenses involved if he had to spend the rest of his days in a convalescent home. Plus they'd go bankrupt and lose the shop if Aer Lingus had to take him home on a stretcher that would take up the space of three regular seats.

'What are they doing for money?' she asked in a voice worn ragged with worry.

'They're spending it.'

My Mam let out a tinny yelp. If somebody had come up behind her and strangled her with the telephone wire she wouldn't have sounded more distressed.

'Your Dad wants a word with you,' said my Mam, when she wound down on her beagle yelping.

'Is that you, Nellie?' he asked, as if my Mam had been speaking to Nellie the goat, or the talking chimpanzee.

'No Dad, it's the Bride of Dracula.'

My Dad laughed. Yet he sounded so wistful. As if he had really aged since I'd left home.

'Nellie, I miss you. We all miss you. So much,' he said, and even though he was still laughing (it doesn't take much to get my Dad going), there was sadness mingled in with it.

'I'll hand you back to your Mam,' said my Dad. Always to the point on the phone or otherwise. Just say what you have to say and get it over and done with. That's my Dad. It's due to spending all day beaming at the Horgans and the O'Briens and an army of locals who come into our shop. Smile and chat with those customers for 12 hours on the trot and non-verbal communication takes on amazing allures.

'You'll let me know the minute anything happens,' was my Mam's parting shot.

'Mam, there is nothing to worry about,' I told her.

Nothing to worry about! The famous last words, as they say.

I blame all further developments on that Room 317, Madame Roussard's love of a real Paddy poured by appreciative hotel guests, the proximity of Montmartre and the Sacré Coeur. The magic of real Montmartre doesn't hit you first time around, mainly because you think you've seen it so often before. People who have never left Alaska could identify the Sacré Coeur and parts of Montmartre. It is more recognizable than American Presidents who also appear on mugs, chocolate boxes and ashtrays. But American Presidents are replaced every few years, whereas the Sacré Coeur has stayed the same since 1868.

The two had been spending lots of time wandering around Montmartre, taking it at a very slow pace because of all the hundreds of steps that lead up and down the hill. They went to all the places that poor Utrillo had frequented - with the exception of the asylum. Belinda always referred to him as poor Utrillo despite the fact he married a woman who was loaded and didn't have to worry about money for most of his life. Belinda thought it much more romantic to dwell on those years when poor alchie Utrillo had been locked in a room by his painter mother Valadon and forced to paint instead of drink. When Belinda and Granddad strolled the side streets of Montmartre at twilight, after the noisy tourists had left, they felt as if they were living in those Impressionist paintings. It was during one of those walks that they came up with Their Great Idea.

They invited me to their 'local Montmartre bar' to tell me all about it. When I arrived the two were perched on bar stools looking mighty pleased. The bedraggled 'painters' who hassled tourists on the Place du Tetre were knocking back the cheap brandy.

'Those are real working artists,' said Belinda in a reverential tone of voice.

I was about to say: 'Most of them are real drunks too.' But I didn't want to burst their bubble. They wouldn't be in Paris for much longer. They couldn't possibly afford to stay on their slim pensions. My Mam's long-distance worrying was pointless. Belinda and Granddad would go home when they realized that it was one thing to splash out on a holiday but it was a totally different nightmare to scratch by in beautiful Paris when the funds ran low.

'What's this great idea?' I asked them.

'First you must have a little something. Then we'll show you our Great Idea,' said Belinda, and swayed on her stool as she pawed Granddad's arm so he would remember his duties as a gentleman - i.e. order the drinks. The stool was high but I also think Belinda was weaving because she and Granddad were doing in Paris what the Parisians did (drink French booze every time they had something to eat - with the exception of breakfast).

I ordered a small Kir (that's crème de cassis and white wine). The small Kir is about the size of a thimble. I had the small size because in an authoritative magazine I read that it was dangerous for foreigners to drink large Kirs. That was the sure way to becoming an alchie in Paris because large Kirs went down easier than fruit juice. For me it was going to be one small Kir until I made my mark as an actress. I didn't want to end up like the 'real artists' in the bar who had forgotten that alcohol usually drowns talent instead of enhancing it.

'Your Granddad always has Great Ideas, doesn't he?' said Belinda. Her stool wobbled like an insecurely tethered boat at high tide.

'I know all about Granddad's Great Ideas,' I reminded Belinda.

In Dun-mo-Croi, Granddad was legendary for his Great Ideas. He had the first grocery store in the West of Ireland to serve take out coffee to tourists who descended in droves from buses to snap up leprechauns made in China. When he 'retired' Granddad's ideas became more ambitious. He tried to raise free-range chickens in the back garden so he could rake in a fortune from the eggs. I was the one who fed and cleaned up after those chickens who were dispatched to a watery grave when the storm of the century hit Dun-mo-Croi and blew the hen house to Kingdom Come. Granddad's next Great Idea was strawberries. I planted a few thousand plants in the back garden. Fifty million slugs ate Granddad's dream. Undeterred, Granddad decided there was a hidden fortune in seashells. I picked up several tonnes of shells so he could make objets d'art that even the tourists looked at twice. My Mam has several hundred seashell mirrors and frames stacked in boxes in the shed.

'We'll show you where we're setting up,' said Granddad as he finished off his apéritif.

Setting up? It sounded as if work might be involved. But this was Paris, I reminded myself. I was standing in a wine bar built in 1769, surrounded by 'real artists' whose grungy clothes were close to the same vintage as the walls. Granddad's Great Parisian Idea couldn't possibly involve me having to work.

'Of course Belinda will be doing all the work,' said Granddad, and put a finger to Belinda's face almost as if he wanted to check where all the red veins had disappeared to under the wine flush.

'But it won't be work. It will be purest pleasure. My dearest dream come true,' said Belinda eagerly. The stool lurched under her.

'Careful now. We can't have you injuring yourself before we start to rake it in,' said Granddad and grabbed Belinda's stool.

To rake it in! Words that used to send ice slivers through my veins. Again I had to remind myself that this was Paris. It had nothing to do with me.

We left the café. They shook hands with the barman like real regulars and said they'd be back the following night. We turned into the Place du Tertre which is the highest little square in Paris and packed year round with tourists and artists in various stages of work and non-work. Belinda mentioned that poor Utrillo had painted that square back in the days when not a single tourist was to be seen. They led me into a side street off the Square. We stopped at the wrought-iron railings in front of a perpendicular flight of steps that ended in a café a long way below. Granddad pointed to the corner where the railings dovetailed into a little nook of a wall about two feet across.

'This is the spot,' said Granddad and pointed to the little nook. 'It's sheltered so you don't get any breezes here. The idea is that Belinda will set up her easel here and paint the Sacré Coeur and the views. When people come along I'll ask them if they want their portrait painted. Belinda will do them in water colours. You don't see too many of the artists up here being able to do that. Belinda will be raking it in.'

It is a miracle - due only to the control I have acquired from acting - that I didn't topple off the top of those steps and land down at the bottom in Café Utrillo when Granddad dropped that bombshell.

TWENTY-EIGHT

I tried to say something but only a croak came out.

'No. We are not taking any of your help,' said Granddad. 'We can do this on our own. You have your own career to concentrate on.'

'For all I know poor Utrillo could have painted on this very spot,' said Belinda with tears in her eyes.

'Was he the one with no legs?' asked Granddad with a twinkle in his eyes. Honest to God, having been told 500 times at least, surely by now Granddad could distinguish between the poor boozer and the poor guy with short legs.

'No dear, that was poor Toulouse,' said Belinda with a purr in her voice. 'Maybe he painted here. Or maybe Renoir. Or Monet. Any one of the Greats could have painted in this very spot.'

'Shall we go and eat?' I asked, because I thought they'd come to their senses if they had food in them.

'Great Idea! Let's take the darling girl to that place Gauguin used to have his dinner in,' said Granddad.

'Before he went to the South Seas,' said Belinda.

She took my arm as if I was the one who needed guiding along the cobbled, twisted streets of Montmartre. I had a Large Kir in the place where Gauguin ate his dinner before he went bonkers and took off for a desert island in the South Seas in search of naked women. The décor didn't seem to have changed much since Gauguin's day. It looked like a cross between an old Kerry pub and a dilapidated stable. Montmartre had once been deepest country and this was one of those restaurants that didn't want you to forget those distant days. There was a rusty plough in the corner. The walls were covered with cow bells and harnesses. Real hay was stacked in racks that went around the room. All that was missing was the manure. The Americans sitting next to us said, 'Well, gee, isn't this just the cosiest place?' as if they'd always wanted to dine in a stable.

'We shouldn't get too fond of this stuff,' said Granddad as he ordered a bottle of medium red (medium as in price).

'But this is a celebration,' said Belinda.

'Well, good luck,' I said and polished off my large Kir.

I didn't add that they were going to need truckloads of luck. All Belinda and Granddad could see was the romance of artists out on the picturesque little Square, painting away and raking in the money. We could do the same, they thought. They didn't know that you needed a permit in order to paint in that particular Place (that's French for 'Square'). In order to get that permit you needed about fifty different kinds of official documents, from your great-grandparents' birth certificates to paid-up gas bills. Getting one of those permits was about as hard as getting nominated for the Nobel Prize for Literature. I knew all about it from Hansi who had voiced the opinion that the paint robots (his description) on the Place du Tertre should be forced to eat their own fingers for inflicting so much appallingly bad art on the world.

I sipped the red wine and felt better. Maybe the other artists (the artistic Mafia as Hansi calls them) would allow the two old people to have a bit of fun for a week or so. Maybe they wouldn't shove them down the steps of Montmartre for trying to nose in on their lucrative business of extracting dollars from tourists. The really cold weather would soon set in. The two could then say - at least they'd done it. Once upon a time they had set up shop in Montmartre. They could go home and reminisce about it - which is what old people live for. As long as they are romancing the past they are OK.

'We must try the snails,' said Granddad decided.

'D'you think that's wise?' Belinda asked anxiously. Belinda isn't a bad old soul but when it comes to food she is all British - bland as wet bread.

'But of course we must have snails. We're in Paris,' said Granddad authoritatively.

'That's right. We're in Paris,' said Belinda, as if she had momentarily forgotten where she was. Well, surrounded by all the hay and barn trappings, could you blame her?

'How do the French come up with their ideas for food?' Granddad asked nobody in particular as we waited for the waiter to notice our presence. 'Ireland and England are teeming with snails and nobody ever thought of stuffing them with garlic and a bit of butter.'

Finally the waiter slithered over. He was tall, full of muscles and ill-tempered.

'I'd recommend the escargots,' he said. They always recommend the most expensive things on the menu.

'And you'd advise us to steer clear of the rest of the stuff?' said Granddad, being his usual jovial and friendly self.

'I recommend everything,' snarled the waiter.

'Are the snails fresh?' Granddad wanted to know.

By the time the waiter had taken our order some of the moodiness had been stomped out of him. He had to explain everything on the menu to the two. We all had escargots and they were very tasty. Granddad said he'd have to take a few shells back to show my Mam as actual proof. When the waiter came for our plates and saw that the shells were missing from Granddad's he gave a gasp of horror but said nothing. He thought Granddad had eaten them too. It was a jolly meal. Every time we saw the waiter looking at Granddad we had to laugh. We ordered a second bottle of red. Granddad said ten times, 'We shouldn't get too fond of this.' Belinda wondered if poor Toulouse or poor Utrillo had ever come to this restaurant to get roaring drunk and do wonderful paintings on the paper tablecloths. Granddad wondered if paper tablecloths had been invented in poor Utrillo's time.

There was a huge moon over Montmartre when we left the restaurant. The artists had all left the Square. There was something like magic and champagne bubbles floating in the air. Old Parisian songs floated out from some of the touristy places.

'Ah, see Paris and live,' said Granddad.

I could hardly break their hearts and tell them that even if Napoleon came back from the dead and wanted to paint in that cosy corner he'd still have to apply for a permit and produce proof of Parisian residence plus a paid up gas bill.

TWENTY-NINE

The pigeons woke me up prancing around on the tin foil
I'd put on the windowsill to make cleaning a little easier.
It wasn't going to work because the scrunching of the tin
foil against the window was worse than a tractor
crushing glass. Mr. Uno was yowling out his dawn 'let
me go' mantra. As always my first thought was: why
can't pigeons go shit and screw in places that are
roomier than my narrow windowsill? My second
thought was: today the two set up in Montmartre. I
rolled over, put my head under the pillow and pretended
I was lying on a deserted beach in Fiji with Jean-Claude
beside me kissing my hair and telling me I was
remarkable. I drifted off into a pleasant nap until the
knock on the door woke me again. My third thought that
morning was: 'Good! Paul can shoo those pests away
and make us coffee.'

Then I looked at my watch. It wasn't even 8 o'clock.
Paul, like all real writers, was allergic to hopping out of
bed so early. There was another gentle knock on the
door, quite unlike Paul's hearty thump, thump, thump.

'Who is it?' I asked, putting my mouth to the door.

This wasn't difficult, the bed being smack up against
it. I put my eye to the keyhole. What I saw was not the
other eyeball of the Farkas kids but the very fine and
expensive material of a man's trousers.

'It's Monsieur Duchamps.'

I leapt so suddenly from the bed that some of the pigeons were startled and lost their balance off their companions' backs.

'Just a moment, please,' I shouted to Monsieur.

I jumped into my jeans. I didn't think it was quite appropriate to welcome him into my accommodations in my best Tipps nightwear - their Jailhouse Line of Night Attire. What was Monsieur doing up here at this time of the morning? It could only mean bad news. Granddad and Belinda had conked out from excitement during the night. Or they'd gone out to the balcony to get the full effect of the Sacré Coeur. Belinda had finally toppled over on those high heels. She'd gone *SWOOSH* over the wrought-iron balcony railings. Granddad had been so startled he'd plopped over the railings after her. All their broken bones were now lying in some horrendously expensive Paris hospital. I opened the door trying not to think of worse scenarios.

'I do apologize. I didn't realize you'd still be in bed,' were Monsieur's first words. 'But I forgot you keep irregular hours.'

He looked embarrassed. As if he wasn't up to breaking the awful news to me.

'May I sit down?'

'Sure.'

He sat on the end of the bed. His attention was drawn to the pigeon activity out on the windowsill. They were back in force. Ten of them. Five on top and five on the bottom. Playing find your mate. Hopping from one back to another and intermittently indulging in full-time pigeon business - pooping and coupling.

'The pigeons like you,' said Monsieur with a sad smile.

I tried not to think of the two toppling to their deaths down the steps in Montmartre. They'd get a mention in the Guinness Book of Records. Monsieur was gently leading up to the bad news by overlooking just what those pigeons were doing not two feet from his face.

'Pigeons don't like everybody, you know,' he said.

'Well, the feeling is not mutual,' I told him. 'I don't know why they come here. I don't feed them.'

It is amazing how the brain can split into so many thoughts in one second. Maybe the pigeons didn't like to dine and sleep in the same area. So if I put out crumbs they'd regard this as a dining room and would fly off elsewhere to perform their bedroom and bathroom activities. Another part of my brain was wondering just when Monsieur was going to explain his early morning visit. Yet another part of me was weeping for Granddad.

'We all like you very, very much indeed. You know that, don't you, Nellie?'

BINGO! I got it! They'd found out about the ketchup on the Persian carpet and the scratches on the Louis desk and drinks cabinet. Madame knew it wasn't the aliens who'd been molesting her expensive flowers. I was being shown the door. This was how the French did it. Politesse oblige. They'd found out about Paul and the mattress that wandered up and down the corridor.

'Maude and Claude do love you so very much.'

'That's very nice of you,' I said, not knowing what I was saying.

Two of the pigeons hadn't been pleased with round one, or had missed the strategic area or just felt like another go. They were poised for action. There was no use trying to draw Monsieur's attention to something else. There was nothing else in the room except for one of Hansi's paintings which was so godawful I had hung it face around to the wall. I couldn't very well get rid of it in case Hansi came to visit. It was rather difficult being the hostess with the mostest given the lousy décor and the randy pigeons.

'You are a very lovable person, Nellie.'

I had the sudden gut feeling that maybe Granddad and Belinda were doing fine, thank you, and that they'd live to take that cab up to Montmartre to set up their painting enterprise.

'It's not bad news about my Granddad, is it?' I asked, so that I could get some release from all the tortured flashes of their double death in Paris.

'Is he still in Paris?'

'Yes. They're going to paint and sell stuff in Montmartre.'

Monsieur sighed. A look flitted across his face which was just like the one he had that evening in the salon. A fleeting look of helpless poignancy and regret.

'You must come from an extraordinary family,' he said. 'I joined the bank to please my parents. I continued to please my wife. Now I must continue so as not to disgrace my children. Most of my life I have never done anything to please myself.'

'Why not?'

'Because that would displease everyone else.'

He sounded weary. Just like my Mam when she goes through her 'I wonder why we are alive' chant, which ails her about three days before her period. In Monsieur's case this could hardly be the contributing factor.

'I'd like to invite you to lunch with me one day, Nellie.'

My heart did the strangest thing. It started knocking. Well, it was a major, major shock to hear those words.

'That would be nice. I haven't spent much time with Madame.'

'It would just be you and me, Nellie. Paris has the best restaurants in the world.'

THUMP! THUMP! THUMP! THUMP!

It wasn't my heart. It was the hearty *THUMP! THUMP!* of a man who'd obviously slept very well on Monsieur's other mattress.

'You are a very popular person, I see,' said Monsieur with his sad hangdog look. As if Nellie's dog-box topped the list of 'Must See' places under the Paris rooftops.

'Those kids! They're at that lark all the time. Real pests,' I said, and opened the door a notch.

'Just *GO AWAY*!' I shouted while putting my finger to my lips to convey that he wasn't to speak.

'Entertaining your new lover?' Paul whispered and nodded to the mattress under his arm. 'This will come in handy when you wear the other one out.'

I banged the door in his face.

Monsieur got up from the bed and said: 'I should be going.'

'No, please. Stay! What else is new?' I said, meaning that he should stay for as long as it took Paul to disappear with his mattress.

Monsieur didn't look like the type who would immediately link a man and a mattress near my door as 'interfering with his property'. But if Madame saw it! And if Madame ever got wind of Monsieur's invitation to lunch I'd be joining the Paris pigeons.

'You're right. Maybe you should be going,' I said.

I opened the door just to double check there was no sign of Paul, the mattress or Madame.

'When are you free for lunch?'

'I'm very busy looking after my Granddad at the moment. As soon as they go back home, though!'

'I'll come up again another time. May I?'

Well, why not? I only have a million and one worries right now in my life. A little extra stress wouldn't even make a dent!

'We'll speak then,' he said, and wafted down the back stairs, looking so very much out of place in that elegant suit on those unswept, cobweb infested stairs.

Five minutes later Paul was back minus the mattress.

'I made us coffee,' he said and plonked himself on the bed.

'Why can't life be smooth?' I asked him. 'Just occasionally I'd like a smooth and even life.'

'Got a touch of PMS again?' said Paul, nonchalantly sipping his coffee. Or my coffee to be precise. I had bought the last two jars of Nescafe although we had agreed to take it in turns.

'Paul, I'll burn you in that mattress if you ever use that word with me again.'

'Hey, my life isn't all heavenly music either.'

I opened the window and shooed the pigeons away. I removed the tinfoil which had about four inches of droppings on it.

'Two days worth,' I said in amazement to Paul. 'Two days.'

'I'm not into pigeon poop as much as you are,' he said arrogantly.

'If you knew those pigeons were descended from the ones Mr. Mighty Hemingway had skipping along his windowsill, you'd probably adopt them.'

Paul stretched out full length on my bed and graciously left me a few inches at the end.

'What are your plans for the future?' he asked.

Why do people always choose the least appropriate moment to pester you about your future plans?

'Now that the play's finished you're not doing any acting. You can't limit yourself to just teaching English. That's a dead end road.'

'Thank you for that enlightenment.'

'I'm just saying it for your own good. You could keep doing the same thing for years. Then one day you wake up and your life is over.'

Yes indeed. It was going to be THAT kind of day!

THIRTY

After Paul's brutal reminder that I was going nowhere even Jean-Claude's postcard and his words 'I compose thinking of your green eyes' did nothing to lift my spirits. It was sweet of Jean-Claude to send me those poetic cards but they wouldn't do a darn thing to advance my theatrical career. I tried not to let my foul mood affect my lessons with Antoine which we now had in a café close to the library where he worked 'part time'. Not only did I have to contend with Antoine but also with his wife Camilla whom I had yet to meet. She was conveniently unwell during the run of the play but that didn't prevent her misleading Antoine when it came to his English. Camilla in her youth had spent two months in London working as a ball picker upper during Wimbledon where she 'perfected' her English. Need I add that Antoine's tonsils nearly came out his eyeballs when he tried to give due justice to Wimbledon? Camilla, the ball breaker, was not bowled over with Antoine's progress and had the temerity to challenge my knowledge of the English tongue and argue that 'what do you do in the evening?' was wrong. In Camilla's views, after her in-depth immersion in the English tongue picking up stray balls during Wimbledon, Antoine should be saying: 'what are you doing every evening?' By the time I had explained the difference of the present tense and the present continuous tense to Antoine (and they'll be making Montrachet on Mars before he actually understands it) I was almost too exhausted to haul myself up to Montmartre and break Granddad's and Belinda's hearts. But I had to get there before the permit police carted them off to jail.

The heavens opened as the little bus swung up towards the top of Montmartre. The harsh Paris rain dribbled down the fancy facades and erased some of the city's magic. The rain finally cheered me up a little. Standing out in the rain painting portraits is not romantic. Maybe I wouldn't have to break Granddad's and Belinda's heart by telling them about permits. They'd give up their nutty idea of their own accord. With new hope flowing through my veins I skipped into the Place du Tetre. Only half the usual number of artists were outside working under gigantic umbrellas. The more established painters were not in their usual spots since they could afford to stay in their warm studios knocking out a few more paintings to hawk the next dry day.

My heart nearly stopped when I saw Granddad and Belinda right smack in the middle of the Place. This was prime, exclusive terrain. They'd have asked Mitterrand for proof of identity before they'd give him a permit for a spot like that. The two had probably seen the empty spot complete with chairs and a large awning and had settled in. How the two hadn't been run off already by the permit police was a miracle on a par with seeing Josephine Bonaparte posing for Belinda instead of the elderly American woman.

'Is it nearly done, Steve?' asked the woman who was posing for Belinda.

'Now Joanna honey, you're not to move,' said Steve, the American who was standing next to Belinda observing the process. 'It's coming along real nice.'

Joanna fluttered her eyelashes up at the man. She was in her near eighties. Her eyelashes were not her own.

They were also longer than the Liza Minelli brand. Unfortunately, Joanna didn't have Liza's looks. She merely looked as if somebody had attacked her with a black bristle broom and had left half of it sticking to her face. Joanna also had a plump, red, bulbous face. Poor Belinda strained to capture the hidden beauty (the 'inner beauty' that my Mam insists everyone has) of Joanna in delicate water colours. She toned down her tawny facial colouring so that Joanna's round face did not immediately remind you of a traffic light stuck on red. She added a masterly touch of pink and gold to the hair so Joanna's hair looked normal instead of the colour of spit.

'There! That's finished!' said Belinda, and cocked her head to look once more at Joanna and then at her painting.

'Gee, honey, you're gorgeous!'

The satisfied Steve glowed all over. Belinda smiled just like those women in the ads who are plagued with migraine headaches until they take Brand X and are immediately flooded with relief. The picture did the rounds. Nobody paid much attention to Belinda's pleas to be careful since it was not totally dry yet. Joanna herself was entranced with the new and improved rendition of herself.

'Another satisfied customer,' said Granddad and patted Belinda's shoulders.

'You look great, honey,' Steve repeated and began pulling out the francs.

'Like I said, if you're ever in our part of Ireland, that pink shell frame is waiting for you,' said Granddad. He took the portrait and assessed it as if he were Art Critic for the National Gallery. 'Yes, a pink shell frame would bring out the tones. Now you've got our address in Ireland.'

'If we're ever in Ireland we'll certainly get that frame from you.' said Steve and handed over the francs which Granddad put into his money belt - a new acquisition.

'You and Lily should have yours done too, Jack,' said Steve to his friend Jack who was standing next to him. 'How much would it be for the two of them in the same picture?'

'I think we could make a special price, couldn't we, dear?' said Granddad and looked at Belinda. 'How about 170 francs and when you're in Ireland we'll throw in the frames for free.'

Done!

It took Belinda a good 20 minutes to complete the portrait of Jack and Lily. She had them posing like the King and Queen of England in official documents - from the side, showing their profiles. Belinda gave Lily a nose job so that her profile didn't immediately holler out the last of the bald eagles. She gave Jack a chin tuck, sliced off a healthy wad of jowls so that he had a neck that didn't instantly remind you of a water buffalo. During those 20 minutes Granddad stood tall and proud giving the little group hints on where to eat in Montmartre. He told them about the places he and Belinda had visited in London, including all the restaurants they should steer clear of. The fact that the American group were not doing England didn't seem to matter. They all listened enthralled as Granddad waffled on to his heart's content.

As I watched Granddad up there in the Place du Tertre that rain-splashed afternoon it was like watching the Granddad I used to see standing outside the Church on a Sunday morning, when he towered high and mighty the way grown ups always seem tall as steeples when you're a child. He looked exactly like the Granddad nobody would dare pass without dropping something in the collection plate for some group of unfortunates who were even worse off than we were. He was the only man who made Paddy Madigan stand and deliver a pound into the collection plate, when Paddy Madigan never parted with a penny, and still owes all concerned for his own mother's funeral and nobody is going to bury his father when he dies. When you're small and you see your Granddad standing tall outside the Church making everyone wilt, it's impressive.

But as the years went by, I grew taller and Granddad got smaller like the shrinking man. I had my doubts I'd ever seen Granddad standing tall and forbidding. And there on the top of Montmartre on that afternoon, with every inch of me drenched and dripping, Granddad was looking taller than all the Americans.

'Now, like I said, when you're in Ireland there's a frame that goes with that,' said Granddad.

'Well gee, this is real kinda unique,' said Steve all smiles. That's another thing I like about the Americans. When they're pleased about something they're not afraid to show it. They just radiate.

'In fact give me your address,' said Granddad. 'I'll send you the frames. I still have a few left. And it won't be missed.' That was a mild understatement. All 235 are now stored away in the shed waiting for that meteorite my Mam prays will fall on them and rid her of those monstrosities.

Granddad turned around and saw me standing behind him. He beamed, pulled me over and introduced me to the little group as his talented actress granddaughter who had trodden the Parisian boards to rapturous applause.

'But the show just closed,' Granddad informed them sadly.

'Aw gee, that's too bad. We'd have gone to see it, wouldn't we, Steve?' said Joanna.

'You should try and get on the 'Young and the Restless', honey,' said Lily.

'It's her favourite soap,' Steve explained.

'Nellie is a Shakespearean actress,' said Granddad, insinuating that the makers of all American soaps might as well spare their money in making a telephone call to Nellie Flanagan.

The Americans began to tear themselves away from Granddad and Belinda and the square in Montmartre, which they said was the most romantic spot they'd seen in Europe. Granddad repeated his advice about not touching the eggs in England in case of salmonella. As a parting gift he gave them his secret tip to an excellent home made chicken liver paté. Substitute the brandy with Irish whiskey - Paddy of course. The rain skittered off their rain hats. Steve said to be sure and visit them one day in Montana. There were more 'au revoirs' and 'see you agains' than on a normal morning in Dublin airport.

'How about a bite of lunch?' asked Granddad, very delicately extracting a fleck of paint from Belinda's hair. 'Hinlu will keep an eye on our stuff.'

Hinlu was the Chinese painter who was doing a very brisk business next to them in cut out portraits. When Granddad placed the easel and paints next to Hinlu's chair, he smiled and nodded as if this was an arrangement that had already been agreed to.

We trooped into 'their local' and ordered three different sandwiches and three small glasses of wine. It was now or never. Granddad and Belinda had to be told about the permit situation. I reminded myself of some tragic heroine in a very poignant film who had to break awful news

'You're not really supposed to paint in that part of the square, you know,' I said, approaching the subject from a delicate angle, instead of vividly describing just how brutally the two could be run off that place.

'We know that,' said Granddad and crunched down on his sandwich jambon (that's the French for ham sandwich). Belinda smashed down on her crispy sandwich paté. There was a pause while they both accustomed their dentures to the extra crunch in crisp French bread. Granddad sipped his red wine.

'Paris is so invigorating, isn't it?' he said. 'It really makes the mind come alive, and think that anything is possible.'

There was a scrunch and a munch in stereo while they again smashed down on their sandwiches. Granddad paused in mid-bite and did a quick probe with his tongue to check that his dentures hadn't cracked under the crispness of the bread. The smile on his face conveyed the good news that the dentures had weathered the attack.

'Ah Paree! Paree!' they chanted in unison.

'What about a permit?' I asked, trying to haul them into the reality zone. 'Those regulars don't mess around.'

'We had a marvellous stroke of luck,' said Granddad.

He was about to take another bite of the super crispy sandwich but decided otherwise when he saw the look I gave him.

'Go on,' I urged him.

'Madame Roussard's eldest is a painter. Charming girl. She's married and has one little girl and she's expecting another any day now.'

'Granddad, how did you and Belinda get that spot?'

I had to keep him on the topic at hand or else we'd have to go through the case history of everyone living in the hotel and everyone who had passed through in the last decade.

'I am in the process of telling you,' said Granddad, a tad miffed. 'Now, where was I?'

'One daughter has a kid and is about to drop another,' I prompted.

'Sylvana is the painter. Charming name, don't you think? The French have such poetic names.'

'Granddad!'

'Oh, sorry. I'm digressing. Well, last night we told Madame Roussard and Sylvana about our little idea of setting up shop for a while. We have them in for a little Irish whiskey and they enjoy teaching us a few useful French words. Of course they've seen Belinda's work and they know art when they see it. They're very fond of Irish whiskey and it's a pity we didn't bring more of it. And to cut a long story short. Since we all know that brevity is the soul of wit,' Granddad leaned across the tiny table and patted my hair affectionately. 'It seems you just can't set up and paint anywhere you like in Paris. Strange country. But Sylvana has a permit for that spot you saw us in. Said we could share it with her. She's expecting like I said, any day now, so she doesn't use it as much.'

'People would kill to get the kind of spot that Sylvana is letting us use,' said Belinda, and scrunched merrily away on her sandwich.

'So then, tell us,' said Granddad, and waved to the waiter to bring over another round of sandwiches and drinks. 'What are your plans?'

'They lie in the stars,' I joked.

I didn't add, 'And right now those stars ain't shining too brightly', because I'd never seen a happier pair than Granddad and Belinda as they scrunched and munched their way through their lunch in 'their local' off the Place du Tertre, Montmartre, Paris, France.

THIRTY-ONE

'Lucky! Lovely Surprise!'

I was trying to duck past Madame's Favela's lookout without being seen but her gnarled hand clamped itself on mine with the tenacity of a barnacle on a boat and dragged me inside her little den.

'Lucky! Pretty! Beautiful! Lucky!'

This is the shortened version of Madame's bout of adjectival ecstasy. For somebody who refused to understand my French when I said I was running late, she could certainly trot out the adjectives. I waited for Madame Favela to exit from her adjective fit about the giant bouquet of orchids on the table. They were as Madame Favela said: exotic, magnificent, and very expensive. 'Expensive' hit the jackpot five times. I wondered if it was her birthday. Then she handed me the orchids and the note which read: 'For my green eyed orchid. With all my love. Jean-Claude.'

I could see him going into a small town in Tipperary and ordering the bouquet; the girls in the flower shop sighing inwardly and wishing this wistful Frenchman would send them orchids instead of some Nellie in Paris. I have no memory of running back up those stairs. One minute I was prying Madame Favela's claws from my arm, the next minute I was chatting away to the pigeons and arranging my bouquet in a large empty jar of coffee. The room looked so different with those flashy orchids.

I turned Hansi's painting right side around and even that looked better and blended in with the bouquet. I would dry each one of them and keep them forever.

There was also a long letter from my Mam. At this stage she was writing daily demanding I tell her the whole truth. Her bones were informing her that something dreadful was going on with Granddad and Belinda. For once her instinct was way off mark. The two had moved out of Room 317 and were now residing *FOR FREE* in a smashing apartment with an even better view of the Sacré Coeur. Once more they had struck gold - thanks to Madame Roussard and Granddad's generosity in sharing his duty-free authentic Paddy. Madame Roussard was best buddy with an old couple who went South for the sun every Winter for the good of their bones. They were ecstatic to have a mature Irish couple who would look after their plants and wouldn't wreck the place with all night parties. Granddad and Belinda made friends with the rickety old couple next door Lisette and André who simply *adored* Ireland, something which called for untold 'little celebrations'.

Belinda usually sold about four water colours every morning on the Place du Tertre which just about covered their booze bill. Belinda was also best friends with a VIP painter who headed a gang of free lance painter/thugs who 'cajoled' tourists into parting with their Francs in exchange for portraits. This lot did not like newcomers but Belinda reminded them all of their sweet old grannies. They couldn't do enough for her and even put business her way. A ten kleenex happy weepie Hollywood movie could not have improved on their lot in life. Sometimes there was a P.S. to my Mam's letter. She wasn't in the least worried about me now. I had a regular job with a nice family in a lovely part of Paris and had a nice boyfriend who played Irish music. As far as my Mam was concerned it was almost as good as me making it to head cashier in Tipps.

Now that the play was over and my French lover was extending his stay in Tipperary, I was back to making one citron pressé last all evening in the brown on brown café. The conversation left a lot to be desired. Diana spent hours praising Granddad and Belinda's entrepreneurial spirit in earning more money in Paris than the four of us combined and living in an apartment with two showers that worked. Hansi grunted. He finally cracked and told her to shut up with her infernal American obsession with soap and money. Paul was not in a scintillating mood either and didn't even bother to leap to the defence of American values. I had run out of day dreams about playing Juliet in London and being feted on Broadway. Every time a plaintive piano piece wafted from Henri's old TV set I could feel my heart go sour with pain. I missed Jean-Claude so much listening to that piano music that I felt like cashing in what was left of my Drama Fund and buying a ticket to Tipperary.

The only other one who had anything to smile about was Antoine. After 25 years of inactivity his agent had finally landed him a non speaking part in a British film as a French salesman hawking sexy lingerie door to door.

'Ma chance! Ma chance!' yelled Antoine when he told me his news as he leapt up and down like a ballet dancer with severe gout.

When he calmed down I translated the English script for him. It was a horrifying pile of shite bordering on the porno. Antoine wasn't perturbed as long as he wouldn't have to do anything too energetic which would make his bad back flare up again. Lingerie played a major part and from the amount of space devoted to describing peepholes in bras and gaps in the knickers, the lingerie was definitely entitled to a credit. It made me think of Tipps! If the marketing manager had equated rips, tears and bits missing to French sex he could have pulled in a fortune because 98% of Tipps underwear always had something missing.

Despite the wall to wall sexy lingerie there wasn't any sex. Neither was there a scintilla of sense, action, excitement or plot development. In essence this was the 'story'. The French salesman (in this case Antoine) kept going back to the same customer, a woman who lived on a dreary housing estate. She made him tea and gave him biscuits. She told him about a piece of land in the South of France that didn't have any water (most of the dialogue had been lifted from the English version of the recently released 'Manon des Sources'). The woman never left her house. Not because she was lazy or suffered from agoraphobia. No, the woman was staying indoors until there was a change of Government in Britain. This was 'protest performance art'.

She bought a lot of the Frenchman's knickers. Towards the end of the film her husband tries on all her frillies and prances around the apartment in them. The woman gets so upset by this, she runs out of the house, destroys her performance piece and is run over by a bus. Inside the bus one of the passengers is the Frenchman with his wares. In the crash his suitcase flies open and all his goods come flying through the air. The final scene in the film shows all the French underwear covering the dead woman's body.

'Open to interpretation,' was Antoine's verdict. 'English intellectualism?'

'English crap,' I corrected him.

'MMMMMM! Crêpe!' said Antoine, licking his lips.

'Crap,' I corrected him. 'Crap!'

'Crêpe. Crêpe.' Antoine went on until I began to see

all varieties of crêpes with delicate fillings of apple, and chocolate and apricot dancing in front of my eyes.

Antoine picked up the script and clutched it to his chest and rolled his eyes to heaven.

'Ma chance! Ma chance!'

His eyes glistened like snow under the moonlight. The guy who'd won the lottery the week before hadn't looked this ecstatic. It was a huge relief to me to know that Antoine's only dialogue would be in French and not in English.

'Mai Hang-leash mass be flea ant.'

Antoine danced around the room and left me to figure out why he was inquiring about fleas and ants. After he repeated that same sentence six times I understood. 'My English must be fluent' was what Antoine was aiming for.

'We must do 6 hours a day now.'

That's the fast variety. It actually took Antoine about seven attempts before I knew where he was aiming. I didn't say anything. He went on dancing his dizzy waltz of happiness, praising God and all on high for giving him this wonderful, unexpected chance. It wasn't the moment to tell Antoine that I would prefer to have boiling lead injected into my veins rather than teach him English for 6 hours a day. Or to remind him that he didn't have to say one word of English in the entire film.

'Shave antsy francs an hour!' he added. I let out a strangled moan. Antoine knew his pronunciation of 70 was a bit off. So he went back to mangling 'seventy' again. He hit every single variation from 'sing', 'sweet', 'sewer' and then eked in a few things that sounded like savants or shave ants. I could only nod and smile. Six hours a day with Antoine. I'd be ready for the loony bin.

The pact was struck and the man who sold his soul to the devil had a better deal that I did. I sold my life away for 'shave antsy francs an hour'.

THIRTY-TWO

I knew it was a complete waste of time but I still paid that weekly visit to CAT where Madame Flore smiled sadly at me and reminded me how many years some of France's finest acting elite had to wait to be discovered. That morning when I strolled into CAT, Madame Flore was looking more anxious than usual. I almost ducked back out again. I couldn't take anymore of her upbeat encouragement. But she spotted me and came running from behind her desk squawking like an agitated old turkey. She pulled me over to the bulletin board and jabbed her fingers at a notice on the board.

'Wanted: English speaking extras for American film. Must be at least 5'10', 19-23, attractive, vivacious female.' The auditions were being held that very day which was why Madame Flore looked so anxious.

I gave her two bisous (that's French for 'kiss') of thanks and ran to the métro. I always carried several copies of my CV and a glossy with me just in case a producer spotted me on the Boulevard and offered me a job. This open call was being held in a highly inaccessible part of Northwest Paris. The film company had taken over an old bread factory and you'd never guess you were in the land of dreams and fantasy when you walked through the huge grey entrance hall. Masses of women darted to and fro like excited fish in an overcrowded aquarium. Some of them were even taller then me. There was a cacophony of 'chéries' and the smacking of kisses. But the most frequent word I could make out was 'rien' (that's French for 'nothing') and that's what every hopeful in that room had been doing since last they'd last seen one another.

There was a desk in the middle of this bright and breezy gathering manned by a self-important, arrogant girl who looked as if she'd consider smiling if you paid her a giant amount. I presented my CV and glossy. She stamped them, then handed me back my glossy plus a number.

'Put your glossy on the relevant pile,' she said, when I continued to stand there.

'Of what?'

'Do you have problems with your eyes?' was her next utterance.

'I have 20/20 vision.'

'So use your 20/20 vision and put your glossy on the pile which includes your number. Over there.'

With a gesture Lady Macbeth would have envied, she pointed to the long table. There was a row of little piles with signs that went 1-20, 21-40, 41-60 and so on. I placed my expensive glossy and all my life's experience on the 161-180 pile.

'Thank you for being so helpful,' I said sarcastically. But she was too busy lacing into the next candidate asking her if she now finally understood the simple fact that she was number 179. Number 179 did not indulge in any outburst of sarcasm. However, when she placed her glossy on top of mine she said, 'Mais quelle garce!' This is a very useful little phrase in French. It means 'What a bitch!' Given the appropriate intonation it can also mean 'What a fucking bitch!'

In a far corner a jolly looking group were having their breakfast. Being French they weren't going to be separated from the meaning of life, i.e. good food, for any serious period of time. There was a free spot on the windowsill directly behind them so I perched myself there and listened to their conversation. It was a bit of a letdown. They looked so intense I thought they were intellectualizing. In fact they were analyzing the quality of the croissants. The woman nearest me opened a giant flask and poured another round of coffee. She held out a styrofoam cup to me.

'Want some?'

I got down off the windowsill and joined the group.

'D'you come here often?' I asked, taking the coffee from Sophie.

'Hélas! Hélas! Hélas!' (This is French for alas! This seems to have died out in the English language. Not so in French.)

'We're all regulars!' Sophie explained. She sighed so vehemently that all the croissant flakes floated down the front of her artsy black dress. She introduced me to the regulars. Hélène, drama school graduate, but no work. Maire Claire, nurse and aspiring actress, no work. Charlotte, night-time secretary and day-time acting student, no work.

'Hélène has been in a TV commercial,' said Sophie.

'Wow!'

For the first time in my life I was sitting next to somebody who had acted on TV.

'It was a commercial for haemorrhoid cream,' said Hélène, with commendable dignity.

There wasn't much I could say. It was not in the same league as starring in an ad for Paul Newman's Salad Dressing.

'At least you got on TV. You must remember that,' said Sophie. She seemed to be the mother hen of this group.

'Use Magnifest and your bum will get that rest,' said Hélène in a droning monotone.

'Hey, I know that ad. It's the one where you use that cream Magnifest and then it's like your bum is floating in a champagne glass,' I said.

'What have you been doing?' Charlotte asked me. Charlotte was visibly tired of all the attention that Hélène's rear end had brought her. Later I found out Charlotte had been rejected for that same commercial. Rejection itself is sore enough. When it is a rejection for intoning the glories of haemorrhoid cream - that smarts.

I told them about my triumph in the Arab section of Paris. They were all suitably impressed. I also told them about all the people who had rejected me in Ireland and France.

'Cons!' They all choroused.

As I've mentioned before 'con' is one of the most frequently used words in France. It means 'jerk', 'dickhead', 'lowlife', 'bastard'. Judging from the frequency with which it is used 99% of the French are 'cons'.

As the morning hours dwindled by the 'regulars' reminisced about auditions past and how their hopes had been whipped up only to be dashed by some low life director. One such specimen had told Marie Claire she'd be perfect if only her eyes were green instead of brown. She bought coloured lenses which a) scratched her eyeballs, b) gave her double vision, c) nearly perforated her cornea and d) she didn't get her the job.

'Cons!' we all muttered darkly.

Mid-day came and went. They were up to number 103. At one o'clock on the dot the regulars unpacked more packages containing lunch. There were cold pork chops, cornichons, salad, fresh bread, wine, cheese, fruit. Sophie passed me a plate.

'I didn't bring anything. I never knew it would be like this,' I said and hesitated before I took the plate.

'None of us thought it would ever be like this,' said Sophie gently. 'You'll know next time.'

For the next half hour they did not mention their aspirations or failures: all their energies were concentrated on the food and wine, which was perfection. All over the room little groups were also eating and drinking. It was quite amazing.

'I'm going to shoot myself if I haven't made it by the time I'm 30,' said Marie Claire. Lunch was over and they were now up to 113.

'You're a nurse. You've got all that access to pills and stuff,' said Hélène. 'That's easier than shooting yourself.'

The afternoon hours ticked by. The numbers were called out at a faster and taster pace. Of our group, only Marie Claire and I were left.

'Number 178.'

It was 4.25 in the afternoon when they called my number. I walked into the adjoining room. I was suddenly so tired I felt like stretching out somewhere and having a long siesta.

There were five of 'them'. Three men and two women. They were all ancient crocks. One man was bald and kept running his hand over and over his skull. He'd probably pawed his hair off. Another man had the biggest belly I'd ever seen. I felt sorry for his belly-button, which must have been stretched beyond human endurance. The third man was seated between the two women and he was so thin and nondescript he looked like the filling in a very stingy sandwich.

One of the women wore giant specs which kept sliding down her nose. She jerked them back up in front of her eyes with an acrobatic hoist of her honker. She did this every eight seconds or so. The other woman was sporting more necklaces and bracelets than an entire Masai tribe. Every time she moved she sounded like an exploding shed. She was also sporting a giant fur hat made of synthetic leopard. This woman wanted the world to know she was really weird.

I could have been a standard lamp standing there for all the attention they gave me. They continued to argue about the previous candidate and analyze her bad points. It was beyond boiling hot in that room. The sweat poured down my back. I was beyond the point of being nervous. After a ten hour wait you don't have the energy to be nervous too. Finally the slip of a man picked up my glossy from the pile in front of them.

'Number 178,' he said.

'That's me,' I told him, grateful that somebody had taken note of my presence up there on stage.

'Don't fucking cut me off,' Leopard Lady snarled at him.

'Darling, we don't have time to analyze all the dopes we see,' said monster belly man. 'Whoops! Sorry sweetie' he added for my benefit.

I smiled at him. He didn't fool me for a minute. The only way this ugly Goodyear blimp of a man could get through life was to insult everyone else in the world.

'It's 4.30. I suggest we get on with it,' said the little man who looked as if he wanted to rush to the nearest bistro and fling himself into a vat of calvados after a day spent in such non exalted company.

'I've prepared a selection of Shakespeare's Sonnets.'

'*QUOI*! Mais non! Je rêve! Mais merde,' yelled Leopard Lady.

She sounded like a bulldog being castrated by a gorilla. The exact translation of her squealings was: 'What! But no! I dream! But shit!'

Not what you could describe as the epitome of eloquence!

'No shit no,' she continued. 'Just read the passage marked in that script. What rock did this one crawl out from under?'

'She's Irish,' said the wispy man and smiled encouragingly up at me.

'That explains it,' said Leopard Lady. 'Shit! Sonnets!'

'Is it because you can't understand the Sonnets?'

That was all I said. But I had their undivided attention. I stared them down. That person trying to impersonate a leopard reminded me of that half human who had me fired from Tipps. The fact that she had me fired from Tipps never bothered me. It was a 'blessed release' to quote one of my Mam's little phrases. But she had insulted my interpretation of Shakespeare. And I will not tolerate anyone who uses 'shit' and 'sonnet' in the same breath.

The thin slip of a man laughed.

'Eh merde alors,' he said breaking into French. (That's French for 'Eh, bloody shit'.)

He said 'Eh, bloody shit' three times. Obviously he never got a word in edgeways with this pack. When he got the chance he couldn't help repeating himself.

'There are still eighty of them out there,' said the bald man, and went back to caressing his pate.

'Let her say her Sonnet,' said the little man and gave me a nod of encouragement.

Except I didn't want to waste the most beautiful words ever written on that pack of ugly slugs - with the exception of the wispy man who seemed to have some feelings left. Something wet dripped down my face. I didn't know if it was sweat or tears. Of course inside I was weeping with the realization that this was probably what I'd have to do for the rest of my life. Be tested by morons. In the end I'd probably leap at a commercial for asses' milk that would do wonders for blackheads, if that would vault me onto the stage. Hasn't everyone compromised at some stage?

'Do you know the sonnet that starts with … 'Like as the waves make towards the pebbled shore'?' asked the wispy man and again gave me an encouraging wink.

Heck, I knew I didn't have a chance in hell of getting work as an extra in that film. Leopard Lady was looking at me with eyes that could spit out razor blades at will. The man pawing his skull couldn't spell Shakespeare. Obese man was only interested in feeding his face. But they were an audience. And any audience is better than none. So I let loose and let them have my seven top favourites. By the time I got to number six it was a real challenge just to be heard above the racket the Leopard Lady was knocking out of her jewellery. But her jungle accessories were no match for a voice that had been trained in the Tipps Zoo. My voice pealed out like the bells in the Dun-mo-Croi church (built 1876) which are always rung by over enthusiastic school kids.

I was far away from that Parisian studio and former bread factory. I was the sound of that bell, piercing the blue sky, skimming over tree-tops and turning birds upside down when they got in my path. Those bags of flesh in front of me were so many clumps of sea-weed that were being thrashed by an angry sea that would make bits of them and scatter their guts to the bottom of the ocean - with the exception of the wispy man who said 'thank you' when I finished.

'The Irish never know when to shut up,' said the Leopard Lady.

'It's not exactly what we want. But we've seen you,' said the bald man.

Monster man leaned over and pressed the intercom.

'Haul in the next one, would you, sweetie?' he puffed through his sausage sized lips.

Haul, I thought. Like a manager in a feed store asking the guy in the back to haul up another sack of medium-sized chick feed. I walked over to the door. You don't say 'goodbye' at auditions. You just go. You carry your heart around your knees. I was about to go out the door when the little man called out after me:

'Does it always rain as much as they say in Ireland?'

There was a soft tone in his voice. As if he really wanted to say something totally different. Before I could answer Leopard Lady leapt in.

'Of course it rains that much,' she sniffed. 'That's why they've all got webbed feet and have to tuck their tails into their knickers.'

She honked with delight. The others sniggered and tittered. Except the wispy man who looked at her in anger.

'At least our assholes aren't where our mouths are,' I shouted back at her.

Oh, thank you, Paul. Thank you for your vulgar American joie de mots (that's my invention - joy of words).

She looked more surprised than if she'd been kicked in the kisser by a kangaroo. The little man looked radiant. Even if he didn't clap with approval, his eyes said it all. He winked one last time. Marie Claire, who was on her way in, heard the whole exchange. She couldn't figure out how or why I would say something so vulgar to the judges. She was so busy wondering what had happened to me that she forgot to be nervous.

Marie Claire got the job. Which is great and all. Now she won't have to blow her brains out or take a selection of pills when she's 30.

And me? For the first time in my life I felt a swish of something like despair knocking at my heart looking for a place to nestle and settle in - if I let it.

THIRTY-THREE

The brown on brown café was closed for the annual staff holiday and decontamination. For several evenings Diana and I endured hanging out in another dive owned by ancient Ella who looked like something that had floated off Easter Island. Hansi was very welcome chez Ella, particularly by the 8 cats to whom he fed shrimp and fish. Paul explained that Hansi couldn't make this his local because he didn't want to make his own cats jealous by coming home smelling of other felines. One evening Diana and I agreed we didn't want to spend another evening being grossed out by Hansi pulling bits of fish out of his pockets, or opening tins of tuna and feeding the ever scratching cats. I invited Diana for an apéro. After my torture sessions with Antoine I had enough to invite both of us to a more refined café. I suggested we go and have our apéro in the Café des Impressionistes which is located in the ritzy part of Montmartre. It is also the café where Jean-Claude used to take me before we went on to dine in all the gourmet restaurants. The minute they got wind of our plans the two lads invited themselves along even though Hansi has a grunt attack even at the mention of the word 'Impressionist'. Paul wasn't too keen on this café either. There is no connection to Hemingway: no plaque on the door saying he dined there; no name plate at the bar; no dish on the menu à la Hemingway. But when Nellie agreed she'd spring for a small carafe from the Antoine torment funds, those lads would go anywhere.

Café des Impressionistes was where Jean-Claude introduced me to Kir Royal (that's crème de cassis and champers). But apart from the Jean-Claude connection, I loved this beautiful café because it reminded me of that famous painting by Manet with the sad-looking girl in front of all the rows of champagne bottles. When my Mam and my Dad come to Paris I will most definitely bring them to this café even if my Mam will go into a dead faint when she sees the toilet which is still the hole-in-the-ground variety which they keep for authenticity to prove that this café is genuinely old. The only other jarring note in the café are the strange dog paintings all over the place.

Café des Impressionists was busy. But we didn't have to worry about not having reserved a table. One look at Hansi and a secluded corner table was immediately ours. The first thing Hansi did was bum a cigarette off a guy at the next table and order the waiter to bring us a carafe of Chateau Chirac while 'the girls decided what to order'. Chateau Chirac has nothing to do with wine. This is what some Parisians call 'plain tap water'. It's their way of insulting the mayor Jacques Chirac. They also wear T-shirts with the logo – 'I drank Chateau Chirac and lived.'

Diana and I were still discussing which sophisticated apéro we'd order when suddenly Jacques Fontenay rushed in waving an envelope at Paul. Jacques was grinning from ear to ear.

'The Philadelphia Enquirer bought one of your articles,' Jacques gushed to Paul and handed him an envelope that had already been opened.

He then plonked himself next to Diana and explained that Ella and 8 very disappointed cats had told him where we were. Jacques still lived with Jean-Pierre in the flat that Paul used to occupy before he was thrown out.

'You opened my mail,' was Paul's response, instead of flinging himself on his knees and singing a Song of Thanks to the Good and Discerning Lord of writers.

'Jean-Pierre opened it,' said Jacques calmly. 'What's the use of tracking you down if it's just the regular reject?'

'Now that philistine opens my mail too.'

'They bought your article,' I reminded Paul.

'It's probably one of Jean-Pierre's sick jokes,' he replied. 'The guy's a jerk. He opens other people's mail.'

Jacques shrugged his shoulders and continued gazing sideways at Diana's breasts. Suddenly, without any warning at all, Paul leapt up, grabbed the nearest waiter and whirled him into a wild waltz.

'I've sold an article! I've done it! Yeah! Yeah!'

The poor waiter nearly expired with shock on the spot. He was 5'2' and Paul was 6'3'. The Frenchman went limp as wet seaweed and clutched his tray in bewilderment. The Manager trotted over, yelling out about not tolerating customers who molested the waiters. Paul waved the letter at him shouting: 'I've done it!' The Manager gently guided him back to our table muttering: 'On se calme. On se calme.'

If Hemingway had floated up through the floorboards and held his hand out to Paul he couldn't have been more ecstatic. Jacques said this might be 'it'. Diana said this was 'The Breakthrough'. I didn't want to repeat all these simplistic banalities and was delving for a more appropriate quote like 'fiery chariots bearing him aloft to literary immortality'. But Hansi distracted us all by ordering a bottle of Viognier for the girls and a bottle of Beaujolais Nouveau for the boys. Everyone's thoughts zoomed back to earth - namely, who was going to pay for that? Not Hansi unless he had come into an inheritance that afternoon. As I've mentioned before, Hansi gave up currency long ago. If he wanted to make a phone call he asked a 'flic' (that's real French for policeman) to help him. He read his newspapers at kiosks. If the owner asked him to stop reading and buy the newspaper, Hansi gave him that Look - the one you'd get from an irritable gorilla if you took his banana away. But we were sitting in the kind of upmarket café where they rang their friendly local flic if a client didn't pay.

Since it was Paul's Big Day he couldn't be expected to contribute to the bill. Jacques' lips tightened. These foreigners were going to make him pay his share. Jacques is one of us until he doesn't like the prevailing situation. Five glasses appeared on the table along with the carafe of Chateau Chirac, a bottle of Viognier and the Beaujolais Nouveau which Hansi immediately poured out without grunting at the waiter that it was drinkable this year. Diana poured herself a glass of Viognier.

'I'm totally broke,' she said, with New Jersey forthrightness, which according to Paul is even more direct than the average American variety. 'I'm down to my last 20 francs.'

'Stop boring us with your financial shortcomings,' said Hansi.

He turned to another guy sitting at the next table and asked him for a cigarette, since he wasn't too keen on the brand he had bummed off his friend. The guy generously gave him three cigarettes. Hansi winked at him. I wondered for the millionth time how he got away with it and why his parents had never instilled in him the need to pay for himself and not expect the rest of the world to do it for him.

'The Philadelphia Enquirer is a top flight newspaper,' said Paul very grandly. 'Up there with The New York Times, the Washington Post.'

'Hey, they paid you, that's the main thing, isn't it?' said Diana.

'That is the stupidest statement I've heard from you,' said Paul pompously.

'So, tear up the cheque then!' said Diana.

'I repeat, money is not why I write,' said Paul icily.

'If money isn't the main thing, burn it,' said Diana defiantly.

Hansi leaned over to the guy he'd just bummed the cigarettes from. The guy looked pissed off. Obviously he was a three cigarette man. Up to that number, no bother, but after that forget it.

'Could I borrow your matches again?' asked Hansi.

'Oh sure,' replied the guy. He looked so contrite for even thinking that Hansi was going to bum another cigarette off him, he picked up his pack and offered it to him. Naturally, Hansi saw nothing amiss in accepting this unexpected bounty. Hansi put the box of matches down between Diana and Paul. She picked one up and lit it.

'So what's the verdict? Is money the main thing?' asked Diana.

'I'd like to keep the cheque as a souvenir,' said Paul and pocketed his cheque before Hansi and Diana got any other bright ideas

'I detest people who say that money isn't the main thing,' said Diana with that confident air that came from years of duelling. 'Next you'll be saying you don't mind sitting in a cold room for the rest of your life writing your guts out for nothing.'

Just then a gigantic man came in with dogs as big as ponies. The dogs zeroed in on Hansi. Dogs always go to people who have a whiff of dog on them. But all dogs are attracted to Hansi. These two settled cosily down on either side with their heads on Hansi's knees. They were very old dogs with white eyelashes. Judging from the amount of 'Bonjours' that were flying about the café a lot of people knew this man and his dogs.

'Those dogs are higher than kites,' said Diana and squeezed her nose with her thumb and forefinger. '*GAWD!* Why can't people wash their dogs?'

At the sound of her voice the two gigantic dogs lifted their heads off Hansi's lap and made a show of flashing all their teeth at her - not in a nasty way but like a kid showing off her teeth after brushing the living daylights out of them.

'It's OK, boys,' Hansi told the dogs and caressed their gigantic heads. 'Say, Diana, you should apply for a job sniffing people's underarms. They'd pay a lot to somebody with a nose as sharp as yours.'

'I'll keep that in mind,' said Diana without turning a hair. She turned her attention back to Paul. 'Now there's an article idea for you! Why don't you write about those people who work for deodorant companies? The experts who sniff people's underarms to test how effective their deodorant is.'

If she had stuck a rapier through his left eyeball Paul could not have been more insulted. Duelling Diana had suggested that Paul, the bearer of the Hemingway torch should lower himself to write about people sniffing body parts like dogs in a park.

'Which article did they buy?' I asked in an attempt to elevate the level of conversation.

Paul pouted. He sipped his wine as if he hadn't even heard my question.

'Hey, forget it, if you don't want to talk about it, just shove it!' I snapped.

Immediately I had his attention. Because I was asking him *NOT* to talk about his writing which to a writer is worse than shoving a rusty tube down his nose and out his bellybutton.

'It was about that exhibit at the Musée d'Orsay on historical architectural drawings from Chicago,' said Paul and refilled his glass, looking more solemn than Mitterrand addressing LA FRANCE. 'You do remember, don't you?'

Could I forget was more to the point! We had both gone to an exhibition featuring Paris-on-the-Prairie (that's Chicago, USA but frenchified) after the Great Fire of 1871. The walls were full of architectural drawings of the first skyscrapers that were ever built on the globe. Paul's first draft of his article was a pack of lies making our visit to this exhibition sound as exciting as the Great Fire itself when all we did was walk around and gaze perplexed at the drawings. He showed me the article and I agreed it was good. In draft number two Paul tried to evoke the impression that the walls and the drawings were doing the actual narration. Oh yes, writers are cuckoo. I told him so at the time. I'll never do that again because he was swamped with self doubt about his writing talent and I had to spend hours bucking him up again. Draft no. three was fiercely anti-American. Paul criticized the Americans who streamed into the Louvre so they could impress people back home but wouldn't dream of going to their own museums. When he proffered draft no. four I said I'd read it in my spare time. It was more diplomatic than saying – 'Show me one more word about those fucking architectural drawings and I won't be responsible for my actions'. There was a sixth and a seventh draft but by now Paul realized that if he talked about his art he'd have to give me equal time to talk about my art.

'So which draft did they take?' I now asked since it was Paul's Big Day and there are always exceptions.

'I don't know,' said Paul and a look of concern flitted across his face. 'I sent them all seven versions just to demonstrate my range of style and diversity. Editors are supposed to be impressed by stuff like that. Since they can't write themselves, they like writers who can approach a topic from several angles.'

'What a load of crap!' said Diana, who was still unaware that writers' egos are more fragile than butterfly wings.

Lord only knows where that remark would have landed us but things took a dramatic turn when yet another bottle of red landed in the middle of our table. Hansi naturally didn't find anything strange about this wine arriving out of the blue. He had probably signalled surreptitiously to the barman to bring on another one. The dogs on Hansi's lap sighed petulantly at being disturbed while Hansi poured the wine.

'I may as well tell you guys now,' said Paul, picking up his glass. 'I've got 8 francs on me.'

'I'm not having any red,' said Diana, 'And I'm broke.'

Hansi tasted the wine. 'Now that's a real nice wine.'

A 'nice' wine translated into a very nice price especially in this fancy place.

'I must be going,' said Jacques. 'Thanks for the wine. Congratulations Paul. Give us a call some time. Jean-Pierre would like to make up, you know.'

The gigantic man who had come in with the dogs loomed up next to our table and looked down at his huge dogs who were now snoring on Hansi's lap.

'You like the wine?' he asked and smiled.

'Oh Lord, it's the bouncer,' said Diana under her breath and gave him her most seductive smile.

But the giant only had eyes for Hansi and the dogs.

'My dogs have taken to you, I see,' he said.

'This poor guy has a bad cavity that could be right on the nerve,' said Hansi and plunged his hand into the slumbering dog's mouth.

All of us - including the giant owner - stopped breathing. You should have seen the teeth in that dog. An alligator had sunflower seeds in comparison. I expected Hansi's hand to be instantly severed from his wrist. But there was no blood, just a whimper from the old dog when Hansi located the miniscule cavity.

'Pauvre Tarzan! My poor Tarzan, Papa didn't see that,' said the burly man and crouched down next to his dogs.

'Brandy would help,' said Hansi authoritatively.

One click of the guy's fingers and a waiter floated over with a glass of Hennessey. Hansi daubed the dog's gums. Then he took a swig from the glass himself and gave the dog another daub. Diana, who thought she had seen everything in rock-bottom European non-hygiene, was goggle-eyed. The other dog tried to put his snout in the snifter, so Hansi daubed his gums too.

'They like Hennessey,' commented the owner.

'So do I,' said Hansi, and took another gulp from the common brandy dog trough.

The huge man did his finger-clicking and almost magically a bottle of Hennessey, another bottle of superior wine, and a huge plate of hors d'oeuvres materialized on our table.

'Eat, drink. My place. My treat,' said the man.

Diana fell on the hors d'oeuvres as if she hadn't seen food in a month. She apologized to Paul about her remarks. She said it was her stomach acidity. In Paris she was crippled with it since she couldn't afford to eat every few hours as she was supposed to. Paul smiled at Diana and proceeded to give her a verbatim account of all seven drafts of his article. The dogs were getting happily drunk on either side of Hansi. Their tongues lolled out of their mouths and they repeatedly tried to put their snouts into the snifters. Hansi and the burly owner discussed animals and brands of alcohol. There was a happy feeling in the air. I was thinking that the soppy things you read about in trashy magazines sometimes do happen.

I was just about to close my teeth over an exquisite piece of smoked salmon and dill when … I saw him. It was Jean-Claude.

THIRTY-FOUR

I could not believe what my eyes were filtering through to me. Jean-Claude was sitting at a discreet table for two holding a blonde's face between his elegant fingers. The salmon and dill snack dropped down onto my lap with the shock. Last week Jean-Claude had sent me a postcard from Tipperary saying that he saw my eyes 'in the glistening morning dew-kissed web of the spider'. Now he had his nose half an inch from the blonde's nose and was gazing adoringly into her eyes. It was one of his most exquisite little tricks. I'd always fallen for it like a hungry goat going for the carnations. Obviously Jean-Claude's technique was having the same galvanizing effect on the blonde. Then he started kissing her blonde hair.

'Are you alright?'

Paul was shaking me. For a few seconds I didn't know where I was and who I was. My heart was pounding as if somebody was sitting on my throat. My breath was coming out in gusts - like an old car trying to make it up a steep mountain.

'Is she allergic to dogs?' asked the concerned owner.

'I have to go,' I said and darted from the table in the direction of the toilets.

One of the dogs gave a little hop as I flitted by him. I was going so fast, the old half-blind dog could easily have mistaken me for some kind of giant hare speeding past him. As my body hurled itself through the toilet door, I felt as if I had been speared by the utter tragedy of existence. All the clouds of the universe wanted to come rushing out of my eyeballs. I was no longer Nellie Flanagan but the tragic heroine who had been deceived by the limpid-eyed hero, a naïve Nellie who had never suspected such base deception could dwell in those watery blue eyes.

But this Turkish loo in this expensive, authentic Montmartre bistro was not the right setting. Those hole-in-the-ground loos are fine for men in a hurry, but most inappropriate when you want to sob your heart out in solitary suffering. In the first place I couldn't sit down anywhere and sitting down is a requisite in tragedy. I couldn't concentrate fully on my grief because as I gazed down at the hole in the ground looking at the two iron plates where you are supposed to put your feet I wondered why in God's earth the women of France hadn't demanded the replacement of those smelly contraptions decades earlier. Who cared if they yelled out 'authentic, old fashioned'? They were as outdated as believing in true love.

To distract myself I flushed the contraption and the water gushed down the wall and made a beeline for my shoes. Tragedy or no tragedy those were my best shoes. I couldn't afford to ruin them. I leapt back to avoid the gushing onslaught of water … and fell right out that door, which in my distraught state I had forgotten to lock. There was a wild clatter as I tottered backwards. All the people at the nearby tables looked up to see who was the loony hanging onto the loo door. The commotion travelled as far over as Jean-Claude's corner table.

I caught his eye. First there was non-recognition, then surprise, then guilt. And I hated every single one of those emotions. I disentangled myself from the doorknob as regally as I could. Like one of those straight laced characters from an Edwardian BBC mini-series I strode from the Café des Impressionistes with my head held high making it pretty obvious that one lying, cheating, deceiving French composer/director (who was never going to make it in either profession) was merely an insect of utter inconsequence.

Outside it had stopped raining and the cobbles of Paris glittered blackly under the lights. The water gurgled merrily in the gutter and sang a sad song as it disappeared down through the hole near the pavement. Just like Love, I thought. Skipping and hopping merrily along and then swoosh, up comes a big hole and you land down in the sewer. I suddenly remembered how often Jean-Claude told me that I brought meaning to his life, and that my eyes were more attractive than the rarest orchids in the jungle. It was nice to listen to all that kind of stuff and I'd really have to hypnotize myself into believing that I was a jungle orchid. But I had swallowed it hook, line and sinker when Jean-Claude said so. Just shows you. Fall in love and go utterly bonkers.

I suddenly realized I'd left my pocketbook back in the Café des Impressionistes. Even if I would have to live without amour, in the capital of la belle France I couldn't do much without my valuable I.D. cards. I was about to turn back when I saw Paul running up the street after me. He was waving my pocketbook. He wasn't even out of breath when he stopped in front of me. All that walking up my 127 stairs had done wonders for his physical condition.

'Why did you go running off like that?' he demanded. He ran his hand through his hair as if it was too demanding for this writer to understand the traumas of the betrayed soul. 'I could have told you the guy was a jerk. He's a wimp. You don't need him.'

In the distance the neon Art Deco lights over Café des Impressionistes were throwing bleeding red images across the wet black cobbles. For a moment the reddened cobbles reminded me of my own heart - squashed and squeezed to death.

'He's a very average guy,' said Paul, and clucked his tongue at me as if I were a silly kid crying over the loss of her favourite bear. 'He doesn't deserve you.'

I began to shiver in the wet night air. Paul clucked again. Then he took off his jacket and clapped it around my shoulders.

'That no-talent jerk couldn't have an original thought if you paid him,' said Paul, giving me healthy pats on the back which were border-line wallops, the kind you'd give a pillow to plump it up. 'You deserve better.'

In between sobs I remembered how Jean-Claude had promised faithfully - his very own words - that he'd do all in his power to help me get work in the theatre after he returned from Ireland. Now it looked as if he couldn't do anything faithfully.

THIRTY-FIVE

November! November! The wind whistled sharply like a bitter old person who hasn't enjoyed life and hisses at everyone and everything. I spent hours gazing out a city that was greyer than an old cat wondering why my First Love had turned out to be a lout and a liar? I cried when he sent me those bouquets of red roses with lying notes: 'I can explain', 'please let me explain' and 'she means nothing to me'. I convinced Madame Favela I was allergic to roses and when I gave her the bouquets she sobbed louder than usual. I cried during the day and even had moments when I rather enjoyed my melancholia. I cried in my sleep until the morning I woke up with what looked like a nasty nappy rash all over one half of my face. If I'd been auditioning for Juliet this would not have enhanced my chances. I tried to cut down on the weeping and remembered wryly what my brother Brian had said about heartbreak: 'You'll find out soon enough.' A pity he didn't tell me how to get over it faster.

November was also a nasty month for Hansi. One evening he strolled across the field to his caravan, opened the door and was met with a most distressing sight. The dogs and the cats were all flaked out in a pile behind the door. There was a fierce smell of gas in the place. It later transpired that Carnation had chewed through the rubber gas connection in an attempt to get at her dog biscuit which she'd foolishly flipped behind the tiny heater. It was a miracle the cats hadn't been smothered and flattened to death by the two large dogs flaking out on top of them. But after years of surviving life with Hansi those cats had true grit and resilience.

Every time we met in the café Hansi rehashed the tragic tale yet again.

'They could have died,' Hansi would begin.

'They didn't. It was a freak accident.'

We had already been subjected to untold accounts of how Hansi had given mouth to mouth resuscitation to his beloved cats. When the cats' eyelashes quivered he stuffed them into the pockets of his jacket with their heads hanging out and ran to Henriette's café. He didn't have to inflict the kiss of life on Carnation or Schopenhauer. The night air brought them around. Marcel, the owner of Hansi's local, almost refused to let him in. He'd only thrown him out ten minutes earlier. But his wife Henriette didn't like the look of all the animals dangling out of Hansi's pockets. She had a feeling he'd finally flipped his lid and she'd have enough proof for the RSPCA to separate him from his 'family' and get him off that field. Marcel regretted opening the door. He had to spend the next hour convincing Hansi that the animals were in fine fettle. All six cats were gobbling up plates of minced chicken provided by Henriette. The dogs were chewing on bones bigger than Hansi's thighs.

'They could have died,' Hansi would begin.

'They didn't,' Diana would remind him. 'So stop grossing us out with how you gave those beasts the kiss of life.'

November also brought bitterness to Paul. His vision of wandering the world writing what he wanted and spending gigantic sums on expenses ground to a halt with the letter which stated: 'We cannot encourage you to submit your work. Please do not send us any more. We will not use them. We wish you luck in placing your work elsewhere.' If the Philly Enquirer had suggested that he go to Antartica and have himself immured in an igloo for the rest of his days, he could not have been more distraught.

'It's too typical! First they boost you, buy an article. Then wham! Cut your heart out and go shove your brains out your ears!'

Nobody wanted to listen to my problems.

'Monsieur keeps asking me out for lunch with him. What am I going to do?'

'He's an old pervert trying to squeeze fresh flesh. Tell him to go fuck himself,' said Paul who didn't pause to think that if I did indeed tell Monsieur to take a flying fuck then Paul would have to seek shelter elsewhere under the rainy Parisian skies.

'Maybe I should put a muzzle on Carnation,' was all Hansi said.

They got on my nerves. They didn't want to listen to my fears that I'd end up worse than Antoine, playing a moronic part in a porno art film. Of course I could have taken Michel the sculptor up on his offer. This time I wouldn't have to pay to model for him. He had discovered the mother lode of rusty bike frames in his favourite dump and told me they were ideal for his broken women series. I told him to 'eff off. In French this is: 'va te faire foutre'.

THIRTY-SIX

One night towards the end of November it was worse then usual. Paul received four rejections that day and wanted to dump all the editors into a radio active waste bin and jettison them in the middle of the ocean.

'I've spent five francs on this citron pressé,' I told Paul. 'I want to enjoy it. I'm sick of listening to your literary gripes.'

'Hey, all you do is bellyache and moan about that wimp and weep ...'

'I do *NOT* weep,' I protested

'Sure you do.'

'I do not weep.'

'Everyone weeps. My Granddad weeps. Anyone with a heart weeps! When we were growing up my brothers were the biggest bawlers ever.'

We were then distracted from our discussion (if you yell and holler in France you are always having a discussion). Four *very elegant* French people squeezed into the table next to ours. They all had that Parisian trademark look - snooty, smart, chic women with earrings the size of chandeliers and men who looked better than models in glossy magazines. Elegance in the brown on brown café was as rare as true love in Paris. Paul immediately flashed his Crest nourished gnashers at the two women who did an agitated old hen feather flutter with their eyelashes. Then they clawed the air like out of work ballerinas who've spent a lifetime perfecting hand movements they have no use for - except when they see guys like Paul goggling at them.

Men are weird. One minute Paul is mentally maiming the American publishing world, next he's ogling French women and then he's back to demanding my attention.

'I've got a fabulous idea for an article,' said Paul and tapped the hand I had clasped around my citron pressé.

'They said they couldn't encourage you to submit,' I wearily reminded him.

'I'm going to write an article about shit mashers.'

I let go of my citron pressé and flopped back against the wall. Shit mashers, for people who haven't lived with French plumbing, are devices you install in renovated medieval apartments (most of Paris!) when you want your toilet inside the apartment and not outside in the common corridor like in Diana's and my own set up. You can dispense with this shit masher if you can afford to gut the entire building and replace all the tiny pipes with bigger ones.

'Why the shit mashers?' I asked him feeling weak at the thought of having to listen to him rave his way through several drafts.

'It's something Parisians talk about. It could be part of my series: 'What They Talk about When They Talk in Paris.'

I reached out for my citron pressé. But it was already half way to Paul's mouth. He took a gigantic swig. Then he leaned forward and spoke in a whisper.

'Listen to the next table,' he ordered.

The elegant foursome were sipping their Kir Royales (that's the expensive variety of blackcurrant liquor and champers) and discussing the price of shit mashers.

'My uncle knows a man who sells them wholesale,' said the guy nearest to me. 'We got ours from him.'

'It's noisy of course,' said his wife and delicately sipped her apéro. 'But we've never had any problems.'

Paul had finished my citron pressé before I could grab it back.

'A lot of people don't know you might need a shit masher if you want to bring the new john inside old Paris,' Paul exulted.

'Most people don't know what happens down in the sewers,' I said nastily. 'They certainly don't want to read about them over brunch on a Sunday morning.'

'I'll start off my article with a snappy history of Paris, then segue into the architecture and explain why they need the shit mashers plus a paragraph on the guy who invented them.'

'Maybe it was a woman.'

'Maybe,' said Paul. He never argued when he knew he was treading on dangerous ground.

'They probably had a most interesting life,' he said.

'A very deprived life, from the sounds of it,' I said.

'And I dare those jerks to reject my article. I can earn 150 bucks first time around. Then I'll slant it in a few different ways and sell it for 100 to the less important papers. OK, so it's not what I want to write. Maybe I should give myself a pseudonym.'

I ordered another citron pressé. I told him he'd have to pay for mine. We argued a bit. He relented because he was going to be earning so much money from his article. On the strength of all his future earnings he changed his own order to a red wine. This did not augur well. Mingle a glass of red wine and a deluded writer and you're guaranteed to be deluged with outlines of future epics. He gave me a synopsis of the film script he'd do on the life of the shit masher inventor. I let him waffle on while

I pondered why a Frenchwoman could wrap herself in half a roll of wallpaper and still look soignée and chic.

'Maybe I could write a series on all the strangest French inventions.'

The elegant 'le tout Paree' people had long since left. They had real homes to go to with installed Shit Mashers and they'd have real evening meals. It was only the likes of aspiring actresses, poor writers and mad artists who hung around café tables during the dinner hour because they couldn't afford dinner.

'What am I going to do about Monsieur?' I asked Paul. Since he seemed to be percolating over with bright ideas he might as well do something useful for me.

'Ask him to take you to Bofinger. Order the entire menu,' Paul said with a wicked smile. 'Then ask them for a few doggy bags to take home with you. That'll shake up the old pervert. Bofinger!'

Paul hooted with hilarity when he said 'Bofinger'. This restaurant he told me was classified as an authentic piece of Parisian history and under a conservation order. Zola and Victor Hugo used to dine there. These days it was frequented by the likes of President Mitterrand and Mayor Chirac and very popular with business people on fat expenses who didn't know what doggy bags were.

'Thank you for your brilliant input,' I snapped.

With that Paul opened his note book and began scribbling. He didn't stop until Diana and Hansi arrived almost at the same time. Hansi finished Paul's wine and Paul ordered another.

'What's he writing this time?' Diana wanted to know.

'Parisian plumbing,' I told her.

'People don't know you sometimes have to install a shit masher for your john in Paris,' said Paul, his eyes all alight and sparkling.

'Some of us do not want to discuss Parisian

plumbing,' said Diana whose main topic of conversation was exactly that.

'What d'you think?' Paul asked Hansi.

'Since when am I a plumber?' grunted Hansi.

Diana settled in to read her magazine about the kind of people we are never going to meet in Paris. The kind who give soirées with 35 sorts of cheeses instead of your usual Brie and Bleue. Diana loves to read about people who give so many parties they keep files on what they served and who sat next to whom. She thinks this is real life and that we are all orbiting in the unreal zone.

She finished the article on Christmas gift tips for people who had everything. This year a few Peruvian Llamas or a flock of camels were considered the perfect gift to jazz up the front lawn of your French country retreat.

'So what are we all going to do for Christmas?' she asked.

THIRTY-SEVEN

'I said, what are we all doing for Christmas?'

Paul shrugged. Christmas was not very high on his list of priorities. I myself had imagined Christmas in a black and white apartment with my French boyfriend and a tree all frosted in silver with exquisitely tasteful gifts dangling from it. Now it looked as if I'd be in the Home for the Aged with Granddad and Belinda since you are constrained to spend Christmas with your family.

'D'you have any extra space?' asked Hansi.

'I beg your pardon.' said Diana, trying to make the connection between Christmas and extra space.

'I must move some paintings,' said Hansi and leaned across the table, almost in a threatening manner, just like a gangster in a movie referring to a dodgy shipment.

'Just sell a few,' ordered Diana. '*Gawd,* you're not going to keep on painting like some nut case until the day you drop dead and have more paintings than the Louvre.'

'Aw shit!' sighed Paul and erased a sentence he had been composing. This particular 'shit' did not refer to the mashing machines he was writing about, but rather to the fact that Diana always rubbed Hansi the wrong way.

'What's the big deal? Just sell a few.'

I suddenly began to doubt Diana's gift of perception. With her dazzling rapier sharp eyes couldn't she grasp that if Hansi (Son of Kong) ever tried to approach somebody with a few of his paintings they'd gallop away to safety?

'You're probably sitting on a goldmine out there in that caravan of yours,' persisted Diana.

She was worse than usual after reading the articles in the glossy magazines. They convinced her there was an easy way to earn those million. There was surely a handsome millionaire waiting just for her if she only wore the right perfume. Hansi must have been in a very advanced state of November depression because he didn't snarl back at Diana. He just went on gnawing off the paint encrusted hairs on the back of his fingers. This is one of Hansi's more disgusting habits. He sucks and slurps on the painted hairs for a lengthy period. When that doesn't dislodge the paint, he chews off the clumps, spits it back between his thumb and forefinger, rolls it a bit then flicks it up into the air with a snap of his nails. Once, after an unusually exuberant flick the clump landed in the glass of red wine two tables away. The man examined the coloured ball in his drink, then gazed up at the ceiling wondering if part of the décor had plopped down into his drink. Then he called Henri over and they examined the bottle of wine against the light. The couple insisted on a new bottle without any 'bête' in it. Bête is the French for 'insect'.

'Give me one good reason why you can't sell those paintings,' said Diana.

That's another thing about Americans. They can never leave well alone. Paul says it's because they have been indoctrinated since birth never to take 'No' as an option. Anyone can become President. Therefore there is no reason why you can't get a rational answer out of Hansi.

'I wonder where I could get a picture of one of those

shit mashers,' said Paul and tried to change the subject. 'It would make things so much clearer if you could see the device itself.'

'Can your toilet crap. OK?' snapped Diana, annoyed at being interrupted. 'And write something sexy for a change instead of your usual loser shit.'

Hansi grunted. Or maybe he was trying to dislodge a hairball. Nobody ever took any notice of Hansi's grunts any more. They were part of the scenery like the noises of a mangy old dog who only wakes up to scratch himself before nodding off again. Hansi resumed his beaver and woodchuck activities. I thought of all the elegant seafood I'd have when Monsieur took me to lunch. I was mentally sprinkling a little lemon on a sea urchin when Diana waved her magazine in Paul's face.

'This is what people want to read,' she informed him.

This was too much for our resident literary master. He snapped his notebook shut.

'Diana, you're such a cauldron of helpful suggestions. Why don't *YOU* sell Hansi's paintings? Then when you're a Parisian art sensation I'll write a sexy article about you.'

Paul smiled all the way back to his molars. He spoke sweetly but there was a healthy trace of non-American disdain which Paul had picked up as a result of living under the impoverished Paris rooftops.

'OK. Fine,' said Hansi as if the deal with Diana was already cut and dried.

'I'll even draw you a map on how to get to Hansi's residence,' said Paul. Before Diana could blink he ripped out a page from his notebook, scribbled down directions to Hansi's caravan and handed it to her.

'*WOAH!* Hold on here,' said Diana.

'Not going to put your money where your mouth is?' mocked Paul. 'Doers do. Wafflers waffle.'

Diana looked at him as if she wanted to dice his nuts with her dagger. Then she regained her poise.

'I'm not doing this for less than 20% commission,' she said.

Hansi shrugged and flicked a multi-coloured hairball into the air.

'I'll sell those paintings by Christmas,' said Diana. 'When you want something badly enough you always get it.'

On the strength of ending up as a celebrity art dealer exactly like the people in her glossy magazines she ordered a carafe of red and paid for it - an unprecedented gesture from tight-fisted Diana. She was perkier than a Pekinese outlining how she would go to the American Embassy, the American School, the American Church and organize art exhibits just in time for the prime Christmas buying period. She would go back to 'our friend' the owner of the Café des Impressionistes who had very thoughtfully permanently barred Jean-Claude from his premises. Hansi topped up his glass of wine and moved to a table far away from Diana's waffle.

'You have to be hungry to get anywhere in the arts,' she then informed Paul. 'You're obviously not. Otherwise you'd get up in the morning, look at yourself in the mirror and say: Today I'm going to force that publisher to take my work. I'm going to sell, sell, sell.'

Paul poured himself a large glass of red and joined Hansi at the distant table.

'Look at those two losers!' said Diana, contemptuously sniffing in their direction. Hansi was yet again bumming cigarettes off the poor demented waiter who had already told him he'd kill his own mother before he'd give Hansi another cigarette. But Hansi nettled him to such an extent that the waiter flung a full packet at him.

'Maybe I'll open my own gallery and exhibit all of Hansi's works.' she said.

I had to have a second glass of red myself when I had this vision of *all* of Hansi's works hanging in the same space. It would be a terrifying experience. Viewers would come down with the bends and vertigo all at the same time - a condition hitherto unheard of in art viewing.

'I'll come by your caravan at 3 tomorrow,' Diana shouted over to Hansi. 'Have those paintings properly strung together. Time is money.'

She got up to go.

'Hey, you wanna come along?'

No thank you. I did not fancy a trip to the Outer Weird Limits to add that 'je ne sais quoi' to my life. The following day I could already look forward to hours of verbal combat with Antoine, then dinner with Granddad and Belinda, mainly to check up on them and write a report to my Mam telling her that things couldn't be rosier in Paris, France. Claude and Maude were busy at school practicing their Two Musketeers scene for the school play so at least I didn't have to put on a brave face with them for two hours.

Diana left me with the half empty carafe. Paul and Hansi returned to the table. I wasn't surprised. Nellie plus a few glasses of red was downright irresistible.

THIRTY-EIGHT

When I arrived the next day for our lessons, Antione was in a very stressé frame of mind. Next to 'Con' (dickhead) and merde (shit) stressé ranks third in the frequency of words used by Parisians. Antoine's reason that day for being stressé was the letter he received from the Film Company. They wanted to shoot a Christmas scene and take advantage of the gaudy decorations strung up all over London. They reminded Antoine in case we could forget that the 'film' was an indictment of commercialism.

Here is an exact breakdown of the little scene that was shoving Antoine into an early grave. *Antoine's character stands outside a world renowned London store and looks 'frightfully' (their word) dejected and sad. Shoppers walk by and ignore him. Santa takes a break from ringing his bell and driving everyone crazy. Antoine moves into his spot and opens his suitcase of lingerie with the bits missing. He is a very pathetic creature standing there. (An explanatory note again pointed out that this would symbolize the crassness of a British Christmas). Nobody takes any notice of Antoine's character as they all dash headlong into the fancy store. It's raining. Santa returns from his lunch. He sees Antoine in his spot, goes berserk and whacks him with his bell. Antoine drops the frillies and runs off shouting 'Au Secours!' (that's French for 'help'). Santa takes off his beard and his face dissolves and changes into that of Margaret Thatcher's.* End of new scene.

It was abundantly clear that Antoine would not have to declaim excerpts from 'King Lear' or even squeak out as much as a single f*** in English in this new scene. But he was so stressé he insisted we'd have to leave the present tense and zoom forward to the future tense. Because of the urgency involved, Camilla had already introduced him to her version of the future tense. Yes, the same Camilla who 'perfected' her English picking up stray balls during Wimbledon month. She got the job because she was an outstanding French student - of gymnastics I might add and not linguistic ability. Camilla benefited fully from her stay in England. After she had watched thousands of yellow balls sailing through the air she extended her stay to 'perfect' (gimme a mega break!) her English. Camilla would have to spend a century in England to perfect her English. But try and tell that to Antoine. And try telling Camilla that 'to improve' is the correct translation for the French verb 'perfectionner' and not 'to perfect'

The night before Antoine had received the full benefit of Camilla's teaching. For the future tense in English all he had to do was add 'shall' to a verb – I shall, you shall, he shall, we shall, etc. I listened patiently as Antoine lectured moi, Nellie Flanagan, mistress of the English tongue, sublime Shakespearean actress on how to 'perfect' my future tense in English. I smiled back at him. I could hardly sit there, rip the teeth out of my head one by one and pepper him with them.

'Let's continue, shall we?' I said to Antoine and opened the manual to the Teacher's Guide.

'Aieee shell,' said Antoine. With my eyes closed he could have been a one year old on the beach complaining about having sat on a sharp shell.

The Teacher's Manual advised that 'At first the students *may not* seem to understand the subtleties of the many forms of the future tense'. That phrase made me downright hysterical. Obviously the writers of that Manual had yet to encounter an Antoine. There would be no *seeming* about it. I gave it a whirl. The Manual suggested starting with the simple phrase 'I am going to the theatre tonight'. Simple? For Antoine 'I am going to the theatre tonight' was about as simple as expecting an afghan puppy to get up every morning, whip out a pair of scissors and clip those annoying hairs that always drooped into her eyes. But Antoine gave his all to 'I am going to the theatre tonight'. Two hours later he was still saying:

'*Aiee GAWING tutu tutu* (once is never enough in Antoine's book) *zeehhahaursur* (A hyena would have made a better hand of 'theatre') zits … zits … zits (by now Antoine is visibly fatigued from all that effort and has to take a giant breath) …EVENNIGHT.'

I smile. I think I am going to be the only 18 year old in France with wrinkles three inches deep from smiling at Antoine while I am suppressing this urge to have a gigantic fit, tear out all the pages of the Teachers Manual, go totally berserk and shriek at the top of my voice that it is not ZITS .. ZITS … ZITS … but THIS .. THIS … THIS.

'Brick?'

I smile. I don't have the energy to correct him and say 'break'.

He rattles around in the kitchen. I sit there and think that a few more weeks with Antoine and I'll be mad, raving, babbling away to myself like those oddballs you see in doorways clutching their bottles of booze and rambling on about 'gawing', 'zits' and 'tutus'.

'Voodoo lickey snick?'

He was back proffering a little plate of 'snicks'. I could forgive him the 'voodoo'. At least Antoine had remembered that you could use the word 'would' when asking a question. It was a milestone for Antoine. I had already reminded him approximately 25,000 times that 'like' was *NOT* pronounced 'lickey' so 25,001 times wasn't going to make a darn bit of difference.

I ate my 'snick' and wondered how in God's name I could contact the Australian woman who taught the chimpanzee 250 words.

THIRTY-NINE

Later when I got off at Lamarck Caulaincourt, night had fallen over the city and the black trees outside the picturesque métro station looked so sad in the twilight. They reminded me of that great line in one of my favourite sonnets 'Bare ruin'd choirs where late the sweet birds sang'. In front of the pastry shop three girls in their school uniform jabbed the window with their fingers and pointed to the cakes they'd like to buy. They had long, laughing debates about which ones they really, really felt like eating. They chose about ten each, then satiated in their imagination, they skipped up the steps to Montmartre. I felt older than Granddad looking at those kids. They could stand in front of a pastry shop, gobble it all up in their imagination and then hop home like happy sparrows. It seemed like only yesterday I used to do the same myself. I went into the shop and bought three of the most luscious-looking pastries. They put them in a real fancy box, and tied it up with a huge golden ribbon.

There were choruses of 'Oh, darling girl!' and 'this is too expensive' when I handed over the box of pastries. Homey smells of sizzling roast pork and rosemary and fragrant French bread wafted around the gloriously spacious apartment Granddad and Belinda had lucked out with. I sank into the nearest sofa.

'You're not burning the candle from both ends now,

are you?' asked Granddad and winked. They always assumed I never told them about the all-night parties I attended seven times a week.

'I'm jaded,' I told them.

'Sit. Rest. You're the guest,' they ordered.

I stretched out on the sofa in front of the TV. But I couldn't keep my eyes open even though there was the funniest cartoon on about a dog trying to ice skate. In the kitchen Granddad whistled and made clackety clink noises with the kitchen implements. He dropped the volume of the whistle when he came into the living room and saw me lying there with my eyes closed. Then he let out a gigantic fart and went back to whistling loudly. I nodded off and dreamt that Jean-Claude and I were waltzing together in a musical version of the Bible. Then I dreamt I was back home, feeling safe and protected on our worn-out sofa. In my dream I could hear the seagulls shrieking as they took mouthfuls out of a bright sky. But it was only the sound of Belinda putting the cutlery on the table.

'Oh, let the girl sleep. She's so young and still growing.' I was still growing at almost 6 feet? There will always be somebody to dent even those moments when you take a pause from the rat race of reality.

Granddad had gone all exotic and we had snails for starters. You could buy them prepared in the local supermarket. All he had to do was pop them into the oven.

'They're in season now, it seems,' said Granddad as he placed a sizzling platter of 5 dozen snails on the table.

I was too tired and too busy mopping up the garlic juice to ask how snails could be in and out of season. I ate 27 snails which is almost a record, I'd say, for a young Irish actress. Granddad beamed.

We were halfway through the roast pork and potatoes

dauphin when I heard about the chance encounter between Granddad and Madame Martinet three doors down. They met when Madame was taking out her little bag of garbage. Granddad being Irish naturally said 'Bonjour. Comment allez vous, Madame'. It came as a shock to Madame Martinet to be greeted so heartily by such a polite neighbour. She dropped her little bag of garbage. The ground coffee beans, fruit peelings, cheese rinds and several empty wine bottles plopped over Granddad's shoes. Granddad 'leapt' to her assistance and 'darted' back to the apartment to get another garbage bag for her.

'Your Granddad was very impressed with Madame Martinet,' said Belinda between clenched lips.

'Her apartment is so tasteful,' said Granddad. He indulged in a lengthy description of the afternoon she had invited him over for a cocktail to thank him for clearing up her garbage mess. 'She's got two dining room chairs that are early Victorian if they're a day. But the legs are shocking. Riddled with woodworm. I offered to treat her legs – well, the chairs' legs. Of course her own don't need any treatment.'

Belinda kept crushing the guts out of a piece of crispy baguette. Granddad - being a man - didn't notice. Men of all ages never realize that it is always upsetting to listen to rhapsodies about other women.

'She's in the theatre,' said Granddad and nodded significantly. In other words now that we knew somebody in the theatre my career was a sure thing.

'Madame *WAS* in the theatre,' snapped Belinda and her dentures sliced through a mouthful of potatoes dauphin with the verve of a guillotine blade cutting through young neck.

'Yes. Now she's retired from the theatre,' said Granddad.

'She's been retired for an extremely long time,' said Belinda. It was obvious that Belinda was trying to overcome a smouldering dislike for Madame Martinet. Being British Belinda has an extremely slow fuse but three years in Ireland have done wonders for that fuse. She's become quite sparky.

'But the point remains that she could have contacts in the theatre,' said Granddad. 'And we know how vital good contacts are.'

He shuffled off to the kitchen to bring in the pastries and the coffee.

'He went over to have tea with that woman twice,' said Belinda and smashed what was left of her baguette to dust.

'You weren't invited?'

'Of course I was invited. But it was obvious I wasn't that welcome. Besides I do have my painting,' said Belinda. 'And knowing your Granddad he'll do all that work for her for nothing.'

'He likes doing stuff,' I told Belinda in case she had forgotten how Granddad had fixed up her little cottage and turned it into a 'showcase' to quote my Mam.

'I know. Your Granddad is the very best,' said Belinda and there were tears in her eyes. 'I am not a jealous woman. That would never do. But I can't compete with a Frenchwoman at my time of life.'

Granddad came back in with the pastries and the coffee on a tray.

'Belinda and I agreed we'd invite Madame Martinet over so you could meet her. That way she can divulge her contacts,' said Granddad and began to pour out the coffee. 'But she's gone to a spa for a week. I wonder what it's like in a spa?'

'Probably most painful with that woman around,' said Belinda under her breath.

'I must be off,' I told them finishing off my raspberry delight. Go while the going is good is my motto. 'I'm shattered. That Antoine is killing me.'

'But we can't have that,' said Granddad forgetting all about Madame Martinet.

'He isn't improving any?' asked Belinda gently.

'He's thicker than a reinforced concrete bunker,' I told them. They laughed.

'But what about your acting career?' asked Granddad. 'You don't seem to have much time for it.'

'You can say that again. One hour to get to Antoine's. Six hours in the torture chamber. Thank God my kids are busy duelling in that school play. I'm flat out exhausted.'

'We can't have that,' said Granddad. He took a deep breath. 'Now this is just a suggestion, mind. Would you like me do the Antoine lessons until he goes to London?'

'The girls needs the money,' said Belinda.

'Of course the money would go to Nellie,' said Granddad in a scandalized voice. 'I'd just do the lessons until Antoine goes on his England trip. Give the girl a bit of a breather.'

Sometimes in life the proverbial sun does break through. It was an offer I couldn't refuse. We called up Antoine. I didn't beat around the bush. I just said I'd be unavailable and that Granddad would be taking over for the next 10 days. Antoine wasn't a bit put out. He was ecstatic in fact! There is no such thing as loyalty, I thought. But maybe he thought that Granddad would reassure him that there was only one present tense and one future tense in the English language and that he could forget about using those little words 'do' and 'did' when asking questions.

They walked me down to the métro stop and brought

me up to date on the new bistros they'd discovered. They rhapsodized about a wonderful fish place they'd found. Granddad had given me the Chef's secret recipe for salmon terrine with sorrel sauce before I even thought of Jean-Claude who used to tell me that my eyes were greener than sorrel.

I passed the bare black trees near Lamarck Caulincourt. Two birds were singing in the top branches. Not being an ornithologist I couldn't tell if they were singing or complaining about the fact that their wings had given out before they could fly on to sunnier spots like Morocco. But they didn't sound sad. Their whistle was a merry contagious one. I skipped down the steps of the métro. I'd get paid for Antoine's lessons without having to endure the agony. I was about to meet a distinguished woman with fabulous contacts in the theatre. With all the luck that had come Granddad and Belinda's way since their arrival to the City of Light and Romance maybe some of it was finally rubbing off on me.

FORTY

Afterwards as far as Paul (from Hansi's side) and myself (from Diana's) could piece things together, this is what really happened when Diana went to pick up those paintings in Paris South West, West. It took Diana and Joel (the guy who only took daily duelling lessons because he wanted to sleep with her) over three hours to locate Hansi's field. Joel's hopes were high. He thought that once out in the green, Diana would somehow drop her drawers and be his. That's what Diana said later. By the time they found the field Joel was in an advanced state of excitement at having been seated so closely to the object of his desire for such a long period. Diana got the feeling that the guy was trouble and it would take all her dazzling duelling art to keep Joel at bay. Since it was his car and he was driving, she was somewhat at a disadvantage.

When they finally stopped driving around in circles they popped into a café to ask for directions and the owner pointed to the field just across the road from them. Henriette came out of the kitchen and had a good look at Diana and Joel. They both looked washed, tidy and normal. Henriette went back to the kitchen praying they were from the local Government and had come to remove that eyesore of a zoo from the field.

'This is simply unreal,' Joel kept saying as they advanced towards the door of the caravan. 'Unreal.'

The caravan as I have explained before had nothing in common with the luxury kind that the Americans retire to when they spend their twilight years in Florida. Most of those caravans would not have the mini fridge, cooker, sink and most of the interior décor piled high on the roof like Hansi's. The grass around the caravan was about 3 feet high. This lush growth was no doubt due to the copious amounts of organic fertilizer donated by two gigantic dogs and six cats. Diana was livid because the grass was wet and she had not anticipated needing thigh waders for Hansi's part of Paris. But she kept a lid on her anger.

'He's got some fantastic paintings in there,' Diana told Joel for the fiftieth time so she could keep him sweet.

Part of her marketing plan was to have Joel walk into the American Embassy with one of Hansi's paintings and say that it was a gift for the Ambassador from the German Foreign Minister. Since it was a Christmas present they'd have to hang it in a prominent part of the building. Diana's strategy was to follow this up by spreading the rumour that the Americans had bought some of Hansi's paintings. Which nation could always smell an art bargain and herald in a future world art trend? Who had first bought up all the Impressionists while others only scoffed? Answer: the Americans. They were the only ones on the globe who would see 'art' in messes made with the assistance of cats that looked like explosions in a dog food factory.

As they approached the caravan the dogs started growling and the six cats tuned in with wild yowling. Joel again said that he didn't like the sounds of it. Diana reassured him the animals were little angels. They arrived at the door of the caravan and Diana knocked timidly. Joel cowered behind her. The door slid open sideways. Normal caravan doors either open IN or OUT. Hansi's slid sideways thanks to the pulley device he had installed to cope with the constant traffic in and out of the caravan all day long. When the dogs barked to indicate they had to go poo poo al fresco, Hansi just pulled the lever and the door slid back. That way Hansi didn't have to move from his perch in front of the easel. Since claustrophobia was a permanent feature of the cats' lives they were addicted to to-ing and fro-ing, given the choice of frost bite of the tootsies outside or warm claustrophobia inside. The minute they had one they wanted the other. That door got quite a work out.

Unfortunately, neither Diana or Joel were expecting that kind of door. Neither were they ready for the sight of Carnation and Schopenhauer filling the doorway. Diana knew the dogs were on the large size but she hadn't expected them to be the size of ponies. However, what made Diana emit a blood curdling scream was the sight of three large cats dangling from a tiny ledge over the caravan door. Hansi had never mentioned that his cats were the only ones in Europe who could dangle backwards exactly like bats. Diana's screams alerted the three other cats who came flying out over the heads of the giant dogs since their view of the action was obstructed by the dogs' haunches. Hansi had also forgotten to mention that he owned cats that could *FLY*. When that door opened those claustrophobic cats simply flew over whatever obstacle was in their way.

The first three cats did their flying routine over the heads of the two gigantic dogs. The dogs leapt for the flying objects and threw Diana sideways in their forward flight. Joel turned and darted across that field almost as fast as the first three cats. Diana saw three more cats flying over her prostrate body. Then to her amazement the door slid shut again. Out of the corner of her eye she saw Joel take off in his car. But before she could get up and run after him, one of the cats came back and started walking all over Diana's winter coat and refused to budge. Let us remember that these were deprived cats. The one clinging to Diana's coat was poor Jelly Bean who had all her fur shaved off. The thick fur collar of Diana's coat reminded Jelly Bean quite nostalgically of her own lost glory. She clung to that fur with the tenacity of that glue which can hold up to 20 tons with only one tiny drop. Diana with the cat affixed to her neck crawled to the door and knocked. But because of Jelly Bean (who was also the biggest cat Diana had ever seen outside of cartoons) Diana was barely able to scratch the door. It slid open.

Hansi had totally forgotten that Diana was coming to pick up his paintings at three. When the door slid back it gave Hansi quite a turn to see Diana crawling her way into the caravan with Jelly Bean slung around her neck and bosom. By now Jelly Bean was so in love with that fur collar she clung to Diana's neck in a firm embrace. When Hansi finally placed Diana he was quite intrigued and immediately assumed she was there to offer herself to him. Back in Hamburg it happened all the time. Women considered him a challenge. The change in temperature was suddenly too much for Diana. The caravan was stifling hot and there was a debilitating smell of paint. Combined with the heat of the cat pressing on her neck Diana was suddenly overcome with a malaise. She tottered a bit and stretched her hands out in the direction of Hansi to break her fall if she fainted. Hansi advanced towards the pleading woman.

Diana was whimpering. She was about to faint into the Son of Kong's arms. There were days and there were days! First Joel trying to paw her. Then the cat falling in love with her. And now Hansi advancing towards her looking as if he was about to – *GASP! HORROR! UPCHUCK*! - kiss her. Hansi still hadn't remembered their arrangement. He couldn't quite figure out what in Hell Diana was doing there with the cat slung around her neck. Back in Hamburg when he had his successful atelier and had been a stunning looker (his own words) lots of women had come avisiting bearing gifts of food and alcohol. But he was somewhat surprised at Diana doing this since she had never expressed any overt interest in him and was far too involved with the useless trivia of life for Hansi to be interested in her.

Yet, there she was gasping for him with her arms outstretched. So he decided to be brave and take her in his arms. Diana was not Hansi's kind of woman. Mainly because she smelt like a chemical factory. Hansi could distinguish every chemical in her shampoo, hair conditioner, the mousse she used to fluff up her hair, her hairspray and the product she used which was supposed to weld her split ends together. That was just her hair. Then he could distinguish the chemicals in the lotion she used to cleanse her skin, the astringent to keep blackheads at bay, the special eye cream, foundation, lip cream, lip gloss. Diana had more chemicals on her body than all the canvasses that were piled high in the caravan. Hansi decided to overlook his aversion to chemicals because it looked as if Diana was in a bad way for him and she had after all come such a long distance to visit him.

Diana decided to go with the flow and faint into the Son of Kong's hairy armpits. The last thing she expected was to be kissed ever so gently. It also came as a major surprise when Hansi's lips tasted like fresh raspberries. Somehow she had expected them to be most unsavoury. But Hansi drank raspberry tea all day long. His mouth was tastier than any raspberry mousse. Also he had the gentlest touch she had ever felt in her life. Naturally being American, brash, vivacious and a dazzler with the dagger most men thought they had to be tougher than wrestlers when they embraced Diana. They mauled her - her own words. Clawed her - her own words. Squeezed the living daylights out of her to show just how masterful they could be too. More than once she had to belt those men away and remind them that she was a woman, not a punching bag. Hansi on the other hand removed Jelly Bean off her neck with the delicacy of her mother who was convinced insects and baby spiders could be reincarnated relatives. Hansi treated her as if she were some kind of Daddy Long Legs where just the slightest rough touch would lop off the thin legs. That was how gentle Hansi was with Diana. She kissed him back.

KABOOM! KARAMBA!!!

Jelly Bean was once more relegated to the cold and wet outdoors despite her protestations. Hansi pulled the lever and they were alone in the caravan. About half an hour later Marcel in the café was a bit perturbed by the wailing sounds and the clamour coming from the field. Normally when the dogs and cats cried, Hansi let them back in immediately. When he looked out the front window of his café he could see the caravan moving in the breeze but there wasn't any wind that day. He called Henriette to come and see. Henriette told him she hoped the two strangers were pounding the living shit out of Hansi and went back to the kitchen with a satisfied smile on her face. Marcel lit up a Gauloise and pondered whether or not to rescue Hansi. He dropped the cigarette when he saw the caravan door slide back and a naked Hansi and a naked woman came prancing out into the field. They frolicked and rolled around in the grass.

Marcel watched as the dogs and the cats stampeded over one another to get back into the warm caravan. One of the animals must have triggered the lever because Marcel watched as the door slid shut locking the animals inside and Hansi and Diana outside without a stitch on them.

Five minutes later Hansi walked into the café with a few bushes strung around his waist and very calmly asked Marcel for a screwdriver to open his caravan door. Later on that night, Diana and Hansi came back for dinner. Henriette hardly recognized the same groomed, washed woman who had been in earlier that day. Diana had patches of green on her face and there were bits of paint in her hair. Diana paid for dinner. Hansi didn't say much. But he spent a lot of time licking Diana's fingers even after they no longer tasted of roast duck. Diana had read about men licking women's fingers adoringly but it had never happened to her until that evening. It was something she had always longed for. She decided to spend a few days with Hansi.

It's as if Diana just changed magazines. Now instead of the glossies she's pouring over the artsy magazines. She couldn't care less if all of New Jersey came to visit her in the caravan. She is living with a genius painter, reading the life of Modigliani and sees herself as the face that will replace all the famous Modigliani women. Hansi has already painted horrendous depictions of Diana and she is convinced one day they'll be lining up around the block in Manhattan to see them. Oh, and by the way, she's in love with Hansi. He's in love with her. They carted off most of the canvasses to Marcel's garage to make room for Diana.

I want to know how such things can happen. As if I didn't have enough to worry about in life! Worrying if I'll ever get to work on stage again; worrying if

Madame will find out about Monsieur's early morning visits and lunch invites; worrying if they'll find out about Paul and the mattress and evict the two of us; worrying about all the horrible things that could happen to old people in Paris. Now I can go to bed worrying that some day I'll flip out and go loony like Diana and fall in love with somebody completely off the wall like Michel the sculptor.

It could only happen in Paris, city of loony love, France.

FORTY-ONE

Granddad very graciously invited my friends to his little soirée where I would meet Madame Martinet and she'd give me all her theatre contacts. I refused on behalf of Hansi and Diana and said that the painter and the 'spritely' girl they'd met at Mahmouds on Closing Night were otherwise engaged. It sounded more elegant than telling them that the two were 'living off the fruits of love in a caravan and banging each other blind'. I'm quoting Paul here who still maintains they've both had a brain snap and any day now the ambulance will cart them off to the nuthouse.

Diana has certainly lost the plot. She bought (tightfisted Diana had truly flipped!) *FOUR* giant kennels. One each for the pony sized dogs and the other two to be shared between the six cats. The two dogs lie in their kennels with their snouts hanging out in the fresh air looking as if they've died and gone to Doggy Paradise. After years being locked up in the caravan they can now enjoy the pleasure of having warm bums and still have their freedom to pursue any action that might manifest itself in the field. If they merely want to stretch their limbs they can do so on the length of clean linoleum in front of their new homes.

The cats also thought they were dreaming gorgeous luxury dreams. Now instead of dangling upside down off caravan hinges inside the cluttered caravan they had endless space with wall to wall super high shag carpet. They didn't even have to go outside to do their business. Diana placed small litter trays inside their homes so that during the harsher months (this could mean that Diana was considering the long-term with Hansi) they wouldn't get their fur wet and get furuncles in their paws from wet grass. The animals were crazily in love with the rescuer who bought them new plush homes. The dogs drooled and the cats purred up a symphony every time they sniffed her. Diana who had never known she wanted to be Mother Earth is feeling quite fulfilled in her new dual role as companion Muse to the Genius Painter and St. Francis of Paris South West, West.

I assured Granddad my good friend Paul would be delighted to grace his soirée. Paul was always up for a free meal even if he wasn't very good company these days because of the mouse who had moved in with him. This was probably the same little mouse who darted out from its hole five minutes after the Mamadous started cooking their pungent Central African delicacies. The mouse packed up and moved to Paul's less flavoursome zones. One little mouse! I reminded him that Hemingway probably had platoons of mice living with him. Maybe he'd even given mice pie a whirl. That was the worst thing to mention. It reminded Paul of 'What They Ate' and his crushed hopes for the bestseller that would never be.

I didn't want to get my expectations up too high with regard to Madame Martinet but things were looking pretty grim on the pounding the pavement front. Fifteen agents recommended to me by Antoine had now rejected the talent packed Nellie Flanagan. So I was sort of hoping that Madame Martinet had a son or a daughter who owned their own theatre and were desperate for a tall Shakespearean actress who could also do a divine Cyrano. I wanted to impress her so I went to a lot of trouble with my appearance that evening. Even Paul noticed my new nice black classic/not overly dowdy dress which would make just the right impression on Madame Martinet. He stopped raving about having his feet gnawed off by sick rats while he slept. He looked most admiringly at my new black dress (10 hours of Antoine lessons) and said: 'Very nice! Who died?'

Antoine had also been invited. They were preparing the soirée food together. That way Antoine would learn very useful English phrases and Granddad could get French recipes. Antoine was bustling around the place like a happy gnat when Paul and I arrived carrying our cheap bottle of red wine. Antoine opened the door with a regal flourish and said:

'*Yuuuuu argh waaa-well* …

He was still struggling to finish his sentence but Paul got there first.

'We're well, thank you,' said Paul at precisely the second Antoine finished his sentence.

'*Vell-konun. I say yuuu arghhh VELL Kom.*'

We were hardly inside the apartment and I could already feel my temples tightening to hear the throaty gargle that was Antoine's interpretation of the English tongue. Granddad was looking very rough around the edges as anyone would after being verbally pummelled by Antoine. For the first time ever in his life Granddad used the word stressé when Paul asked him how things were going for him in Paris.

Belinda looked totally different. At first I couldn't quite make out why. Until I realized that Belinda was wearing more make-up than half of Hollywood. Most times Belinda was a woman you didn't really notice. She was a bit like a fireplace you'd only notice if the room was very cold and the fire was out. Tonight she'd have won first prize in 'the world's worst make-up' competition.

Madame Martinet was late so we started on the avocado dip without her.

'Madame Martinet gave me the recipe,' said Granddad.

'It looks like her too,' volunteered Belinda. 'Green slime.'

'Wot iz .. schleeem?' asked Antoine pulling out his new acquisition, the notebook where he jotted down all his new useful words.

'Oh, that's one you must learn,' said Belinda reaching out for Antoine's notebook with a verve that was most unlike her.

The doorbell rang and Granddad said: 'I'd better go open.'

'Unless she's going to ooze her way in through the keyhole,' said Belinda.

'Oooooo-zzzzzz,' said Antoine and struggled to understand.

'As in Booze,' Paul said to me under his breath. 'You could have mentioned the marital conflict, you know.'

Madame Martinet came as a bit of a shock. She looked as if she'd been pickled in preserving juices for several decades. She was scrawnier than Jane Fonda and had that sinewy look of ancient ropey African trees. Her teeth were the exact shade as our mahogany table back home. You could only understand a tenth of what she said because of her smoker's wheezing voice. She wore false eyelashes and her perfume preceded her the way you can smell the airline fumes long before you can see the planes at the airport. She immediately honed in on Belinda. She *LOVED* her dress, she said. She even had cushions in the same fabric. She grasped Belinda's hands with the sincerity of a drowning person clutching a life buoy and when she let go of them, Belinda tottered back into the chair like a floppy dog. Everyone tittered which of course was the wrong thing to do.

The first course was mussels in white wine and crème fraîche (that's French for 'sour' and not 'fresh' cream - try figure). Every time he tasted a mussel Antoine said:

'Zits ees a muskel'

When Granddad ladled out a second helping Madame Martinet did a wild flutter with her hands like somebody playing an invisible violin. Belinda looked as if she wanted to shove the ladle and all the shells down Madame Martinet's gullet.

'I don't know if I should,' wheezed Madame Martinet.

'Oh go on. Have some more,' said Belinda rushing her words together so only the Real English speakers could cop on. 'With any luck you'll catch hepatitis B.'

Granddad's eyelashes fluttered up and down in total astonishment. Granddad being a man couldn't for the life of him understand why Belinda wasn't her usual sweet, sugary and boring self to the old buzzard who was pawing Granddad. Being Granddad he probably thought Belinda would be thrilled to see that a sophisticated French woman liked him. Granddad stopped offering around the mussels. Antoine took up where he left off.

'Voodoo lickey more muslekes?' he asked Paul.

Paul hadn't a clue what he wanted. Antoine decided to attack the question from another angle.

'Zoo lickey muslekes?'

Even with the ladle poised over his plate Paul couldn't decipher Antoine's simple question 'Would you like more mussels?' This was most upsetting to

Antoine because he was now getting paranoid about his pronunciation. It was even more upsetting to Paul because the mention of 'zoo' reminded him of the fleets of offspring that one little mouse could have if there happened to be a mate lurking nearby.

'Madame Martinet, we're wondering if you have any tips for Nellie,' said Granddad. 'Given your own vast experience in the theatre.'

'I hated those Germans,' said Madame Martinet dramatically reaching for the wine bottle and pouring herself a huge glass of wine. 'Rotten Germans.'

'What Germans?' asked Paul.

'The Nazis! They made me perform for them,' said Madame Martinet with true tears. 'Mamman was very sick and Papa was dead. The Nazis threatened her and my sisters. We had no food, nothing. After the war they said I was a collaborator. The Nazis ruined my life.'

'Isn't that tragic?' said Granddad and patted her hand. Madame Martinet hopped on it and clasped it to her chest.

'You'd believe anything that old bag told you,' said Belinda, and reached for the wine and filled up her wine glass.

'Bag? Beg?' repeated Antoine, vainly trying to catch a word he could relate to.

'I think our ragout de lapin is ready,' said Granddad. He left the table and gave a hurt look in Belinda's direction.

'I'll help,' said Madame in her special blend of wheeze/cough croak. She was more than well on the road to inebriation. Being rake thin it didn't take much to get her going. We could hear her wheezing away in the kitchen and laughing like a horse with a bad case of bronchitis. Belinda sat at the table snorting through her nostrils like an asthmatic bulldog.

'We don't eat rabbit much in the United States,' said Paul trying to salvage this disastrous meal.

'Ze Emarrrraghikans only it sheeeet,' said Antoine.

From the way he twirled his wine glass you could see Antoine was in seventh heaven and loving his evening with the English speaking community. Paul smiled over at Antoine until he pieced together what he had just said: 'The Americans only eat shit'. Now this was something Paul himself had said on many, many occasions but he was deeply insulted to hear a foreigner malign His Homeland's cuisine. The cordiality plummeted on that side too.

I sat there thinking that to my knowledge the Nazis had invaded France about half a century earlier. That was one of the reasons Paris hadn't been bombed to the ground and why those old buildings still had maids' rooms with communal loos in the corridor which Diana would no doubt fondly remember after a few weeks out in the caravan. But if the Nazis had ruined Madame Martinet's career 50 years earlier what were the chances of any red hot tips from her? Granddad came back with the rabbit stew and Madame Martinet managed to put the platter of veggies safely down on the table despite swaying like a dingy in a hurricane.

'But you're still active in the theatre aren't you?' I asked.

'I severed my connections in 1945. It broke my heart,' she said and attacked the red wine again.

'You never worked in the theatre after that?' I said. It was so long ago it was like the Middle Ages.

'The French are a cruel people,' said Madame. 'Explain to them how it was Antoine during the war. How they hounded all of us in the theatre. How they called us collaborators.'

'Antoine was born after the war, weren't you?' asked Granddad.

'I was an actress. I acted. They destroyed my life. I hate Germans. Horrible, ugly Germans.'

'Voodoo lickey rib it?' asked Antoine completely ignoring Madame's histrionics.

He ladled rabbit ragout onto my plate. Then he went around the table intoning his '*voodoo lickey rib it?*' Since it was the only thing on offer everyone immediately said yes. He beamed. At least there was one happy person at this sorry soirée.

Madame decided to forget the war years and attack the rabbit instead of the Germans. Belinda pushed the bits around her plate. Granddad said it was just like chicken which upset Antoine and that changed the direction of the conversation for a while. Paul said it was disgusting what the French could eat, paying Antoine back for his earlier insult to The Land of Lands. Paul wanted to know how the French could eat those tiny little birds you saw in the market, birds so small they could fit into the palm of your hand.

A bit of rabbit fell onto my new black dress. But what did it matter? My heart was heavy. Another road blocked. There would be no magical contacts from Madame Martinet. Maybe I should give serious thought to changing my name to Redgrave or maybe I could claim to be related to Olivier. Maybe I should give up?

Non, non, non!

FORTY-TWO

Another giant glass of red and Madame Martinet was swinging from the rafters. She moved closer to Granddad and fluttered her false eyelashes at him.

'What is your recipe for rabbit, Jimmie Joe?' she asked Granddad.

She pronounced it the French way - 'Shimmey Show'. Belinda gazed at her and you could see she was repressing the urge to pelt her senseless with the rabbit bones. But the old British sang froid conquered. Belinda got up from the table and said she'd get the dessert. I put the plates on a tray and followed her into the kitchen. Here she went straight for the drinks cabinet and poured herself a very healthy glass of Crème de Menthe.

'I'm going to kill that bitch,' said Belinda. 'Then I'm going to kill him.'

Paul came into the kitchen with the empty serving dish. He put it into the sink before turning his attention to Belinda.

'Why don't you tell us what the matter is, Belinda?' he said acting like a doctor in one of those old TV series.

Belinda burst into tears. For the first time in my life I saw somebody 'burst' into tears. (Afterwards Paul agreed with me on that). One minute her face was dry as a rock in the desert. The next it was wetter than an Irish morning.

'He doesn't love me anymore.'

The snot flowed from her nose. I got a length of paper towel and handed it to her. She buried her entire face in it as if suddenly ashamed of the way she was behaving.

'It's good to get in touch with your feelings,' said Paul. 'Feelings are very healthy. The closer you get to them, the better.'

'You couldn't possibly be jealous of Granddad talking to Madame Martinet,' I told Belinda.

Paul frowned at me like a renowned psychiatrist being interrupted by a heretic during a therapy session.

'Are you jealous of Madame Martinet? Tell us,' said Paul in his best counselling voice.

'He goes over there for tea all the time. He's mending her legs,' said Belinda.

'But you don't mind them having tea now, do you?' asked Paul in an oozy voice that wasn't a bit like his own. Paul would never have made it as a therapist. Couldn't he see that Belinda was going ballistic at the idea of Granddad and Madame Martinet having afternoon tea?

'I most certainly do mind,' said Belinda.

'Well, yes,' said Paul somewhat taken aback by Belinda's snappy vehemence.

'But he tells you about it, doesn't he?'

'How else would I know?' snapped Belinda.

'Belinda, please, there's nothing that Madame Martinet has that you don't have,' I said. It was a very complimentary way of saying they were both old dodo birds about to kip off their perches at any minute.

'You are an artist Belinda,' said Paul approaching the problem from another angle. 'You are fortunate and can occupy your time. I know. I'm a writer. Artists never feel alone. We have no problem filling up those 24 hours.'

Oh yeah! So why did the guy spend hours in my dog

box every morning bellyaching about how impossible it was to get into the flow or out of the block, find the 'mot juste', kill off a character or invent a new one.

'Poor Madame Martinet is not so fortunate. She's alone at home all day. She does her shopping, discusses the merits of a piece of plaice or cod for half an hour in the market. She buys the paper. Maybe she has an apéro in the bistro in the afternoon.'

'She goes in the evenings too,' snarled Belinda and ripped off another length of paper towel. 'She props that mangy dog of hers on the chair opposite her and the waiters don't say anything. In England she'd have to tie the dog up outside.'

'But that proves it, doesn't it?' asked Paul.

'It proves she doesn't know where to put the dog. If she were living in America she couldn't bring that mongrel into a nice restaurant with her. Could she?'

Paul furrowed his brow trying to remember what the rules were in the US with regard to dogs in restaurants.

'Belinda, she takes the dog because all her friends are gone. They're all dead.'

I broke the news as gently as I could. Surely she must have realized that nobody in their right mind would sit in a café with a dog sitting across the table from them. Unless of course their husband was worse looking than the mutt.

'Now if Mr. Flanagan ever died you'd always be able to keep busy painting,' said Paul repeating the one word that is anathema to the old - 'Die'. 'But Madame Martinet is not a painter or a writer. She was probably going out of her head with loneliness until your Mr. Flanagan came along to chat to her over a strawberry tart during the long, bleak afternoons, reminding her she wasn't dead yet and she could still do some living.'

The way he spoke I suddenly thought that maybe

Paul was lying about his age. He sounded like a much older person.

Then Antoine appeared in the doorway.

'*Aiee bring triffel*,' he announced beaming from ear to ear. Granddad had probably spent 10 minutes teaching him how to pronounce 'trifle'.

'Trifle,' I corrected him automatically.

'Triffel,' he said.

We all left the kitchen. Belinda's eyes didn't look too bad. With half a ton of makeup wiped away she had improved a bit. She gave Granddad a watery smile and he rubbed her hand.

Antoine was most effusive in his description of the trifle.

'*Zits ease triffel*,' he said putting down the large dessert bowl on the table. '*Zits has zello end FRRuitZZZ end spinges end JIM.*'

Even Granddad looked pained at the mention of Jim.

'Jam,' Paul corrected him since neither Granddad or I had the stamina left to do so. 'It's Jam. Jam. Jam.'

'Jim! Jim! Jim!' said Antoine adamantly.

'What did you do after you left the theatre, Madame?' asked Paul politely.

To everyone's utter horror Madame Martinet started sobbing. Madame Martinet's way of crying was totally different to Belinda's. The tears rolled down her face like melting ice. Antoine got up and went over to her and said a lot of French words of endearment. He patted her back as if she were an old relative. All the while he shrugged his shoulders wondering why on earth she was sobbing.

'I hope I didn't say anything to upset you,' said Paul shooting from his American hip.

'Mais non,' she said and removed one of her false eyelashes that had come adrift. She placed it very carefully next to her plate. Then she peeled off the other one. Minus the false eyelashes she looked worse than anything facing a firing squad.

'I was a hairdresser for 45 years. I should have been a major star. Instead I washed and cut hair all those years. It was cruel.'

'I was a hairdresser too all my life,' said Belinda. 'Isn't that something?'

'Instead of acting I had to deal with cretins coming in with no hair and asking me to give them big bouffant hairdos,' said Madame Martinet and blew her nose quite delicately into a linen handkerchief.

'I hated hair dressing,' said Madame Martinet. 'I was an actress.'

'I hated it too,' said Belinda. 'I wanted to be an artist.'

'I should have gone into dog grooming. At least with dogs you don't have to listen to them and pretend to be interested in their dreary lives,' said Madame Martinet.

'Did you miss the theatre?' asked Paul. Just like a writer.

Not knowing that to leave the theatre is to die.

'It broke my heart,' said Madame Martinet. 'And I was not a collaborator.'

Belinda suddenly got up from the table and walked behind Madame Martinet's chair. She toyed with some of Madame's scant hair. For a split second I thought she was going to yank her hair out or do something wild.

'Madame will need a protein pack on this,' said Belinda still fingering Madame Martinet's hair. 'Our split ends are in an appalling state.'

Paul and I looked at one another. Had old Belinda finally flipped? It was only when Madame Martinet hooted with laughter that we understood. The two were play acting.

'I'd like it really high on top this time,' said Madame Martinet and pulled up her own wispy hairs from the top of her head. 'So I can wear my new tiara at the Opera.'

'I really like this trifle. I think I'll make it for Camilla at Christmas,' said Antoine.

Silence fell on the room. It was a silence that was palpable, the kind of silence that is said to come after a volcano or a tidal wave when there is that pause when everything goes abnormally quiet before life trots on again at its usual pace. Everyone looked at Antoine. Madame Martinet was less shocked that the rest of us. She was smoothing back her hair and looking happy again. Granddad was the first to react.

'What did you just say Antoine?'

'I like this trifle. Would you give me the recipe? I am going to make it for Camilla.'

'He's speaking,' said Paul in amazement. 'Hey, the guy's talking English.'

'Of course I am speaking English,' said Antoine in a miffed tone to Paul.

'As I live and breathe!' was all I could say.

'Shall I make the coffee?' asked Antoine.

'You did it, Nellie,' said Granddad.

'No way, you did it, Granddad,' I said.

'No. You both did it,' said Belinda. She gave Granddad a kiss on the cheek. She had obviously shared a few torture sessions with Granddad.

'Oh, it's just like My Fair Lady,' said Belinda.

'Heck, it's better,' said Paul.

'Halleluia!' I said.

Antoine still hadn't quite grasped that he was the cause of all this display of affection. Granddad and Belinda hugged and kissed.

'Ah love is grand. No doubt about it. Love is grand,' said Antoine with the thickest Irish accent I'd ever heard.

I didn't want to burst his bubble. Still smarting from the Jean-Claude kick I would have told Antoine that Love was far from Grand.

'You are such nice neighbours,' said Madame Martinet. 'So kind, Belinda.'

'And you're an even nicer neighbour, Paulette,' said Belinda.

As Shakespeare so aptly put it - all's well that ends well.

For accuracy sake he should have added – 'even if it isn't for very long'. I am referring here to Antoine's brief encounter with linguistic clarity and fluency.

FORTY-THREE

Once a month Paul and I did a joint wash in Le Pigalle Wash Shop. Between us we had enough whites and coloureds to do two washes and once around in the dryer. Le Pigalle Wash Shop was nowhere near Pigalle. The 'Wash Shop' was tagged on because it is part of the French tradition to use English words in order to add a bit of class to something that direly needs it. Le Pigalle Wash Shop was managed by a trio of Sicilians who acted like hallucinating bulls every time anyone faintly resembling or masquerading as female passed in front of the window.

I used my time in the Wash Shop to catch up on the fascinating goings-on of the minor royals of Europe, their 'fairytale' weddings and expensive divorces. But Paul was distracting me, jawing on about the one little mouse that had moved in with him instead of getting claustrophobia staying with the Mamadous where there were seven in the one room. One teensy weensy little mouse! The way Paul bleated about it you'd think he'd been parachuted into the jungle.

'Maybe I should do an article on the hidden wildlife of Paris?'

I ignored him. Paul was traversing a rough patch of writer's block. This bout started when he dreamt that Hemingway came to him in a dream and told him that his writing was crap. I told him the interpretation of his dream was as clear as day. Paul had spent a lot of time concentrating on Parisian shit mashers. It was inevitable that the two things he thought most about in his life, i.e. Hemingway and crap, would appear in his dreams. Naturally he wouldn't listen to my words of wisdom.

He pulled out a letter from his brother and asked me to read it. This was a very bad sign. Paul usually exaggerated on letters from his family. The fact that he gave me the letter meant that he didn't need to exaggerate which is quite traumatic for a writer. The letter said:

'This will be the third Christmas in a row you've missed. Mom doesn't say anything but it's killing her. If you don't have the money you can always ask me. I won't hassle you about it. I'll just add it to the 354 dollars you already owe me.

Becky and I were discussing your attitude and questioning your outlook on life. Paul, this may sound harsh but you are too old to live like a bum and imitate your dead idols. You do have a brain. Just when are you going to use it? Becky and I are having the basement turned into a separate apartment so we can rent it out. The house will have paid for itself in three years. It's always a risk renting out part of your property but the mortgage has to be paid. We are buying a piece of land up North where the prices are bottoming out at the moment. If we buy at the bottom we'll be able to sell with a tidy profit when the market turns around in a few years. We are also going to put a down payment on a place by the shore when we find something reasonably cheap.

Becky and I are on schedule with our lives. In three years time Becky will start having babies. She will be 27. The perfect time to have a family is when you have a paid roof over your head, an investment in a place by the shore and a piece of land maturing. I mention all this, Paul, to let you know that with a little planning you too could lead an orderly life. I too would prefer to fritter my life away in glamorous Paris. But Becky and I will only treat ourselves to Paris when we have saved for the kids' college education.'

Next to me Paul sighed so loudly it drowned out fifteen rickety washing machines all spluttering and vibrating on the premises of the Wash Shop. Paul sagged forward worse than any bag of old laundry. The exuberant Paul with the flashing gnashers who had leapt onto the Ireland-France ferry with the alacrity of a kangaroo exploding with joie de vivre and endless hope was like a picture I'd seen once in a film I could no longer place.

I could hardly concentrate on the article about the Bavarian Princess who went to bed with a tiara glued to her coiffure. One night the tiara clobbered her lover in the eyeball and he sued her for astronomical damages. The Princess spent another fortune in therapy trying to find out the reason behind her tiara in bed fetish. The Bavarian tiara trash took my mind off the fact that 47 theatres had said 'NON' to me for the second time despite my highlighting the fact that I'd played Juliet at Théâtre du Zivot.

'Au Secours! Au Secours!' (That's French for 'Help! Help!').

A desiccated old man was freaking out in front of the washing machines. Foam cascaded from several crevices in the old machine that was supposed to be hermetically sealed. Obviously the old man was a newcomer to the Pigalle Wash Shop. He didn't know that the machines were prone to having all sorts of different attacks.

'Help! Help!'

The Sicilian baboons took no notice even though they were paid to see that the place operated efficiently. The poor old man was so distressed at the sight of the water gushing towards him he could have been one of the stragglers left behind when the Red Sea was going to close in once more after Moses and his followers had reached the other side. Paul moved as fast as any Hemingway obsessed writer can. He bodily lifted the old man away from the flood and deposited him in a safe area in front of the dryers. Then he came back, gave a healthy kick to the front of the machine, smashed his two fists on the top. The machine stopped imitating Niagara Falls.

The old man gazed at his Saviour, flapped his arms a bit more, tried to get up the energy to curse the three Sicilians who were kissing the window and rolling their tongues at a passing tank of a woman. The foam and the bubbles disappeared away through a vent in the floor, which hopefully did not lead into somebody's basement. Paul put his hand over his face.

'Will I ever get to be a writer?' he asked dripping with self-pity.

'Will I ever get to be an actress?' I said joining him in the self-pitying duet.

'Ça brûle! Ça brûle!' (French for 'fire! fire!')

But you could see the old man's heart really wasn't in it. After all it wasn't his wash that was being burnt to a crisp in the dryer that had only 2 heat settings: 'Keep Wet' and 'Set on Fire'. The woman whose wash was being incinerated did a record breaking twenty yard dash to the dryer yelping like a giraffe giving birth while being chased by a herd of wild hyenas.

'There are days I have to remind myself I'm actually living in Paris.' said Paul with a long, long sigh. 'It's so different from what I expected.'

'Stop exaggerating!'

'I'm living on a wandering mattress that I have to pick up in the evening and deliver back every morning. Nobody wants my work.'

Paul was momentarily distracted from his ode to self pity because the little old man was wailing pathetically as he gazed at his wash which had turned varying shades of emerald. Obviously he was not entranced with the surprise new shade which was a permanent feature of the Wash Shop. Paul and I never knew what alluring shade of underwear we'd be wearing until the next wash.

'I share my accommodations with mice.'

'Mouse, singular,' I reminded him.

'They could easily bite me during the night. Those rats could have rabies. I'll wake up one morning and I'll be stark raving mad and for the rest of my life I'll have to listen to my Dad droning about how he told me so. Oh Dad, you were so right. Just why am I doing this to myself?'

At the other end of the Wash Shop the woman now let out a yell which was worse than any giraffe giving multiple birth. She was holding up what had probably once been a serviceable piece of clothing (nightie, I surmised). It would now immediately pass the seconds' test at Tipps since there were strategic pieces missing which the dryer had gobbled up or melted. This woman had yet to accept the capriciousness of the dryers in this place. When you tossed your wash into one of them it was like playing Russian Roulette - Win Some, Lose Some, Say Goodbye to Some Parts.

'Hey lady, hold it down, wouldya?' Paul yelled over to the woman. 'I mean there are people here who are trying to find a logical explanation why anyone with half a marble left would stay in this city. The only reason it exists is to mislead people and drive them mad, mad, *MAD.'*

''Fou' is the French word for mad, insane, crackers, nuts, loony, bonkers. After 'stressé I'd say this was a pretty good contender for fourth place in the French word frequency hit parade. Paul screaming out *FOU FOU FOU FOU* at the top of his voice and freaking out in the Pigalle Wash Shop drew about as much attention as a flea in an animal shelter. The lady volubly mourned the bits missing from her clothes. The wisp of an old man whined about his all new frog coloured wardrobe. Paul marched over to the Sicilians and asked them to explain to him why he was still in Paris. I took the clothes out of our machine. The white wash was still in the white range - a positive miracle. The coloureds were a fascinating shade of plum which was a colour we hadn't had up to then. I dumped the lot into the middle machine. This was the one which either dried your clothes properly or ate your money. The machine started to hum. Wash wise it was my lucky day. The Sicilians *NEVER* reimbursed your money even if they actually saw you putting it in and getting no service at all.

I sat there bored with the minor Royals of Europe and watched the clothes go round and round in fleeting dashes of white and plum. I listened to the Chug Chug Chug of the dryer which could change any minute and decide to burst into flames, or stop entirely. Chug Chug Chug. It was like the sound the train makes when you hear it speak. And the Chug Chug Chug of the dryers were saying 'You'll never be an actress in this city. You'll never be an actress. You'll never be an actress.' Chug! Chug! Chug!

I was suddenly reminded of the evening Jean-Claude and I went to see the film adaptation of *Cyrano de Bergerac*. As we strolled to Chez Jean for dinner I let loose with a sprinkling of my favourite Cyrano bits. We were half-way through our starter - salmon terrine with sorrel sauce for Jean-Claude and scallops in Pernod for me - when he asked:

'Was Cyrano on your school curriculum?'

'No, I just love it. One day I'm going to play Cyrano. I'm going to be simply fabulous.'

He let out a gale of laughter.

'I don't see the joke,' I said frostily.

'You can't be serious. Cyrano's a man's role.'

'So? The plot is about a poetic guy with a big nose falling in love with a pretty woman. A modern version would be about a poetic woman with a big nose falling in love with a pretty guy'

He nearly choked on his frizzy lettuce. In French this is called 'frisé' which also means 'permed' or 'curled'. In the background Aznavour was singing about coming back to Montmartre and finding that all the lilacs of his youth had died. It was the song of a broken heart. I had told Jean-Claude my dearest dream and he had laughed. By the time I had finished the noisette de veau, with the tapestry of autumn vegetables I had come to the conclusion that Jean-Claude was not going to make it to the big time if he didn't have the breadth of vision a Director needed to interpret a play in a multitude of ways. So why hadn't I clocked it that he was a lying, cheating, bastard who was never going to give me all his theatre contacts? Just because he lit candles and wrapped himself around me on the white sofa?

Paul got tired of asking the Three Baboons to explain the meaning of life in Paris to him. They were too busy helping a blond girl sort her intimate wash - a service Paul and I never got. The dryer stopped turning. Paul unloaded all the dry clothes and bunged them into two black plastic bags which he slung over his shoulder. We walked the seven blocks home in silence. Twilight was falling as slowly as gum from a tree. There was a moon climbing up over the distant outline of the Sacré Coeur. A gaggle of kids dashed past us giggling to themselves and munching the flaky pastries that the French adore. Paul looked at them and smiled. I linked my hand fondly into his arm.

'Have you heard anything from Hansi and Diana?'

'No.

'I wonder how they're doing,' I said.

'They're probably doing it as we speak,' said Paul. He hooted at his own smartness. I laughed along. Diana and Hansi - it was too weird for words.

Diana no longer spends much time in her Parisian hole with no phone, no shower and the fridge at the end of the bed. She refers to it now as her 'city residence'. She doesn't care if all of New Jersey knows she's living in a caravan with a zoo. This is Diana's La Bohème. She's in love with a genius painter whose portraits of her will soon be hanging in the Musée D'Orsay.

'Jacques gave me invites to a new jazz café,' Paul said as he watched me make my bed with the freshly washed sheets that smelt of burnt chemicals. I gave them a quick spray with the expensive Eau de Cologne that Madame had given me because it reacted badly with her body chemistry and made her smell unbearably cheap (her very words).

'D'you want to check it out?' said Paul, still standing at the door with the mattress under one arm and his plastic bag of washing slung over his shoulder. If he hadn't looked so daft I'd have sworn he was asking me out for a date.

'Why not?' I said.

Everything was perfumed and fresh in my dog-box. Paul and I were going to a different café which was like converting to Buddhism for Paul. I decided to wear the new black dress I'd bought to impress Madame Martinet.

'You should get decked out more often,' said Paul approvingly as he opened the door for me. There was an unusual sheen to those eyes. I'd suspected it all along. The guy was probably madly in love with me! That's when he said:

'You don't have any rat poison on you, by any chance?'

FORTY-FOUR

Christmas was coming to Paris. The city was gearing up for another round of excessive eating and drinking that would tax livers to breaking point and induce several million crises de foie (that's French for liver Kreezes). The Champs-Élysées glittered as if the Milky Way had fallen on it. When I dropped by CAT to check on the bulletin board, Madame Flore smiled at me for the first time and told me to relax. It was holiday time. All the theatres were booked out, CAT was closing down until the New Year. Everyone was thinking of family. She herself was off to visit her grandchildren in Savoie and hoping for snow so she could go ski-ing. I couldn't believe it. She was almost as old as Granddad and Belinda.

It was mainly in the food departments you could see the difference between Christmas in Dublin and Christmas in Paris. There were so many pheasants in those Paris shops, the forests must have been cleaned out. I saw boars for the first time in my life. In some 'very high quality' butchers the entire boar was hanging from a hook looking like something out of 'Robin Hood'. But most butchers only used the head of a boar as decoration to add that 'Festive' touch. Oyster and seafood stands sprung up where none had been before. Of course Paris is wall to wall restaurants with such seafood stands outside. But during the Christmas period these stands cropped up everywhere and displayed dazzling selections in all things fish.

One evening I was standing in front of the largest display of oysters I had ever seen in my life. There were about 20 different varieties and prices. It was in the fancy part of town and a lot of businessmen were buying the oysters. All that fish reminded me of Jean-Claude and I wondered who he'd be conning and having oysters with under the Christmas tree. Hopefully the tree would topple over on him when he was decorating it. Or maybe the lights would electrocute and fry him to a crisp! Or maybe he'd get gastric poisoning from a bad oyster. Or maybe ....Suddenly somebody grabbed my elbow.

'What a wonderful coincidence!' said Monsieur and beamed at me.

'How are you, Monsieur?' I said. I really didn't feel like breaking into a jig of delight at the sight of him.

'Oysters and champagne are a most felicitous combination,' he said.

'Most felicitous,' I said.

'Let us have some then,' he said.

Before I could say 'nay' or 'yeah' he had chosen 6 of the ugliest and the most expensive and 6 of a less ugly looking variety. Then just as efficiently he guided me into the bistro beyond.

The décor was the kind I'd only seen in the glossy magazines that Diana adored. There were antique lamps and tables all covered with linen as white as Paul's teeth. There were built-in mirrors and paintings from the turn of the century which showed tall, willowy women wafting about with chiffon scarves trailing behind them. In some panels equally tall women were encased from head to toe in thick furs. From this fin-de-siècle place you could easily get the impression that all women had once upon a time been semi-giants.

In my black dress from the Monoprix that I had jazzed up with a long red scarf not unlike the ones the Art Deco ladies were trailing behind them, I thought I was elegance personified, sitting there with my flûte of champagne. I just love that word 'flûte'. It has such a refined twang to it. The open oysters lying on a bed of seaweed looked silver instead of the colour of old spit and brought moonlit seascapes to mind. The only fly in the ointment was Monsieur. I wished I could have been sitting there with somebody my own age or somebody who wouldn't jaw on about missing the boat of life.

'You are very busy these days,' said Monsieur, delicately swallowing an oyster with such ease it could have been ice cream.

'Yes, very busy,' I told him. Very carefully I tried to unglue my oyster from its shell. When I finally succeeded I then squeezed the lemon. Unfortunately some of the juice hit Monsieur's right eye. He mopped his weeping eye and looked peeved.

'You leave so early these mornings, I never get to see you,' said Monsieur, twirling his flûte and sniffing at the expensive bubbles.

'I have to leave early,' I told him.

It was more diplomatic than saying that Paul and I had our knock code.

'How is your acting career progressing?' asked Monsieur. He daintily mopped a mist of oyster juice from the corner of his mouth.

'I'm still looking.'

Our waiter came over and poured out more champagne. He was tall and gorgeous and my heart gave a little flip-flop when he smiled at me in a very special way. He lingered at our table asking Monsieur if there was anything else he could do to serve us, but Monsieur waved him away. He walked back across the restaurant. He was wearing one of those long white aprons. It was a miracle he didn't trip over it. He was taller than me and had lovely brown hair, thick and luscious.

When I tried to pry off the next oyster, Monsieur leaned over and put his hand on mine. It was very kind of him to want to show me how to eat an oyster without spraying all and sundry and making the oyster do the high jump. But with his hand over mine all I could think was - this is where Madame makes her grand entrance. I'll lose my job. Paul and I will end up under the bridges of Paris. My Mam and Dad will remind me that I lost a wonderful job at Tipps and then I went and lost an even lovelier one with that nice family in Paris.

'There! That's it!' said Monsieur and released his grip on my fork. I ate the oyster. It tasted oily, slimy and slithery with a dash of elusiveness, due no doubt to the fact that you have to swallow it so fast you only get a fleeting impression as you knock it back. It reminded me of Granddad's saying that 'you had to eat a lot of gourmet stuff before you could really appreciate it'.

'Madame is having her hair done today,' I said.

'Oh, mon Dieu!' said Monsieur. (That's French for 'Oh, my God!'). He put his flûte down and clucked his tongue in irritation. 'I'm supposed to pick her up at the salon. We are going to the theatre.'

Monsieur rubbed his forehead and looked so stressé he could have been an actor in one of those nuclear holocaust films where he had to find the right button and save the world or push the wrong one and send it down Memory Lane.

'What are you going to see?' I asked excitedly.

'*Cyrano de Bergerac*,' said Monsieur. He gave a long, bored sigh.

'But they're sold out,' I told him. About six weeks earlier I had tried to buy the cheapo tickets but there were none left.

'Why do they keep reviving that old horse?' asked Monsieur. 'Marie-Ange dragged me to see that dreary play a few years back. Why is it necessary to see the same play again?'

'To discover some of the subtleties you missed the other times.'

'I usually miss most of it,' said Monsieur and waved the tall waiter over. 'Theatre puts me to sleep.'

He took a thousand franc note from his wallet and snapped it down on the silver plate the waiter had placed at his elbow. Behind Monsieur's back the tall waiter winked at me in a salacious way. I decided that even if he was the only person taller than myself and Paul in Paris I didn't like him. Right at that moment there were very few men in Paris I did like. Monsieur was going to see *Cyrano* only to fall asleep while the actors poured out their life's blood up on stage. The waiter gave me another wink as he walked away.

'Please have lunch with me next week, Nellie,' said Monsieur.

He arranged the few bills left in his wallet. It was just like the one they showed in the ads for the man who thought he had everything. My Dad would have gone clean ape over a wallet like that. But it wouldn't have suited him. The wallet's elegance would have shown up the lack of sophistication in his fingers, his wash-and-wear shirt with the frayed collar, the V-neck sweater he always wore that had the faint whiff of bacon from the shop.

'Have you been to Bofinger yet?' asked Monsieur.

I had to laugh. Bofinger, the ritzy resto recommended by Paul! Hello! Bonjour Monsieur!!

Bofinger was not the kind of place a 'resting' actress living in a maid's room with a platoon of pigeons would be in a position to pronounce on.

'No, I haven't been to Bofinger yet,' I said.

'Then you must. Won't you have lunch with me there next Monday?' he asked. He checked his watch to see just how late he was running and how furious Madame would be.

'Suits me,' I said.

Monsieur stood up. He wrapped his exclusive Ana Costa Tayassu scarf around his neck and gave it a little caress. Again I thought how entranced my Dad would have been with that burgundy scarf. He'd run his hands over it, put it to his cheek and wonder how many silkworms had gone into making it. Then once or twice a year on a major occasion like a funeral or a trip to Dublin he'd wear the scarf with his best blue coat which had cost a 'fortune' and was supposed to last a lifetime, but had started to fray around the buttonholes after only 15 years of solid service. I suddenly missed my Dad. I wished he could be sitting opposite me and I could be the one showing him how to pry off stubborn oysters. He'd only laugh when the lemon juice hit him in the eyeball and he'd say: 'That young man is admiring you' when the tall waiter looked my way.

'I'm not in any hurry,' I told Monsieur.

It was a more stylish way of saying that I had no intention of letting the tall waiter guzzle the rest of the champagne and gobble the last three expensive oysters.

'Goodbye then, Nellie,' said Monsieur.

He picked up my hand and kissed my palm. His tongue flicked quickly three times, reminding me of somebody ringing a bell with a secret code. Then he patted his gorgeous Ana Costa Tayassu scarf and elegantly weaved his way through the tables.

Two sips out of my flûte later and the tall waiter was back.

'Your Papa has left?' he asked. He cheekily lifted the bottle from the silver bucket to see how much was left. My flûte was already full to the brim.

'Are you referring to my husband?' I asked and gave an imaginary lift to a huge piece of fur around my shoulders just like the women in the paintings. 'Why do you wish to know? Do you perhaps wish to contact Monsieur?'

'Pardonnez moi, Madame!' said the tall waiter, blushed and scuttled across the restaurant.

If he hadn't winked so many times I wouldn't have been so heartless. I put him straight out of my mind and sat there drinking in both the champagne and the atmosphere of a place I would not be visiting too soon again. On my way up to my dog-box I had to sit down twice. The thing about champagne is that once the bubbles wear off you get this very droopy feeling. I was ready to crash on the bed and sleep until the New Year. But Paul's note changed that plan. His note said:

URGENT!! COME TO THE CAFE. THIS COULD CHANGE YOUR LIFE AND GET YOU STAGE WORK.

I didn't feel like going. But I went. It's that pull of the unknown. Maybe Paul had met an American heiress who owned her own theatre and was putting on *'Barefoot in the Park'* and needed a flamboyant leading lady. Luck strikes - *WHAM* - out of nowhere, for no reason. I had trundled down the 127 steps and was half way to the café when I remembered that luck striking out of the blue and changing your life always happened to *other* people.

FORTY-FIVE

In the café Jacques was sitting at the table with Paul, which made me think that Paul had sold another article but that wouldn't mean a darn thing to my life.

'You smell weird. What did you eat?' Paul asked as I sat down opposite him.

'Champagne and oysters.'

'Here have a piece of gum,' he said. 'Maybe you should see the dentist?'

'What's so urgent it couldn't wait until you came for the mattress?' I asked instead of having a discussion about oral hygiene.

'Jacques got a great job for the two of us,' said Paul. 'We'll appear on TV'.

Lady Luck had finally found my address and was putting an end to my Parisian Purgatory. I'd be on TV. I was on my way. Stardom would soon be mine. And rightly so!

'Well yes', said Jacques with far less euphoria and enthusiasm than Paul. But that's only to be expected. When it comes to being pessimistic and expecting things to go wrong the Irish and the French are on the same wavelength.

'When do we start?' I asked, eager to fly to my destiny.

'The day after to-morrow,' said Jacques. 'The two workers who were going to do it got a better offer. So they cancelled at the last minute.'

'Hollywood called them?' I asked merrily.

'No,' said Jacques with a look of total incomprehension. 'They got a better offer from the fish department in the Monoprix.'

As I mentioned earlier the Monoprix is a great little chain of supermarkets in Paris where I got my elegant black dress at a most reasonable price. I hadn't noticed their fish department since I do not cook scallops à l'armagnac in my dog box. Therefore I had difficulty reconciling selling fish in the Monoprix as a better offer than working on TV.

'Jacques' uncle needs two sales people,' Paul explained. 'He owns a charcuterie company that takes part in the Alsace Christmas Food Fair here in Paris.'

'So what would the two of us be doing?' I asked. I still couldn't see how all this fitted in with working on TV.

'We'd be selling his charcuterie,' said Paul patiently.

'Charcuterie?' I repeated so there would be no misunderstanding. 'Charcuterie' is French for 'cold cuts'. The French can make 500 different things from a single pig so they call it 'charcuterie'.

'So we'd be selling these cold cuts on TV, is that it?' I asked.

'No. We'd be selling the stuff in the Gare de l'Est. That's where the Food and Wine Festival is. They come around and film it and you could be on TV that evening. And you could add it to your CV.'

'That I sold pig parts in a railway station in Paris,' I said bitterly. 'You're *CRUEL!*' I was about to storm out the door.

'But the TV teams will be there. They wouldn't dream of missing the Fair,' said Jacques in his most ponderous tones.

I sat down again and thought this over. Jacques is the kind of pedantic Frenchman who would never say that green was green because there are too many different shades of green and he'd like to specify the precise one.

'They always film it for 'Events in Paris'. It's up to you to avail of the opportunity.'

'Events in Paris' is a half-hour programme that goes out every night on Channel 3 before the news. And if Jacques said we'd get to appear on that programme, it was a sure thing.

'He'll pay us 100 francs an hour.' said Paul. 'It'll be a gas.'

'Why are you doing this?' I asked Paul, since he was always adamant that a writer wrote, and didn't do anything stupid like go out there and earn a living.

'I'm thinking of being a food critic,' replied Paul, picking up his glass of very rough red and sniffing it as if he were already the food and wine correspondent for the New York Times. 'I'll interview Jacques' uncle and find out all about French charcuterie. I'll talk with all the food producers at the other stands. Brush up on recipes for my book. And I wouldn't mind being on TV either.'

'I have to call my uncle and tell him if you're taking the job,' said Jacques and tapped his watch and pursed his lips. 'Otherwise he'll have to get two other seasonal workers.'

'You could make lots of contacts,' said Paul.

'In the Gare de l'Est?' I said sarcastically. 'In a railway station? Especially in that railway station.'

'I said I'd call my uncle before 9,' said Jacques with a plaintive whine reminding me of a cat reluctantly joining the kids in the bath.

'It's just gone 8. What's your rush?' asked Paul.

'Look, I was the one who suggested you two to my uncle. If you don't want the work, just say so and I can go on home and continue with my studies.'

'Easy money and lots of free food and wine,' said Paul trying to persuade me.

'It's a 12 hour day,' said Jacques lugubrious as a gravedigger doing overtime.

'Count me in,' said Paul.

'OK. Me too,' I told Jacques.

That way I could also afford to have a new load of glossies made. And when Jacques said that the TV people came around and took shots, you could believe him. Jacques, being French, was constitutionally unable to tinge up on the facts. If Jacques said that a hairy, blue elephant would fly in through the window at 21.14 you could put your house on that happening.

'Maybe, I'll get my hair done,' I told Paul as we waited for Jacques to return from his phone call to his uncle.

'You don't need to,' said Paul looking at my hair critically. 'It's fine.

'Thank you, Paul,' I said, giving my locks a frivolous flip.

'You'll be wearing an Alsatian costume so nobody would see your hair anyhow. Why go to the expense?'

'What Alsatian?' I asked. Going on French TV dressed as some half baked dog wouldn't outshine the BBC on my C.V.

'I'm going to be dressed as a male Alsatian,' said Paul looking delighted at the prospect.

'Why didn't you mention we'd be doing a double dog act?'

'You won't be a dog. You'll be an Alsatian.' said Paul with that insufferable 'tut tut' in his voice.

'I've no intention of going on TV dressed as a dog.'

'You won't be a dog. You'll be an Alsatian,' said Paul.

'An Alsatian is a dog.'

'An Alsatian in France is also somebody from Alsace,' said Paul, slowing down his words in that manner he knows infuriates me. 'They have a traditional costume which we will both be wearing. I'll be dressed as a male Alsatian, i.e. a man from Alsace, and you will be dressed as a female Alsatian, i.e. a female from Alsace.'

It was better than being a dog. But it still wouldn't outclass the BBC on my C.V.

FORTY-SIX

Mr. Uno hadn't even started on his release me from Paris mantra when we tottered from our beds that first morning to go out into the cold grey city to sell pig bits otherwise known as 'charcuterie'.

'Winter kills,' said Paul morosely as he heaved the mattress on top of my bed. Then he stood at the window looking out at the gloomy grey landscape of pigeons' bottoms and Paris rooftops. The clouds were wrapped around Paris like a moth-eaten chinchilla around the spindly legs of a frail old lady. The grey dawn clouds leaked their weariness into all the buildings and into the hearts of every living creature.

'Christ, even the moon is grey and tired,' he said.

He waited for me to comment on his flight of poetry. But I wasn't in a downbeat poetic frame of mind. Because during the night I had come up with a fabulous idea. While they were filming the Alsace delicacies on our stand I would go into full acting mode and ask the people of Paris to open their hearts and give me a job in the theatre. This was Christmas after all, the season for giving. I'd appear on 'Events in Paris'. This was the day I was finally going to be discovered. Fame was only a few short hours away.

'Winter kills,' said Paul once more as we trudged down the 127 steps and did an instinctive dodge past

Madame Favela's lodge even though there wasn't a sign of light or life anywhere.

But the métro station was packed with people all anxious faced at the thought of getting to work a few minutes late. Paul gazed at the surging masses and said to me: 'Jeez, imagine some people do this every single day of their life, for as long as they live.' He spoke like a man who'd had a major revelation. The clodos (that's real French for 'winos/tramps' and not 'clochards' which foreigners erroneously use) were occupying the only four benches in the station. They could have stamped their names on those seats the way they emblazon Director, Producer and Star on the backs of chairs on a movie set. Only unsuspecting tourists ever dared rest their bums on those seats. Every regular commuter knew that the clodos used those seats night and day and no matter how much perfume the Paris Authorities might spray around the tunnels there was no way of eradicating the stench of their sad lives. That was another thing Paul and I always argued about. In his opinion they were not 'sad' but accepting and at peace with their lot in life.

Paul always hung around the clodos and listened to their ravings. He could always 'use it as material' which goes to show how dumb writers are. Drunken elephants yahooing through feet of dung in the jungle made more coherent conversation than the boozed up bunch of winos. But in the early dawn even the tramps sounded almost coherent. Paul pulled me closer to the group so we could hear what they were saying. That's why we were hovering around that smelly area acting as if the clodo group were some kind of exclusive clique at a party that we wanted to get friendly with, but didn't quite dare.

They were all holding steaming cups of coffee in their red hands that always reminded me of lumpy hamburger meat. At this hour of the morning even the clodos looked worried and peeved as if the thought of hustling for their booze money was too stressful for them at that ungodly hour of the morning. Like everyone who used this métro stop we knew the names of the clodos. Pierre was the tallest and the leader of the group. He could have looked as handsome as Cary Grant if he took a bath more than once a year and looked at something other than a bottle. Marie Marie was the accident prone member of the group. Marie Marie had a different wound every week either from falling off the bench during the night or tripping down the métro stairs in a drunken stupor. In the course of the past few months alone, Marie Marie had broken his arm, three fingers (and wore black bandages that looked as if they too were festering), and an ankle. He'd also cracked several parts of his face and skull - and never together but in sequence. He was only in his 30's but looked about 70. He was the closest thing I'd ever seen to a war casualty.

Marie Marie wasn't his real name. He got it from his incessant incantations to 'Marie, Marie, Marie, Marie.' Paul and I also argued about why the clodos called him Marie Marie and why he kept calling out for Marie. My opinion was that the accident prone slob had taken to drink after Marie had broken his heart, or maybe he'd killed her accidentally. Paul, in that insufferable haughtiness that so ill becomes an American, said that nothing as trite as heart break could turn a man into a self-destructive clodo. Paul said that Marie Marie had never been able to satisfy his querying of the meaning of life and that's why he spent his life with a gang of clodos in the gutter calling out to Marie, the Mother of God, since very obviously God had not deigned to hear his pleas.

Something verging on revolutionary had happened to

the clodos during the night. You could distinguish most of the words they grunted to one another.

'The quality of life is really dropping and fast. And me, it worries me.'

This was Pierre speaking, whistling through the half dozen chipped teeth he still had in his head.

'Galeries Lafayette isn't what it used to be,' said Marie Marie.

The other clodos agreed and nodded into their coffees. Galeries Lafayette, I might add, is a very swish department store which sells everything from gourmet quails' eggs to gold eyebrow tweezers – according to Diana who spends half her life in there.

'Once upon a time, you could rely on it for quality,' continued Marie Marie. 'But now the quality is ... *BOF.....,*' Marie Marie grunted and scratched the plaster on his wound, searching for a word. Since he rarely bothered with real speech he was somewhat on the rusty side.

'.... it's going to bloody hell. That's what's happening to quality,' said another clodo who looked just like a human rat. You could understand why he spent his days hidden in the métro. He had rodent features, eyes, nose, colouring, hands.

'Even coffee isn't what it used to be,' said Marie Marie with blossoming fluency.

'Don't touch the bananas in the Printemps,' piped up the fourth clodo. 'Try the oranges. The last shipment was real juicy.'

'That guard took them away from me last week. He even tried to stop me going in there another time,' said Pierre pulling his neck up out of his filthy shirt in a flash of indignity.

'He should be reported,' said Marie Marie. 'We're people. Aren't we?'

He looked at his other miserable companions for some sort of corroboration.

'I'll get some lamb chops today,' said the Rat Man. 'They still have that gas ring and a pan in Jules Joffrin.' (Jules Joffrin was another métro station beloved of the clodos where small groups cooked on small stoves).

'And stick it into your pockets. Don't shove it down your trousers and lose it like last time,' ordered Pierre.

Marie Marie yanked off the dirty plaster from the side of his head and showed his wound to the others. They said it was healing nicely. He threw the bandage on the ground and started to pick silently at the bloody crust of a scab. The train slithered into the station on its rubber wheels. The surge of air whipped the bandage with it and blew it down the platform.

Paul had that strange light in his eyes I knew only too well.

'Maybe I should do an article about being a clodo,' he said as we got on the train.

'Since you're not too far from there yourself,' I said spritely.

That doused the sparkle from his eyes and I felt sorry.

'What I mean is they have dreams too, even if most people don't know that,' I explained to him.

'Point taken,' he said. 'Yes I think I'll write an article on the life of clodos. Or maybe a series about the history of poverty in Paris, pauvre cuisine and a guide to clodo Paris.'

He was so pleased with his new idea, he started whistling 'Paris s'éveille' which is his favourite song about waking up before dawn in Paris, something I doubt he has ever personally experienced. That first time we met he taught all the words of this song to those rugby drunks on the train. They were amazed that an American could know that the line about the bakers making 'bâtards' at dawn in Paris referred to a type of baguette and not an increase in world population. It had been months since Paul had hummed let alone burst into exuberant song. The commuters glared at him as if they didn't want to be reminded that they were waking up in Paris. They all looked so old and worn. The horrifying thought of being old and weary like them one day just didn't seem possible. To cheer myself up I started singing along. We stood near the door singing that happy song again and again, cheering ourselves up and getting on everyone's nerves. At one stop an old woman got off and gave us a franc grunting that she really loved that song.

I could now truthfully add singing in Paris to my CV.

FORTY-SEVEN

The Gare de l'Est is a beautiful station with gigantic sweeps of glass and iron structure that covers the station and platforms. On a postcard the Gare de l'Est looks enchantingly beautiful. That morning the stunning foyer Hall had been transformed into a Christmas Market cum Festival of Food and Wine from Alsace. Wow! Unfortunately, all this beauty was marred by the Artic wind that whipped in from the open air station beyond. We'd be frost bitten before midday.

We had no problem finding Jacques' uncle Felix. He looked just like Jacques but only 30 years older. He was also a lot merrier than plodding Jacques. Felix wore a red shirt and blue jeans and had a knotted yellow and black scarf around his neck. He didn't even look French, just mildly daft. I knew straight off that my Dad and Felix would have a lot in common. They were both devoted shop keepers with intense professionalism. While all round us people at the other stands eased into the day, drinking endless cups of coffee, smoking and chatting as if they were at a cocktail party Felix rearranged his stand several times until he was pleased that his attractive mounds of black and white puddings and his 30 varieties of salamis all with weird names looked better than a painting in the Louvre.

Paul and I changed into the traditional Alsatian

costumes provided by Felix. In his blindingly white shirt, his embroidered velvet jacket and trousers and his chic hat Paul looked quite fetching. But even the Hunchback of Notre Dame would have looked alluring in that costume. Nellie on the other hand looked like Benny Hill's twin in a dizzy dress of ruffles, lace and petticoats worn over several woolly sweaters underneath to ward off frostbite. The traditional headdress was a velvet bonnet with nightmare giant ears flopping off both sides like black airplane wings. I'd have looked more seductive dressed up as an overweight hyena. Paul, a man with no taste whatsoever, said I looked great.

Felix gave us a crash course in selling pig parts and a quick background explanation for the various sausages. The dried up square shaped scarlet ones, sold in pairs were called 'gendarmes' (that's French for 'policemen'). He hadn't a clue why they were called policemen or why they were only sold in pairs. Paul tried to flaunt his knowledge of Latin and said that the sausage called 'cervelas' probably had brains in it. Was 'cervelas' a bastardization of 'brains'? Felix was shocked. He told Paul that 'cervella' might mean brain in Latin but no Frenchman would ever churn up brains into a sausage. I asked him where the 'Museau Pressé' (Squashed Face) got its name. Felix was visibly moved by our interest in the behind-the-scenes in sausage making.

'It is called 'Squashed Face', he said gazing lovingly at the platter, 'because they cut up a nice pig's face and set it in a tasty gelatine.'

Paul gave me a look, which translated meant: 'Ask a dumb question, get a dumb answer.' But I was looking at the eyelashes in the Museau Pressé, something I hadn't spotted before.

Felix finally had one word of advice for the two of us

before he left us. Unlike other nations, a lot of French people always wanted to know what went into the different sausages, salamis and fancy meat pies. Felix suggested we always say: 'The choicest of pork, marinated in different wines and exclusive herbs.' I agreed with him. That definitely sounded a lot better than 'ground up dead pig bits'.

At 9.00 Felix left us and said he'd be back in the afternoon with another load of delicacies from Alsace. At 9.02 the guy at the next stand offered us a glass of warming Schnapps. We declined. The guy was really miffed. Since we'd be working close to one another for a week Paul decided it might be diplomatic to get back into his good books. At 9.30 he made up a tasty ham sandwich for himself and the guy at the next stand. This time Paul felt obliged to take the Schnapps. The guy told Paul he understood. The only reason Paul refused the first drink was because the boss was still close by. During the next hour Paul refused at least 10 more offers of different drinks. By that time the guy was fully crocked and lolling over his stand. But he wasn't frozen purple like the rest of us.

Mid-morning Christmas lights went on in the Arrivals Hall and Christmas music came on over the loudspeakers. The first time we heard those festive songs Paul and I hummed and sang along. Listening to Rudolf the Red Nosed Reindeer, Paul said he couldn't understand how the Finns could consider Rudolf's balls a culinary delicacy and actually eat them. By 11.30 we realized the Christmas songs were on a 7 minute non stop loop. Santa Claus, angels, roasting chestnuts and snow in the city were giving us a royal pain in the gut. We felt an all-embracing hatred for Rudolf and his kin and couldn't care less if the Finns made Bolognese sauce out of every last reindeer in Lapland. When he wasn't serving customers Paul kept muttering about reindeer torture under his breath. I tried to concentrate on the little speech I had prepared for that night's 'Events in Paris'.

The TV cameras were due at mid-day. This was the only Alsatian Festival in Paris. It was the media's patriotic duty to report on the state of Alsace food and wine. The film crew would be there to film the thousand and one delights that Alsatians can whip up out of one single pig. They wouldn't be falling over themselves to include Nellie Flanagan's ode to Unemployment. Being French given a choice between filming Nellie's Tales of Woe or Tarragon Pig's Ears I knew which one they'd go for. Oh yes, competition would be stiff. But I know my worth. Those Alsatian delicacies might be magnificent. But when Nellie Flanagan acts even the allure of fancy pig's farcie fades away.

'Check out where the toilets are,' said Paul petulantly. He was running out of gruesome Rudolf recipes.

'Felix said we could use the ones in the restaurant. They've got lots in there.'

It is an affliction with Paul. He can remember the exact dates and addresses of Hemingway's séjours in Paris. But don't ask him to remember anything mundane like where the jacks is located

'I'll go and check it out,' I told him. I wanted to freshen up for my TV appearance and escape from the infernal Christmas tape for a while.

The restaurant had that dingy odour that always clings to railway eateries. With their suitcases piled up next to their table all the diners looked tired and wilted. The lovebirds kissing feverishly in the alcove were the only exception. The pressure they put on each other's faces! That was definitely the way to unhinge jawbones and loosen a few teeth! It made me think it would put a damper on a snogging session if you had to interrupt and say: ''Scuse me lover, I gotta remove a few broken teeth.' The woman had her back to me, but I couldn't help thinking that I'd seen that expensive coat from the sable or squirrel family many times before.

When I got back to the stand the official mid-day opening festivities had started. A band had arrived and was playing the same kind of Christmas songs we'd been enduring all morning on the tape. The TV crew composed of one cameraman and sound man were already filming the wine stand next to ours. The dipso owner was drunker than the proverbial skunk. He wanted the cameraman to explain to him why he wouldn't have a drink with him. He was so far gone he refused to understand that the cameraman might find it useful if he could focus.

'Shall I take my headgear off?' I asked Paul in a sudden panic.

I didn't want to be immediately typecast as a giant actress with floppy, black elephant ears.

'You look real cute,' said Paul.

I dithered with the strings of my bonnet. I had major reservations about what Paul classified as 'cute'. Once we saw a mangy, half-dead, rain drenched cat slouching home and looking as if it had just survived the wash and rinse cycle. Paul had called that cat 'real cute'.

But it was too late to adjust my toilette. The film crew were standing right in front of our counter. They were annoyed because of all the drunken insults the dipso was still shouting at them, telling them they were a disgrace to France if they wouldn't taste the wine from one of its finest vineyards.

'D'you mind standing closer together?' asked the cameraman in a bored, long suffering tone. 'You're the typical Alsatian couple.'

'That's great,' said Paul enthusiastically. 'Cause I'm American and she's Irish.'

The cameraman went on doing his work.

'I'm a wonderful actress and I desperately need your help,' I said. 'Can I say something to the camera?'

The cameraman took his eye from the lens. He looked at the sound man. The silent language between the two of them translated into: 'There are days. Then there are days like this one.'

'The foie gras looks good,' the soundman said to the cameraman totally ignoring us while they gathered up the strength to get back to work and produce some footage.

'We're just here to take shots of the food and wine,' said the cameraman as he continued taking shots of the charcuterie.

'Connards, enculés, enfoirés!' yelled the dipso at the TV crew.

These are probably the crudest words you could possibly use in French - unless you wanted to be more specific and say that the cameraman's father preferred chimpanzees to more normal sexual partners. But I suppose if you work in TV you've heard it all before. They were done with our stand and the crew were nonchalantly moving on to the next. And if they did that Nellie Flanagan's Christmas plea would not be broadcast on TV and I wouldn't be discovered.

'You must try the foie gras,' I said and ripped open a packet of the stuff and began spreading it on nice crispy bread. Paul looked at me as if I had suddenly become unhinged. I was about to give away our week's wages.

'Et voilà!'

I handed a full plate of foie gras snacks to the astonished crew. The price of foie gras is about the same as caviar and it isn't an everyday occurrence to get a plateful pressed upon you. The soundman sucked back the saliva at the sight of this unexpected bonanza. He reminded me of a dog we used to have called Spitface. The poor dog got that name because it drooled uncontrollably after it cut a vital nerve leaping after a rabbit through a hedge with hidden barbed wire.

'For you,' I repeated.

After a few bites they told me their names were Roget (camera) and Marcel (sound). They smiled gratefully and we all ignored the dipso who was getting most repetitive in his insults. Paul looked disapprovingly at me then at Roget and Marcel. He finally threw in the towel and tasted some foie gras himself.

'Mmm, not bad,' he concluded.

The two Frenchmen were beyond shocked but decided to ignore the slur on French finesse and went on relishing the foie gras fest. Not even the original owner of that liver could have pounced on it with more pleasure. Roget and Marcel looked at me, then gazed at the outrageously expensive foie gras and their eyes said there was nothing they would not do for Nellie Flanagan.

'Just a few words to the camera?' I asked sweetly, and ripped open a second packet of foie gras. They nodded with glazed eyes.

Roget and Marcel were renewed men. Roget put his eye to his lens. Marcel double checked that his batteries weren't running low.

'OK. We're rolling,' said Roget.

'I am a wonderful actress,' I said, glowing for that lens. 'But I have now been looking for acting work in Paris for six months. Luck has not been with me. It's up to you to change that. I want *YOU* to hire me. Happy Christmas.'

Because of the foie gras they let me repeat it three times.

'I have no say in what they gets broadcast,' Roget said sadly. 'The editor has all the power. The rest of us are just lab rats.'

'But you'll try, won't you?' urged Paul, obviously forgetting how much cash he'd have to contribute towards the foie gras sandwiches.

'I'll try my best. I'm just warning you that most of the stuff I shoot goes straight into archive,' said Roget meekly. 'They'll pull it out in 50 years' time as historical archive for some programme or other.'

By the time Roget and Marcel had finished filming, the crowd in front of our stand was like something you'd see in Cannes. They all wanted to get their faces on TV. Roget and Marcel had to fight their way to the next stand. The dipso was having a siesta, snoring with his face down on the counter. Things returned to normal. Paul discovered that three expensive jars of rabbit ragout had disappeared from the front of the counter.

'I've got to go,' I told Paul.

'You just went.'

'I gotta go again. I do hope that meets with your approval.'

'A guy can't say a single word.'

On the way to the restrooms I worried about Roget and the wimp factor. He didn't seem in the least bitter that nobody would see his work in his lifetime. Thus, despite the memory of the foie gras he wouldn't commit Hari Kari trying to get Nellie's plea on TV. In desperation I got on the hotline to the Lord and begged Him to infuse a bit more Umph into Roget's personality before nightfall. And if He did me that little favour, I'd never have to bother Him again.

The urge to go to the bathroom immediately evaporated the minute I set foot inside the restaurant. It was so cosy and warm. I let my mind go into its usual positive mode and imagined how I would look that evening on 'Events in Paris'. I stood there dreaming of all the offers which would pour in as a result of my heart bleeding plea. I could see my name blazing on Broadway, all those lights twinkling, my Mam and Dad and the brothers getting out of a stretch limousine for Opening Night.

I glanced over at the lovers in the alcove. They had taken a breather from mauling one another and trying to crack each other's jaws. The man must have said something about my hilarious costume because the woman turned around. I nearly went into a dead faint when I saw her. So did Madame. Why hadn't I recognized that coat? It wasn't as if I knew anyone else with a sable or a fancy squirrel coat in their closet. The smile literally fell off her face when she recognized me. Then she swivelled back to the young man. The happy expression on his face changed. All joy just went *PLUFF.* The young guy put his hands up to her hair and she snapped them away. He looked over at me with a sort of loathing. I ran back to the stand. Business was booming. The rush wouldn't stop until 6.30 that evening.

All that afternoon, while half of France pestered us for pig-bits, wanting to know exactly what was in the gendarmes, my brain just split itself into three. One part of me concentrated on slicing and weighing and getting the prices right. Another part was praying that Roget would act like a man for a change. But mostly I was trying to block out the look on Madame's face.

FORTY-EIGHT

After locking up the stand for the night Paul and I raced from the Gare de L'Est to be on time to catch 'Events in Paris' which comes on every night at 7.15. The café regulars who are scratching by in the real Paris with all its pits hate this fake, glammed up version of our city. They only watch it because the presenter is a blonde dolly bird they've nicknamed 'Tweetie Pie'. Her plunging necklines are sometimes lower than her waist. Recently, there was mention in the news that a government committee was being set up to standardize female necklines on French TV. But Tweetie Pie has yet to hear about the committee to stop the plunging neckline. That evening she was in low plunge and had more wattage on her tight fitting top than the Christmas tree on the Champs-Élysées.

Tweetie Pie always read the story links with the same moronic, non-blinking, all toothy style. This evening was no different. The first item was a gruesome fire that had wiped out an abattoir in the North of Paris. Half-crazed animals which had been lined up for slaughter stampeded through the flames and ran amok in the streets. There were close-up pictures of two burnt, dead goats with their legs straight up in the air. It wasn't a pretty sight.

After the smoldering goats it was back to Tweetie Pie and her breast plate of sequins and her glittering earrings that were bigger than lamps. Item no. two was about a high society wine auction where one bottle had been sold for the price of an apartment that could house a family of fifteen. The next event was the Christmas Fun Fair in the Tuileries - a tradition that went back several centuries. There were lots of shots of the antique carousel. My heart was going round and round like the carousel. There were usually four items on 'Events in Paris'. Number four just had to be …. had to be … and it was - The Food and Wine Extravaganza in the Gare de l'Est!

My heart was pounding so loud I couldn't hear what Tweetie Pie was saying. But my eyes were still functioning. There were long shots of all the stands and the hundreds of delicacies stacked up in the Hall. Paul was yelling his head off, shouting to everyone in the café.

'It's us! They put us on! It's us!'

And for one fleeting half a second there we were. The 'Alsatian' couple smiling and toasting each other. This was followed by a close up of the foie gras, the paté en croute, the prize winning pig's 'squashed face' and a swirling artistic dissolve to bottles of wine from Alsace. Then Tweetie Pie was back with her asinine smile and cooing something about getting over to the Gare de l'Est to stock up on the glories of Alsace for Christmas.

Paul grabbed my hand. He gripped it so tightly it hurt.

'Look, I really didn't expect them to put it on anyhow,' I said.

'You tried,' said Paul.

For about a second he looked sad. Then he cheered up.

'At least we both got to appear on French TV,' he said and tried not to look too pleased with himself.

'And not even our own parents would have recognized us,' I reminded him.

'You can now truthfully put on your C.V. that you appeared on French TV.'

'That will definitely revolutionize my life.'

'Is it my fault they didn't put you on?' Paul looked as if he could burst out crying any second. 'If I could do anything for you I'd do it. Oh hell … what can I say?'

I told him I wasn't going to drop dead with the disappointment. I hadn't really expected anything to come of my inventiveness and only a moron could expect a theatre to respond to my 'I want *YOU* to hire me plea'. I had to spend ages cheering him up. After that Paul felt much, much better. We both had hot tea with rum and suddenly we felt wearier than farmers who have just hauled in the harvest single-handed.

It took us ages to trudge up those 127 steps. I could have conked out on the steps and slept. I suppose that's what disappointment does to you. It drains all the energy and hope you need to get from day to day. There was a note under my door. Madame certainly didn't beat about the bush. 'Nellie, this is to inform you officially that we will not need your services as English tutor after Christmas.'

'We're going to be homeless,' I informed Paul.

'When?' asked Paul, which was most unlike him. Obviously the novelty of putting in a long day's work had drained him dry too. His monosyllabic attack made me screech with laughter.

'Now don't get hysterical,' he said, and put an arm around my shoulder looking worried. I kept on laughing because I had just remembered the time that Paul had begged me to tape-record Monsieur's early morning advances. Paul wanted to get more insight into the workings of a jaded middle-aged man since he had such a long way to go before he himself reached that point. If Paris kept hitting both of us in the jaw we'd be middle-aged before New Year's Eve.

'We've got options, little one,' said Paul. He put his arms around me and patted my hair. 'We could stay in my room. Nobody would have to know.'

This time I let out a yelp at the thought of us sneaking past Mme Favela's eagle outlook and creeping up the back stairs to sleep on the floorboards with the choosy family of mice that were now firmly entrenched in Paul's woodwork. Paul swore he could hear them dancing the night away. A Parisian mouse disco!

'We could use Diana's place,' said Paul.

Move into Diana's place? Look what that had done to Duelling Diana. She raved constantly about the water level in showers until she completely snapped and shacked up with Hansi in the middle of a field with a zoo. If Paul and I did move to Diana's we'd have a roof over our head. We'd also probably go mad. But Paris would do that to us anyhow. Moving into Diana's room would only accelerate the process.

'We've come this far, haven't we, little one?' said Paul and patted my back like I was some kind of child.

He didn't say anything for a good while. He just kept on stroking my hair the way my Dad used to do many years earlier when he tried to console me through a childhood disappointment. I must have fallen asleep on my feet because the next thing I knew, I was stretched out on the bed without my shoes and Paul lay next to me fast asleep. We still had all our clothes on under the duvet.

The good part was that the next morning all we had to do was pull back the duvet and get over to the Gare de l'Est. The bad part was that I sort of liked it. Especially the fact that Paul didn't snore.

FORTY-NINE

'Winter kills!'

At least this time he accompanied his dawn poetry with a cup of steaming coffee, made the way I like it and not the way he likes it. Then he went over to the window and stood there reminding me of a Dark Knight prophesying death and pestilence.

'Winter kills,' he repeated.

I almost expected to see the pigeons landing just to die on my windowsill. They'd pile up high as Winter killed them and I'd become an expert on pigeon burials.

'I wish you wouldn't say that, Paul. Winter is Winter. And besides, it's going to be Christmas any day.'

'That sure is going to come as a major surprise to us,' he said with his sweet smile and hummed the first few bars to 'Rudolf the red nosed reindeer'.

I had to laugh despite my gloom.

'And don't let me sleep with my clothes on again,' I said.

'No problem,' he said and blew on the windowpane. He doodled on it while I went to the communal bathroom to wash my face and teeth.

The city that morning was greyer than any ancient cat. The air made us shiver. In the métro the clodos silently smoked and drank their coffees. Paul was annoyed because he couldn't pick up any more nuggets for his article on the Parisian clodo 'lifestyle'. The métro was packed. The endless tunnels echoed with the sound of armies marching to work. The old man hawking his pathetic hand puppet called 'Freddie the frog' slumped in defeat against the wall.

That morning was much the same as the day before. Felix dropped off half a tonne of merchandise before disappearing back to Alsace. The dipso at the next booth gave us a bottle of white wine and said we should always taste wine on an empty stomach. The dreaded Christmas tape came on at 9.00 instead of 10.00. During the quiet morning hours Paul tried to do some note taking while honing his gruesome reindeer recipes. At mid-day he had to put his notes aside. That's when the doddering brigade descended on us. Flocks of old men and women loitered for ages in front of our stand looking for 'a thin slice of Alsatian ham', or 'half a black pudding', or 'one Alsatian gendarme' even though they knew they were only sold in pairs. The ancient brigade usually spent about 10 minutes deciding which delicacy they would purchase. I'd say very diplomatically – 'I'll attend to others while you decide, shall I?'

Having watched my Dad in action down the years I was eligible for a PHD in doddering customer relations. My Dad would win prizes in dealing with dithering, old fogies. He used to say to me: 'Just remember, Nellie, you'll be just like them one day.' I always told him I would *NEVER* be like them. He used to retort in that hurt voice of his: 'The least you can do is be polite to them.' I suppose I felt as if my Dad was watching me and would have been most disappointed if I told a customer what I was really thinking – i.e. 'Lady, I ain't got all century. Could ya speed it up a bit?'

That day Granddad and Belinda, Madame Martinet and her decrepit hound Haut de Gamme (rechristened Hopalong by Granddad although his hopping days are long gone) paid a visit to our stand. They took photos of us selling to the hordes. Granddad was bursting with pride to see his granddaughter exercising the profession he himself had proudly served for decades. I smiled for them. I am a brilliant actress after all. I just kept on smiling. If I stopped smiling for a second, the dam of pain would break and I'd see myself homeless, penniless, begging in a métro corridor in my old age or selling hand puppets and yelling out 'Buy Teddie the toad!' to the dawn commuters. Other times I'd see myself like Madame Martinet, a heartbroken, shell of a woman whose only daily highlight was to sit in a café opposite the dog. I tried not to think of the 'alternative careers' I'd have to pursue in dumps like Tipps to keep the teeth in my gums and clothes on my body. I might as well start accepting the fact that I'd never play Juliet. Outside I looked like sunny Summer all beaming bright, inside Winter had already murdered all hope.

Every night after work Paul made us hot chocolate. Then he settled himself next to me on the bed and told me charming tales of Christmas in Philadelphia. It was the best part of the day. He was too weary to drag the mattress down the hall to the room where the mice danced and pranced the night away. The prospect of being homeless in two weeks had drained both us of everything except the will to survive the night. I was so dead of soul that I wasn't bothered that Paul saw me in my Tipps nightie. We just huddled close, the way the pigeons did during the cold weather. Before dropping off into a dreamless sleep I'd think of pigeons and the way they shivered and snuggled all together on the windowsill - all cheekiness and perkiness gone from them - as if they couldn't fathom why life was so awful in Fabulous Paris. When the pigeons fluttered their eyelids you could see the same helpless look that had crept into Paul's eyes. I'd catch it when he'd glance up from his note taking. His eyes would fill up like massive puddles during a rainstorm. They were swamped with desolation and trampled hope. Maybe he saw the same in my eyes. Maybe that's why we had to huddle close together to keep the cruelty of that Winter from killing us.

FIFTY

During our first week on the stand in the Gare de l'Est Antoine left for his filming in London. Granddad went with him to the airport - to keep his English flowing (I use the word very loosely) right up to the last minute. Granddad just had enough energy left to wave him a heartfelt goodbye and good luck. After 2 weeks verbally wrestling with Antoine, Granddad was longing to be a fulltime pensioner again. It was far less stressé. Soon he might even be able to sit down and enjoy doing the crossword without being haunted by the memory of Antoine's mangling of the English tongue.

Antoine arrived in London. No problem there. He successfully got from Heathrow to his B & B near Sloane Square by tube. This was all thanks to meticulous planning on the part of Belinda and Granddad. The Bed & Breakfast was efficient and central. No problem there. He got the royal treatment (bacon, sausages, tinned tomatoes and tinned beans for breakfast with toast and tea and marmalade all of which he didn't want but felt compelled to eat). The owner was a dear old friend of Belinda's. Like they say it isn't *what* you know but *who* you know. As a result of all those connections Antoine got a cheap bed in Central London which didn't sink in the middle like a boat. He woke up refreshed instead of feeling shipwrecked which is how most people feel who stay in English B &

B's - at least according to ever picky Paul – the failed travel writer.

Antoine met the film crew at the appointed spot. No problem. Handshakes and hellos all around. Antoine was cool as a breeze. They all piled into the mini-van. Betty, the make up lady flirted with him, complimented him on his beautiful English and said his gorgeous French accent was a real turn on. She said it was terrible that none of them knew a word of French except for 'merde' and 'cher' which is French for 'expensive'. She then did a wonderful job of enhancing each and every one of Antoine's features so that he looked absolutely stunning with just a sophisticated touch of tristesse (this is Antoine reporting back).

They set up outside the famous store. The cameraman first took long shots, wide shots and mood shots of the Christmas shopping hordes to cut into the film during the edit. No problem. Looking gorgeous in his makeup Antoine stood on the designated spot with his suitcase of frilly goods getting the feel for the place and his role. The actor playing Santa was ready with his bell. Everything was going exactly according to schedule when a very annoyed Store Manager stormed out and demanded to know just what they were up to. The director said they'd cleared it with Management. They had been given permission to film that day. The Store Manager said he'd have to check with his superiors.

While the director was inside sorting out the problem of filming clearance, Antoine being the committed actor that he is, decided to get into character. He put his suitcase of frilly goods at his feet and began to 'sell'. Totally immersed in his role of struggling salesman Antoine stood there in front of one of London's snootiest stores (unfortunately, I can't name names) waving his wares in the breeze, demonstrating the frilly knickers and the bras with unnatural holes in them. It was a bit unfortunate that his goods were the kind they were. Because the Christmas shoppers were not prepared for a salesman who excitedly put three fingers through knickers to show how seductive they could be. He showed how sexy the bras would look if worn by the right person. I cannot elaborate any more. But Antoine said his sales technique drew gasps from the audience that was growing in front of the store.

The cameraman and soundman were standing nearby smoking and complaining about stupid secretaries and bosses who couldn't even sort out something as simple as a filming permit. The crew hated hanging around doing nothing. It made work tedious. Suddenly two men in decorative uniforms stormed out of the store and advanced on Antoine in a highly threatening manner. The first man whipped the knickers from Antoine's hand and shouted at him for being a 'filthy pervert'. The camera crew snapped into action. Finally something they could film! Those two guards could have stuffed those knickers down Antoine's throat (such better footage really!) and all the crew would think about was capturing the action on film.

Naturally Antoine couldn't understand what the guards were yelling at him: 'dirty maniac', 'kinky kook', 'monstrous mockery of Christmas'. But when one of guards tossed the knickers over the heads of the onlookers, Antoine caught a glimpse of the crew filming him and thought it was all part of the scene. His first thought was that maybe he hadn't understood the new script or maybe (later he even had the temerity to express this) Nellie had mistranslated the script. Antoine acted up a storm to do justice to this new twist in the scene. The guards tried to take the suitcase away from him shouting that it was full of filthy wares. Antoine hung on to his suitcase thinking it was all part of the action. The suitcase spilled all its sexy goods over the pavement. The onlookers sniggered. This sent the guards into a rage. One of them got a bra and began to wind it around Antoine's neck. Antoine stumbled against the glass window and nearly got concussion. But that wasn't enough for a few loony self righteous shoppers. One pounded the suitcase over Antoine's head. Another whacked him in the stomach. At this stage Antoine got the eerie feeling that something was very wrong somewhere. Another righteous member of the public punched him in the face a few times and said this was the 'holy season'. The guard yanked the bra tighter around Antoine's neck. He was seconds away from being publicly strangled when the Director and an apologetic Store Manager raced out of the store.

The footage of the brutal Christmas attack went around the world. Antoine had to be hospitalized for the night. The evening papers had a front page picture of the French film star who had been attacked by British shoppers and kicked by guards employed by one of London's top stores. By noon the following day Antoine, the unknown French actor was the French star everyone wanted to interview. All the representatives of France in London and the British political elite went to his bedside to apologize for his bruised and battered face. The store wants to settle out of court. But Antoine's British and French lawyers are advising him to hold out for much more. Antoine the actor whom nobody wanted for 25 years is suddenly flavour of the month. Thanks to the advance publicity the film will probably sweep the boards in Cannes by the time it is finished. Antoine will be able to choose his roles from now on. A world famous Lingerie Company called him in hospital to offer him a ludicrous amount to endorse their wares. He's considering all offers.

He didn't have to take the métro home. A limo was waiting for him at the airport courtesy of the London store. Awash with cash he took Granddad and Belinda out for a real classy meal in Montmartre to thank them for their help. They went to a place that was ritzier than Bofinger. As usual Granddad had snails for starters. As usual he slipped two of the shells into his pocket. These were the biggest shells so far in the enormous collection of snail shells he had purloined from French restaurants.

Granddad was very surprised when the owner of the restaurant came over to them and began apologizing profusely for not giving them six snails. She begged Granddad to forgive her staff for short changing him in the snail department. She placed another six snails in front of Granddad. And finally Granddad realized that you were not supposed to take a few shells with you. The empty shells were used in preparing the next batch of escargots. There was more to this French delicacy that just stuffing a bit of garlic into a garden snail.

They spent the evening drinking to Antoine's good health. They even had the high priced vintage wine. It was a most enjoyable evening. Later Granddad said to me: 'You see Nellie, that's life. Your luck will turn too - just like Antoine's!'

Just like Antoine? In which case I might just as well take to my bed and get up again in about 25 years time.

FIFTY-ONE

On Monday Belinda came by the stand at midday. She looked as worried as a wet week and wanted to know if I could possibly have lunch with her. I felt duty bound to say yes to Belinda which meant I had to cancel my Bofinger assignation with Monsieur. I was a bit miffed with Belinda because I had decided that since there wasn't a ghost of a chance of me being an actress in Paris or anywhere else on the globe I might as well go with the flow and do what the rest of the world was doing – i.e. having expensive, furtive lunches with their married employers and doing jobs they hated. I found a phone, called up Bofinger and had him paged.

'How about next Monday?' asked Monsieur.

'Madame doesn't want my services after Christmas,' I told him.

'Marie-Ange had no right to do that,' he said in a half-hearted whine. 'But her parents unfortunately own our building.'

'I must go now,' I told him.

'Next Monday?' he asked hopefully.

But I had hung up. At that moment I didn't know who to feel sorrier for – Madame or Monsieur. But the thought of being unemployed, homeless and having to move à deux into Diana's grotty cell of a room in the most unsavoury district of Paris changed my mind. I decided to save all my pity for myself and Paul.

Belinda and I had lunch in the station restaurant where Madame and her lover no longer met. Belinda spent ten minutes pondering the merits of a grilled steak with frites or a grilled chicken with frites. As I waited I gazed at the hordes of Christmas visitors pouring through the station restaurant. I envied them. They could still listen to a bar of Rudolf the Red Nosed Reindeer without having the savage urge to maim everyone within reach. They could enjoy the tinsel and foie gras. Christmas was a holiday full of cheer and charm. For Paul and myself it was worse than a stint in a damp dungeon. But we had 'options' as Paul reminded me. We could celebrate Christmas in the caravan listening to Hansi grunting his way through the dinner he'd buy from Henriette's Café on Christmas Eve with the understanding he wouldn't come near them on Christmas Day. This would be accompanied by unwashed Diana's rhapsody about the fascinating toilet habits of cats and dogs. If that wasn't thrilling enough for us, we could spend Christmas in the brown on brown café drowning our sorrows with the rest of Paris' drunk, coughing losers. Or we could go for the streamlined Zen version and recover from our exhaustion by crashing on our separate mattresses until they rang in the New Year.

'I have to ask you a favour,' said Belinda when she had finally placed the order for an omelette with fried potatoes.

'Go right ahead.'

'You know how attached your Granddad is to his Christmas rituals,' said Belinda.

'Yes,' I said even if I've never understood them. Every Christmas Eve he visits his parents' grave and it is so strange to think that Granddad was ever a child let alone a baby. Another ritual is waiting anxiously for a telephone call from his friend Jack in New York. For the past 45 years Jack has never yet missed calling Granddad on Christmas Eve. Every year Jack says the same thing: next year he is coming home and he'll be there in the flesh.

Another ritual is attending Midnight Mass. This year it was Granddad's turn to read the lesson. Fr. Foley always gave the old people a chance to get up on the altar and have their moment of glory before they were dead. The choicest days were Easter Sunday, Saints' days, Holy days and top of the bill - Midnight Mass. Everyone was always in rollicking form at Midnight Mass. That's because most of the faithful rolled out of the pub shortly before midnight singing 'The Kerry Dances'. In Church they belted out 'Silent Night' and 'Come all Ye Faithful'. In Dun-mo-Croi the weather was usually crisp and cold for Christmas. The natives called it 'the miracle of Christmas'. When we came out from Midnight Mass the stars always dripped from the skies like huge blobs of molten metal. Granddad's other Christmas ritual was to go into the garden, point up at the Milky Way and quote the Thomas Moore poem 'At the dead hour of night when stars are weeping'!

'Christmas means a lot to your Granddad,' said Belinda. 'You're too young to understand about traditions. But when you're old!'

Belinda smiled happily and sipped her hot chocolate, which was the strangest thing to have with an omelette and potatoes.

'I am old,' I told her.

But she only went on smiling indulgently. The old never understand. They think just because you're young that life hasn't yet had the chance to wallop the guts out of you. A lot of them think you have to be in your dotage before you can ever know what despair or disappointment is.

'Would you like to go home for Christmas?' asked Belinda.

I shrugged nonchalantly. Of course I longed to go home for the holidays. To that security and love that would envelop me like an invisible cashmere cape. My Dad would ask me if the tinsel looked better draped around the tins of peas or around the Christmas hams. My Ma would listen entranced to all my stories of Paris and sigh pleasantly now that I had survived them. We'd have home made Christmas pudding fried in butter.

'Of course I can understand why you'd prefer to stay in Paris,' said Belinda. She was radiating understanding. 'Paris is much more exciting for young people.'

'You mentioned a favour?' I said, before I told Belinda what I really thought of Paris and its dynamite attractions.

'We're going home. We miss Kerry,' said Belinda. 'Madame Roussard wanted to know if there was any chance of you looking after her friends' apartment.'

'You mean the flat where you and Granddad have for watering the plants?'

'You'd have a free phone and all the amenities,' said Belinda. The owners won't be back until May.'

'A free flat?'

Spots were jumping in front of my eyes. My heart did a weird flutter. Was I about to have that heart attack at 19 that Auntie Betty was always blathering about?

'Madame Russard knows how dependable you are. Would you be interested?'

I took a long sip of my Chateau Chirac and the heart fluttering subsided.

'Oh thank you, thank you, Belinda,' I said and threw my arms around my saviour.

'Wonderful!' said Belinda.

She took a long sip of her chocolate and took a deep breath as if she was about to embark on something embarrassing.

'I don't know how to ask you this.'

'What?'

'Does your friend Paul like dogs?'

'Dogs?' Paul definitely didn't go ape over small animals if his reaction to one teensy weensy mouse was anything to go by. 'I honestly don't know. Why?'

'You see, Lisette and André would like to come to Ireland with us for a few weeks. They've always wanted to see Ireland. If they wait any longer they might never go. None of us are getting any younger.'

Belinda was coming down with Granddad's disease. Give you a million details and then forget what you wanted to say originally.

'Paul and dogs?' I prompted her.

'Why, yes. You said he was between apartments. And Lisette and André don't want to put Balzac into a kennel. Balzac likes his comfort and doesn't settle easily.'

'And Paul?' I asked again.

'Paul is a writer so I'm sure he'd appreciate a quiet apartment in exchange for walking Balzac. Lisette wouldn't worry. And the two of you would be close in case of emergencies.'

I couldn't help myself. I burst into loud, clamouring tears.

'Oh, you mustn't cry, Nellie. Is it because it's Christmas? You're homesick? Is there a problem? Can I help in any way?'

I was laughing and crying all at the same time, slurping back the snot and jabbering my effusive thanks in English and French. Well, they say good things come in pairs. But this was too much. We'd have two of everything. Two free apartments. Two bedrooms. Two fully equipped kitchens. Two bathrooms. Two balconies with geraniums. It was like fifty Miracles of Christmas all wrapped up in stars and heavenly tinsel.

FIFTY-TWO

There were lots of au revoirs last night down in the pink Salon. My kids insisted I come by for a Christmas goodbye drink. They wanted to show me their Two Musketeers routine from their school play. They were fabulous. Afterwards Maude and Claude sat at my feet in a most touching tableau while Madame sat on one petit point armchair and Monsieur in the matching one. My kids wanted to give me every last detail of the Fun Fair in the Tuileries and how many of their pals threw up on the carousel and how one of them almost got sucked into the centrifuge airplane.

'Say goodnight to Nellie,' ordered Madame as the kids filled up my glass to the brim with champagne. 'Take them to bed, would you, Henri?'

Monsieur leapt at this excuse to leave the domestic scene. But my kids lingered around my neck and whispered their love for me into both my ears. I whispered back, tears poised just to come plopping down. Like I said, I can't stand kids. But Claude and Maude were different and it was difficult not to be touched by their overwhelming adoration, of which there was too little in this world.

Then I was alone in the Pink Salon with Madame. With the warmth of the kids gone, the room was like an Ice Salon and Madame was frostier than any ice sculpture. Her manicured nails beat out an imperious rhythm on the wooden arm of her chair.

'Will you continue with your acting career?' she said. Madame had never before inquired into my personal or professional interests. It was rather disconcerting.

'I'm doing the best I can,' I told her. 'It's not easy.'

'Nothing is,' she said in a doom-laden voice. 'You'll see when you're older. Tout passe, tout casse.' (Everything passes, everything breaks)

This was high philosophy coming from Madame. She stared at me sadly across the expanse of finest pink silk of a rug. Her emerald and diamond rings twinkled splendidly under the chandelier. Even her nylons had that sheen you'll only get in ones that cost as much as my dress from Monoprix. Madame looked like an ad for material happiness.

'It can't be that bad,' I said, bravely picking up my overflowing glass of champagne.

'Believe me, Nellie. Just remember. Tout passe, tout lasse, tout casse.'

'That's very depressing,' I said.

'Mais non! It's reality. It is only when we try to escape reality that we end up depressing ourselves.'

I kept on sipping my champagne. For once I thought this might be something I would understand when I was older. At that moment it made no sense at all.

Monsieur came back into the room. Madame got up. Very formally she skirted the delicate silk rug instead of walking across it. She shook my hand and gave me an envelope.

'Thank you for teaching the children so well,' she said coolly.

'I'd like to see Maude and Claude occasionally if I could, keep up their Shakespeare,' I said, sounding like a character in a divorce case wanting some custody of the kids.

Madame nodded oui and began to leave the room. Almost as an afterthought she said over her shoulder, 'See Nellie to her door, would you, Henri?'

For the last time Monsieur came to my dog box. I didn't ask him in.

'You will have lunch with me next Monday, won't you, Nellie?'

'No, I won't,' I told him.

'Why not? Oh, please!'

'I'm sick of you pestering me,' I said. It was mainly the champagne bubbles talking.

'I'm sorry if you thought I was pestering you,' said Monsieur huffily. 'I enjoy your company. You are a very attractive woman. Such a beautiful woman.'

You could have felled me with a feather. Recognition at last! But then the French have taste. They can recognize quality and beauty. They are trained to.

'I find you so different! So very fresh and brave!'

He began to spoil things a bit there. I would have preferred if he had gone on to tell me I had skin like satin, hair like a rabid sun, the kind of rubbish that Jean-Claude had spouted. I suddenly remembered that Jean-Claude had been a pathological liar. Which didn't necessarily mean that Monsieur was one too. But it is best to be cautious.

'I can't see you again,' I said, insinuating that it was all very tragic but nothing could be done.

'You're sure?'

'I must go now,' I said. I leaned most dramatically

against the open door just the way the heroines do in poignant black and white films. 'Adieu!'

Monsieur was about to kiss my hand when the Farkas kids came hurtling down the hall on their skateboards. Monsieur beat a fast retreat down the back stairs.

I very nearly didn't open Madame's envelope, thinking it was a Christmas card or something politely French. When I saw the 1,000 franc note I felt very strange indeed. I thought of Madame and Monsieur down in that Pink Salon with its 10 foot chandelier, the tapestries and silk rugs, and how they were choking to death while pretending to be alive. I felt like returning the money to Madame. But reason prevailed. I kept it.

FIFTY-THREE

Today is going to be our last day selling charcuterie. Paul and I smell like liver paté no matter how hard we wash. Paul has lived exclusively on a diet of smoked ribs, gendarmes and liver paté for the past ten days. Today the pork feast ends. Tonight Granddad and Belinda are having their farewell party. It's going to be a real geriatric affair. Lisettte and André and a few more doddering oldies from the outdoor bowling team will be there. Madame Roussard of course. And her artist daughter Sylvana whose second child is now a week overdue. Granddad keeps saying that maybe the party 'will do the trick' which is a very new approach to obstetrics.

Antoine, the future star of French film will be gracing the party. So will Camilla who still thinks her English is better than Nellie Flanagan's. Madame Martinet is coming with the old man who sat in the same café with his dog for the past ten years. They never spoke until last week. It was Madame Martinet who took the initiative by inquiring about the age of his old dog. Madame Martinet got 'a new lease on life' once she discovered that Granddad and Belinda wanted her to go with them to Ireland for an extended holiday. It wouldn't surprise me in the least if the old man Marcel joined them as well. So Paul could be in charge of a mini-kennel. Which should give him a few more ideas for his articles.

Naturally Paul and I will be in attendance at the geriatric soirée hopping around the place like jack rabbits keeping everyone's drink topped up. Hansi and Diana intend to drop in. They are going to an art event nearby. There is 'splendid news' on that front. In a moment of severe weakness Henriette agreed to hang some of Hansi's paintings in the cafe. Diana persuaded her it would be fabulous exposure. Once Hansi's work began to sell he'd clear off that field in no time. That's how Claudette Moreau (art dealer) discovered Hansi. She popped into Henriette's for a quick espresso and an even quicker dash to the facilities on her drive back from an art auction in Geneva. She stopped in her tracks (shock no doubt!) when she saw Hansi's godawful paintings. When Claudette went weird and started gesticulating and babbling about the paintings, Henriette offered her a calva telling her it was the only cure for that first encounter with Hansi's oeuvre. Claudette tossed back the calva (now that's one hell of a feat!) and when she recovered the power of speech she told Henriette all her Christmases had come at once. She had discovered the most revolutionary French painter since Henri Rousseau! Henriette didn't mention that Hansi was German. Besides after several years in Paris Hansi had mastered the Gallic grunt to perfection and could easily pass for French.

To cut a long story short Claudette is organizing Hansi's first exhibition in Paris in March. The prices for his art are sky rocketing. Since Hansi doesn't want anything to do with finances, Diana is in charge. All her dreams are coming true. They've been swamped with invites to all sorts of swish arty events. Hansi insists on wearing his jacket with the 23 safety pins and some morons think it is an expensive fashion statement. He has no intention of moving from his caravan or the field where he gets all his inspiration. But Diana is at peace with that. Hansi is going to finance Diana's academy for the Duelling Arts and restore stage duelling to new glory. She is eagerly awaiting anyone who might drop in unexpectedly from New Jersey. She may have time to squeeze them in for an apéro. And once the Academy takes off she can buy a ticket home to New Jersey without having to admit to that most awful of secrets, 'I am a loser.'

Beside me on our super high bed Paul gives a satisfied grunt into my ear. After today we'll go our separate ways again. He is one happy man. The sparkle of hope is back in his eyes. He's back in total love with Paris and scribbling non stop when he should be selling pounds of bacon. He has dusted off the old manuscript of 'What They Ate' and is going to bombard publishers with his epic of hungry artists in 1920's Paris. He is sending a deluge of articles to hundreds of American newspapers on a whole range of topics, from 'How to get the best in shit-mashers' to 'Recipes for squashed face'.

The moon outside my window is no longer grey. It is the gold lamé kind and it gives a silver polish to the pigeons on my windowsill. I know that I am not going to miss them in the least. But I want to lie here and watch them and store up this memory to look back on in future years. After today things will be completely different. Paul gives another gleeful grunt. Since he heard about Balzac and the free flat the guy is so elated he wants to find that mouse in his old room and kiss it goodbye. So joyful, he reminds me of the old Paul. So chirpy, he is getting severely on my nerves. He's sleeping next to me like I'm some kind of old hound he can snuggle up to for a bit of warmth. For some reason

I want him to realize that I am not some rolled-up old carpet that he can put his arms around when he is world weary. I know the first thing he'll say when he opens his eyes is: 'Winter tries to kill you. And then you just bounce right back.'

So if I didn't love that guy I'd really, really hate him.

FIFTY-FOUR

It's been a roaring success of a day. Felix paid us and even included a bonus for efficient and friendly service. We felt duty bound to mention the occasional theft of the very popular rabbit ragout and the packets of foie gras. Felix said that the loss due to theft was usually three times higher. It's now four o'clock and the commuters are thronging around our stand. Already we've had two who hollered out: 'Could you serve me first, I've got a train to catch.' Paul and I just love it when that happens. It gives us a frisson of nasty pleasure. We try and beat one another to hollering back, 'Monsieur! Madame! This here is a train station. Last I checked there weren't any planes or boats.' We always get a loud laugh and then it's back to pig business.

Because it is so close to Christmas people are buying more and more. Which of course annoys those people who only want to buy a slice of 'Squashed Face'. A short little man took his turn in front of the counter and pulled out a very long list. The customers catching their trains looked as if they wanted to throttle that guy with a list as long as his arm. But I like people with lists. They know what want. They don't spend half the day dithering between two and a half slices of ham or one and a half ounces of black pudding. The first item on the thin guy's list was 2 pounds of ham. And he didn't add the annoying specification of 'very, very thin'. When they want it thin it falls to bits like a cobweb and then they blame you for making a mess of their ham. The next item was two pounds of paprika salami. I was slicing the huge mound of paprika salami when it struck me that I had seen that wisp of a guy somewhere before. But when you are operating an electric slicer it is not the most suitable moment to study the customer. You could slice off more than the paprika sausage.

Next he wanted two pounds of liver paté. Hey, I was beginning to really like this little guy. None of this 'Half an inch of paté' stuff. And none of that 'what's it made of?' nonsense. Hey, listen, bozo if I told you, you'd never eat salami again. Or that gem: 'how long will the salami last?' 'Hey, if it starts opening the fridge door all on its own, it might be trying to make a statement.' None of that. This guy was the perfect customer. Two dozen gendarmes. Done!

The other customers were getting pissed off with this guy and his never ending shopping list. It is truly amazing how irate people get if they have to spend two extra minutes of their lives waiting in line whereas these are exactly the kind of people who go home and watch all those working actresses on TV for an average of 6 hours a night. Three pounds of cervelas! Every time he placed the next order he looked at me in the strangest way. His voice reminded me of somebody. But I still couldn't place him, since I had to concentrate fully on slicing pig parts. Finally he came to the end of his list. I was half way through totting up the damage when he leaned over the counter and said in an excited voice:

'It is you. I wrote to you yesterday,' said the whispy little man. He had switched from French to English.

I looked up from my computations. Paul was hogging

the calculator and that meant I had to do the totting up all over again.

'I wrote to you yesterday,' the little man repeated.

This time Paul heard it too and looked over at me. I smiled. When in doubt, smile, is my motto. Then I went back to adding up his list. Paul sidled over to me.

'Another weirdo admirer?' he said under his breath.

I kept on smiling. My policy is keep smiling even at the weirdoes. They probably have a very good reason for being weird, especially if they live in Paris.

'I wrote to you yesterday,' the little man said one more time.

That was the straw that broke the camel's back as far as the woman next to him was concerned. She decided to have an almighty mother of a Kreeze. She started yelling at the top of her voice informing everyone in the Gare de l'Est that 'un espèce de con', an 'enculé', an 'enfoiré' was flirting with the Alsation assistant and making her miss her train home. She banged her fat fists on the counter top and demanded half a pound of liver paté.

'Mademoiselle, I am going to report you to your boss unless you start serving the other customers instead of entertaining your boyfriend here,' she snarled.

'Mais Madame!' said the little man in a most indignant voice. He was a bit like Mitterrand, ever so stiff but you knew he could relax if he had to.

'I know your kind all too well!' shrieked the woman.

'But Madame!' said the man again, just in the same tone of voice as Mitterrand if somebody had accused him of being a kangaroo masquerading as human.

I had to add up my figures all over again. I wrenched the calculator from Paul's grasp. Then I fed in the wrong numbers. For some reason I couldn't do the simple task of adding up those numbers and had to ask Paul to help.

I hate admitting I can't cope – especially to a man and particularly to Paul. But I needed a moment to remember who the wisp of a man was.

'I want half a pound of liver paté now,' yelled the woman. Again she smashed her fists down on the counter making the piles of salamis quiver and shake.

That's when it all came back to me. This was the wisp of a man who had listened eagerly to my sonnets and who asked if it rained in Ireland as much as they said it did.

'I'm sorry, I didn't recognize you,' I told him.

'I certainly had a hard time recognizing you in your costume.'

'I won't be wearing it after today,' I told him, ignoring all the hollering customers who were acting like crazed animals at the other side of the counter.

'But this is simply extraordinary,' said the little man. 'I wrote to you yesterday to the address you had on your glossy.'

'Why?' I asked cautiously.

'In Spring the New International are putting on a completely radical version of *Romeo and Juliet*. We want you for the role of Juliet.'

PLONK!

I dropped the giant knife I was holding and narrowly escaped chopping off my own toes.

'You want me to play Juliet?'

'We want a flamboyant Juliet. I'm sure Shakespeare never meant Juliet to be just sweet and saccharine. His Juliet knew what she wanted. Are you available?'

It was suddenly overpoweringly hot in that hall. I couldn't breathe. I tried to loosen the strings of my bonnet. Earlier we had accepted two small Schnapps from the dipso next door. Maybe that was why I was hallucinating, hearing this wispy man offering me my life's dream on a platter right here knee-deep in sausages, liver patés and 'squashed face'.

Paris had finally done it to me. Crack up, breakdown time! My legs quivered under me. I can remember swaying the way women do in Edwardian serials on the BBC when they swoon softly onto a velvet sofa or into the arms of a gentleman wearing more ruffles and lace than most modern women on their wedding day. But I wasn't in a BBC costume drama. I was in the middle of half a ton of pig parts, dressed up as an Alsatian with giant black ears flapping from my bonnet. It was only fitting that I fainted snout down into the mound of gendarmes (which as I've mentioned are the dried salamis called 'policemen' since they always come in twos). A few of the policemen went flying out over the counter and since it wasn't every day that customers in the Gare de l'Est were pelted with salamis they very philosophically accepted this Christmas bonus.

I was out for about 5 minutes, according to Paul. Since there wasn't a bed or a love seat behind the counter Paul settled me as best he could on the cold station floor and shoved a pile of his notebooks under my head to elevate it. The dipso next door vaulted over the partition brandishing a bottle of brandy, which he tried to drizzle down my throat. Paul had to beat off the dypso and his bottle. The little man who had offered me the part of Juliet was most concerned and came behind the counter but without indulging in any vaulting.

The crowds kept clamouring for their sausages before their trains departed. They were rowdier than the crowds around the guillotine during the Revolution. And wouldn't you know it? That was precisely the moment that Granddad, Belinda, their lovely neighbours Lisette and André and their doddering dog Balzac came by to pick up a few more delicacies for that evening's party.

Granddad at 6 foot four is taller than most of France. He had a bull's-eye view of his darling girl stretched out like Ophelia in *Hamlet* but not quite that classy. He also saw Paul trying to keep the dipso at bay, and the wispy man tapping me on the cheek asking me if I was alive. King Lear could not have equalled his cry of distress on seeing me prone on the cold floor. And not even Henry on his stallion blazing once more into the breach could have cut a faster swathe through that mob of Parisian shoppers. Granddad vaulted over the low part of the counter, knocking over another stack of rabbit ragout and two packets of foie gras (never to be sighted again). Balzac, the old beagle who'd been brain and body dead for about a decade, suddenly felt a stirring in her genetic programming and flew over the counter after Granddad and landed next to me. If that dog had landed on top of me, my chances of ever playing Juliet would have been severely curtailed. Ecstatic to realize that there was still a modicum of vigour in her old bones, Balzac the beagle let out a yodel of delight.

Somehow the dog's high-pitched yodel sliced through some layer of my consciousness. I still wasn't 50% in the reality zone. When I opened my eyes and saw all those people bending over me, the dog licking my face, the customers yelling and peering down at me through mounds of cold cuts, I thought it best to close my eyes again. It was then I felt Paul's hands caressing my head. Except now he's muttering and sobbing to me. He's even kissing my cheeks and my neck. I'm beginning to like this, even if the cold of the station floor is seeping through my costume and tickling my back.

'Darling, my sweet one,' Paul is saying between

kisses. 'Wake up, mon amour. I love you, Nellie. Everything is going to be alright. I'm here, mon amour.'

This is really nice, I think, even if the customers are still baying like bedlam. But I must double check on one thing. I open my eyes and turn to the little man.

'Am I really going to play Juliet?'

'But of course you are, mon amour,' says Paul and covers my face in kisses.

'Most certainly. If you are available,' says the little man.

I close my eyes again. Paul thinks I am having a relapse and yells out for a doctor, a nurse, an ambulance.

'I'll be fine,' I reassure Paul who starts kissing my neck again. It is wonderful lying there, being kissed by the guy I love with all my heart, and knowing that soon I'll be on that stage speaking the most beautiful words ever written.

'Give me my Romeo and when he shall die
Take him and cut him out in little stars.'

'Take it easy now, honey,' says Paul.

'And he will make the face of heaven so fine
That all the world will be in love with night.'

Behind me I can hear Granddad tell Belinda that they'll take me back to the apartment in a taxi but there's nothing to worry about. On the contrary! He tells Belinda it's very re-assuring to see me indulge in a fit of dramatics again. It proves I'm back to normal.

The ice of the floor is seeping through my bones. I don't want to get pneumonia before I send those Paris critics into paroxysms of praising prose. Or before I can get dressed up in my nice black dress and maybe buy some flashy ear-rings and tell Paul how much I love him too, but in a more romantic setting than knee deep in smoked, boiled, fried and freeze dried pig parts. I want us to sit romantically on one of the two geranium filled balconies of our 'free flats' where we will kiss and raise our glasses to the place we love and brought us together – Paris, the most gorgeous city in the galaxy.

'I'm fine now,' I tell them and they help me up.

Granddad puts his arm around my shoulders and says: 'Darling girl, you had us worried there for a bit.' I put my arm around my Granddad. Balzac licks my ankles. The dipso is busy cutting up liver paté and massacring it into bits for those customers who would insist on getting served even if all of Paris were crumbling around them. Still holding my hand Paul removes the knife and the liver paté from the dipso's grasp.

And Life goes on.

Lightning Source UK Ltd.
Milton Keynes UK
30 January 2010
149323UK00001B/2/P